Erotic Memoir Presents

Summer in the Garden of Eros

By Hormonius Young

Erotic Memoir is an imprint of Clocktower Books, San Diego

Summer in the Garden of Eros

Erotic Memoir™ is a publishing imprint of Clocktower Books™ -world's first publisher online (1996) of true, full-length, proprietary (not public domain) digital novels for download.

Clocktower Books
www.clocktowerbooks.com/
P. O. Box 600973
Grantville Station
San Diego, California 92160-0973

Contact: editor@clocktowerbooks.com

Contents

Notes on the 2014 Edition

Editor's Note: For the 2014 (effectively, third) edition, we decided to replace all instances of the f-word with a symbol. For reasons of typesetting, markup languages, and portability, we settled on the @ mark. By all means, when you see @, substitute the f-word in your thoughts as desired--or simply enjoy the sensual humor and coyness of the @ mark, knowing its secret in context. Think of it as an extra layer of seduction and spice. Hear gods and goddesses laughing in the Garden of Eros as you read...

Added Note: For good measure, we also replaced all instances of the c-word with the word *oyster*. The author agreed to these changes, and with our feeling that the expressive needs of the text had evolved over the years since its first publication. We felt it impracticable to place fig leaves over other vulgarisms in the author's long ago exuberance. Therefore, much vibrancy of his free expression remains.

Prolog: Poignant Arpeggios

This memoir, based on true events, is constructed as an erotic alphabet, from **A** to **Z**, detailing man-woman sex and affection, straight sex in other words, with a few auxiliary woman-man-woman triangles as things get hotter and hotter toward the end. It is not a memoir of sexual recklessness or immorality, but a track-map of the delicate maneuvering and nuanced mating dance of those who really have no plan to mate, but just crave a good, wet, noisy @ with all the strings cut loose.

It is, at the same time, a memoir that is graceful and elegant, celebrating the beauty of youth amid the chaos and strain of life.

If I were to choose a music for this memoir, it would be a solitary trumpet, playing jazz, the way you would cut paper into origami shapes. Trust me. This is good.

It's not one of those pulp books some men go out after midnight (often, sent by the woman in their life) to buy from a clerk in a small bookstore smelling vaguely of semen, paying for the book which the ragged man with the runny nose slides across the counter, wrapped in a plain brown bag. No, this is a more intellectual memoir. The Summers and I were all young thinking people, with educations, feelings, ideas, sometimes wild and crazy ideas.

It started with a standard slightly older woman, who taught me the simple things, like licking her clitoris in a certain way until she lost consciousness during her orgasm (honest, it really happened). There was the blonde surfer who liked just a bluff you-me let's get down and do it. There was the woman who cried because she was too loose, and the animal she had just divorced tormented her about it, but I was able to soothe her anguish with my thick dick. There was the woman who liked to @ in public places, while pretending to be eating an ice cream or observing pigeons on the Green.

There was the woman who had silvery weights hanging from her labia, hoping to stretch them (and I'm all for big labia; they are like steaks to chew). There was the woman in New York City, who was so wealthy she could run her own sex diorama, complete with actors in costume, and a guy with a dick curved like a banana who was the final period on her evening drama. And more stuff. Well, read the book.

My memoir is a string of episodes in the lives of good people, a man (me) and the beautiful, sensitive, erotically starved divorcees and librarians whose proper makeup and carefully designed clothing hid a howling wilderness of hormonal adventure let loose for the first time. Oh yes, it could be humorous and we had a good time, too. We have to stop taking ourselves so seriously.

Someone once told me that the expression on a woman's face, when she is orgasming, is similar to that when she is in pain. I would differ slightly, saying it is more similar to the look when she bites into a fine chocolate with a raspberry or caramel liquid center. She rolls her eyes up and gets a dazed look. Someone else told me that the stuff in chocolate is the same complex array of carbon and other atoms that is in our brains when we @ like bunnies. So I must be on to something.

In those days, I strangely never seemed to make love to a woman my own age. I lived two separate love lives, one with younger women, the other (to which this memoir is lovingly devoted) slightly older women. They were, in fact, all young, as I see it today, long after the fact. Perhaps I will write a memoir some day about my younger women. My memoir about women my own age would largely be a blank book. The real treasure, I believe, lies with my Summers. That's what I call them. I was Spring, and they were Summer. That's the memoir that this book is about: Summer in the Garden of Eros.

Limerence is that state of madness that newly in love couples fall into, which lasts a few weeks or a few months, and then they either marry or move on. If we all remained in limerence, there would be no skyscrapers or airplanes or post office boxes. There would only be men and women, @ing in the woods. There would be no Camembert, no white wine, not even beer. We'd all be too busy @ing in caves to take time out to invent the pencil, or the telephone, or spoons.

When you are young, as I was, and reasonably attractive without overstating it, you have the event horizon of a mosquito. Tomorrow is already years away. Like a child, you can only plan for the next hour. Mostly, it's can I get laid now? Or do I have to wait another hour? Geez, can I endure? Here I was, in a perpetual state of either confusion and depression, complete with English degree, curbside guitar, and long flying dark hair, or I was in a state of limerence with some woman for whom I felt moments of love, hours of affection, and, well, that's as far as I could see. I loved them all, in my own way. I certainly respected them. This is a memoir of, if not quite love, affection and deep respect. In thee I see myself.

I was that guy most of us are at that age, who would panic, would escape out a tenth-story window down the fire escape, at mention of the word Commitment. It was like saying Communism to Joe McCarthy, only I wasn't frothing at the mouth or biting people. All you saw was my pale face, and then a puff of wind, and then nothing. I had vanished.

My Summers understood that, for the most part. Some were still bruised and tender from their failed marriages. Some still confused limerence with true love. I was not ready for true love. I wasn't even ready for true life. But I was ready for true sex. People are wrong to call sheer sex an animal act. That's not what interested me. I could wear that famous author's meat glove and have sex in a minute or two, as if clearing my throat or gargling. What my Summers and I had was freedom, sex, and wild affection. They were done with some horrific relationship, and they knew they were just going to find another relationship with the same exact guy, just a different name. But meanwhile, in the interim, they left their baby with grandma and lied about going to the movies with Sally or Biffette. Then we went to her place, unplugged the phone jack, turned off the lights, and, well, read the book.

Into many a lucky young man's life comes a slightly older woman—and into her life comes a slightly younger man. At their young ages, a slight difference in years is a significant bridge between spring and summer. Theirs is often a unique and important relationship that leaves its tender mark on each for life.

He is about 20, a Spring. She is two to five years his senior, still quite young—Summer to his Spring. He thinks of her as older—forbidden fruit, the Establishment, the possessor of knowledge and rituals he has not even dreamed of. She brings a wisdom and erotic experience (or curiosity). Each is a lock, and the other the key.

He steps through a mysterious door into the delightful garden of that amazing, more mature angel and her secret knowledge. She does much to initiate him into full adult sexuality when younger girls had not a clue—or, having escaped an pleasureless marriage, maybe she comes to him like an innocent, an empty cup thirsting to be filled with the wildness of the young berry.

All the doors are open to a carefree, lusty involvement with virtually no strings attached. For many a Summer it is a flawed relationship that she will remember through rose-colored glasses as the most romantic, free, and lustful of her life. For the Spring, it is often the wildest erotic experience of his life, and he will never forget her. She may be a cool and skillful player, or she may fall in love and get hurt when he runs. There are risks for both, but anyone who has had a good relationship of this nature knows how special and unique it can be.

If she is wise, she will avoid getting involved with an abusive Spring. The last thing she needs is more sadness or ugliness in her life. If she picks carefully, she will have, however briefly, a handsome, if bumbling, and zesty toy she can hop in bed with, in a relationship where she is largely in control. She will first put her Spring through a testing process before getting too involved—she may invite her Spring to dinner with friends, and get some third-party opinions. She may walk with him down a dark street or a remote corner of the mall, to see if he displays predatory or undesirable traits. If she intends to sleep with him, she'll adhere to the not-on-the-first-date rule, or maybe a rule that says goodnight kiss on the first date, light petting on the second, romp from the third going forward. A Spring worth his salt will respect her pacing, and will show some class by being patient and not pawing her. She can instruct him in this, and he should be eager to learn new subtleties in life.

This book is my erotic memoir. Both I and my Summers, seen in these pages, are still in the blush of youth, as seen from the perspective of the now much older man I have become, who looks backward in time at a very different person he was long ago. I'll have more to say about this, later, but briefly. I make no excuses for who I was, nor how I lived. I am grateful I could share those wonderful long-ago moments with the Summers who allowed me into their intimate and alluring gardens.

Summer is the most alluring, primal, and sexually gratifying event in a Spring's life. The affair may last a few months, or a year or so at most, but it leaves its imprint on both for the rest of their lives. In a sense, she is the standard by which he gauges all his later amatory experiences. He may leave her, for any number of reasons—he often does love her, truly and deeply, in his muddled manner, but he may dump her because he isn't ready for commitment—or she may decide to move on, when she has tired of playing, when she has healed from her bad time, when she starts to need a man of means who is ready to launch a new family with her.

My stories are from a period in my early to mid-twenties, when a year or a few years makes her the 'older woman.' Maybe there are guys who go on living in this mode beyond their mid-twenties, but I know nothing of that, and I know nothing of May/December. She isn't strictly what we call a cougar today. The age difference generally isn't that great. In this context they are each a cougar cub, though she is the older and more cunning.

During that phase of my life, I was still living life in a chaotic, primal fashion. I lived from day to day, month to month, job to job, place to place, woman to woman. I had finished college—had a B.A. in Liberal Arts, was beginning to pick up the thread of Graduate School. I chose not to teach, and stayed out of academe. I was a rather lost soul. I careened from one affair to the next. There was not a ready paycheck for what I had studied. I could not show any Summer prestige or high pay. She usually did better in those things than I, and wasn't looking for that in me. Quite often, she was still wounded from her bad marriage or relationship, and needed time to heal—so why not play and have fun during those months?

Aside from some immature self-centeredness, I was a charming and kind enough guy. I didn't have a car, being an urban animal adept at getting around the city on foot or by public transportation, although I worked as a taxi driver at some points. I was blessed by a reasonably cheerful nature, a certain quiet confidence, a mixture of integrity tempered by total cowardice in the face of any sort of commitment. I had the blush of youth on my cheeks and the taut, trim lines of a twenty-something body. One Summer told me I was the youth in her dream who bicycles, sails, plays guitar on the sea wall while his hair flies in the wind. She, as was typical, did not let me take over her life, not that I sought that; nor did she take over mine, but she made a niche between child care, work, and social commitments for a candles by the tub, walks in the park, romps in the hay romance.

This is a loving memoir of a time and its women. I was never intentionally unkind or thoughtless (although the nature of being the younger man in a woman's life makes it almost inevitable). Nor is this a series of prurient titillations, though it fondly recalls, in explicit detail, the minutiae, the sounds, feelings, and excitements, of each relationship. I remember each woman with love and respect, although in varying degrees and ways. Some deserve more than others. Some cannot be thanked enough. In each case, it is a true portrait of a moment in time, of lives entwined however briefly, and deserves to be captured on the photo film of memory.

There was a short story I once wrote. It was called 'Piano Music.' It was about a young man living in a large house with many other boarders in a New England city. It was a story about how the young man was lonely and drifted from job to job, from one lone meal to the next at a diner, just to be close to a certain pretty waitress for a short while. Lest you think this is a rake's tale, think again. The younger man lives his own life, most of it actually separate from his dalliances with the older woman. He does meet and enjoy younger women and women his own age. The story 'Piano Music,' is dry and autumnal as one of those Swedish movies in which the actors do nothing but talk and make bored or tragic faces while walking along dismal canals under black and white skies. That's enjoyable in its time and place. In the house on which I based that story lived a piano player I never saw, probably a university student, who practiced night and day. He or she was quite good, and on some days the concertos just rolled out under the hammered keys in great swirls, whirling down darkened hallways whose walls glistened with underwater light. On other days the notes were as sparse as the distances between crows on a telephone wire in winter. It might be Chopin or Satie or Pharaoh Sanders. Poignant arpeggios and solo notes and carpets of chords minor, major, augmented, diminished, Persian and Western, rolled around the bleak corridors of that great empty house the way October leaves roll and circle on gray streets. The younger man is attracted to his older young woman because they are at the intersection of her hunger and thirst with his, maybe at a place like that—a house of loneliness and longing, near an intersection of fulfillment.

The Story of A

A was the first June in my life—almost a July really, at 7 years older. I was utterly inexperienced in matters of love and much else, until instructed by *A*. I was 23 years old, just out of college with a B.A. degree in Liberal Arts, and no idea how to live a practical life. I had pretensions of being recognized for a minor poetic gift I did in fact possess, but this (ahem) cruel world offers little reward for such things. I was driving a taxi for a living, and I soon discovered, to my amazement, that many women see the young taxi driver, with his slender body and long, flying dark hair, as a kind of doctor, artist, shrink, authority figure, what have you. For a few fleeting minutes as you navigate the streets, you are the captain of the ship. To be honest, only one or two liaisons came from this source, but the few that did were firecrackers. So, one day, I was taking this 29-year-old woman home. She was divorced, had a child I never met (as was often the case in these affairs, amid their juggling of people and times to give us space), and lived in one of those huge apartment blocks that smell of Dry-Fluf and carpet cleaner.

How did this come about?

I recall the swirls of snow on the darkening streets as I drove her from the school, where she taught Music (if that's not ironic; and maybe it's what made me think of the title of that dreary short story). How did it happen? She talked animatedly all the way. She was Italian-American, and beautiful in an understated, 'cute' girl next door kind of way.

Oh, and this you must realize: once a young man finishes college, the blender of constant young chicks vanishes overnight. If he is smart and studies something for which society pays, and he makes a nice salary and circulates among offices in which many women work, then maybe a newer, still lesser blender begins. After all, he is now more responsible, and his event horizon goes from 'the next moment' to 'tomorrow,' 'next year,' or even 'when I retire someday.'

I was driving a taxi, and at a loss to share with anyone the meaning of the circles in Dante's Hell, or the underlying Weltschmerz of Waldo Gassoff, poet and longshoreman, and all the other obscure things on which I had written papers during my undergraduate years. When people asked, I sort of fibbed and said I had applied to graduate schools. I hadn't yet, at that point. A young man could not be more lost in life than I was during those years.

A was in control of the situation. She had a wry mouth and a sense of humor to match, and brazen brown eyes in a smooth oval face. I can still see her as she leaned over the seats with her arms crossed and her chin on her wrists as she asked: "Would you like to have a drink with me?" Her insouciant grin gleamed handsomely from smooth olive skin.

It took me a moment or two to close my mouth, which had dropped open. I had several working hours yet to drive, and I couldn't think of having anything on my breath.

"You are a good responsible man," she said (was she teasing me? Of course).

"How about later?" I asked.

Blah, ...di Blah, ...di Blah, ...di Bloody Bla-Bla.

Skip to eleven o'clock that night. By now she knew more about me than I knew about her. Actually, I cared less about her background than she did about mine, to be honest. I was flying blind. She seemed like a nice person, and I had nothing better to do. She seemed 'older,' and I wasn't interested in her for that. We found ourselves in a nightclub around eleven. I got carded on the way in. She laughed. "You are tall, and thin, and good looking of course, but that thick dark hair and those wavy, flying curls, you look so damned young that it makes my mouth dry."

We had one drink each; beer for me, some mucky looking ladies' thing with chocolate in it for her. We danced to a absolutely horrible band of Mediterranean-looking men in Mongolian-looking suits, playing the worst kind of lounge music imaginable. Understand that this was near a highway on/off ramp, and all sorts of brief encounters flickered on the movie screen of this hotel's existence. For her, it was a convenience because she lived within walking distance.

It was good to hold her, and I became interested. As my hands moved with surprised fingertips over the smoothness of her slender waist and the generous curves of her hips and rear, I stopped thinking of her as 'older.' She had a body under that dress, a figure that was as smooth and soft as any girl's. I had an erection and a wet spot soon after. She cut us off after that one drink, and nursed us out into the lounge, which was less intimate. She told me once after: "Don't you get it? A woman tries you out. Sees how you act. If you're an animal. If you can't keep your hands off. If you are dangerous, and she's smart, you won't see her again." With that, she touched my nose, brushed a kiss on my lips, and swished away. She wore a purple ski parka which made her look athletic and young, and she wore a dark skirt that came to just above the knees, with some kind of grape-colored hose and then mahogany loafers. Very high school music teacher. There was, of course, the never-on-the-first-date rule, of which even I was aware, so I had patience and got a sense of where the game was headed. I mean, I had an inkling, or maybe let's say a hope. Here I was, just past 22, a veteran of plenty of college adventures with girls as young and inexperienced as myself. I was still experiencing things like blue balls and unplanned, early erectile launch. Smooth I wasn't.

Third time around, same lounge, she adjusted the rules. We were dancing a slow dance that squeezed like toothpaste out of the sound system—a slow motion mazurka with yak butter. It was dark in there, and a ball twirled slowly in the ceiling sending glitter in all directions. I found myself looking into her eyes and falling in love, and starting to panic. This wasn't supposed to be happening.

I had a few friends in town, and I couldn't tell any of them I was seeing a woman with the earliest signs of crows' feet around her mouth and eyes. All I knew was, I had not gotten laid in months, and my loins were like panthers running across the veldt—directly at her. Here eyes were full of glitter and veiled desire, not to mention the lead singer's unintelligible moaning. I did what I had done each of the previous times—I slid my palms down the narrow isthmus of her waist, to feel the branching out of that river delta in whose channel I longed to blow my steam whistle—loudly, and often. On previous occasions, she would shove my hands away—no, roughly place them back on the fine and proper line of her waist. Don't think there weren't jaded and cynical eyes watching our every move like snipers across the rims of whiskey glasses in the dark recesses with their red plastic (torn) bench seats studded with brass tacks. This time, she responded by saying, "Let's go have one more drink."

Surprised at this change of vectors, I allowed her to lead me back to our own dark nook, where she ordered a 'little bit more interesting drink' for me. It was a Rusty Nail, which is a Drambuie with Scotch (insist on Chivas). One of those will rattle your yurt. Two... She looked at me with those amused, calculating eyes, and the pink lipstick on her wry mouth glistened: "You can't drive home yet. Why don't you come up to my place and I'll fix us coffee?" Good strategy, *A.* If I was aware of being finessed, I calculated and ended up not caring.

The equation was loaded in my favor (and hers, each for our own reasons). There was that long, brisk walk arm in arm, with chattering teeth, for neither of us felt fit to drive. It was cold, and wisps of dry snow swirled on frozen asphalt. The street lights looked Arctic and distant. By the time we reached her apartment block, our ears were numb and our lips blue. That's when I first smelled the Dry-Fluf and the carpet cleaners, which remain sexual excitants to this day. I'll skip the coffee and conversation. Actually, she made tea and put a little shot of rum in each. More strategy. We sat on the couch together, watching some musical variety show. Then the TV was off, and she was sitting closer. All I had to do was reach over and put my arm (hesitantly) over her shoulder, and she scooted close so she could snuggle against me. It amazed me that so ancient a woman could be so much like a college date.

The only sounds in her apartment were those of the refrigerator dropping ice cubes now and then, and distant movement of water in pipes. Oh, and grit hitting the windows as an occasional snow flurry kicked in. I like this part. The fumbling. The trembling. The ache and the desire. The help from her. Oh, but first, the kissing. It is a long meeting of tongues. We find that we are compatible kissers. This is important. It has to be just right, and this was.

We were in tune, in rhythm. Maybe her being musical helped. Our tongues worked against each other, left, right, top, bottom, purple, moist, hungry. Our bodies grew more horizontal and I maneuvered more on top. My hands wandered over the sweatered contours of her body, her small breasts, her taut stomach and full hips and thighs. She was voluptuous, ripe, needing. She maneuvered me like a big boat and got my anchor caught in her bay.

So it turned out—a glance at the clock, which was close to one a.m., and the fact we both must be at work early—and she said something like "Let's relocate." That brought us to her bed, and, tired as I was, a stubborn insistence on getting under her flimsy (pink) silk night gown. "You have so much energy," she said as she pulled up her nightie, and I plunged upon that wonderland like a swimmer into an Olympic pool. And here's the critical thing, which makes this memoir worth telling. The woman had passion. After preliminaries—which included licking the soft pink nipples of her small, uneventful breasts—I pushed her knees back and rose against her like a bus parking.

She pulled me to her at the same time, hands around my buttocks, then helping my pointing prow through the gate. There was a momentary dryness, before her labia sweated themselves wet, instantly, and she barked with passion as she urged me on, or in. I slipped into that good sweet container that fit me like a body glove. I exulted as if I'd just been won an erection, been erected president. We were a great fit, *A* and I. We went to work the next morning, each of us with barely a few hours of sleep.

We met again the next evening (she was getting her little one babysat by grandma) and, after a nap, started in again. We could not get enough of each other. Understand that, until now, making love had seemed to me a quick thrash in the bedding with some girl as inexperienced as I was. This woman had seven years on me. In that time, she had wed and divorced, and undoubtedly had more than one relationship. So it was now that she introduced me to a few new things. She brought out the rumba, the passion, and the poetry in me. When she lay there on her back, pulling her knees to her breasts to open the gate wide for me, I developed a kind of rock 'n roll of the hips, a mechanical jam-bam action like a windup toy. I loved the wideness of that basin under me, the richness from thigh to thigh, the wealth that opened before me.

She liked to play. She had fire and imagination, and she enjoyed letting me look up her skirt as she did dishes. We had fun together. I remember crawling into the kitchen and looking up her skirt and playfully biting one buttock that was palely visible in the shadows. She knew I was there, and let me.

In the same vein, I remember walking into her house from a trip to the grocery store, blowing her a kiss, and starting to telephone a friend. She was wearing only panties and a hugely oversized sweater. Meanwhile, she was on her knees before me as I spoke on the phone. She got my cock out and sucked on it with energy and enjoyment, while laughing. Soon my conversation with the friend petered off as my voice grew faint and he said "Are you okay?" while I said "Call you later" and hung up. I closed my eyes and just stood there, enjoying the sensations while she licked my cock and my balls and pleasured herself with the fingers of both hands under her sweater. I noticed the panties now lay crumpled in mid-kitchen.

When she couldn't stand it any longer, she pulled me down by my cock like a pull-toy. As I got on my hands and knees over her in the small hallway containing the phone, between kitchen and living room, she held her labia apart with thumbs and forefingers and whispered over and over: "Get in, @ me, get in, @ me..." until I was in and @ing her and then she held me tightly by my buttocks and moaned, "@ me, Peter, @ me," over and over again until she came. Sometimes, she told me she momentarily passed out as she came during our sex. I believe it. *A* and I were a recurring item for several years. We became @ buddies after the initial passion cooled. It's more than that. We cared about each other, though her temper and my immaturity and our age difference wreaked inevitable havoc.

Sometimes, when I was unable to come visit her, she would call me. I was always glad to talk, so she only had to ask a question or two about the arts, about history, and I would recite all that I knew. She would listen quietly, and sometimes even cry out in wonder. One time, I asked her a question, and she was silent. I grew impatient and said something unkind. She said, "No, no, just talk, talk to me, Peter, I want to hear your voice. You have the most wonderful, soothing voice. It's like listening to music..." So I went on talking, and pretty soon her cooing noises and gasps told me finally that she called me to masturbate to the sound of my voice. Now who could feel slighted by such a compliment?

She had an absent habit of lying on the couch watching television, and lifting her dress slowly to rub her clitoris with her middle finger. At first, in my naïveté, I thought she was just scratching an itch; well, she was, but a different kind. I don't think she was aware of doing this most of the time. She would be engrossed in watching some handsome man on television, and start rubbing herself. When she then held her breast, and sighed heavily, and occasionally licked her finger, I understood that she had become very turned on. She liked it when I would come over, lean over the back of the couch, and help her with my finger. Sometimes our fingers took worked together on opposite sides of her clitoris. Sometimes together we brought her to a little shuddering climax that way. We enjoyed each other's company for many months and played together every time we got together.

Since this is a celebration, I won't dwell on how or why relationships sour. Leave that to the sociologists and anthropologists who study us as if we were a race of chimps wearing designer clothing. I was at that time intent only on hopping on her bones, as they say, and the bones were more than eager to get hopped on.

The Story of B

It was summer, and I was past that first wonderful May/July relationship with *A*, when I met *B*. I was walking a friend's dog on the beach, when this tall, attractive woman sort of towered over me. I think she fell in lust almost instantly. She had this glow that beamed out in all directions. She was a tall blonde in her early 30s, 6 feet tall to my 5'10" with that modeling agency poise. Great face, squarish but soft. Great hairdo, done professionally and amplifying her noble lines.

She wasn't a movie star, but she worked for a motion picture production company, and had actually done some modeling in both New York and Los Angeles. She had married a company executive, made trips to places like Bimini or Antigua and what not, and became a photo shoot producer herself. As with *A*, the perennial symbol of this paradigm (for a young twenties guy) was the incipient crows' feet around the corners of the mouth and the eyes. But geez, I soon began to compare the experience of the younger man/gorgeous older woman to driving an incredibly expensive car that was just a few years past its production date, having come into its prime.

Women seem to get started rather slowly in the passion department. They are so intent on dating right and marrying right and @ing right and cooking right, and above all obsessed with their diet and figure, that it usually takes a brisk, awful divorce and some soul searching for them to let go—at least for a while—and say the hell with it all. Which is when I, the younger guy, step in. Face it, she's between geeks. First there was the guy she divorced, and next will be a guy just like him, but in the meantime we have a little of what I call wedge time, in-between geeks. She'll whisper in my ear, as we lie naked and entwined, that I am just a cute behind, a full mass of wavy dark hair, sweet in my naïveté, and I look good on a bicycle or playing my guitar on the sea wall.

There might be some truth to that. Tanned, relaxed, muscular, I had to laugh quietly to myself when cars would crawl past in beach traffic, and women nearly fell out the window as I took their breath away. Don't misunderstand me—I don't say this to brag. It was all an illusion. I was still the same poor church mouse working crappy jobs and almost hating myself. I was ashamed to tell people I shoveled shit for a living. I was still writing poetry, but starting to think of switching to songs. That was another illusion, or delusion, but I think it made me interesting. I was passionate about my pipe dream, if not about my lousy jobs. One or two Summers told me they thought I was a young stud who looks like he stepped out of a jeans commercial.

B didn't appreciate poetry as much as she liked my flat stomach, which she liked to palm with her hand at odd moments. Like I'd be driving us to the movies or to lunch or the beach, and her hand would sneak over and rest flat against my stomach. There were like these waves of sensuality that emanated from her hand as she did this. Apparently it really turned her on. I'd glance over and see her half-closing her eyes. She'd be looking around at crowds, at people passing as I drove, but I would swear she was in stage one of a ten-stage orgasm. She'd lift my shirt and reach underneath and put the palm of her hand against my stomach. I don't know if she rubbed back and forth, or if it was the molecules in her hand marching in step, but I could sense her sucking sex out of me. Women do stuff like that. Men have to stick it in and @. Women can suck sex out of you with their eyes, or even by not looking. They can be turned on by seeing out of the corner of their eyes, while pretending to be aloof, that you are staring hungrily at them.

Talk about hungrily. *B* had breast implants. Why, I have no idea. Sometimes she just wanted me to hold them, squeeze them gently, to ease the discomfort. I love small breasts. I love breasts of all sizes, but small is a specialty for me. *A,* the first older woman in my life, had small unremarkable breasts with wimpy pink nipples, but she made up for it in other ways. *B* had maybe had small breasts once, but now they were bazooms. They were the kind of bazooms that hang a little, are a little long, and not balloons. Talk about hungrily. When she wore a bikini, and we walked along the beach, I could feel the laser-like searing beams of men's eyes following her. She was tall, and her blond hair was long and straight and flipped this way and that. Being a model and actor, she conveyed that surfer look. Did I mention that she had a few freckles? She had them on her boobs, too. Her boobs terminated in these brown nipples that pointed right at your loins if you stood there talking with her.

B was taller than I, and this helped us have an interesting sex time together. It turns out that if a woman is slightly taller... a matter of proportion, her legs, her torso...I'm talking just the right combination of strengths and lengths...then you can @ her while dancing, and she will enjoy it just as you will. If you are capable of standing up and having an erection, and maintaining that boner, you can enter that tall woman and dance with her while @ing her. We did it all the time. It was addictive. This is what tears me up. In each of those relationships, there was at least one remarkable, wonderful aspect that I miss to this day. This was one of the things I missed about *B.* She had the hots for me, which meant that she got wet right away. I could drive to her place and get out of the car and knock on her door, and as she opened the door, she'd get wet. She didn't get on her knees and start sucking me like *A,* but I knew. Early on, in the time when a woman is at her hottest in a relationship, I came to her apartment once and saw that she was wearing this navy blue bikini. I noticed that the crotch had a dark spot. Being bold and very intimate with her, I wrapped one arm around her and scooped her to me, while reaching down there. Being nimble-fingered, I penetrated through the webbing in her bikini bottom and into the moist folds of her oyster. "You are very wet," I said, and she pressed against me with a kind of guilty moan. She said:

"I was looking out the window and when I saw you pulling in, I felt myself get all hot and wet below."

I learned that *B* was passionate, in a way different from *A*, especially at certain moments. Like the time I walked in on her while she was bent over looking for something under the bed. I just walked up behind her, lifted her skirt, got my Wang out in one quick motion, and penetrated her. She was wet and ready in an instant—she'd heard me coming, and some ESP must have radiated my desire to her on a subliminal level. As usually happened when we dance-copulated, she'd weaken in her passion and beg to be laid down.

Now, @ing her oyster from behind, I let her toss that long body of hers onto the bed, never falling out of her because I was so hard for her. My dong isn't extra long, but it's extra wide. I have what you might call a thick dick rather than a long dong. When a man inserts his cock, it fills an emptiness that desires filling, the way a napoleon longs for custard. So *B* liked it when I pushed her forward, bumping my hip against her butt, so that she sprawled across the bed.

How long her legs were! I was in her oyster, pumping away, while feeling her buttocks with my fingers. She didn't want me to penetrate her anally though. That would be another day, another lady. I did glimpse a nice tight virgin bum. I remember that much, and some clamorous orgasms together, and not much else about that relationship. It was the Paleolithic period of the Spring/Summer epoch in my life. I didn't quite know how to draw things out and make them exquisitely breathless, hungering, delicious. I do remember that *B* wanted to be in love, and I honestly admitted early on that I wasn't ready, and she moved on. She was the one who stopped calling. In a way, I was glad she rescued herself before she fell too hard.

The Story of C

C entered my life one day when I was out for a walk. It was an autumn day, and leaves rustled knee-deep on the streets. It was mid- afternoon, which meant the sun was vanishing amid smoky gray clouds and the smell of burning wood was in the air. In this gray world, I stopped at a convenience store to buy a soda, and there she was in the dairy aisle. I'd stopped into the store more out of desire for its cozy lights than out of thirst. In particular, I didn't want to take my eyes off the blue and red neon beer signs because some receptor in my brain associated that with warmth and everything that was opposite the gray, dreary New England November and the light of a failing day, the failing light.

She was tall, not as much so as *B*, and shapely. That wasn't immediately evident since she wore a heavy black coat, jeans, sweater, wool cap with light brown hair sticking out. She trailed a long scarf as she walked to the counter with her milk and a few cans of food. We had a brief brush at the counter. Each would let the other go first. I won, and she went first. Her eyes gave me a long, lingering look and she smiled invitingly as she left the store. I paid for my cola and was on the sidewalk seconds behind her. "Hi," I said.

"Hello," she said. She was fumbling with her car keys, and I rushed to hold her groceries while she unlocked her car. She thanked me and put the groceries inside. I had to think fast. On the back seat of this great big old black car was a book. "Have you read his other books?" I asked—anything to keep kindle conversation. She smiled. "Yes, I think I have read" (she scratched her head and laughed) "all of them. Now have I? Am I missing any? Do you know what they all are?"

"How about joining me for a cup of fancy Java tea down the road at that little place, and we'll make a list together?"

She gave a little shrug. "Okay, that would be nice." She stuck out a hand in a pink mitten. "I'm *C.*"

"I'm Peter," I said. "I was out for a walk. Can I ride with you?" And that's how it went. We had a very pleasant tea in a kind of boutique where people in scarves came and went. There were barrels of oats and other seed things, plus groceries and flowers, and a small section of books and magazines. *C* liked to read and was impressed with my poetry, so we lingered over the books a while. She was single, and lonely, so we agreed to wander to her place. She lived in a cozy little apartment behind a larger house, but she had her own driveway and privacy. She was an accountant, a very bright lady with much patience and a good head for numbers. We spent a pleasant hour or two, until it was time to make dinner. We ate lightly, and then watched a movie. Somewhat later, she was very close on the couch and I kissed her. She was not very aggressive, but her breathing changed and I sensed that she wanted to be loved. "Why don't you spend the night?" she suggested. Taking our time, kissing, petting, we slowly undressed each other. Even in the near dark (lit only by stray light from the living room beyond a half-closed door, and by a night light in the bathroom nearby), I marveled at the smoothness of her skin and the perfect form of her limbs. Here was a treasure that had been concealed in modesty and heavy clothing. She was transformed from a gentle, easy going doe into a hard-breathing, hungry forest animal. She pawed my back and my ribs. She planted kisses in my ear so that I felt the heat and moisture of her sharp breaths. We lay side by side as we kissed, deep penetrating kisses, plunging wet tongues like sea animals rubbing together in the deep.

Her breasts were full and pleasant, with large plum-colored nipples. They hung slightly in their fullness. As I sucked on her nipples, I had my fingers in her. Her quiz was so wet with desire that when I moved my fingers around, faint little wet sounds smacked in the quiet air around us. It turned me on further. She giggled with embarrassment, but not for long, because I could feel the hard little bud of her clitoris against my finger, and I rubbed gently the damp, smooth furrows on either side.

The little clit swelled and pressed against my finger seeking my touch. *C* was intent on that clitoris pressure, and seemed to be moving her body around as if tracking the fingertip she at first desired, then needed. I moved my fingertip down under it, and *C* moaned under me. I rubbed two fingers up and down, one on either side of her clitoris, capturing it between my fingertips on each swing and exerting a tiny amount of pressure that made *C* writhe and thrash her feet on the sheets.

She gripped one of my upper arms with one hand, while her other hand held my balls and with one finger she stroked the shaft of my penis until I too was ready to thrash. I knelt closer, offering myself to her hand, and she cupped my balls in both hands while she took my penis into her mouth. We worked our passion up to white heat, and it was clear we could wait no longer. Then she did a strange thing.

I lay beside her getting ready to enter, when she pushed me away and turned her back to me. She lay breasts-down and reached behind to grasp my arm and pull me toward her. "Come in me," she whispered, "behind."

"From behind?" I whispered in puzzlement into her ear as I lay behind her, slightly over her, with my finger still in the wetness. She shrugged and pushed her hand down so that her fingers rose up to cover the pink cleft. She made a sniffling noise.

"What's wrong?" I asked. I sat back and beheld the breathtaking sweep of her body—her long back and waist, and the fine melon-like widening of her buttocks. It was like looking at a painting. She extended her free hand behind her to pull on one cheek so that it parted from the other, revealing a fine dark pucker. "You want me to come into your butt hole?" I said. My cock longed to plunge into the other pool, but maybe she had some reason... She did have a fine bum hole, and I regarded it with pounding heart. She still covered her oyster with delicate beige fingers, and held open the back door with the other hand. But she had begun gently sobbing, and when I saw tears on her cheeks I embraced her from behind, spooned her, held her tight and close. "I don't want to do anything you don't want me to do," I said.

It took me a good half hour to coax the terrible secret out of her. I was amazed that she would have such a complex about so insignificant a thing. She had what might delicately be termed the opposite of a tight oyster. I suppose that makes it a loose oyster. In other words, she'd had a few bad experiences starting when she'd lost her virginity in college. One or two gruff, indelicate college boys had somehow hurt her feelings. She explained: "I had no idea what it was all about, why I didn't feel much down there, and then I got it from a girlfriend who had overheard the two boys, jocks from the varsity swim team, talking locker room talk.

They'd been talking about tight oysters versus loose oysters, and mentioned her name. Poor *C* had nearly died in mortification at her own indiscretion in dating two boys from the same fraternity house. She'd thought about leaving that university entirely to attend another, but decided to tough it out. She never went near the part of campus where these two lived. Later, her husband had started giving her a hard time about it before dumping her for a younger woman—with a squeaky tight oyster, no doubt.

"So that's what it's all about," I whispered in her ear while she burst out crying. "Baby, baby, baby..." I repeated while rocking her gently back and forth. In ten minutes her sobs had turned into hard, heated breaths. "Let me show you something," I said. "Baby," I said again, to coddle her as I gently rolled her onto her back and hovered over her. "Baby," I said while I grasped my cock and moved it toward her. She regarded me like a starving wolf with white eyes as I slid the head of my cock into her vagina. Yes, it went in easy and there was little friction in the extreme wetness of her desire. She repeatedly raised her head to kiss my nipples. She kissed my nipples in short nips before falling back helpless with moans, to gather her strength and suck my nipples again. I said: "Your little oyster is just fine with me, but to make you feel better, let's do this." I placed my knees outside her thighs, so that the strength of my legs pressed her thighs together. She massaged her breasts with one hand while reaching down to briskly massage her clitoris. She breathed: "Can you feel anything?"

"Oh yes," I said. Her oyster was tight around my thick dick, with the meat of her thighs pressing firmly inward from both sides. "I can feel it, baby. It feels great."

"Oh thank you." She came in a cascade of jerking motions—the first time of several that night. Later, I rolled her over and stuck my dick into her oyster from behind, same thing, with my knees pressing inward against her thighs. We also invented a position in which she sat on top of me with my dick inside of her.

She faced toward my feet, and wrapped her arms around her knees to keep them together, which made her lower legs point away. As she leaned back a bit, I wrapped my arms around her thighs so that her pussy was squeezed together around my cock. She was light, and I was able to rock her back and forth until we both came again. She got up, walked to a dresser, and returned with an object she kept hidden in the back of her underwear drawer among pink and blue, green and yellow silk undoes. "What is that?" I said.

"You don't have to try it if you don't want to," she said in that gentle way she had. I laughed, and she laughed too. I was careful not to embarrass her, because she was very sensitive in this matter. "It's a strap-on that I bought years ago for my husband, thinking it might save our marriage." I rose and embraced her. "Sweetheart, what was wrong with your marriage wasn't the looseness of your oyster. It was the looseness of his brain cells." We both laughed. She walked into the bathroom with this huge, imposing thing.

I followed, palming the cheeks of her butt. She padded nakedly to the sink and ran warm water. This thing she held was all black, and had straps to go around a man or woman's waist. It was an ingenious solution to a perplexing problem. She said matter of fatly with dry humor: "It's not a dildo for laziest or anything. I found this in a catalog and ordered it by mail. It is specifically designed to solve the problem of loose, wet oysters." She showed me the tunnel that would contain my dong, and the little spigot on one side to fill the tube with hot water. "Makes it feel like you have a tight oysterie around you, while you are ramming me and I actually get to feel like I'm tight."

"Does it work for you?" I asked while she knelt and strapped it on.

"I have no idea," she said. "He refused to try it." She lubricated my head thoroughly with spit. She dribbled spit into the tunnel for good measure, a lot of it, until it was gooey. I thought it was going to feel nasty putting it in there, but it was warm and moist, a pleasant feeling. Not as pleasant as her oyster itself, but my dong was so vibrant from all the sex we had already had that this was just a sort of dessert. "Take me," she ordered, as she climbed onto the bed and waited for me on her hands and knees. The rubber was surprisingly light as I walked toward her holding it in both hands. My dick felt cozy inside. "Do you need some cream or something?" I asked.

"No, can you feel how wet I am? Turn me on. Spit in me."

I knelt at the foot of the bed, savoring her rear with my eyes. I ran my palms over the curves of her butt cheeks. I rubbed her clit with my fingertip. I used both fingertips to part her oyster lips slightly, and I spit into the pinkness. Her fingers slid down, this time not to close her oyster to me, but to rub her clitoris while I spat into her. "Am I dribbling yet?" she asked.

"Any moment now," I said, and just then a fine thread of silvery spit dribbled out of her hole and over her clit and down onto the bed. She had a fine little light brown bush, and it got full of spit. She slid two fingers into herself, then pulled the fingers out and put them in her mouth to taste both my spit and her oyster juice.

"Baby," I whispered. My cock was hard as a rock inside the firm oysterie tube. She said: "Ram me. Go on. Ram me. Stuff it in me and slam me."

I rose and moved toward her. She helped guide the thing into her hole, and then cried and sobbed loudly as I grasped the fine china points of her hips like jar handles and slammed her repeatedly against my groin. "Does it hurt?" I asked at one point, and she just managed to swallow hard, saying "No, feels good, ram me, ram me!" The popping noise of her soft buttocks slamming against my hard, flat stomach and groin filled the air. It was a wet, soft, flopping sound that kept on with machine-like determination. Her knuckles grew white as she gripped the tangled sheets around her.

"Turn," I said. She swung one leg almost over my head and pushed herself down toward the edge of the bed. Still standing, I @ed her while holding her waist. Then I crawled up on the bed, pushing her ahead of me, so that she swung her lower legs onto my shoulders. She pulled me up over her so that she could tongue my nipples while I kept flopping her. She had one huge, final climax as the dark shaft shot back and forth inside her. We took off the engine and I came inside her one more time for good measure. Then we lay exhaustedly side by side.

The Story of D

D was a surfer chick in her mid-20s at the great University in our city. She was from Long Beach, California and studying pre-med in New England. She had never been married and had no hang-ups about men, young or old. She had short blond hair with sun-touched (and frosted) highlights, and a square, bluff face. Her eyes were hazel, her nose a cute little ramp, her chin small and angular. She had a high, intelligent forehead and a way of looking fearlessly into one's soul. Her problem was that she was studying organic chemistry and didn't have much time for socializing, especially with men who had agendas and were demanding. She didn't cook, she didn't clean, and she didn't do much foreplay. She liked to @ and then have someone warm sleep beside her. I didn't blame her a bit. We met one day while I was walking through a park downtown and she was hustling past with an armload of books. She was short and muscular, with a swimmer's body—broad shoulders, muscular legs and arms, and places with firm meat or fat.

"Gonna read all those today?" I joked.

She was equal to the situation. "Want to carry some for me?"

I shrugged. "What's in it for me?" even as I held out my arms and she started piling them on me. They were library books about esoteric chemistry and microbiology subjects.

"You're cute. Help me out and I'll buy you a soda."

"Sounds like a fair deal."

We walked together. This was on a balmy spring day around noon. I carried her books to her dorm room, met her roommate—a dark-haired girl of 22 from up north, who wore glasses and sat amid her own mountains of reading material in a dark little cell they shared in a neo-Gothic campus building. *D* was true to her word and took me to a diner, where she treated us to sodas and ice cream. We talked about our lives, and she admitted that she missed having someone to hug. So I hugged her, and we drove down to the beach. "I miss surfing," she said. "It's hard to find a place with good waves in New England."

"I don't surf," I said. "I hardly even like to swim, but I hear there are great waves up at Cape Cod."

She grasped my bicep in hard fingers. "You look pretty buff. What do you do for a workout?" "I bicycle, walk a lot. I have a degree in English and am saving up for grad school, but I have a miserable job right now as night watchman. I walk miles on my rounds."

"Sounds relaxing," *D* said. She was ever one to look on the bright side.

"You must work very hard," I said. She sighed, "yes," and I slipped my arm around her waist. She slipped her hand around mine in a carefree, thoughtless motion. "Poor kid," I said, and hugged her. She stood frozen, with her eyes closed and her chapped lips slightly parted, waiting for me to kiss her. Which I did. It was like eating tangerines. Tangerines that fought back with energy of their own.

She spoke on her cell phone. When she took me back to her room, the other woman was gone. *D* locked the door and showed me the nook where they had a sturdy wooden bunk bed. "I'm on the bottom," she said. She plopped down. "Like it?" I slid in beside her. "Cozy," I said. We sat looking at each other. "You can kiss me," she said. I said: "What a deal. First a soda and ice cream, then kisses. Can I carry your books again?"

"Mm," she said. She took my face in her hands and pulled me toward her. Her tongue entered my mouth and flicked around as if looking about and seeing where to get comfortable. I guided her so that she stood before me. Her tongue never left my mouth. I took my time loosening her jeans and working them down over her solid thighs. I unbuttoned her dark blue flannel shirt one button at a time, until I could open it to reveal two pendulous white breasts like a pair of melons—laced with tiny blue veins, and with enormous flat pink nipples that puckered as I touched them.

She pulled my head against her breasts and waited as I suckled them alternately, palming them, while she pressed my head into her shirt and held me to her. I glanced up and saw that she tilted her face skyward, eyes closed in ecstasy, while a faint blue light from a clock shone on it like on the moon. She looked beautiful and almost unearthly that way. I pushed her panties down so that she stood up to her ankles in heaped clothing. I kept nuzzling those heavy breasts with my lips, while my hands run up and down the smoothness of her calves and thighs. She was not very tall, and this gave her a nice ability I will mention in a moment. She had nice wide buttocks and firm, ripe thighs that begged to be handled. When I touched the little blond tuft of hair on her Venus mound, she readily took it as a cue to part her legs slightly. I pressed my fingers between her thighs. This was a girl who soaked easily. Her oyster was drenched. I had her part her legs more, and then more, while I worked two fingers up into the jelly that she made for me. All the while, she hugged my head to her breasts. Finally, she began to weaken as I stroked her clitoris. She exhaled loudly from the heat, and slipped her shirt off. She looked blue and cool now in the dim room. I swung her gently around and laid her backwards on the bed. She was not acrobatic in the sense that long-limbed, thin women are, but she breathed loudly in and out. She made small moans, and I confess I moaned to have her. My cock was stiff and hard like a wooden bowling pin, and began to hurt from being dry and unsheathed.

When I say she wasn't very tall, I have to be more precise again. It's not just a woman's height or shortness that can make a difference in how she makes love, or how she plays with herself. It is interesting how a shorter torso on longer legs, or a longer torso on shorter legs, can affect what she does and how she does it.

Because her torso was short, and her arms long, she was able to put her fingers into herself. I learned from each of the women in my life. I think a younger man is intrigued by older women because he senses that they have lost the shyness of young girls, and if they weren't shy girls, they have lost the brashness and indelicacy they may once have had. A younger man senses the mystery of what he doesn't know. He sees the mysterious smile of the older woman, even if she is partly laughing out of amusement at him, and he longs for the adventure she takes him on. She takes him into a dark unknown that can only result in pleasure and orgasms. Each woman has her own world, her own flavor, her own nuances, her own way of inventing her place to be. Some are more interesting than others. I'll say more of this later.

D was fascinating because of her directness. You could watch how she took you to her, and, as with many women, you could readily guess what she did alone to satisfy herself. When I slipped my cock into her tight little hole, we had to go slowly. Wet as she was, her sphincter was like an athlete's muscle. She couldn't control its strength. It guarded her precious entry like a warrior. Slowly, working together, we appeased this warrior. It seemed to hurt her a little, forcing this wild thing to open, but we got through. "You're so big," she whispered at one point. "You have a cock like a car."

"Compact and convertible," I quipped. "Sorry if I don't put the roof down. It's raining."

She nodded. "I'm very wet for you." When I did slip inside, we both gasped at the pleasure of it. She was tight and good. We both felt the meeting of our flesh in that perfect passage. The train and the tunnel loved each other and roared together. I came almost immediately, and retreated just a bit as I went limp. "Sorry." "No matter," she whispered. "I'll get you going again. Just rest a little."

"I'll rest inside of you."

"Oh yes, and suck my nipples. I love having my nipples sucked."

So I nuzzled her nipples, which had puckered up and grown into pink button mushrooms. I lay relaxed beside her, with my cock limp in the entrance. She took care of herself for a bit, and I enjoyed watching. She slid one hand down under her heavy buttocks so that she got two fingers into her oyster from below, and massaged the lower entrance where fluid pooled. As she did this, the mid-knuckles of those two fingers stroked up against the swollen area on the lower side of my erection. With her other hand, she massaged her clitoris from the front. She had a rhythmic way of doing this. She would pinch her clitoris firmly and shake it from side to side, like a lion killing its prey.

Then she'd spread two fingers and rub them up and down with the clit riding high between them. In the blue light, I saw it getting hard. I watched the little bud grow and peek out from under the clitoral hood. I listened to the lapping of waves and I put my hand on her wide belly, which shook with contractions racing through her as she came for the first time. I could feel myself getting hard again. Still sucking on one tit, I reached down beside her fingers and imitated what she did to her clitoris. I felt a firm little bundle between my index finger and thumb. "O God yes, do it that way," she said. Her eyes were closed, and her face looked upward in ecstasy. Meanwhile, the hand that had rubbed her clitoris now slid down under her butt and up so that she had one little fingernail slipping in and out of her rectum. I thought of *C's* delightful ass and bum hole, but how loose she was compared to *D.* They are all so different, these women, each a world of delight to explore!

D was the first woman I knew who was not only great at masturbating, but also liked playing with her behind. It was a novel idea to me at the time. I'd always been attracted strongly to a pretty behind (like *C's* exceptional ass and curvature) but I thought it was just eye candy. It never occurred to me that some women derive extra pleasure from stimulation down there. I held her breast but stopped sucking so I could get a better look. I stopped rubbing her clit and put my fingertip down there, replacing hers at the butt hole. "You can go down and watch me," she whispered. "Go on, I want to see you watch me."

I pulled out and slid around so we were head to toe. I pushed her legs up—which I find erotic, because it is such a pose of invitation—and gently inserted a finger lubricated with spit into her rectum. "Oh yeah," she said in a low groan. She now had both hands free to fan her clit and simultaneously run a five-fingered crane beak rapidly in and out of her pussy.

The crane beak is a martial arts metaphor of putting the five finger tips of one hand together in a point, almost forming a kind of cone with the hand. Her wetness made smacking sounds as she masturbated. I played with her butt hole, using two fingers to open it just a crack, and to massage it this way and that while looking at its puckered beauty. Some women are brownies, while others are pinkies. She was a pinkie—tits, oyster, and even the inside of her ass. It was so little, and yet so great to play with. She struggled up the slope of passion and came with a wail. She thrashed around, slapping the sheets beside her and rocking up and down.

Then she grasped my cock. "Are you ready, baby? You helped me out so great. You were a good boy. Now I want to see about getting you up there for a second orgasm. Are you ready, baby?"

"Oh man," I said. I was still at her lower end, and pushed her legs back up so I could soak my face in her wet oyster. I got my tongue all the way up where the birth canal starts (or ends, depending on who you are and which way you're heading). With her mouth on my dong, she had a lip-seal that was first class. She could suction a dick with precision like a German motor. I had never imagined such an exquisite blow-job. Better call it a suction-job. Several times, she released vacuum, and there was a loud popping sound. My dick almost went numb, but it stayed hard as a surfboard. After one such popping noise, she said: "You're hard as a rock, Peter. Get in me, quick."

We did a quick shift around, and I popped into that tight little oyster of hers. We rolled over so I was on my back and she rode me. I reached up to squeeze her orbs. She played with them, then reached down to gently twist my nipples. Here's a little secret. My nipples are the most sensitive part of me (aside from the head of my erect schwantz). If a woman touches them, I come. As I now did, and she came again, so that we moaned together. She rode up and down with her full breasts flopping out of control. I was afraid she would hurt herself, and pressed my palms against them for her to contain them. She wrapped her arms around my hands and her tits and then collapsed in a final orgasm that drained her. She lay limply on top of me, a firm, heavy girl. Older woman. "Just stay there," I said while kissing her face. She laughed like a drunk in her weakness while I pressed her full buttocks down and enjoyed the feel of being inside her.

The Story of E

Stranger than fiction are some of the people you meet in real life. One such was *E,* the freckled and cute librarian with the horn-rimmed glasses. I was in the university library one day, doing some research on Kit Marlowe, when I noticed this slender librarian in a loose-fitting dress laughing as she read a book. She was in her late twenties, about five or six years older than I. She had dark coppery red hair, thick and braided, and freckles to match. Under the neo-Gothic vaults and stained glass windows of a major university's main library, a cathedral of learning, I heard her laughter peal out. As I looked up, she caught herself and made an oops face while bringing her fingers to her mouth. She shrugged self-consciously and looked left and right. I had only to turn and take two steps, which put me before the dark wood of her counter. "I need a laugh today. Can you share?"

She slapped the book shut. "Not on your life." Then she took another look at me and leaned her fine little chin on her fist. "Say, you're cute."

"Thanks. So are you. You know what the fine is for laughing in a library."

"No, what is it," she said buying into my come on.

"I get to torture you with coffee and pastries until you confess and tell me what you were reading that was so funny."

"Where?"

"Shartenberg's."

She thought it over, just for a second. "Well, okay. Will my sentence be long and hard?"

"It depends on how modest and remorseful you are."

She laughed. "Then we're going to fry in hell for all eternity, because I'm neither."

E was in some ways the youngest of all the older women in my life. To me at the time, being 23, she seemed like an older woman who had not grown up. With the thick, round

horn-rimmed glasses off, she could pass for younger than I—
unless you noticed the first streaks of gray in her hair before
she rinsed it. I felt older than she seemed to be.
Chronologically, she was older, but in every other way she
was a giggly ditz. She was fun to be with, kind, patient, and
sexy. She was one of those women that men turn around on
the street to look after. I'm not sure what that quality is in a
woman. Other women, too, stared, sometimes out of desire,
but usually out of envy. Envy, masked as disapproval, is one
of the ugliest traits a woman is capable of. I'll dwell no more
on this, except to say that *E* and I hit it off. Her attitude was a
bit like in your face, which is what I would have liked if I
were more forward and less of a wall flower guy. I'll skip
much of the preliminaries. We did meet for coffee and pastry
at this fine (now extinct) American imitation of a European
style coffee and pastry shop. She wasn't complicated, and she
related early the usual palaver about my being tall, thin,
handsome, thick wavy dark hair that she couldn't wait to get
her fingers into. It didn't take long to get her into bed, either.
She'd never been married, had not settled down yet, was me in
a sense but female and five or six years older.

Before I discovered her most unique trait, I enjoyed low
key sex with her. She was not a starfish, meaning she was not
one of those women who believe sex is something the man
does while they lie limply and sprawled out waiting for the
end. She humped and pumped like a champ. She liked the
foreplay and steamed up a few car windows with me (because
both of our apartments were too small, with thin walls and
nosy neighbors, for much frolicking). She was a slender, soft
woman, not an athlete. She was too lazy to be an athlete. She
ate what she wanted, but had a metabolism that burned off
calories like a furnace, with the result that she was skinny.

She was pale and skinny, with many freckles, and with
hair the color of reddish copper. Irish, she was, through and
through. She wasn't a drinker, but a @er. *E* thought of @ing
the way most people might sip at sodas. A day without a @
was a day missing its sunshine. I might have said that a day

without a @ was [plug in any old somber philosophic thing] but *E* was light on her feet and didn't read much into things. *E,* with that dark red copper hair and quizzical funny expression and cheery if slightly nutty brown eyes and skinny freckled body, was a woman in fifth gear and cruising down a highway with more entrances than exits if that makes any sense. I mean she saw more opportunities than barriers, while she struggled to make more of her life financially. She had a degree in German, of all things, and could say Guten Tag or Wie Geht's but couldn't remember a line of Rilke or Brecht. She was a good @ buddy. In her own way, she was true. I mean, she didn't pick up men right or left. She was actually quite selective. We talked about all this. God, this Irish girl could talk. Put a bottle of beer in her hand and hang her feet over the edge of a dock, and this girl would put you to sleep. I loved her. She was dangerous. No man could ever tame this wild banshee. I felt sorry for her. I worried, wondering how she would land as she got older, because she'd soon be pushing 30 without a man or a real job or a coherent thought in that funny head of hers.

I'll cut you in on a little secret, knowing what I know now: *E* retired from the university system a near millionairess many years later. You see, she had this one quality nobody saw in her. She was loyal, and she stuck to it. That was the meaning of her loyalty to me. She didn't want or need another man. She knew we weren't a permanent thing. The minute I told her my age she turned that page. Still, she had that sense of who she was. In her stealthy manner, the freckled wine-dark redhead may yet outlive us all. I don't believe she ever married, but I'm sure she was never lacking for a companion.

She was a good @, as things go. Nothing complicated. The trick was to spend two or three evenings a week with her, and to make sure she had at least one good orgasm. Here's the deal. She had a pale, freckled body slim and lean almost as a boy's. Her breasts were full and white like milk, though small. Her nipples were red like the copper of her hair. She wasn't a pinkie or a brownie, but that rare thing, a reddie. Like her freckles, her oyster was orange. It was a dark, stained orange, like juice that has sat too long after being spilled.

Many redheads suffer in their beauty, not realizing what autumn leaf delights they are. This girl was the dark end of the leaves, the burning red, the bloody finality of the freckle before it gutters out like the ember that it is. If you don't understand that, @ you. I am a poet with Irish and Celtic blood in my canals, and this woman *E* put me in touch with the wild fox in me. The fox, you'll recall, is a red animal with a thick tail, a pointy snout, and a clever mind. So what was it about *E*? She had a delightful little ass, buttocks that I loved to grab, each a handful. She liked being grabbed if she happened to be in love with you.

What was it about *E*? She had a good little oyster, nice and tight, with a respectable hood and a button of a clitoris under it—orange as her freckles. Roll her over, and she had shapely buttock buns with a nice little pucker down below. She didn't let you @ her heinie, as she called it, but you could play with her buttocks and put your finger, just one finger, slowly, ouch, not to hurt her, just one finger, in there if you must. And must you must, because she had a splendid white ass pale as a half moon, gorgeous in its round lines, lean as a boy's, soft as a girl's, tight as a fresh-baked bread loaf.

Another delightful thing about her, you could @ her in front and roll her over, @ her in the oyster from behind, and she was equidistant if you see what I mean. She was a rare girl, this *E*. Rock her in front, rock her in back, and it was about the same. You noticed that she was cooperative, breathed a little bit harder, maybe groaned a little, but she didn't really come in the cum sense very much. Something was missing. And I learned what it was.

One day, *E* and I were in this dark pub on a side street between the university's music school and residential colleges. It was a windy spring day, and the windows were just open a crack. She and I were in there like a pair of wraiths in the smoke, shadows, in the dark while outside it was sunny. She was sitting on the bench with her back to the window, while I sat opposite her in a chair, with the heavy oak table and its scarred top between us. Some instinct made me kick off my sandal and raise my foot so it grazed her soft white thigh.

She reached down and took my foot in her hands. That is when I learned the secrets of her inner life. *E* guided my foot toward her twat so that my big toe touched her clitoris. She was wearing a short skirt. Under that she had fine silk panties. Here we were, in this place smelling of coffee and echoing with conversation, and under the table she guided my big toe into her oyster. She pulled her skirt up, pushed her panties aside, and rubbed herself to make her oyster wet. Then she pulled my big toe toward her until it entered her oyster. She slid forward an inch or two to help my toe get into her.

With a little wriggling and sliding, she got the upper half of my foot into her oyster. What does this feel like? Well, first of all, your cock is on fire. Your dong is a motorcycle revving at max RPMs with flames shooting out of its pistons. Here is this beautiful girl @ing herself with your foot in a public place. We have to stop a moment and think about what you look like when you are a woman @ing yourself in a public place with a man's foot. She leaned forward, looking rather pale and concentrating, and her eyes wandered out of focus. Her mouth was slightly open, and she was breathing harder, but in a subtle way, and that is important. You are just there— you might as well be just a huge dildo, for all that it matters. You are a sex object. She has learned the art of concealing these public orgasms. As the spasms roll in waves across her belly, she just looks momentarily dazed as if realizing she should bend over and tie a shoelace whose knot has come loose. What an art! What a skill!

Later that evening in the privacy of her bed, I asked her about this event. She grasped my dick and pulled it into herself. "How did it feel?" she asked.

"I was going to explode like a hand grenade," I said.

"Did you come?" she asked while working the inner muscles of her oyster so that my dick felt massaged and I could only moan. I nodded. "It turns me on."

"What?"

"Getting worked up in public. You know, secretly?"

Now I had the whole cycle of *E's* arousal down pat. She was a good little sport when it came to plain @ing. She was good at that, make no mistake. But she didn't shout. Now take after we went someplace public and I orgasmic her. Take her home now and @ her. What a different gal. She reared up in an arch, as if her back was made of rubber, and she wailed as I sucked on her clit and made the juice flow.

God, when I got my thick dick inside of her and whacked it back and forth in her fluids, she had orgasm after orgasm. It was the public thing that set it up. She loved being secretly @ed in public, a matter that can land you in jail and certainly will cause the other patrons of restaurants and movie theaters to become irritated.

There is a whole art to this. The French in fact have dubbed a corner of it frottage, the act of rubbing against the other in a public place. But the art of @ing the other publicly, that was *E's* special skill. That was what turned my little dark-red coppery vixen on.

She had his long dark green olden overcoat. She sewed a slit into the back of it. We measured carefully where this needed to be. Then we would go into a public place, like maybe a crowded trolley. Positioned in the back, with our fronts to the people ahead of us, I could open my fly and push out my rod right through the slit in her coat. What wasn't obvious was that she wore a tiny skirt underneath, which was easy to lift, so that her ass and oyster were accessible.

My cock hungered after her oyster. Given half a chance, my cock would race through a hole in any overcoat to get to her wet little tunnel. She in turn had learned she could lean forward a bit and clamp down some muscles inside to grab that dick and make it sing. So there we were, while the trolley hummed and rumbled along its tracks, and my dick was bursting inside of her slippery oyster tunnel. All the while, she kept a straight face and pretended to be reading the train schedules.

She liked to have sex with this danger all around, this air of imminent discovery. The best part was that when we got back to her place, she was ravenous, throwing her clothes off, tearing mine off, to get my in her mouth...and that didn't last long because she would pull me to the table, bend over it, and pull my dong toward her openings. She liked being @ed from behind, and I enjoyed kneading her pale long buttocks with my hands while sliding in the slush with her moaning, hands splayed on the table as if she were body surfing. As I say, she enjoyed the danger and pushed it to the limit. Once, we were in a restaurant. She had on a pleated tartan skirt. Three middle-aged construction workers with pot bellies, white hair, and red faces sat two tables away over their beers and sandwiches while a juke box played loudly. *E* pretended to read the menu (we had already ordered) while she massaged my foot on the edge of her chair between spread knees. The men must have noticed a single shoe and sock on the floor under her seat. The fact that it was a man's shoe and pointed to her must have added to the evidence.

I didn't dare glance toward them, but I thought I heard a snicker or two. *E* pulled my foot toward her under the skirt. I felt the folds of her vagina on my toes. You don't feel it as much on the big toe, but when she gets going, is wet, is loose and open, and your little toes go in, it's like being gummed by a huge frog. It's a uniquely delightful feeling, especially if the woman has those little oyster muscles that open and close on you like a gasping mouth. We were going good. I never actually masturbated in public, but I had a rod on that ached and required my shifting in my seat.

She was just getting good, with her face flushed and her eyes closed. Just as she gasped, they started laughing loudly. They were crude, stupid men. *E* grabbed her purse, threw a twenty on the table, and ran out the door. I grabbed my sock and shoe and ran after her. The baboons were hooting and making gestures. I saw their red faces and little mouths full of rat teeth and food on their tongues, and wondered if they were of the same human race. My anger subsided when I saw her a block away, bent over a newspaper dispenser, laughing herself silly. I had to start laughing too, and forget the morons—after all, I had more sex in a week than those dumb drunks had in their lives. If they were smart they could have enjoyed the show. Oh well.

Another time we were in the back room of a dark lounge—the kind that advertises itself as a bar & grill. They serve steak dinners to a lunch business crowd but also cater to the beer and sausage crowd a few cuts above the dumb shits mentioned above. So there we were, in the back room, waiting for hamburgers and savoring a mug of beer each. The waitress, herself a tall cute woman in her thirties, with wear heavy in her features but youth still in her eyes and smile, took our orders and flounced away in her flight attendant-like dress. *E* slid around beside me, kissed me, looked around mischievously, and then vanished under the table. I slid down a few inches to give her space to work. She had my zipper out and my erect dick out. I felt the edges of her little teeth on the head, then the shaft. She worked the tip of her pointy little tongue around the opening on top, catching the first stray leaks and squirts. I must have looked like I just swallowed a mouse as I turned purple and sat pushing at the edge of the table. Just then the waitress came back to say "Your order will be just a few—." She paused, looked at me (I immediately acted nonchalant) and then leaned forward with her head tilted so she could see under the table. I don't know what she saw in the dark, maybe *E's* pale hands, my pale dick, and the glint on *E's* glasses from a distant light, but she turned pale herself and said, "Sir, that will be your last beer, and I trust you'll finish up and leave."

"Yes," I said, "make those burgers to go."

She could have done all that Puritan crap people do—call the police, turn us in, fetch the manager, get the local curate, dial E for Exorcism. I commended her silently, within myself, for still being young enough to understand how it is. My dong had gone limp, and I sat up so that it appeared to withdraw of its own volition like an eel pulling back under its rock. I pulled *E* up from under the table and had her sit meekly beside me. She did, except for one moment when she uttered this huge, sucking sigh and swept her lips up behind my ears and whispered "I'm going to tongue @ you as soon as we get home." Minutes later, burgers in bag and bag in hand, we hustled out the door and I sensed the whole waitress contingent staring after us. I think there were a half dozen of them, all looking dour with longing as they watched *E's* tight, girlish ass sailing off on bare, fresh legs.

It was exciting, but scary, and I had trouble getting erections in public with her. We tried having me diddle her, and that worked for a while, but she liked having it in her. I sensed that she was starting to see someone else, and we drifted apart. I did see her once, a few months later. She was with this tall, muscular black man. He had short hair, a small head over huge shoulders, a gold earring, and big hands the color of raw coffee. They stood on the marble steps of a public building in plain sight downtown while the leaves twirled through the air and the October sun shone like wildfire. They each had on long coats. I recognized hers—that long dark green olden with the slit in back. She was leaning over the marble banister halfway up the broad steps, pretending to coo at the birds in the grass below. People were walking by, busses came and went, taxis honked, cars sailed in and out of traffic. I watched for a few moments. He stood behind her with his groin pressed tightly against her rear. His long arms and big hands were in her hair, gently combing it with his pink fingernails, a pretense, as my eyes caught the furtive bumping of his hips against hers. I could imagine that sizeable slick cheroot sloshing back and forth in her bubblegum-colored channel. Wistfully, remembering the feel of her, I turned and walked away. I never saw her again, not even on my occasional trips to the library.

The Story of F

Speaking of librarians, *F* was another of those prim women in early middle age who are full of surprises. *F* was a tall black woman with a frizzy, glistening hairdo (it would have been called an Afro long ago). She had a beautiful face the color of dark wood. Not black, like licorice, but very dark brown, and soft. Her features had a streamlined, almost airbrushed proportion that made her face one you could stare at for long bouts of time. She had dusky, violet lips and gorgeous teeth when she laughed. Her eyes were exotic, almond-shaped as if she were Asian.

She liked to wear big, dangling earrings because she was a tall woman and not afraid to step on six inch heels to add to her glory. In heels, she was taller than any woman I ever dated. We met at a public library when I was doing some research and needed to go into an unfamiliar back section. It as an older, stately building with wood paneling and WPA murals high up painted on plaster. All these muscular men and women had been painted there by Communist-influenced New Deal artists imitating the raw concrete formalism of the Russians in Stalin's time.

Their features were rudimentary and brutal. Even the women's breasts looked tight and muscular. They held tools or sowed grain or did whatever it took to get this mighty economy rolling again. For all that energy, they could have been having a huge orgy up there. They certainly looked like they were full of @ and energy. *F* caught me gaping and said: "Can I help you, darling?" She had a rich, full voice and a tone as if she were the queen of periodicals, addressing the duke of lost looks. I stated my need (the one involving the library) and she stepped out from behind her desk to accompany me. I walked behind that gorgeous swaying wool-clad ass and inhaled the perfume she wore, just a hint of musk in it, but otherwise a complex flute whisper of vanilla and crème citric or something... I don't remember much of what we talked about, but she had that musical voice that wrapped around me like a bassoon. She wore a wool dress, and under that a silk blouse that was fairly open at the top, so that when we stood opposite each other and she leaned over a file drawer to run long purple fingernails over the file folders, I was less intent on her explanation than I was on the full mocha breasts that strained at a black lace brassiere.

She was definitely a principled, not-on-the-first date sort of woman. She was a prodigious kissing partner, however, and her roving hands made it clear there was good stuff to come if I toughed it out on her schedule. When I say her hands roved, I mean that the middle part of my body was off limits.

Likewise, there were limits to where I could touch her. She took me to her apartment in a fine former hotel downtown, the first few dates when she had me come visit on her lunch hour. She was very sincere, and showed me her books and her collection of lithographs (honest; we even laughed that she'd had me come up to look at her sketches). She was an accomplished musician, and played some very touching violin pieces for me. I enjoyed watching her as she closed her eyes and laid her cheek against the pad. Her face became transfigured as she swayed with the music that rolled off her strings. She smiled at the thick, rich notes that poured out from the straining, tight little sound chamber flanked by two opposing clef cuts.

Then, one day, she was ready. Lunch time with *F* had already become a fevered habit for me. I couldn't wait to ride up in that brass elevator, get out in that dark corridor, and walk toward that oak door with a bouquet of dried flowers in a fine little checked ribbon above the spy hole. She had the afternoon off from work, so there was no hurry. First time, we'd go slow and get it right. We'd learn all the right notes and play the augmenteds and diminisheds in slow and stately rhythm like the Gymnopaedies of Erik Satie.

F's furniture was red leather and heavy. She was a tall woman, and wanted sturdy furniture. Her voice changed when we first confronted what we hungered to do. Her voice box tightened with nervous tension, and her mellifluous voice grew light as if she had transformed from soprano to alto. "What do you like?" she asked in a thin, sweet voice as she stood before me while I sat on the couch. I rose and took her in my arms. She stepped down from her heels, still two inches taller than I was. I felt her hands on my back, trembling on my shoulder blades. We kissed deeply, but differently.

"Be gentle," she whispered. In silent reassurance, I held her firmly to me. She laid her head on my shoulder as if we were slow dancing, and I let it be like that for a long time. It was silent in the dark room except for the ticking of a clock and the birds chirping outside. She moved easily and lightly to my touch, but she was big. Not chubby or soft, so much, but a big girl. She had been very athletic all her life. Her legs were robust and firm, almost muscular but soft. Her buttocks were more like armfuls than handfuls.

I could get my arms around her at her widest, so that my hands touched over the dusky crack of her ass, but her hips were in my elbow joints. I had to turn my face up to kiss her—that equaled out in bed, where she soon had me. There, I lay on my back while she straddled me. Her eyes were closed, her mouth distorted with pleasure, as she said: "Lick them. Lick them good for me." Her breasts were not remarkably large, at least not out of proportion with the rest of her.

They hung a bit, pendulous, like grapefruits in a net bag if one wants a comparison. Her nipples were slick and plum colored. They swelled and grew whorls and huge plateau nipples as I sucked on them. "I like that," she said warmly. "Lick them for me. Suck them." She grabbed one from underneath, held it on her palm, and slid it to my mouth. "Suck it, baby. Oh yeah."

With her providing the nipple, my hands were free to roam up and down her long, smooth back. She was slender and shapely. She was beautifully proportioned—just larger than an equally shapely smaller woman. My fingers came to the curly hairs down there, and explored. "Mmmmm," she hummed contentedly. "Yes, baby, that's right." She crawled forward a few inches so that her nipples swung over my mouth while my fingers had easier access to her slit. It too was large, but I was surprised as my fingers discovered how tight she was. She laughed, reading my mind. "I don't often have a man up here. That little pussy of mine is about as close to virginal as you'd expect in a woman of my age."

I said: "I bet all that rowing and tennis and running keeps it tight too."

"You have a point there," she said. "Speaking of which—" She plopped down beside me so that her breasts lay folded in a pile on my left nipple. She reached down and sought my whang. "—you do have a point there. Mmm, that's a good thick dick. Oh yes, it's a good thick dick." She liked to talk a lot during sex, and it was this sensuous rambling, cooing, stream of consciousness, stream of oysteriousness, as she stroked my phallus while her lips descended on my nipples. That's my most sensitive spot. She licked around the outline of my breasts, and sucked on my nipples, while I writhed.

"Baby?" she said.

"Hmm?"

"Baby, what do you want to see?" I smiled at her and whispered in her ear: "What have you got for me to look at?"

She smiled that wondrous flashing smile, brown face, violet lips, pink gums, white teeth, mischievous slanty eyes. She swung around so that she straddled me, bum to my chin, yellow heels by my ears. Her mouth moved down over my cock, enveloping it, and she head-@ed me. She moved her head rapidly up and down while her mouth made itself into a vagina. A less talented woman would inevitably have allowed what the computer jockeys call a head crash. In sex, that's when a woman's teeth bang against the engorged, sensitive head of a man's cock causing untold anguish.

She kept her pearly teeth away, and let that thick dick of mine ride up and down in the shaft of her mouth and throat.

Meanwhile, I had the entire wealth of her ass and oyster spread before me between the beautiful harmonious ovals of her buttocks. When I put my hands down, I was just able to reach as far as her knees, which were round and hard. I ran my palms up the long, firm surface of her thighs, swinging around the orbits of her buttocks, until my fingertips encountered the damp, pink meat between her dark labia.

She had long, smooth labia, not excessively long, but firm and thick like slices of fruit. They would bear much delicious sucking and lip-riding. But first I had to explore the rest of her treasure. Pulling her labia apart lightly, I saw in there the juices glistening on her engorged tissues. Pulling a bit further, I caused the hole of her oyster to part. I could not wait to get my tongue in there.

But first, I lightly fingered her pee hole which sat atop a little cartilaginous mound of its own. Since the whole thing was upside down, I explored downward a little further until I encountered the good strong line of her clitoris. I reached my arms around her thighs and pulled. "What do you want, honey?" she asked in a faint, dazed voice. "Move back a tiny bit," I said. She shunted back a few inches, so that the heat of her meat shone on my face. I inhaled the fragrance of soap and oyster milk. Now I could get my tongue anywhere I wanted. I started at the top. I ran my tongue around and around the rim inside her open oyster, which made her squeal and I felt the first faintest contractions rippling through her. They were just shivers at that point. While I tongued her, I used the tip of one index finger to play with her butt hole. "You can't @ me there," she said primly. "I'm just rubbing it to make you horny," I said.

Actually, I would have gladly experimented with putting my whang in there, but one does not force a woman. One does not go beyond the boundaries of what the woman lets you know is her comfort zone. I had never butt @ed a woman, so I forgot about it, except to keep playing with her sphincter, outside, and she said: "That is nice, honey. Not inside, though." I did discover that, if I rubbed around it with my fingertip (wet with my spit and her juice), and if I pressed lightly while I did so, little tremors ran through her entire body. Maybe she was extra sensitive there. No telling—it would forever remain a mystery zone.

No mystery zone her pussy region, however. She pressed it close to my face, with her thighs spread, inviting me to take her. "Do what you like," she said. "Do what you like, baby. I like whatever you do. Just take it. Play with it. It's all yours." So I buried my face in it, licking her oyster hole and then her pee hole (which is rich in nerve endings and drives many a woman up a wall).

I mouthed her Venus mound and moved my tongue up around the shaft of her clitoris. As I played with her clitoral hood, her clit swelled and began to bulge out. She hissed with agonized pleasure as I touched it with the tip of my tongue. She hissed loudly, and stiffened, as I carefully worked my tongue around and around the mushroom bud of her clit. It waggled stiffly on its stem, so erect was it. She began moaning loudly, as if in pain. It sounded as if a large cat were wailing in the room, over and over again, the same tones.

When her clitoris was fully erect, almost like a little bone, I could work my tongue in behind the head and into her clitoral hood. Only for a second, though—because now she came. And how she came. She reared up, tilting her face back, and groaned loudly. Then a bellow. And a soft, declining wail. Her entire body stiffened. Ripples like ocean waves streaked back and forth through her stomach muscles. I had my mouth fully on her clit, suctioning it as she moved her rear back and forth in sharp motions. I lost my grip on her clit. At the same time she threw herself forward, off me, so that she could reach down and get her fingers on her clit and furiously massage herself to the end point of her climax.

Then she covered herself protectively down here with the same fingers while she lay breathing hard. "Oh, baby," she gasped finally. "That was good. You need something, baby. You need a reward and I have just what you need." She turned on her back and invited me to the good old missionary position. Knees parted, and fingers holding her vagina open, and purred: "Come here, baby, come inside. Get in here, baby, enjoy this good oyster. Come on, honey, get that thick dick in here so I can feel you inside me. You deserve some good candy and I have it here for you."

I got in there and rode on her like she was the ocean. It was tight in there, and my fish swam with it like a minnow in a drinking straw. She lightly slapped my buttocks and played with me. Her palms slapped loudly but painlessly on my butt cheeks—left, right, left, right—as if she were playing tambourine. "You have dimples there," she crowed, and drew circles in the sides of my buttocks with her long fingernails.

She lay under me, an Amazon, mighty and glowing, proud to have me on her breasts and under her smile. It is the only time I have ever come several times in rapid succession. I was limp by the time she was ready for the really big one. "Honey," she said, "I've worn you out." She rolled me on my back and started kissing me from my forehead on down, and from my toes on up. I couldn't move. "You are like a rag doll, baby. Was the ride that hard on you?" Then she came to my dick. "Oh, but look, your other half is still hard as a rock. Does it hurt, baby? Is it sore?" She flopped it gently between her palms and studied my facial reaction. I shook my head. "Go for it," I gasped.

She swung around and come down on me oyster first. I pulled a pillow down under my head so I could watch with ease. I rested my hands on her strong thighs and smooth knees as she rocked up and down. "I'm not too heavy for you?" She wasn't. Even sitting on me with those glorious cocoa cheeks, she was really light. Hard, athletic, but light.

Her stomach was flat with a slight scar running diagonally from some long-ago injury. Her belly button was a large innie stretched laterally in this position. Her breasts swung slowly while she supported herself with her hands on the sheets on either side of me. As her tight oyster rode up and down, I slowly found myself stiffening again. I had been hard, but now I was getting stiff.

I reached out with interest for her long, swinging tits. She breathed harder as she saw my renewed interest. She liked having her titties sucked, and leaned forward. She closed her eyes with pleasure as I pulled her heavy tits to my mouth and licked the nipples alternately. I did this languidly because I was too worn and lazy to do much more. She was an aggressive woman when she wanted something, and now she was reaching for that final gigantic orgasm so she could once again become the sweet little violinist and the quiet librarian standing with her books amid the stained glass light. She reached down and spread her hand over her clit, with my dick between her middle fingers. Everything she did to her clit, I felt on my shaft. "I'm getting so wet," she said. "I hope you can still feel me." I nodded. "Not to worry," I said, "it feels like heaven." And she said: "Oh good. That's nice." She rubbed steadily, faster, harder, turning her hand slightly so the ball of her index finger caught the tip of her clitoris from different angles. She liked to talk, and muttered softly: "Feels like I'm raining on you, baby. I can feel the juice sliding down your peepee from inside my vagina. Does it feel nice?" "Oh yes," I whispered as I started to become passionate again. I put my hands on her shoulders, then down her arms, and pulled her face down so our mouths entwined. She was breathing too hard, babbling too much, couldn't get her breath if we tongue-locked, though she tried, dear girl, she tried to get her tongue down in my mouth, but she ended up raising her face up for air. "Oh sweetie," she said, "oh sweetie, what you are doing to me, baby."

I began to thrust with my groin, slowly at first. Each time, she moaned. She kept sliding her hand in these little figure eights that made her palm glide over her wet clitoris. Then she'd curve her hand so fingers entered her oyster. This pinched my dick a bit because her hole was so tight, and she eased up. I helped her though, by leaning down and sliding one finger up her oyster beside my dick.

That seemed to please her because she made these jerky little nodding motions. Her lips spoke soundlessly. Her breath came in gasps. Her supporting arm strained under her weight, while her oyster arm moved faster, and her fingers slid back and forth around the root of my dick. "Let me help you, baby," I said, and gently tilted her so she fell on her side, off that supporting arm. I reached down and hooked my hand under her knee. I pulled her leg up to me, opening up her underside for her. She reached down—one hand in front, the other in back—and worked her vagina from both ends. She slid two fingers on each hand in and out with my dick in between. I started @ing her from the side, and now she said: "I'm almost there. Peter. Don't stop. Keep it up. @ me, baby. @ me, Peter. @ me. @ me. @ me."

She kept up this mantra, trembling from the fast and wild exertions of her hands, until the great orgasm hit like a storm. I @ed her as hard as I could, hearing the slam of my hips against the solid weight of her basin. She slammed back with that great athletic body, and our flesh made slapping, slamming, wet noises that echoed under the white ceiling. "Give it to me," she cried. Then she reared up, higher and higher, in huge spasms, like a drowning person, pressing her dark tits into my face. Suddenly it was over. She collapsed and lay limp beside me. I stroked her back slowly and gently. It took a few minutes for her to regain her normal breathing composure. With a great sigh of relief and satisfaction, she grasped my dick and balls in her palm as if her hand were a jock strap. With her other hand she pushed my hair back out of my face and raised herself just enough to kiss me sweetly. Brushing my hair with her fingers, she whispered: "That was nice." We had many a lunch date like this until, as happens in life, she or I met someone new and moved on. I think her next man was a wealthy black banker with fine, subdued suits and gold rings and a sunny smile, who worked hard to win her love and then took her somewhere out west, where I imagine she stands before a white wall overlooking the Pacific Ocean and playing her violin.

The Story of G

Speaking of the Pacific Ocean, and windy San Francisco, here in our New England city is a small Asian community. Some are associated with the university, others with the restaurant business, and the rest in various occupations. The grandfather of **G** was an elderly doctor who had retired from surgery but still held a private general practice at nearly 80 years old. When I came to have my tonsils checked one winter day, it was like stepping into a back room in Canton or Shanghai. The building itself was severe and modern, western, but the décor was Chinese. There was even a small shrine with Confucius in the main waiting room. Scrolls with Chinese writing hung from the walls. Sketches from the Imperial era hung in various rooms. I was the only patient that morning, and I felt as if I were walking among ghosts in those many inward rooms. As I sat in the waiting room with a copy of China News, I looked up and saw a young woman working at a desk in an adjoining office. She picked up the phone and spoke in clipped Chinese. After she hung up she looked my way and smiled briefly.

An elderly woman in a nursing aide's uniform with face mask trudged out and signaled for me to follow her. She took me deeper and deeper into this labyrinth of rooms. Bamboo water wheels spilled trickling water into bamboo pipes, which dribbled it onto little pebbles in tubs of green plants. At the end of the hall, a very Confucian looking old man with a goatee and white lab coat stood waiting for me. With decades of skill, he assessed me from head to foot even as I walked down the hallway.

When I stepped into the office, the lady informed him in Chinese of my sore throat. He pinched my nose and lifted it while pushing a tongue depressor down on my lower jaw. I thought he was going to harm me for a moment. He had me sit down, took my blood pressure and temperature, prodded my ribs, listened to my heart and lungs, and said: "Listen, young man, the only thing wrong with you is that you party all night and don't get enough sleep. You don't have anything to worry about—just clean your sinuses and it will step the drip drip drip."

He opened his mouth like a fish, raised his head, and hooked his hand over himself to point down his throat. "That will be eight dollars, and let me give you some tea." He fussed about a steel counter and mixed something up. He gave me a little envelope to tuck in my pocket and handed me a medium sized cup without handles. It contained a steaming green broth. I smelled eucalyptus, fennel, licorice, ginseng, and who knows what else. I sipped this hot stuff as best I could, and it opened chambers in my skull that I didn't know existed. My ears popped as if I were driving down from the mountains.

"Wow!" I said.

He nodded. "Wow is right. You came to the right place. I've been dabbling in herbal medicine since I retired. A lot of it comes from Europe, too." He took my money, thanked me, and showed me the directions to the exit.

Along the way, I got lost and ended up in the young woman's office. She turned and looked at me as I came up behind her. She wore a white lab jacket and sat at a desk with a pile of manila folders crammed with records. She looked very Chinese, with yellow skin, almond eyes, and thick glossy black hair.

"I'm sorry," I said, "I got lost." I gesticulated. "Lost." I made circling motions with my arms and shrugged.

"Rost," she said. I nodded. Suddenly her face crinkled up in laughter and she rose. "That's pig-Chinese for lost. Sorry, bad joke."

"You speak English."

"Yes!" She really was cute, with all these dimples when she smiled. "Of course. I grew up here, just like you." She was compact, with an egg-shaped face tapering in a small round chin. "It's that way," she said pointing to the waiting room and the door beyond. She laughed again. She told me later that I really amused her. She thought I looked gaunt and needed feeding. "Did my grandfather give you his tea?"

"Yes, my head feels so much better."

"Good!"

When I got home that evening, there was a note under my door. Someone had called and left a message about forgotten medicine. I didn't have a phone in my little room, just a bed, a desk, a chair, a small closet, and a wide windowsill that was my pantry in winter. My idea of food to store was packages of freeze-dried soup, and I had a heating coil to bring water to a boil in a cup.

"It's *G,*" said the girl from the doctor's office. "You forgot your tea! My grandfather found it as they were closing up." We discussed the matter briefly, and she agreed to drop it off at the corner. So I bundled up and went out into the dark street. At the corner were a few businesses and bright lights. It was actually a good part of town, a rundown adjunct to the university, and I was not ashamed to tell anyone I lived there. As she had promised, the woman pulled up in a long, sleek black car with skis tied to a rack on top. "Peter?"

I stepped off the curb and approached her driver's side window.

"I have your—" She looked around her, and appeared to have lost the small packet. A car honked behind her, and she pulled over. I jumped out of the way as some impatient person splashed past in a show of immaturity. She signaled for me to get in. The interior of the car was dark and luxurious. An expensive music player poured forth crystal clear soft rock music.

"You have a whole live concert in here, complete with people whistling and cheering," I said.

She laughed that wonderful crinkly smile again. "I have to get under a light. Your tea fell under the seat someplace."

I apologized, and she said "No trouble. I'm on my way to Stowe, Vermont for the weekend, and you're on my way."

I said: "That's great of you."

She drove to a supermarket parking lot, and we dug around under the seats, under the carpets, and everywhere. She looked stymied. "Maybe I forgot it." She laughed, as she often did. "Do you have some kind of amnesia you're spreading?"

I shrugged. "I forget."

She pointed to a restaurant. "Tell you what. I'm famished. You want to join me for a bite?" I was always hungry, and readily agreed. She was a postdoc chemistry student getting ready for a life of medical research, I learned over a matching set of meatloaf dinners with mashed potatoes, gravy, string beans, and lots of catsup. We shared a pot of tea. I told her about my struggle to find a niche, and my interest in certain historical and literary topics.

"I love reading the classics," she said. "I just wish I had more time. I have to squeeze things in. Do you ever do things impulsively?"

I had to admit that I did (most of my current life style was by impulse). She said: "How would you like to come to Vermont with me? I had the trip lined up with a girlfriend, but she bugged out at the last moment, and I'd love to have someone interesting and intelligent to talk to. There is a couch in the lodge that you can sleep on, and food and drinks will be on me."

That's how we got started. It was a long, pleasant drive up there. *G* was a great conversationalist, and I listened carefully because she really was a neat person. Even though (shock) she turned out to be ten years older than I was, she seemed the nearest thing to a regular date to me at that point, compared to other women older than myself that I dated now and then. "When you are Chinese-American," she said, "people think because you look totally Asian that they have to yell or you won't understand them. Sometimes they talk to me in funny accents that they think sound Chinese." She laughed. "Sometimes I get impatient and talk in funny accents just to baffle them and piss them off." We both laughed. "I'm as American as apple pie, at least I think so."

I assured her: "You are extremely apple pie."

G had worked for about seven years at a very high salary after graduating from Stanford and then Yale. She'd been engaged to a graduate student from Hong Kong, of whom her family had approved, but they had grown distant from each other. "Totally different cultures," she said. "At first I was gullible and naïve, and he just worked and studied all the time and had no ideas of his own, no personality, but worse yet— no sense of humor. He was a nice, shy, quiet guy, but I nearly died of boredom. So, to escape, I broke off our engagement and took jobs in large corporations. I kept moving every year or two, until he gave up and stopped trying to follow me around. Also," she said with a giggle, "I had Chinese girlfriends of mine set him up with dates until one day he met one and fell in love. That's when he went back to China and I started my studies at the university." I asked her if she played any sports, offhand, and she said "no, but I won a first place trophy in a beer chugging contest at Stanford."

I said: "Oh-oh, I won't challenge you on that."

I was resigned to just being around her, which was very enjoyable. I couldn't ski to save my life, but I loved sitting in the great lounge with its crackling fire place and watching all the ski people. They come from all over the region to places like Stowe. When the first flakes twirl, the highways are choked with cars heading here with skis on their racks. That night, I slept on a sort of large wooden box with thick Mexican rugs and a quilt on top. "I'm sorry about that," she said. "I'd give you my sleeping bag but it's way too small for you." She laughed. "And it's pink." We both laughed.

Next morning, we had a nice breakfast overlooking sun-bright slopes. "Oh gosh, I hope it snows, or at least doesn't melt before we leave." She went skiing for a few hours. She waved to me, a petite figure in a pink paramilitary suit of some kind (okay, I'm joking, that's what she called it). She waved and pulled these cool tanker goggles down over her face and disappeared among the legions of people in similar clothing dispersed in all directions. Toward noon, she came into the lodge with her tongue hanging out. "Want to stay through tomorrow?" she asked.

"I'd be happy to," I said. She asked, "Enjoying yourself?" I smiled and told her honestly, "It's great up here. What a nice change for me."

She patted my leg. "Good. I'll make the arrangements."

We sat by the fire and drank hot chocolate. She was tired and went upstairs for a nap. I went into a viewing room and saw a movie. When I went up to the room, she was just beginning to wake up. She had fallen asleep in her pink suit, with just neck open a little, and a blanket over her shoulders. Her stockings, protruding from the pink ankles of her suit, were thick, wheat-colored crew socks.

She stretched and yawned. "Hi!"

"Have a good rest?"

"Yep." She patted the bed beside her. "Sit here." As I sat, she rose up and bounded past me. "Back in a minute." She disappeared into the bathroom, where I heard muted tinkling sounds, then the flushing of water, then the rush of water at the sink, and the sound of someone gargling. After a moment of silence, the door opened and she jumped out. "Ta-dah!" She hopped on one leg, with her arms extended like a skater. I applauded. She had stripped down to a flimsy tank top (pink) and equally flimsy panties (pink). Aside from that, she still wore the heavy crew socks.

"Aren't you cold?" I asked.

She shook her head as she walked past me and crawled onto the bed. "I have you to keep me warm." She lifted the covers, crawled inside, and held them open for me.

"I am honored," I said as I started in.

"Take those off," she said, pointing to my jeans, flannel shirt, and heavy socks, not to mention my long johns. I stripped off the jeans, socks, and shirt. "All of it," she said. I complied, and slipped into the warmth beside her. I felt the smoothness of her thigh against mine. She lay on her side facing me. She propped herself up on one elbow, with her chin and cheek in her palm, a pensive pose. She patted my chest with her other palm. "You don't have to sleep on the trunk again."

"Thank God," I said.

She laughed at my rolling eyes and groan.

"It was not only hard, but too short for me."

"I'm sorry about that." She patted my chest. "You did very well though."

"That was a test, huh?"

She nodded. Out from behind the bed came a baseball bat. She uttered that wild, happy laugh again. "I wasn't really gonna brain you—just scare you if you turned out to be a wild-man." The bat rattled loudly as she dropped it on the floor behind her.

I lay regarding her. She was petite, with features I found exotically pretty. Everything about her was compact, firm, not delicate but scaled down. As a skier, she had surprisingly hard little hands as I learned when we intertwined fingers and stared at each other. "I felt," she said, "that I wanted to have you, to help you. I thought you would be a lot of fun to be with, and I'm happy you came along."

"I'm glad I passed the test."

"Let's go slow. We have all day and all night. I'm going to go out on the slopes again for a while before dark, but I'd like you to check out my slopes before then."

"I'll be glad to help you with that. Do you mind if I inspect your slopes first? Get the lay of the land?"

"I think we should light the pilot with a good long kiss."

"I think that's a great idea." I leaned forward and sought her mouth with mine. Her tongue was short, her mouth small, and her breath smelled of toothpaste. I cupped her breast, which was wobbly and pointy in its flimsy shirt. We petted lightly for a good long while. It was quiet in the room with its blond wood theme and its thick storm windows that cut out both the chill outside (minus 40) and the noise from the slopes. A small fire crackled in a black iron fireplace across the room. We had time and attention only for each other. My hands roved all over her small body, from her ankles and calves up her thighs and around the softness of her buttocks. I rubbed her belly button with my fingertip and she giggled. "Push the button and you giggle," I said. She reached down and pushed mine, as if in an elevator. "Nothing happens when I push yours."

"I'm stuck on hard," I said.

She held both hands over her mouth and squealed, her eyes thin squiggles above her (pink) fingernails. I rolled onto my back and pulled her on top of me. She still wore the tank top and panties. Her little titties bobbled provocatively behind the material. I reached up and touched each soft nipple through the cotton. "They get hard," she promised. "You just have to turn me on some more, and I'm sure you will."

"I like it when your titties hang over me like that."

Her breath came hard and hot, and her eyes smoldered over me.

"I'm going to pull up your shirt and look at them. Will you like that?"

She nodded slowly. "Only if you do it slowly, like you mean it." She gritted her teeth at me. It was the first sign of the passion to come.

"I'm going to lift your shirt now." I pulled at the hem, seeing the belly button underneath, and the soft yellow skin. I pulled her slightly toward me, exerting a little power on the shirt.

She gritted her teeth and looked defiant. "Do you dare?"

"You can't stop me."

"I can stop you." She wriggled her ass against my cock, which was hard and naked and pushed the flimsy panty material in to the crack of her ass. "I dare you. I defy you. Are you man enough?" She took my wrists in her fists and pushed them back over my head. I let her, although for a moment I seriously wondered if I had the strength to counter this wiry little bitch. She was small and soft on the surface, but like a steel coil underneath. "Suffer," she said through those gritted teeth as she swung her chest from side to side, and those pointy titties were grayish shadows bouncing under the shirt right before my face.

"You know I am going to end up licking them before we are done."

"I don't know that. Are you man enough?"

"I am going to end up sucking them. You know I will. It's only a matter of time. You can't hold me back forever."

"I can slap you around and hold you anywhere I want." She crossed my wrists, held them with one steely hand, and reached in back of her to take my cock in her palm. "You have a big dick, but I am not scared of it."

"You will have that dick inside of you after I kiss your titties."

"I am not going to let you do that so easily. You think I am small and easy, and because you are nice looking I am an easy @. You will have to beg and work and sweat before I let you touch me." She thrust one breast against my eye.

I raised my mouth and took the cotton in my lips, and with it the cone of her nipple. She teased me by withdrawing it. She turned slightly and brought her other nipple close but pulled it away before my mouth could close on it. So she was a tease. I told her: "You are an expert at this torture. You are a cock tease, bitch."

"@er!" she spat at me. "@er!"

"Is your oyster dripping wet all over me?" I said weakly.

"You wish, big guy. Hah!" She took her hand off my cock and stuck it in her panties and brought her fingers out. She offered them to me.

I leaned forward to suck on them. "I can taste your salty oyster milk on those fingers."

"Oh really?" She laughed and sucked on them. She made a quizzical face. She stuck her hand in her panties again, rubbed two fingers around in her oyster, and brought them to her mouth to lick. "Hmm. You're right. That is some quality oyster juice."

"That is why I must @ you today. You have the finest grade A oyster milk of any cow in Vermont."

"What if I don't let you have my oyster milk?"

"I have some dick milk for you."

"You're lying."

"AM not."

"Are too."

"Want to see?"

"@ you. No." She spat in my face, and little globules of spit hung in my eye lashes and lay on my skin. "Don't wipe it. Leave it. I want to see you with my spit on your face."

"I want to taste your spit."

"Why?"

"Because I already tasted it when we kissed and it's pretty good. Tastes like peppermint."

We both burst out laughing and she almost lost control over my wrists. She recovered and grabbed my cock again. "What if I take this thing and beat you over the head with it?"

"It would probably hurt. I would have to have you sit on my head for a bandage."

"If you are good," she said, "and I mean very good. If you are very, very good, maybe later I will let you do the bowling ball carry on me. But only if you are very, very good."

I remembered the old joke about that. "What do I have to do to show I am very good?"

She wrinkled her brows and folded her arms over her chest. Straddling my waist, she looked down on me and said: "You have to do things I ask. For one thing, let's postpone this game. We can get back to it later. Are you enjoying playing with me?" "I love playing with you." I pinched the strap on her panties and pulled it down so I could get a glimpse. She let me for a half minute. I reached in and put my middle finger against the crack of her snatch to feel her clit. There was a little hard bud there.

She reached down and pulled my hand out and pulled her panties up. She unstraddled and climbed down from the bed. Her buttocks jiggled as she landed on the floor in her bare feet. "First, Peter, let's dance a little." I sat on the bed, while she walked over and put another log behind the fire grate so vermilion sparks rose up the flue in a shower. Then she went to the entertainment center and turned on a radio or DVD.

Soft rock music poured out, as it had in her car. She stood there and beckoned. I went over and took her in my arms. She rested her head against my chest as we slow danced. I rarely slow danced naked, and my hard cock swung around. It slapped against her thigh several times, until she gently pinned it against her soft skin. "All secured, captain."

We moved around like that for a few minutes until we shifted gears again. She was light, and I lifted her so that her legs wrapped around my waist. The cloth with her titties in it jiggled against my cheek bones. I was beginning to wonder how long I could hold out before I had to get my cock into one of her holes, or at least ejaculate somehow. I was getting blue balls. My nuts were beginning to feel like they were on fire. She French kissed me ardently, playing with my ears and my hair with her small fingers.

I danced around, holding my hands under her ass. Those panties were so flimsy it was almost as if they weren't there. I had to hold her high enough so that she wasn't sitting on the head of my dick, which was engorged and very sensitive. I enjoyed feeling the strength of her strong little legs around me.

"Do you want to suck me?" she muttered softly as she pressed her nose against mine.

"Yes," I said.

"You will have to suck your way up to me."

"I will gladly suck whatever you want me to suck, as long as you are attached to it."

"I know you wan to drop my panties and slip that big fine dick of yours up my hole. That would be easy, but I won't let you. First, you have to take me to the bed and I'll tell you what to do." I carried her over and gently laid her on her back. She held my dick in one hand while she said: "I am going to let you see my titties. Would you like to see them?" I said yes, and she stood up on the bed. "You'll have to raise my shirt. Slowly like you mean it." I pulled her toward me. Standing on the floor while she stood on the bed, her pussy was right there by my mouth. I cupped her ass and buried my nose in her twat, inhaling the smell of her hair and her juice. She grabbed my hair in her fists but made no move to stop me. It was clear that if I tried to lick her, or do anything other than sniff, she would yank me away. I closed my eyes, inhaled the smell of her quim, and cupped her ass in my hands. I knew I would have it all, and there was no hurry.

"I like when you sniff me down there," she said. "Is it good?"

"Oh yes, very good."

"What does it smell like?"

"The sea. The forest. A snail."

"It is a snail, dummy. I hope you like escargot, because you are going to be dining on that snail down there."

I pulled my nose out and looked up at her between the points of her tits. "I'm going to have you walk that snail right into my mouth when we get that far."

"What if she doesn't want to go that way?"

"Then my mouth is going to chase her."

"But she can't run very fast," *G* said in a kewpie voice. She reached down inside her panties as if to comfort the snail.

I pressed my cheek against her belly and looked up her shirt. I heard her tummy grumbling with excitement at all that was going on. Up the shadowy slope of her torso, I could see the bottoms of two very cute and interesting titties. I lifted the shirt away and stuck my head in. "This is great," I said. "Help me out here." I crawled onto the bed and had her arch over me while I sat on all fours. She placed her right hand on my neck and leaned forward so I could look directly up her shirt. Now I saw them in full for the first time. They were two longish pointy cones with big bluish cone nipples at their tips. "Do your titties get hard, or are they always firm and pointy like that."

"I train them well. They are always firm and pointy. It's a hassle when I am trying to put my shirt on without a bra, because one always gets caught under my arm or in a sleeve."

"I would love to see that movie," I said. I had her kneel before me with her ass in my face.

"No pulling my panties down yet," she said.

"I have the titties to play with first," I reassured her. While she sat on all fours, and her shirt hung under her, I lay beneath her and slowly pushed the shirt up. She tired of it and briefly rose up to pull it over her head and throw it on the floor. "I like posing for you any way you like," she said as she resumed her four-points pose. I slid on my back under her, until her nipples hung over my face. They were engorged and bluish. I lay under her and sucked on them. *G* moaned softly. I lipped them, first one, then the other. "You are being good," she said.

"Am I being very good? Very very good?"

"Almost."

"What do I have to do to be very very good?"

"Keep sucking my titties and I'll tell you when they have had enough."

I kept holding them in my hands and licking each one round and round the nipples. My rod was hard as glass and threatened to shatter soon if I didn't get some lubrication on it. "Bowling ball," I reminded.

"Oh yeah. When you have been very very good."

I sucked on those blue-tipped titties until they had tight nipples.

"I want you to suck my toes," she said. She pulled her titties from me and lay on her back. She waved one pale foot in my face. "Get a washcloth from the bathroom and wash them first." I did as she asked, thoroughly cleaning her toes, between them, under them, the balls of her feet, her arches, everything up to her ankles. "That feels nice," she said. "Now let me do yours."

She brought fresh washcloths soaked in hot water from the bathroom, and cleaned both of our feet for good measure. Then she lay back and had me suck her toes. I pulled her into position so that her ass (panties still on) rested against the corner between my balls and my cock. I pushed her feet together and took both big toes into my mouth at the same time. I sucked on them as I had sucked on her nipples, and then licked around their edges.

"That is very good," she said. "You can watch me while I make it very very good." She reached down into her panties and played with herself with one hand, while palming one breast with the other hand. Her eyes got a dazed, swollen look as if she were drunk with sex. "This is one of my favorite things," she said.

"What if you don't have someone to suck your toes?"

"Watch me." She took one of her legs, leaving the toes of the other in my mouth, and bent that leg to her so that she sucked on her own toe, all the while her little knuckles rose up and down in her panties. "You squirted a little," she said with a mouthful of toe.

"I can't help myself."

"I'd better catch all that cock milk before you lose it. But first, one more little thing." She had me sit ass to ass with her, so that I still had her toes in my mouth, while she pulled my legs around and put my toes in hers. It was like being nibbled by wet little furry mice. I laughed. She sucked on my toes while diddling herself with one hand, and cupping my balls in her other hand. She was beginning to ripple out of control. The first lightning strikes of orgasm rolled across the soft roundness of her belly.

On the verge of losing it, she tremulously said, "One more little thing..." She let my feet go, and put her feet on my shoulders. Using both hands, and lifting her butt, she pulled her panties up her thighs. I looked down and saw the pretty little bush there, and the whorls of interlacing labia that were stuck together with wetness. "I like doing this," she said in a trembling voice.

She pulled her labia apart and gently stuffed my balls into the entrance of her oyster. "You think I am small and so I must have a small oyster, don't you? Well, it is small inside and your balls would hurt if I pushed them all the way up there like I would like to do."

I felt the warm, wet skin of her vagina under my balls and moaned softly: "Please...I can't wait any longer..."

"Neither can I," she said feebly. "Get inside me. Now. Hurry." To our mutual relief, I just swung my legs back and my body forward, which put my ram on a collision course with her castle gate. She was holding the gate open with both hands as my train slid into her tunnel. We both cried out in relief and joy as her tube closed in tightly around my cock. We embraced each other tightly while I rocked back and forth and our first orgasm came in seconds. I kept rocking back and forth inside her, and couldn't wait until I could be aroused again.

"Oh baby," she said, kissing me and holding my head. "You were very very very good. I am probably full of your juice now, and I love it. It makes you slide around so nice and easy in my little pussy. My juice and your juice mixed together, all this delirious love we have been making for hours." She laughed. "It's dark out. I missed my afternoon ski." She petted me as if I were a hurt mouse. "We still have a lot of time to play. You're going to eat me, and I'm going to eat you, and then we'll play some more." And we did, through much of the night, and again at her apartment the next evening after we had driven home. She was a lot of fun, and we dated for a long time.

I almost forgot to mention about the bowling ball carry. Late in the night, when we awoke for more sex, she turned her ass toward me and waited on all fours. "Spit on my asshole."

I did. She rubbed her oyster vigorously and pushed juice up to make her sphincter wet.

She cautioned: "You can't ass@ me. You are too big. I'm serious. Do me that one favor, okay?" I nodded, and she relented from her anxiety: "You can do anything else you want. Anything. But first, I want you to put your thumb in my mouth." I did.

She sucked on my thumb, and then added her thumb so she was sucking on both thumbs. Then she took the wet, gooey thumb out and reached down for her ass. She slowly worked the thumb in. "It's tight down there," she explained. "I'm getting your thumb nice and wet. Go easy, okay?" When she was ready, she added: "Go slow. I'm very tight and tender."

Spit and juice dribbled from her asshole as I pushed my thumb in. She gasped a bit, and wiggled to fit it in, but then my thumb was in. She reached down to pull my index and middle fingers into her pussy. "Try to get another one in," she said. I felt her fingers pressing on mine. Our hands were dripping wet. "You're too small," I said. I rubbed my palm on the soft curve of her buttocks.

I kissed them, and she mmmm'd with pleasure. "Rock me," she whispered. With my thumb and fingers in her, I gently pushed and pulled. She had her hands on the sheets and rocked back and forth, more and more strongly, until she came in a big series of halting gasps. "Keep them in," she said. In that position, about all I could do was kiss her up and down her back and buttocks.

She lay on her belly with her arms folded under her chin and murmured: "Don't stop." A few minutes later she had me enter her pussy from behind, doggy style. I was hot for her, and slammed her rapidly and often against my groin until it was my turn to shoot up her, gism dripping from her like foam as we came together. We slept well, and she did get a little more skiing in before we left for home.

The Story of H

Probably the most exotic looking (and beautiful) woman that I dated among my older women was *H*, a 34 year old daughter of refugees from Tibet. She was fairly tall, and thin, and had this incredible face with high wide cheekbones. Her eyes were slitty and raised at the outer corners. Her mouth was small, her face flat, her skin like honey. She had a narrow, flat, high nose. I met her while working as a research assistant for the summer to an Asian professor of management and business. My job was to take in paragraphs and chapters of research results, organize them according to a sort of boilerplate model, and format them in Word in preparation for the printer.

H was a graduate student with degrees in Marketing (B.S.) and Business Administration (M.B.A.), working on her doctorate (D.B.A.). Like *G*, she was one of those misunderstood Asian-Americans who causes people to yell to be understood, or to speak in fake accents in the hope that someone they think has an accent will understand them. When *H* opens her mouth, pure American idiom comes out, and she can speak either Valley Girl or Harvard-Smart or the usual imitations of New Yorkers porking their korrs or Bostonians pahking their cahs.

H was kind of shy and quiet until you got to know her. She was born in Chicago after her father, a yak broker from Lhasa, and her mother, a housewife from a mountain village, had fled the Red Chinese. Both parents had made enormous sacrifices, living first in India, then in the U.K., and finally in the U.S. By dint of hard work, *H's* father had earned degrees and insinuated himself in the university system, where he became indispensible as an expert on carpets and textiles. Corporations paid him handsome sums for his knowledge, which involved Iranian and Pakistani goods more than Tibetan ones.

H had been raised in Catholic schools in Chicago and Canada, and now she was a 30-something woman with a divorce and a small child of mixed Tibetan-Italian-American blood. She was a sturdy, cautious woman, and it took her a while to warm up to me, but I sensed her interest in me. She would pass in the hall, while I worked at my terminal, and I could see her looking at me with interest. Maybe she didn't realize I saw her reflection in my computer screen, and she passed more often than one would normally expect. After a while, her lovely eyes had a certain wounded or vulnerable hunger, maybe just a curiosity like a huge itch, and eventually I decided to make contact. I did this one rainy spring day, when everything was that delicate spring bud green, and the rain rattled gently outside the windows. I maneuvered myself into a place of talking with her while we waited for a coffee pot to perk. A bit of casual banter, and she agreed to lunch sometime, and later a movie. Her violent ex was pretty much out of the picture, and her baby was safe with grandma, so for the first time in years she had some freedom and breathing room to explore the world for herself. At the same time, school was putting huge demands on her, even with the fact that her parents provided a monthly stipend. I think *H* needed a part-time, safe playmate of the opposite sex. Someone who had no agenda, was not threatening, was nice to her, and made her feel good. I was that playmate. As always, for me it was a port in a storm. I was choosy, yes, so not any port. This port, that *H* offered, was exceptional.

There were the usual lunches, dates, movies, flowers, bonbons, all the things people do to charm the opposite gender. *H* lived in a small house in the suburbs, funded by the university because they were chronically short of housing. Somewhere in that house, whenever she had me there, was a room with baby cribs and things, but the timing was always such that baby was absent when I was there. That suited me fine, because I was nowhere near ready to be a parent. First, though, we met out of town, secretly.

Intriguingly, *H* made good money on the side as a model in New York. What they wanted above all was the Kachina doll beauty of her face. She was in several perfume ads and some other things. I got to suck on her oyster. That was more than the rest of the world had from her. Her beauty, when skilled photographers applied makeup and lighting, was almost other-worldly. She was a true exotica. And yet the *H* I personally knew was a quiet, shy, vulnerable woman who had been maimed by an angry, violent divorce.

She liked to be held. The older woman is not always the nurturer. Sometimes it is the clumsy pup who is the nurturer. She had me meet her at this friend's apartment in a nearby city one day, when we had gotten to know each other a bit and she trusted me. (She thought I was too good to be true, but admitted later she was wrong in that sad little assessment. She said she didn't know men could be so nice.) She wanted me, for a lot of reasons, but was afraid of herself, her desire, the consequences, the violence of her ex, the disapproval of her parents. That was the reason for the secret assignation.

We had this nice apartment to ourselves. "Honestly," she said while spreading her long arms over my shoulders on the balcony at dusk, "I haven't been able to sleep well thinking of how this would be."

I put my hands on her fine waist and kissed her. "Listen, I've slept like a prince, thinking of what a wonderful fine woman you are and how privileged I am to have a little time with you. Do you have any idea what that means to me?"

She appeared a little dazed. "Does it mean that much to you?" Her tiny mouth hung slightly open with surprise, and her eyes signaled confusion (Tibetans' eyes don't slant up, but tend to be narrow slits straight across).

I sat her down on a blond Dansk stool in the modern kitchen and explained the reasonable realities of life to her. We had a pan of steak, potatoes, and string beans in the oven. The skyline outside was just marvy, with stars over it, and a full moon to make us nuts. "I don't know what part of the Tibetan schema lingers in your brain," I said, "but this is

America, and everyone is supposed to be free. I know we have a fascist pig for a president, and a bunch of criminal swine in Congress, but let's cling to the illusion or delusion of freedom, shall we? Baby, I demand that you be drunk with freedom."

She held a wine glass between her hands, and twirled the glass slowly on the thick glass counter. "I don't feel like much."

"Okay," I said, "the holidays are almost upon us. I have to help you feel better."

"Thank you," she said sincerely. After dinner, she said to me in a quiet moment when our heads were close together, "It means a lot to have you here, and just being nice to me."

"I feel the same way." It was the quintessential moment in my career as a lover of older women. There is a terrible truth at the heart of such relationships, which it is wise for both the woman and her blithering young stud muffin to understand. Almost every single one of these things is a fleeting moment in the great river of love that rushes unseen through the big city.

A wise Summer knows that she is but a port in a storm, and that her youthful movie star will in time settle with a girl his own age or younger. That fortunate (maybe) girl may even be less attractive. It can be the difference between having ten grand to spend on a car—do you buy a tiny new compact with rollup windows, ratty radio, and that new plastic smell? Or do you look around for a five or ten year old luxury car with electric windows, power everything, and a wrap-around sound system?

When you are a lost, broke young soul, unable to afford even a date with two beers, what a splendid thing to be taken in, pampered, fed, clothed, and sucked and @ed by a gorgeous woman. Not an inexperienced, self-centered child, but a mature woman, seasoned in her sexuality, still very young at heart, and best of all, asking nothing substantial in return—not even permanence. If she expects a lasting commitment, even marriage, she is most likely going to be deeply hurt. Unless he lies to her (which I tried never to do), she cannot claim to feel betrayed, because she refused to read her own tea leaves. When there is a reciprocal need, as there was between me and *H,* a lot of pleasure and fun can be had.

H just happened to be a tallish, thin woman who struck most men (and women) as aloof and hard. With her narrow eyes and high cheek bones, she may have seemed chilly—but she was shy and hurt inside. I read all that early on, when I saw her looking my way. It took a bit to break through the defensive walls, but when a woman longs to be rescued from her own defenses. *H* was truly a beautiful woman, which put many men (and women) off also. She was so gorgeous that I found myself torn by serious feelings for her, but the ten year difference loomed just over the horizon. I wasn't dealing with the issue, and she never let on if she was. I tried bringing it up in a tender moment, when I worried about hurting her, but she quickly put a fingertip on my lips and shook her head.

Thanksgiving rolled around—gray, cold, barren. *H* had me drive her car to a place up north, where we had dinner with some college friends of hers. They were even older, three couples in their late thirties, early forties. One was a Swedish engineer and his blonde (graying) butter-churn of a wife, who regarded me and *H* with a certain disdainful sorrow in moments when she thought nobody was looking. Then there was a New York philosophy professor with a bald, gleaming pate and a nut-brown ring of hair, and his loud, heavy Italian wife, both of them extremely kind and thoughtful.

Finally there was a quiet, insular Chinese man with wide cheekbones and a bony face on a bony body, who came and left with a leggy, long-haired woman of mixed Native American-French Canadian extraction—she was the most youthful and fun of the bunch, with her long black hair and saucy mouth. She and the Chinese man left right after dinner, and *H* explained to me that she had been shocked to see the Chinese man show up—he was a cousin of a man she had dumped after being engaged for years; what stories he would tell; what telegrams and messages she could expect to get. We decided, instead of going home that night, to drive up to Montreal. It was a long drive yet, five hours, but we took turns driving, listening to music, talking. "I feel so free with you," *H* said as she drove, and passing highway lights made the surfaces of her face flicker brighter, darker in hypnotic rhythm. I put my arm around her and whispered in her ear: "I want you to be my Christmas stocking stuffer."

She laughed. "You want me to pop out of a stocking? That would be a big stocking."

I nuzzled her ear lobe. "I just want you to pop out of your stockings that you wear."

"Oh, I see." Her eyes began plotting clever and sexy surprises. You see, when a young woman and her younger man are together, they are like children. There is no tomorrow or yesterday—just now, this moment, this day, all the fun we can have before we have to go inside and eat our vegetables. This interlude is youth's last playtime. For both it is the Indian Summer of being truly young. For her, it is a brief, light moment between marriages and huge, heavy years full of responsibilities; for him, the last random flight of the arrow before his heavy years arrive. "I will be glad to be your stocking stuffer. I am also glad that we are planning that far ahead."

"A whole four weeks," I said. Was she thinking that I might run out on her between now and then? Not a chance. Even I could plan that far ahead.

Love making with me, for her, was still in that scared, stiff phase. I wondered if I could help her stop being scared. Sometimes, like in the hotel room in Montreal, she actually trembled as I helped her undress. I was tired of asking her what was the matter. I knew—guilt. She felt guilty about our not being married, about not feeling she could present me to her parents, who lived not far away in Trois Rivieres. She felt guilty about wanting more in our sex than she could readily ask for. I was waiting for the dam to break, for the walls to tumble, for the real *H* to come out.

The first time we made love, she warmed a little bit, which gave me reason to expect more. There was much slow, hesitant undressing, and much looking—she grasped my dong and looked at it as if it were a telephone receiver she wasn't sure she wanted to pick up. I was patient, emptying my mind of expectations and being thankful for whatever I did get. She had a long, thin body. Not ribby or emaciated. Just long and thin, with soft padding in the right places. Her breasts were small and tilted, with brown nipples that rose up like chocolate chips. "What do you like?" she whispered self-consciously. She sat like a statue, wanting me to show her. She held one slender hand over her pubic area. "Let's kiss," I suggested. Even that we had not done much so far. We lay nakedly side by side and kissed. She liked my tongue in her mouth, and pulled me closer to stick her tongue in mine better. Her breathing grew fast and heavy, and I knew there was a tiger in there waiting to come out. She guided my hand to her breasts and signaled for me to play with them. She still looked a bit embarrassed and maybe felt silly asking me in words what she thought should happen in gestures and looks. "It's okay to talk," I said. She laughed. "Instruct me, then, because I am very inexperienced. I was engaged to a man who was rather cold, and I didn't want him touching me, so I spent years pretending to be frigid."

"We have to thaw you out then."

"Okay." She laughed. "I have something nice."

"I'll bet you do."

"Want to see, or want to wait?"

"Can I look, and then we wait?" "Okay. Look." She moved her gaze so I should follow it down the length of her body.

Puzzled, I let my lips guide me, from her dry little lips, down her bony jaw and chin, down her long neck, over the foothills of her dove-like breasts—whose nipples became longer when they grew erect—down the downy furrow of her belly, bouncing over her outie belly button, down a dip and then up over her hairy Venus mound. "See?" I still didn't, but pushed her long thin thighs apart—enjoying seeing the tender meat inside quiver as her thighs moved—and studied what she wanted me to see. I saw pert little buttocks and a pretty brown pucker down below. Above that was a generous region of genitals. She had a brownie, outie oysterie.

"Take a look," she urged. I liked her labia, which were stuck together like hands in prayer. With the tip of my tongue, I shook them and unglued them. I parted them by moving my head up and down. As they unfolded, I saw the loose flesh in the slightly open hole of her oyster. I saw the pinkish hole that she squirted pee with.

"I see it," I said. "Oh God, how wonderful." She had a marvelous clitoris. It was wide, with a massive hood that spread like the clouds over a Himalayan mountain top. Folds of yellowish brown skin formed a generous hood over this prodigious button about the size of my fingertip looking head-on. That's big. It was about the size of a slightly worn, rounded pencil eraser. I kissed it, and had to force myself to stop. I smelled its moisture, its slightly salty body fluids amid the dampness emanating from her open vagina onto my almost-touching face. I was going to work my way down there to that reward, taking my time, as long as I could stand it.

"You like it?" she asked as she touched my cheek and I returned to start kissing her. I nodded. "You have a treasure there."

"The treasure is yours," she said. I knew she meant it, and that was the dark side of Spring/Summer. She was glorious, but the nagging thought of our future kept gnawing at my soul. I suppressed it, just as she had pressed a finger on my lips. She was a woman who fell hard when she fell in love, and she was trying not to fall in love with me. If she had not been so breathtakingly beautiful, I would have run from her just to avoid that.

Maybe I was in love with her in my own broken and incomplete manner. Perhaps the fact that I didn't want to hurt her meant that I genuinely felt something for her. I had never been truly in love yet, so I had nothing to gauge by. Looking back I think some of those passionate affairs are really tragic love stories. What is worse, the dark sense of pain and the anticipation of loss adds beauty, adventure, even high artfulness to the passion the two lovers shower on each other.

Again looking back from far away, I think I understood more clearly than I would admit, amid all my denials—that I was truly in love with her, in moments when the age difference and the inevitable tearing asunder were not in my conscious thoughts. When you are making love, your event horizon shrinks down to the extent of your two bodies. Your time horizon is minutes and seconds, at most an hour or two. She was not ready to let herself fall into that velvet, shadowy room of the soul where clocks do not tick, where the sun does not move in the drawn shades, where no new flower petals drop from the vase to join those already scattered around the base.

That room, which is like a painting by a Dutch master, reminds me of what the poet Thomas Carew (the British Cavalier poet born in 1595) wrote:

Ask me no more where Jove bestows,
When June is past, the fading rose;
For in your beauty's orient deep
These flowers, as in their causes, sleep.
Ask me no more whither do stray
The golden atoms of the day;
For in pure love heaven did prepare
Those powders to enrich your hair.
Ask me no more whither doth haste
The nightingale when May is past;
For in your sweet dividing throat
She winters and keeps warm her note.
Ask me no more where those stars 'light
That downwards fall in dead of night;
For in your eyes they sit, and there
Fixed become as in their sphere.
Ask me no more if east or west

The Phoenix builds her spicy nest;
For unto you at last she flies,
And in your fragrant bosom dies.

Even in Montreal, to jump forward, she was still aloof, though I understood her deepest hesitation and could not argue with it. So I was slow to continue seducing her, knowing that her slide into sexuality would also mean her slide into love, and I was entirely, sickeningly uncertain how I would handle myself there, if at all. Was it cowardice on my part? Some will think so. Nevertheless, this was a fire that warmed, and it was a flame that was meant to burn. Some great bonfires are ill-starred to be lit on an exceedingly windy night, and that probably best describes my love affair with *H.*

I wasn't earning much, but she was feeding me and my expenses were minimal, so I saved up a nice chunk of change. I was going to do something really nice for her for Christmas. I made the arrangements by phone from the yellow pages and some research footwork. "Honey," I told *H,* "I want to help you understand how beautiful you are, so I have a surprise for you."

"Oh really?" From her laugh, I suspected that she was more amused than surprised, and I realized that most women do really realize it if they are beautiful. Knowing you are beautiful, and accepting it, welcoming it, are two different things. If a woman is not happy with herself, it will actually anger her that men look at her in a certain way. If she doesn't like herself, she won't like men who are gentle with her, because they must be bigger losers than she feels herself to be. Such a woman seeks out rough, strong, and sometimes violent men who pay her the treatment she feels she deserves.

I unfortunately was always seen as one of the losers in those situations, and I learned to steer clear of women with such a lack of self-esteem. *H* was not like that, but she was severely wounded somewhere inside. So I drove her down to Manhattan on dry, chilly day. I had already made all the preparations and confirmed everything by phone. We bore wore nice clothes. "I have never seen you in a suit," she said with a mystified air. I told her in the car as I drove: "I'm giving you your Christmas present early."

She seemed delighted, like a girl. "I can't wait. Peter, what have you cooked up?"

I took her to a special place in Midtown, where they specialize in makeovers. Moreover, the deal is for a princely hunk of money, they take you in to a backroom and let you pick out clothing from a selection of thousands of suits and dresses. You can pick out a costume if you want, be Robin Hood or Caesar or Napoleon. I directed *H* to a section of movie star dresses. I have never seen a woman gasp so many times. For a woman who is generally very easy to please, she seemed overwhelmed. "Don't cry," I told her, "because we have a photo shoot coming up, and we can't have your eyes all swollen."

She got a light and very professional makeover that made her look like a Himalayan princess. Her small, even teeth glittered like sugar. She really looked royal that day, more so than her usual regal good looks. In another section of the building, she had a full range of portraits taken in the outfit she had chosen—a long white sheath with a black poufy shawl thing had looked like it was full of air as it floated over her bare shoulders.

She had costume jewelry and a matching purse, and her own high heels. They gave us each a glass of champagne, which made her chiseled cheeks glow. She had dimples by her smile that I had not noticed before. A gaggle of gay men came from several makeup rooms to admire her and fuss over her. Nobody had seen a beauty like her in a long time. She choked down her embarrassment and took it all in stride. The best part was yet to come. I draped a cape over her, that the costume lady had chosen, and handed her a bouquet. Two gay men brought a small tiara with glittering rhinestones that they placed on her head. One of them, holding ribbon in his teeth and laboring mightily, tied a white ribbon from the base of her skull in back to the noble crown of her forehead, which pulled in her long glossy black hair and emphasized the gorgeous curve of her skull. The other placed the tiara on top as the finishing touch. His companion handed me a large black umbrella just in case.

I walked her down six blocks of Midtown Manhattan, and thousands of people must have stopped to stare. I took her to a nice restaurant for a light lunch in elegant settings, and then to see a flustered and bemused little old lady named Mrs. Weinstein who had a little office full of stacked papers, photos, and posters. Mrs. Weinstein smoked incessantly, left red lipstick on her faux cork filters, and also reddened the rims of her paper tea cups. She had a deep burry voice and exclaimed, while examining the first proofs from the makeup place, "I think we can place you in some cosmetics ads. I have a job coming up next week. I'll send your pictures along."

H gasped, and clasped her hands together. Some photographer snapped us, and our picture appeared inside The Daily News with the tongue-in-cheek caption 'unknown princess with escort—arrival a state secret.' A month later, her picture arrived in a department store infold inside the daily newspaper, and I showed it to her. That was when she actually did cry, and kiss me, and said thanks once more.

By Christmas, when she probably felt a bit lonely, I was living more at her place than mine. We slept together at night, and made our brief but juicy sex each evening and morning. She made oatmeal with peaches and milk each morning, along with black coffee and a fat vitamin pill. I gained a few pounds in that period, because she complimented me and told me "you no longer look so gaunt and hungry." She bought me new jeans, a size larger though still skinny in the waist. She rubbed my behind and then patted it. "Nice!"

She was actually Buddhist, and had a wall altar dedicated to her Tibetan religion. She liked Catholicism, too, and had a Bible and some other Christian symbols. She felt that the pictures of both religions seemed alike in many ways, except that the people had different eyes. "Do you mind my eyes?" she once asked me in a hushed tone. "I love your eyes," I said sincerely, kissing each beaded lid. I had a hard time saying "I love you," but I had no trouble telling her how much I loved every one of her body parts.

Christmas Eve, while seasonal choral music played softly in the background, she gave me a few presents of clothing. "I want to see you in those." We had put up a midsize tree, and her features looked like stained glass as she regarded me in them. We sat under the tree sipping hot glogg and munching crunchy cookies from a tin. "You are a sexy man," she said. "Stay here." She left the room, and came back in a few minutes later ringing a sort of cow bell. I jumped, and then gasped in surprise before laughing delightedly. She had donned a red Santa suit with big baggy legs, a pillow belly under a red jacket trimmed in white, and a floppy red cone-hat with a white pompom on the end. She was about half a foot taller—this Santa had very high heels. "I couldn't find enough cotton balls to make a beard," she said. I started to rise because I wanted to hug her, but she put up a hand for me to stay. First she changed the music to something more bumpy and grindy. Then she did a slow striptease. One by one, she peeled off the Santa layers, and I applauded and whistled with gusto. Finally, she was down to these two green and red knitted wool stockings that extended to mid calf. "You want to take them off for me?"

"I'd love to."

As she pranced slowly over to me on six inch high heels, I waited on my knees. Her face looked different, more animated. It was as if a veil had been lifted. "I made a decision," she said, "to let go and love you." She arrived before me, so close that her bare snatch was almost on my nose. "I have let myself fall in love with you, even if you walk out on me tomorrow." She raised her hands and laughed, dropping them so they fell down with a carefree slap against her thighs. "I figured it out! I'm so busy trying to prevent the shoe from dropping that I never get to let myself take the walk!"

She laughed loudly like someone who has thrown all her money off the bridge and plans henceforth to be poor but happy. "I may get hurt, but the best part is that I'm no longer afraid!" With that, she pushed me so I fell backward onto my hands and buttocks. Still in those heels, she advanced on me. Through the bush, I saw that marvelous hood spreading like a snowy hillside, and protruding under it the still flaccid nubbin of her clitoris. "Lick me," she commanded.

As she stood over me, I raised my face to admire the curvature of her buttocks, the longer, subtly curving line of her thigh, and the brownie outtie that awaited me in all of its glory. The prayer-hand labia were dry and slightly parted. A woman making a dramatic and perhaps scary announcement will not have moist labia or a wet oyster (unless she has peed her pants). Rather, she will be bone dry from shock. I was there to help her with that problem. I held her legs and felt the tension in them. Her whole body trembled faintly, and I pressed my hands on the tops of her feet to steady her on the high heels lest she fall. But she braced herself on furniture and looked downward. She noticed a large mirror on a vanity nearby, and took it down and put it near us so she could watch me. I nipped and licked lightly at her labia, which fluttered like fruit peels as my tongue nudged them. "I'm not licking them yet," I said. "I'm waiting for you to send juice down and make them wet." In her excitement, she did squirt a little, but it was pee. I wiped the warm, salty liquid from my nose and upper lip. "Gotta go?"

"No. Keep doing..."

I ran my fingertip along the crack of her butt, along the creases where each cheek tucked a corner into the thigh below it. I traced the ridge between her asshole and her oyster hole. Meanwhile, I ran my tongue back and forth, left and right, over the curve of her hood. Almost before I could miss it, dew sprang up on her labia. Her entire oyster area grew damp, then wet, as in a sudden forest rain shower. I slicked my finger back and forth in the hole, and heard the splash of wetness. "I am so wet," she said. "Oh God."

"What's the matter?" I asked.

She stepped off her heels. "I really do have to pee now. I can't hold it any longer." She took me by the hand and towed me along into the bathroom. She sat on the ring, sucking my fingers while pouring out a flood into the water. When she was done peeing, she dabbed herself with a tissue, dropped that in, closed the lid, and flushed. Then she led me out to the bedroom. We peeled off her stockings. "You are the best stocking stuffer a guy could ever have," I said.

She hugged and kissed me as I lay on top of her, both of us naked. She put her arms around my neck and pulled my head close for a long kiss while her legs wrapped around my thighs so that the head of my swollen cock lay heavily on top of her clitoris. "I love you," she said, "and I want you to know that."

"I love you too," I said.

She smiled wistfully and bravely. "It's nice that you say that. Are you lying, or do you really love me? Oh, I get it." She touched my nose with her fingertip. "You love me this moment. Well, that's something. And you made me into a queen for a day. That was spectacular. I'll never forget that." She laughed. "You rove me. That's special."

I kissed her dove-like breasts with their chocolate chip nipples, and she held her breasts for me to bite, although they were not big. She just wanted to help—sort of an underline or an italic, emphasizing how sincerely she wanted to give herself to me and help me enjoy her.

I liked looking at her long, thin body. Her skin was smooth as a girl's. She had just this little bit of bush atop her Venus mound, and a few curly hairs between her legs below, between the holes. Her knees were up, and she drew her ankles back and partly apart to show me what she offered me. Her genital apparatus looked up at me like a beseeching face.

I fondled her thighs, her buttocks, my fingers working their way toward her labia. "Go down," she murmured in a husky tone. I took my time, brushing her belly with my palm, again and again, like someone feeling a bolt of fine silk. Her hands moved to her groin, and her long, slender fingers with their neat little fingertips parted her labia slightly. It was like holding a door open, welcoming someone in.

I reached down, grabbed her ankles, and swung her legs up onto my shoulders. She slipped a moment, patted the sheets to right herself, and then reached down to part her labia again. The head of my cock thudded against her pee hole. With her middle finger, she nudged the head down so that it plopped into the brownie ring of her hole. The pink, palpitating interior waited for me full of oyster soup. Big as it was, the head rumbled easily over that wet, ready doorway and into that clutching, cloying tube that swirled around it.

I closed my eyes with the delirious pleasure of it, and groaned loudly. I heard her too. When I opened my eyes, I saw that her face pointed to one side. Her eyes were closed and her mouth was slightly open, as if she were in ecstasy.

She had her hands down there to assist. One set of fingers held one labia open, while the other fingertips oscillated over her clitoris and its hood. The labia fingers slid forward and she rubbed her pee hole. She slid it further, down into the brownie ring where my cock was sloshing back and forth like a pump. From there, she repeatedly picked up dripping juice on her fingertips and transported it up to water her hillside. With her legs sprawling up my torso, and her ankle bones brushing my cheeks, I could look straight down and see those fingernails blur as the soft pads of her fingertips worked the hill and the button it contained.

I caught glimpse of its pinkness. The hood was brownie, the clit brownie on top but pinkie underneath. I bumped against her in steady rhythm, and heard the slap of her thighs against mine. I listened to the waters in her pussy.

She began to arch her back. Tremors fled across her stomach. She writhed and whimpered, then moaned and sobbed. She rubbed her clit faster now, and I @ed her as furiously as I could. Suddenly, she doubled over and rolled away, holding her fingers to her oyster. She jerked her shoulders this way and that as she came. She rubbed her hands between her legs as if she were furiously cleaning something with a brush—continuing the frenzy of her climax until the contractions abated and she lay limply before me. Not for long. I still had plenty of pepper in the pot. Seeing her buttock cocked up at me, I walked on my knees and slipped my cock into her oyster from behind. One of the neat and unique features of **H's** build was that her oyster hole and asshole were close together, and her behind was small, so I could @ her oyster with equal easy from the front or the rear. The only slight inconvenience about the rear approach was that she'd get excited and squirm, and somehow her heel would knock into my nuts, sending a testicle rather uncomfortably up into my body.

Then we'd have to stop and wait a few minutes, while I made swallowing motions, and she looked shocked and concerned as she rubbed my back and said she was sorry...and inevitably, the testicle would drop back out into its scrotal sack. She would then spend much time fervently kissing it until both nuts ached, but I enjoyed the kisses on my ball sac. She liked playing with it too, with both hands, gently toying with it, one palm below and the other above. "It's like a little mouse," she said. Still palming my nuts, she would take my cock full in her mouth and warm it, wet it, embrace it with her gums.

I took my Christmas Buddhist from behind, and rode her like the surf. She was like a swimmer, herself, arms forward and chin on the sheets as she cried out for me to take her hard. I fondled her buttocks and her long back as I rapidly slapped against her rear. My cock slipped in and out of her moist oyster with a sloshing noise. I straddled her, making gorilla fists on the bed, while she stretched her long legs out around the outsides of my knees and pumping thighs. When I felt myself going, I cupped my hands under her hips and pulled her buttocks up tight against my abdomen. She slapped her hands on the sheet and sprang backward to help, pushing her butt against my stomach. I was starting to groan deeply, feeling the ejaculation muscles kick in. I glimpsed the brown flower of a slightly open asshole, and wanted to put my fingertip in, but I was overcome with my orgasm. The sight of her flower added to the passion in my climax, and I collapsed on her sobbing with my exertions.

That is how I like to remember us—that, and her prodigious clitoris. Within a few months, *H* had begun to become more and more needy as my own flight became imminent. We started to argue and spend time apart. She still called every day, and I sat there in my dilemma trying to decide if I must cut it off. If the decision was to either commit for life or cut it off, the stark choice was obvious. Something remarkable happened, though. Because of her new modeling contacts in New York, she became interested in a very wealthy and handsome young Canadian Chinese of Hong Kong wealth, a billionaire with a private jet. The last time I saw *H* , she had me over to her modest apartment for tea. We never made it to the bedroom. She started crying and explained that she still loved me, and would stay with me if I wished, but that her heart was torn over this other man. I saw the opportunity then, and knew what I must do. My only regret was that I could not tell her I loved her, which I did, because it was meaningless. Not meaningless in the moment, but meaningless in the world in which clocks ticked and trains rushed on their tracks and airplanes thundered up in to the sky. I had a long, dark road ahead, unknown and fraught with uncertainties, and I could not pull her into that. I rose and took her hand.

We looked into each other's eyes. Hers read the truth in mine, and her eyes glittered with tears. Killing the love in her for me, I kissed the back of her hand, inhaled one last time the pinkness and the gentleness there, turned, and walked out the door never to look back. As far as I know, she is married to that man to this day (he is actually a few years younger than she! Is it somehow symbolic that his age is exactly halfway between mine and hers?). They have several children and live in a great mansion overlooking the sea near the city of Victoria on Vancouver Island. If by some chance she reads this book, and recognizes herself, I hope she will not contact

me, but know that I did love her in my broken way, and still
do. I did not know it then, but I recognize it now—a truth
lives forever.

The Story of I (An Introspection)

This is the story of not one woman, but a type I will call *I.* First, a little recap or introspection about why it seems important for me to capture those golden moments that are now starting to seem long ago. As a writer, I am privileged to capture moments of time in the lens of my words, and preserve them as a kind of personal immortality. In that sense, the women of this book should thank me, though I have protected their identities.

There were over 100 women in the course of my five years as a Spring. Maybe it's fair to say that, during that time, I started as an April and ended as a Summer, while the younger of my older women were Mays and Junes, and the older ones Julys. As the title of my book suggests, this is the story of a wonderful period in a young man's life, when he is himself the younger man in a young woman's life. There are several ways to describe this, and it is important that we understand each because of its nuances.

Item: As a young man, I was privileged to enjoy the mystery and adventure of the older woman in my life. Every young man should enjoy this great delight at least once, and I humbly and gratefully offer that I was able to have it many times. Often the older woman is the best sexual partner a young man will have in his life. The union is impermanent, and carries with it the cachet of danger that it may end at any moment as one or the other partner moves on. It imparts a heavy wine of melancholy that lingers under the surface of all that we do and say, even in our most intimate and passionate moments, for the hard hand of morbidity is ever a chill inch away in these delirious but dead-end couplings. Usually, it is the younger man who wanders off suddenly like an irresponsible and sometimes unfeeling comet into another orbit, leaving the star of his previous joy mourning and hurt. She is still young and will get over it. e years of my education while I was as lost and adrift as a ship without sails. Or she says, enough of this toy, and sends him spinning, but he too will get over it.

Item: Every woman as, or should have, at least one younger man in her life. I have no experience to offer beyond my 27th year, when I settled down and stayed totally true to the woman I married for life. Getting back to the points made above, while a woman of any age may, if she keeps herself well, find a younger man, I can never again (except in memory) re-experience my time as her younger man any more than I can ever become young and lost and irresponsible and handsome again, with the wild wind blowing in my loose dark hair. It is a lost world. Which brings me to the next point. For many women, just as with men, having a good-looking young stud at her side is a trophy that she can show off to her friends and to the world. This book isn't about that.

Item: Every young woman as, or should have, at least one younger man in her life. Notice I say every young woman. Through her twenties and earliest thirties, a woman who thinks young and stays fit and sleeps well, maintains her sense of humor, and does not take things too seriously or excessively feel sorry will remain a truly young woman. Even if she has had children and is divorced from an unhappy marriage, she can still think young. As with my time as a young man, with this older young woman in my life, this is a period that a young woman should treasure and make the most of. If she happens to be single (or thinking about it, though I avoided dabbling in seducing married or committed women), she should choose carefully a younger man who will be kind to her, who is intelligent and a good conversationalist with a pleasant personality, who never hurts her physically or with his words, and who shares fantastic sex with her. The young man should be clean and honest, although he may fib in matters that make her happy to hear, because the whole relationship is a fleeting fantasy anyway.

There is too much to say, that cannot fit within the narrow margins of this book, as Fermat said of his Last

Theorem, but suffice it to say: There is a kind of paradise lost (if by introspection we ignore that warts and bumps that time makes us forget about our imperfect relationships) that exists briefly between an attractive young woman and the handsome younger man in her life. Finally, there is this to say: it is not about the younger man providing the ravishing sex, nor is it about the forbidden pleasure of intercourse with the older woman who brings added spice and passion. Rather, the fact is that it is a volatile mixture—the young woman in her own strength and beauty, and her younger man in his strength and untamed wildness, that couples into an alchemy of sublime sensuality—the true Persian Carpet on which the impassioned couple sail past the moon and the stars.

One could almost elevate such relationship to the level of a gender preference, since it is so unique and powerful in its own right: the young woman, and her younger man. Perhaps it is best characterized as a rite of passage for each, like the chrysalis to butterfly, since it is a transitional age without reprise.

There is an *I* of whom I shall not speak. Call her Inot, rather than I' or I-prime, for she is the one to whom you do not return. She brings a pack of baggage with her. She is ashamed of her desires, and denigrates you while she hates herself. Avoid her.

The *I* worth writing of, without devoting a chapter to her, may be tall or short, thin or wide. She may have a shorter torso that allows her to touch herself more easily below, or longer legs to pleasure her younger man in extra ways—like slow-dancing while @ing. In the latter case, three outcomes are possible. Either both partners collapse in unison, as orgasms ripple through her and lightning screams from his thunderbolt; or, second case, she comes first and sinks down, rubbing himself, and taking him with her to finish pleasuring her; or, third case, she lags a bit but patiently waits while he grips her thighs in his hands and whacks away inside of her until he grits his teeth, shouts, and firehoses his hot sperm all through her shaken pussy. *I* may be blonde or brunette or redhead, or even have her first streak of gray at an early age (easily masked with rinse). She may be Asian or German, Black or Latina, Hawaiian or Amazonian, but she brings her passion and interest to the capture of her younger man. If she is wise, she will be careful not to fall to deeply or hard in love, because it is a fleeting paradise.

Each *I* has her own unique little lessons and secrets to impart. Maybe it is her own little way of rubbing herself as she grows aroused. Maybe she shares with him the secrets of what she does to arouse herself, so that he will be all the more aroused and awed at the mystery she gives him.

Maybe it is a certain object with which she likes to penetrate herself when she is alone, and which she now wishes him to use on her so that she will have both hands free to pleasure herself, or him, or both of them.

Maybe she likes to @ on the floor, or be licked while she rubs her clit, or prefers to spend time sucking your head while you put your fingers in her vagina.

Maybe she most happily comes when she has your cock in her mouth, and you hold her thighs in an iron grip and dip your tongue into her oyster or her asshole. Every time a young woman mates with her younger man, it is an exchange of new information and pleasures.

For him it is a welcome port in a storm, for most often he is adrift and lost, and cannot see beyond the next corner.

For her it is often a time of freedom from obligations. Maybe she does not want to become a prisoner of love just now. Maybe she is exhausted from an abusive relationship or marriage, and wants to enjoy playing for a while. Maybe the younger man's careless and carefree lifestyle infects her like a fever and makes her lose her mind for a while. Maybe she never really felt free and young until she started learning from her younger man.

Then there are the risks. I have already mentioned the peril of the young woman investing too much of her heart and soul in her younger man. There are perils for him, as well. Maybe she is selfish and uses him as a bridge between more serious men in her life (that's I*not* again—but think, some women are on the cusp between *I* and *Inot*, neither fish nor fowl but some measure of both).

Whatever the opportunities and risks, there is passion here to be remembered for life, and that makes these relationships cosmic in their importance.

Maybe she is a one-night stand, by mutual decision. She needs someone just that once, to remind her how pretty she is, and how passionate. Or maybe she just needs some relief during a lonely spell, or someone to masturbate with, one night or once a week or (@-buddy style) occasionally. Maybe she needs someone as a little therapy in place of a week in the Caribbean or a night of too many margaritas. Maybe she hasn't been laid in a while, and just wants a reminder of what it's like to have a oyster full without all the bullshit and obligations. Maybe he feels similarly, though often the younger man knows or cares little about obligations—they slide off his back like rainwater off a blue jay's wings.

There is also the gorgeous Filipina nurse who was a movie star in her own country but fell into political disfavor and decided it was more expedient to become a nurse in the USA. That was where I met her. She was gorgeous, and I enjoyed taking her out because men (and women) stared after us. She only liked the missionary position. *I* is all the missionary position nights and quickies and okay dates that don't need a chapter to regale you in endless detail, but every *I* is a heroine of this book and deserves her place in this chapter. What *I* has in common with every other young woman in this book is that she offers her younger man the sophistication and maturity that his own younger women cannot possess—but will one day, perhaps, when they in turn meet their younger man.

The Story of J

The Gothic one was *J*.

I was in a bookstore one day. The weather outside was balmy, a fine spring day. I wore jeans, tennies, a white dress shirt with fine green stripes, and a dark blue beret. I had sunglasses planted high on top of the beret as I skimmed through the magazines. I became aware, gradually, of a faint patchouli essence. Glancing over to my right, I saw a spiky head of black hair tinged with green and purple, a woman in her late twenties with multiply pierced ears, and under her large black coat lapels, a valley of cleavage between a pair of ripe, freckled breasts. "You are a natural redhead," I blurted.

She laughed. "What?" I was afraid some bruiser would come to thump on me, but she seemed unconcerned. She seemed pleasantly engaged. "What did you say?"

"Sorry, it's a guessing game. I looked at you, and guessed that you are a natural redhead."

"How would you know that?"

"Sixth sense." Actually, I noticed that she had a sprawl of orange freckles over her pale skin. "And I like redheads."

"Why is that?" she said with the same surprised, bantering air. "They're special. I don't think they are temperamental as people make them out to be."

"Thank you. Society has oppressed me all my life. You are a liberator."

"Well, at least a kind soul, I hope."

"You made me lose my train of thought." She glanced at the magazines in puzzlement. "I was just about to pick up a thing on architecture."

"What kind of thing?"

"It had these cool pillars you can put in your garden."

"This?" I held up a thick, expensive magazine with more advertising than content, and an image of a garden with a pool and a pair of white columns.

"Yes! Thanks!"

"Have you seen the Art and Architecture section? It's got more like this."

"Really? Where?" It was a kind, easy day. She was imposing at first, but there was sunshine behind that Gothic façade; and then a darker side, as I would find. But what would one expect from a woman with tricolored hair?

From the A&A section it was a short walk to the coffee bar for espressos, and from there a natural succession to her dark green British sports car (top down) and a pleasant cruise to a white condo complex choked in blue dogwood and pink cherry blossoms. "It's a day for letting go," she said as she turned the key in her apartment. She was a secretary by day, an architecture graduate student in the evenings, and a Gothic club jetter by night when she wasn't passed out from exhaustion.

"Three day weekends," she said. "I love them." Her place was small but spotless, and well laid out. Chrome chairs, leather couch and love seat, a few black and white vampire posters on the walls. The main color was red. The rest was mostly black and white. She kept the appropriate dark rock music growling on low as background music. The place was really sunny and cheery. She brought two low, wide glasses full of something red. "Campari and soda. Hope you like it. I'm out of cola."

I thanked her and sat rather stiffly on the white leather couch. "Put up your feet," she said. "Make yourself at home." I relaxed. "Would you like to go for a swim? The pool is heated."

"Oh sure, that would be great. I don't have a swim suit."

"I think I can find you something from my ex." She laughed as she left the room. A few minutes later, the spiky hair leaned from a doorway, and a pair of light blue trunks came sailing toward me. I snatched them from the air. I changed into them—with a little belt tightening, they fit reasonably well, enough not to come off under water on the first dive. A long ten minutes later, a very different looking *J* appeared. Gone was the spiky hair, now down to very short carrot-red hair. "I was right!"

"You were, which is why I like you," she said brightly as she strode past me. She carried a pair of towels on one arm, and wore a black bikini. She was smallish, trim, shapely. "Come on. Let's go swimming." We carried our drinks outside to a small patio. Leaving the drinks there, we walked down to a medium-sized pool shared by a dozen or so condos in a common courtyard.

We were alone in the pool area, except for an older couple finishing a session in the bubbling, steaming Jacuzzi nearby. *J* and I left our towels on the warm concrete and slipped into the water. As we warmed up, we played together—splashing, ducking, jumping, gradually touching each other more and more. Pretty soon, we were locked into a deep French kiss that just seemed to go on and on. She was not a complicated woman—yet.

We migrated to the Jacuzzi, which was sheltered from view by a high circular concrete wall. It was a twelve seater, controlled by a ten minute switch. We sat in our separate seats in the hot, chlorinated water. I felt a strong pulse of forced water coming out of a nozzle at my back. We leaned close and continued kissing. She laughed and said: "Want to see something cool?" I nodded, and she turned to kneel before the pulsing jet at her seat.

She pulled the crotch of her bikini bottom aside, and maneuvered so that the stream went directly against her vulva. I looked closer in fascination. Her labia were remarkable—large, brown, like underwater things with a life of their own. They were easily two fingers across at their widest. She motioned for me to help. I held her bikini crotch away from her vulva, while she pinched her labia in her fingers and held herself open. She closed her eyes and moaned as the hot stream squirted against her little bud. "Kiss me," she wailed faintly. I leaned close and tongued her. Her mouth vacuumed on mine, so that my tongue threatened to come out by the roots. Turned on, I reached down with my free hand and stuck my finger in her vagina. She pushed my hand away, because it interrupted the stream of water. "It's on my pee hole," she said, "and up and down my clit. There's nothing like it anywhere."

"Want to bet?"

She laughed a little throaty laugh. "You have something better?"

"When you are ready."

She moaned lightly. "I want to come." "Go on."

"I'm a little embarrassed."

"Why?"

"Because we don't know each other very well."

I kissed her mouth, and we each breathed raggedly with raw sexual energy. "We're getting to know each other quite well."

"Will you be nice to me?"

I slipped my hand down her back, along the crack of her ass, and got a finger into her vagina from below. "I'll be very nice."

"Yes, you are very nice." Her eyes were closed. "I hope nobody is coming."

"Only you, honey, and me soon after."

She uttered what can only be described as a mixture of a laugh, a bark, a hiccup, and a cry of orgasm. She shuddered, bowing, bowing, bowing, lower, as the spasms traveled through her. She gripped my hand and pressed that finger deep inside of her in a clumsy move. "Oh my God," she choked. "Oh, that's good." A moment later, we both sat innocently in our seats as a family with several small children came chattering and laughing into the Jacuzzi area. They regarded us with mild curiosity, and it was clear they had just by seconds missed the show of their lives.

I went with *J* to her patio, where we picked up those drinks and hurried into the house. We left them on a counter as she took my hand and hurried me up the stairs. Her bedroom was an octagonal room with a round bed in the middle. On the walls all around were posters of the dark life.

She pulled down the drapes and turned on dim red lights. "I like to be looked at," she said. The soft Goth rock rumbled in the background. "I like to look," I said.

She pushed me onto the bed, where I sat up leaning on my elbows while she showed me her toys. Aside from the usual sorts of penetration tools in various sizes, shapes, and colors, she had an interesting set of objects in a black case lined with green velvet. "These are from Holland. Aren't they great?" As I watched, she took off her bikini top and bottom. I saw those significant labia again. "I want to suck on those," I said. She smiled. "Oh, you will, but first I want to show you this." She took two hooks from the case and pushed them through her labia. "I had them pierced," she said. On these hooks, she hung two smallish stainless steel chains, on the ends of which were two small stainless steel balls. "Now you can lick me," she said while standing before me with her legs apart and her arms akimbo. It was a domination pose, with her small conical breasts sticking out and the long brown nipples on them pointing over my head as I sank to my knees to inspect her more closely. There were more weights in the case, but I wasn't too into this and hoped she wouldn't stretch herself to the floor. She rocked lightly from side to side and the balls swung back and forth. "I'm stretching them. Every day I do this."

"What else do you do?"

"This." She rubbed herself, slowly at first, as if spreading juice around, then faster until her fingers were blurry. "Like to see me play?"

"Oh yes."

"Play with me. Make me horny. Make me come." Her voice was urgent, pleading.

I sat down under her. I turned her slightly so I could work my way under her, and I lay down on the rug. I nudged her until her oyster was directly over my face. She asked: "You want a golden shower?"

I had no idea what she meant. I was about to lick her. I was staring directly into her hole, enjoying the pink frilliness inside, and the view of her little knob hardening pinkly under its hood, when hot pee squirted from the tiny opening above her oyster hole. Startled, I tasted her salty fluid on my tongue. Sputtering, I rolled over and wiped it out of my eyes. "Did I hurt you?" she asked. I shook my head.

She removed the hooks and balls. She pulled on my ear. "Come here, I want to show you something." Taking me by the hand, she led me to the bathroom. "Look, I'll bet you didn't know women can do this. Most women don't know they can do this." Standing with her legs slightly apart, so that her buttocks looked part and grabable as apples, she spread her oyster open and held her fingertips near her piss hole. "Watch, Peter." Out came a nice thick twirling rope of golden pee, just like from the tip of my dick. I couldn't believe my eyes. "Then why don't women use urinals?"

"Because we like to remain mysterious to men. Maybe to ourselves." I watched as the heavy stream rushed into the toilet water just as if a dockworker were hanging his hose out over the harbor water. "Wasn't that fun?" She flushed, and we went back into the bedroom.

"One surprise after another," I said. She wiped my face with a clean, damp towel. "You weren't expecting that, were you?" I shook my head. "Did you like it?"

I replied: "Surprisingly, it wasn't terrible or anything. I like watching you pee. I'm just not sure I want you peeing on my face. I was just looking at that little hole when the pee came out all over my face."

"It's sterile," she said. "In India, people walk up to cows on the street and let them pee in their hands. Then they drink the pee, they wash their hair with it, they wash their faces, even brush their teeth with cow pee. It's sacred. And guess what, pee from a healthy person or cow is sterile."

"All the more reason for us to pee on each other," I said.

She dabbed at my eyes. "I'm sorry I startled you. Maybe later you'll want to try it again. Some people get hooked on it and can't get enough." I was sitting on the edge of the bed, and she stood before me. She wrapped her arms around my head and pulled me to her so that I could kiss the space between her breasts. "Now you can lick me. I promise not to pee on you again."

I lay back on the bed and had her crawl over me. She lowered her oyster over my face so that her wide flaps dangled over my mouth. I blew on them. They wiggled in the air stream. *J* squealed with sensory delight. "Yeah!"

It may seem strange after so many adventures, but I was just at that moment becoming conscious of the exact physiognomy of a woman's complicated apparatus down there. Maybe a lot of women are afraid to touch themselves and know less about their genitals than they should. I have made love to women who feel they should lie passively— what someone I know referred to as the Starfish Syndrome.

So here I was, with a woman who was not afraid to explore and pleasure herself, and feel no guilt about it—and for the first time really staring her sex organs in the face, so to speak. Our instinct to reproduce is hardwired into us. It is the strongest instinct we have—on a par with survival.

That's why, when I could have been home reading a good book or watching a movie, I was staring at this vivacious little redhead's piss hole and turned on as a three year old by a pile of wooden blocks. The best part was, her instincts made her turned on that I was turned on. She writhed low, rubbing her labia back and forth over my lips. "Lick them. Suck them. I love them. I like to play with them when I'm alone."

"Oh..." I groaned, "I love them too." I sucked on them, nibbled them, gently bit them, licked them from bottom to top. I paused only to lick her pee hole, which made her shriek with pleasure. I could feel the orgasm vibrations rippling through her body again. I put my fingers in her oyster and pulled out all the juice there, and started masturbating myself. I kept getting more of her mucusy juice that made my fingers slippery as I tightened my grip on my head and pumped up and down until it began to spurt. She came about the same time—wracked with shuddering contractions that almost made her fall over backwards—and in the last moment, as she yelled out in pleasure, she couldn't help it. She squirted. I closed my eyes and went along for the ride, snorting and spouting as if someone had poured beer over me at a kegger. I felt the shower of warm pee in my hair and trickling down my face, and thought of the cows in India. Maybe they knew something we didn't. *J* and I cried out loud in unison as we came together.

The Story of K

K was one of those perfect, Frisian blondes one sees in skin cream commercials. We met while I was browsing in a large bookstore. As so often happened in these Spring/Summer situations, she had noticed me and maneuvered slowly closer. Like a hunter on its prey, she closed in slowly but surely.

Women generally don't admit such a thing, because it sounds too much like something they think a man would do. In nature, however, females need to be aggressive hunters, and in bookstores it is not much different. When I finished in the Philosophy aisle, and turned the corner into the Eastern Religions aisle, she was waiting. At first, she made a pretense of stretching up high for a book she couldn't reach. Wearing jeans and a tight sweater, both of which emphasized her good figure, she turned her milky face toward me. Her long, straight blonde hair gave a toss, and she gave me an inquiring look. Her eyes were cornflower blue, her lips wide and pink. The faint shadows around her eyes and mouth gave away that she was at least 30, not to mention a stray gray hair or two.

"Which one?" I asked, and she said: "That big one about Tantric Yoga."

As I reached up for her (she was tall, but I was taller) she asked: "Have you ever tried it?"

I had to admit that I had not, as I handed her the book. "Looks interesting," I said. I was interested in it, and in her, and she was interested in me, and it.

We wound up having a close, animated conversation at the bookstore coffee shop. We made a date to attend a yoga lecture at the university, and from the lecture that evening she drove me to her apartment. She was divorced, had been an engineering professor's wife, and had one toddler child who spent Tuesday and Thursday evenings at his grandmother's. *K* was a good mother, but needed a lot of space. The little boy spent much quality time with his two grandmothers, and in fact I gathered that the paternal grandmother thought *K* was taking a class Tuesday and Thursday evenings, which was a fib. *K* still had a lot of youth and mayhem in her. She drove her old Volvo stick shift too fast, and at least once in each journey gave someone the finger. I liked the way her fine, corn silk hair swung back and forth under a well-shaped face as she bent over the stick shift. She was one of those women with a long torso, which made her hunch a little in the car. She had probably intimidated the boys of her age group in high school, and probably would have ignored me in favor of some jock. That was then, this was now, and she was the needier one in this different world of her 30s. I could not tame her, but let her vulnerability, as she perceived it, keep her humble—it is the best way I can find to speak of a woman who has been used to being adored all her life, and now is becoming 'one of us.' Of all the Summers and Julys I dated, I probably had more spats with this one than any several others combined. One day we were in the steamy bathroom, where we had just showered. We had bickered about some nonsensical thing, and then made up, had sex, and she was contrite as we toweled, I confronted her at a vulnerable and appropriate moment and showed her her face in the mirror. "You see yourself?" She started to become tearful, and bit her lip in remorse. "You see this gorgeous face?" She nodded. I pointed to the vertical lines on either side. "If you continue being mean and pouting, these will become age wrinkles. Now let me rub some cream on there to soften them up." You never saw a humbler person as She waited like a child for me to get the white European clinical cream, with its clean, orangey under-essence, which I applied liberally to each cheek.

   K was temperamental, which made her good in bed. She could bicker one minute, and then @ the next. At first I was put off by the roller coaster, but then I learned to step back and let her thunder and lightning. It was harmless, and in fact most of the time she was right—I was a slob, I didn't pick up my sweater, I didn't take my fork to the sink, I didn't see that the trash was overflowing, etc. She maintained that, since I ended up sleeping at her house most nights, and we @ed through the night, as if she were my whore, I could help out. I

assured her she was not my whore, and I promised to pick up. I was intrigued by this fantasy, though, and I think she was too. She wasn't terribly imaginative, but she was very adventurous. She loved it when I created a fantasy, and she would follow me anywhere in it. The whore thing gave us a frequent play topic. It wasn't about the nasty, violent real world. It was more about the Game. That is, the Game of pursue, elude, catch. It was about all those coy exchanges that happen when two people play. I'm not sure that the same Game plays in both people's heads, but pillow talk amid the shadowy pleasure world of the bedroom can reveal some things.

K and I had come home, showered, and relaxed in our robes and underwear for a while. We were watching a sitcom with attractive young people in it, and I noticed that she was rubbing the inside of her thigh with one hand. Leaning a little closer, I noticed that her robe was slightly open. I could see the pink of her thigh and the black of her silk panties.

She was almost absently stroking herself. I noticed that, with her hand lightly curved, she had her middle finger in her panties. She didn't notice me looking, and I didn't let her know how interested I was. Maybe she wasn't even aware of doing it—I have known several women who casually diddle themselves in the privacy of their homes without necessarily masturbating. I think watching handsome men—and possibly women—arouses them to some low-energy state of interest, and rubbing a damp labia or gently pressuring a slumbering bud under its clitoral hood, without actually bringing it fully erect, offers a pleasant background buzz.

I was trying to guess which of the men she was most interested in, and if any of the women added to her pleasure. There was one scene where two young women were having one of those conversations where they say funny things with a straight face, gesturing and grimacing, and the audience laughs every ten seconds or so. I watched her hand, and it may have slowed a bit, but that long finger stayed hooked in her undoes. She turned her hand so the knuckles were up, and the finger straight, and began rubbing with more energy. But she did that in fits and starts, no matter who was on. During commercials, she removed her hand and used it to hoist her steaming tea mug, or to stir sugar in.

She picked up the TV schedule and read with serious, innocent mien. "Nothing but junk," she said to me. I pretended to be lost in thought, and shrugged, raising an eyebrow to signal I had heard her comment. She put the paper down and resumed stirring her tea. The show came back on and she sipped her tea. Two young men were having a dumb conversation in the living room.

One left, and in came a vivacious young brunette. Her little breasts jiggled as she strode back and forth, and her dress flounced under a pert behind. She sat down, sulking, and the young man sat down close beside her to console her. As she sat thus, her dress rode up, revealing the dimpled insides of her knees and the beginning of one lush thigh. *K's* hand moved back into her robe, and her finger went back under the panties. First she did the knuckles up diddle, with the @ finger out straight, rubbing rapidly, as if she had to catch up on her erection. Then, having lubricated and swollen herself just enough, the hand relaxed, went knuckles forward, fingers curled, and her @ finger sort of absently brushed up and down along one dewy lip.

"Which one turns you on the most?" I asked, breaking our silence.

She was startled, embarrassed, and flicked her robe shut and folded her hands together in her lap while squeezing her knees protectively together.

"I think you have cute knees like that woman," I said, looking at the actress on the couch.

"She is really cute," *K* said.

"Does she turn you on?"

K pulled her head in as she coyly raised her shoulders. I put my arm around her shoulder and rested my head against hers. "It's okay if you tell me."

"I'm not lesbian, if that's what you're asking," she said without any rancor. It was a casual statement, like "I am not one of those who put bananas in my peanut butter and jelly sandwich."

"That's fair," I said. I knew that all her rubbing must have stimulated her, and I wanted to see how long she could delay getting really turned on—by the actors, rather than by me. "I didn't think you were."

"Oh? What did you think?" She laid her head back against my shoulder. We were on the verge of another fantasy game.

"I was watching you, seeing that you were getting a little turned on, and I thought you were turned on for me."

She laughed. "For you? How's that?"

"I'm serious. You were turned on by those handsome guys, and I was turned on by those gorgeous women. I think telepathically, in your mind, you sensed that I was turned on, and you tuned into that."

She kissed my earlobe. "You know what? You're nuts." I noticed that her hand had sneaked back into her robe. I could see the outline of her knuckles slowly moving back and forth. I pretended not to notice. I had a huge hard-on by now, but didn't let on yet. "Tell me more," she said.

"Well, not much to tell. Just watch. Look." I pointed to two women in the show, whose titties jiggled in their light sweaters as they circled each other in the living room saying funny stuff that goosed the laugh track. "See how their titties jiggle? The show's producers do all that on purpose. They can't show naked people, so they have women with jiggly breasts and men with huge codwallops." "Cod whats?"

"Codwallops. I made it up, from codpiece, which used to be an item of fashion in the 1500s. Men wore these outer sacs over their pants to emphasize that they had dicks inside."

"You mean like a cod, or halibut, or a fish?"

"I think cod was Middle English for scrotum."

"How weird. That's almost like those Stone Age people in New Guinea who wear gourds on their dicks."

"Same thing."

"What do women wear?"

"Little black miniskirts. Open blouses. Lots of things to turn other people on." We watched the rest of the program. It segued into another rerun of the same show. *K* yawned a bit, rubbing her eyes with her left hand while her right hand stayed in diddle mode under her robe. She honestly did it without thinking. I could almost read the sensuous thoughts that crossed her mind by watching the polygraph of that finger. As a seismometer needle traces the strength of earth tremors, so her knuckles moved slowly back and forth under the robe.

I distinctly saw the hand flip into knuckles up position each time this one dark-haired young man was visible—but it also happened when this very pert young brunette was visible; especially when the brunette's blouse was open at the top, or she wore a fine sweater that showed the unrestrained jiggle of her little boobies when she walked in rapid steps on her high heels. Once in a while, *K* would emit a heavy sigh, or even a tiny cry like some micro-climax. I gave her space, and hung back watching with my own bulge becoming painful from arousal.

K yawned. "It's getting late. Want to go to bed?"

"Sure." As she flicked off the TV with the remote, I rubbed her fanny. She yawned again. She didn't push me away, but said: "I'm very tired, Peter. Maybe we can make love in the morning."

I accompanied her down the hall. We hung our robes on a chair together (the robe had been left by her ex, a highly intelligent looking balding man still gracing her bedroom along with a photograph of their son at age one and a happily smiling *K.* Sometimes she tossed her panties over the portrait as if to shield their innocent gaze. Or maybe it was to insult her ex.

K kissed me goodnight and turned away. "Night, honey," she said, yawning again. She set her alarm for work the next morning, and turned out the light. I lay behind her, in a netherworld, inhaling her scent and enjoying her warmth. I pressed my groin against her buttocks and was pleased by the way her waist curved up into the mandolin-curve of her hip and thigh.

She laughed throatily. "I feel someone." Normally, on the rare occasions when she was really too tired, she would say "not tonight, honey" and kiss me lavishly to make up for the denial. I knew on those occasions I should fall rapidly asleep, for I could take her in the morning. We made love often in the morning—a short, puppy thing, in which one woke first and started humping the other.

More than once, I woke up to find my erection inside a wet oyster, and *K's* face straining above me as she @ed herself with my dick. Or I would waken, roll half onto her, push her knee away with mine so I could get between her thighs—she still sleeping, mumbling in some dream, maybe flickering a smile or licking her lips in dazed confusion, while I slid the ram of my sex into her. If she was dry, she rapidly got wet. Sometimes I had to rub my spit on my cock to moisten it for the initial penetration, but once it was in, it was really pleasurable. A morning @. The cock crows. But now it was night, and she actually felt my erection before I knew I had one. She laughed again. "You can do a quickie if I don't have to do anything."

I kissed her behind the ear. Sincerely, I said: "Thank you, baby. I love you for that." I never told any of the Summers and Julys that I loved them. The words could not cross over my lips, so frightened was I of commitment. But I could condition it like that. "I love you for letting me put my rod into your sweet little sleepy pussy." She liked that, and made a long hum of satisfaction as she lifted her upper thigh to let me in, doggie style. My cock had been hard for at least an hour watching her diddle herself, and I must have been dribbling sperm all over the place. Now, as the head slid between her legs, looking for her moist hole, I was lubricating my way by dribbling ahead. She did one thing: she reached down and diddled her finger under the head of my cock, where that little thin blue triangle of dorsal skin extends from the chin of the head down to the shaft.

I put my hand on her buttock and pushed her an inch or so forward, rolling her hip away to open the space between her legs a little more. As I did this, she lost touch with my dick and I did all the rest from there. I think she was so tired that she fell asleep right then, as her hand flopped onto the bed.

I pulled the sheet and blanket up over us so that we were enveloped in a sheath of comforting darkness and warmth. She sighed happily in her sleep and spooned snuggling back against me. I wanted to see if my cock (my 'little man') could find his own way, and he did. I stretched one arm up above my head as I lay with my face against her spine. I rested the other hand on her thigh.

My little man got into the crack of her ass, pressed against her pink butt flower (she murmured 'no no' in her sleep) but then, moving just an inch further, he slid into that comforting slippery hot hole. Her butt cheeks wiggled in her sleep as if they were happy. I think they were happy buttocks, with that hard meat between them. I waited a minute for my cock to grow to its full erect size.

She murmured snoozily as she felt her oyster expand with the pressure. Oyster juice swirled around my shaft as she got turned on. After all, she'd been watching those gorgeous women and those handsome men for over an hour and playing with herself, without getting near the relief afforded by a great climax.

Or maybe she'd had several tiny mouse-sized climaxes characterized by a sigh or a tiny shriek. Getting @ed in her sleep was, for *K,* a bit like letting sleep itself overwhelm her. It became part of slipping away into a deep, wondrous sleep in which her insides had a sexual implosion—a nearly silent arousal and climax. When I was hard, I started pumping. She was so wet that it caused her little friction and no discomfort. Even her thighs were slippery so that they felt girlishly smooth.

For both of us, the pleasure came not so much from friction but from pressure. My hard cock in her tight oyster— and her ass spread across my groin and my free arm over that voluptuous thigh—I came in shudders and she squirmed with her butt in my groin so that she wiggled as if she were peeing and shaking out the last few drops. It was over in a minute or two, that quickie, and we both fell fast asleep.

In the morning, I woke first. I lay on my side, pretty much as I had fallen asleep. She lay on her back with an angelic look on her face. The lines beside her mouth had softened and almost disappeared, and her eyes were a little shadowed, but she looked relaxed and rested. I liked doing these quickies with her with as little prolog as possible—the very fact that I would take her so quickly and hungrily added its own little frisson. It telescoped foreplay into the play itself. It was almost naughty in a way, because it wasn't supposed to be done this way.

So I got on my knees between her legs. I put my hands under her knees and lifted so that I pushed her thighs back and opened the entire vista of her pink domain. She kept on sleeping, though I'm sure she was partially conscious and enjoying it. She had a pleasant, almost-smile, and she did reach down with one hand, first to scratch the hair on her Venus mound, then to brush her labia to see how open and wet they were. From the smacking sound as she dragged her fingers through the gap between her labia, and from the way her pussy parted limply showing her pee hole and the round opening of her oyster, I knew she was wet for me.

I slipped into her and pounded away. She started to awaken, and held her thighs up for me so that I could rest my knuckles gorilla-style on both sides of her while my entire body turned into a battering ram that made flesh slap noisily and splash with stray secretions. She rested her calves on my shoulders and put her hands on my ribs, as if trying to help.

We came together in a chorus of groans, and then laughed as we rolled and tumbled on the bed.

I pressed her down so she lay on her stomach. I made big playful sucking sounds with my lips on her buttocks, and she squealed as it tickled. I licked her crack and diddled the flower of her anus, but that was her limit. She turned onto her back, and I turned my mouth loose on the fine connective structure between her oyster and her thighs, where I found more loose flesh to suck on. "You're giving my hickeys all over!" she cried as she pushed at my head, though not hard enough to end my contact.

"Who cares?" I said. "Nobody is going to see."

We lay beside each other resting, during a 15 minute interval before she had to get up for work. "I think about you at work," she said.

"Do you get horny?"

"Yes."

"Do you walk over to the copy machine and let it jiggle between your thighs while it makes copies?"

She laughed. "No. I think there is one secretary downstairs who does that, but she is so subtle that you'd never know."

"So what do you do?"

"You really want to know?" She looked at me shamefaced yet eager to tell. It was a 'show me yours and I'll show you mine' moment.

"Yes. I want to think about you while you're at work." I was unemployed at the time, and spent my days looking for a part-time job at a library, which made her feel good.

"Do you ever masturbate thinking about me while I'm at work?" she asked.

"I think about it, but I don't." She looked a little disappointed, and I added: "...because I save it all up for you."

"Aw, that's nice."

"So what do you do?"

"When I'm horny, thinking about you, I have this electric pencil sharpener by my side. I pretend to sharpen a pencil, and

I hold it against my bush, and it sends just the right vibes, right through the hood of my clit, so that I get one of these silent, gooshey orgasms."

"And if someone walks in?"

"I pretend that I have hiccups. I put my fist to my mouth and make a face as I recover from my sex. I can fake it really well. People have walked in once or twice, and gotten all concerned that maybe I was choking. I put a few peanuts on the desk to let them think that. I can almost picture my boss lady walk in and give me a lecture about eating while I sharpen pencils." We laughed together. *K* was very inventive that way.

The whore thing was one of our fantasies. It wasn't really a whore thing, but a sort of verbal foreplay fantasy. The whore thing might go like this, as we lay entwined on the couch in our robes, with the TV on mute and *K* absently diddling herself.

"You have no shame."

"I don't want to have any shame."

"I am here to remind you of your chastity."

"@ my chastity."

"Okay."

"You're not supposed to make it funny."

"I couldn't help it. You walked right into that one."

"Tell me you like my ass."

"I can watch you walk down the street and wonder how much it would cost to touch your ass."

"Not much. I'm pretty cheap." (She laughed: "But you don't have any money.")

"Now now, in insulting the john."

"Sorry. I'll give you a free blow job to show you that I'm sorry."

"Will you do it on your knees while I stand over you?"

"Uh-huh."

"Want to do it now?"

"Come on, whore."

"No."

"Come on, whore oyster pussy."

"I won't unless you pay me."

"I don't have any money."

"Then you have to lick my knees."

"I think the whore should lick my knees." "The whore will lick anything you want, but you have to lick her knees and her ass cheeks first."

"I want to lick the whore's ass cheeks." "You don't touch the whore's asshole though."

"I like the whore's asshole."

"Do you?" (she softens, as if considering...)

I say: "Yes. The whore has a nice ass, just the right size, without too much or too little, just right." I see that her hand turns knuckles-up under the robe, and the stiff @-finger goes into the slot.

"Tell the whore more about her ass. Her whore ass." With her other hand, she reaches under my robe and finds my stiff cock. My cock is near her ear. "Ooh," she says, "what is this, a telephone?"

"Call me, whore."

"Okay." Diddling herself, she caresses my cock with her cheek. She bubbles with laughter. "Busy signal."

"You have to hang up and dial again."

"Maybe I'll push this button," she says, and punches my nuts gently with her diddlefinger hand. I didn't see that coming, and roll off the couch in pain.

"Oh my God," I hear her cry out through the clouds of olive drab, bilious blue, mustard yellow, and ketchup-garbage pain that float like huge bubble bladders in my blinded vision.

"Are you kidding around, Peter?"

I lie in a fetal position gasping for breath, as the pain starts to ease. "Please don't do that ever again, okay?"

She was on her knees hovering over me as if I were a deer she'd hit on the road. Her arms were outstretched as if she wanted to heal me but was afraid to touch me.

"It will pass," I said in a broken whisper. I wasn't kidding.

"Oh sweetie," she said, breaking into tears as she hugged me and kissed my face. "I'm so sorry."

"It's okay. It was an accident, sort of." I felt her tears on my face like lukewarm rain that cools as it falls through the atmosphere.

"I'm so sorry," she said. "Honey, I will make it up to you. I will kiss you anywhere you like, and you can lick anything, even my asshole." She pressed her breasts against me. I felt their fullness, and turned to put my arm around her as we lay on the thick carpeting. I held my hand over my still-aching nuts. My gut felt as though I'd been football-tackled in the stomach. My solar plexus thought it was time to heave, and I almost did. She nursed me back with a concerned face and more tears. I kept reassuring her: "It's okay. It's just a thing in the nuts. I'll get over it." I ended up stroking her hair and consoling her. She hovered over me as I lay on my back. She said: "I'm serious, sweetie. You can kiss anything on me. It's all yours. Want to touch my asshole?" I had to admit that the prospect of playing with her asshole intrigued me. I was still learning from my Summers, and they were educating themselves with me. Older women know more, usually, and the more adventurous ones are more skilful. *K* had shied away from anal play, and I had almost no experience with it, so I was interested in exploring. "I'd like to play with it a little," I said. "If it hurts, tell me and I'll stop."

She pushed my shoulders down. "You rest, honey, and I'll get in position." She rose so that she stood straddling me. "Which way do you want me?"

"I'm not sure. The view from here is great."

She smiled and pushed her thighs apart while opening her labia. "Like that?" I saw the little dot of her pee hole in its swollen button, and the ready hole of her oyster. I nodded. "How about this?" She turned and pulled her ass cheeks apart. I looked at the shadows between them and said: "Closer." She bent over and lowered her rear so that I saw the little pinkish brown star of her sphincter behind the glory of her oyster. "Closer," I said, and she crouched down in a squatting position. "Go easy," she said. "I wonder if I can come when you touch me there."

"I've heard it can arouse a woman." I slapped her buttocks lightly, first one, then the other.

"Am I bad?" she fantasy-asked. I knew the tone of voice.

"I am going to check," I said. I wasn't sure I wanted to play the whore game anymore for the moment. "I think this calls for the doctor game," I said.

She laughed as she squatted over my face with her arms folded on her knees: "Want to play doctor?"

"Yes. I'll be the doctor, and you are the patient." I ran the tip of my index finger up and down her ass crack. She had fine golden hairs all up and down. "You suffer from goose bumps," I said. "Are you cold?"

"No, I'm a little scared. I've never let anyone play with my asshole before."

"You think that's because it is wrong, or because it hurts your sphincter?"

"Well, if I am being bad, then it doesn't matter if it's wrong. I just don't want to tear or hurt my sphincter muscle."

"What if I just put my fingertip in gently, like this?" I licked my fingertip to wet it and then pressed against the little flower. Her sphincter was tighter than a virgin's oyster. "You want me to play with anything I want, because you want to show me that you are really a very nice, sweet girl who didn't mean to almost knock me unconscious by busting me on the balls." "Yes, you can play with anything you want."

"Then how about being a good little girl and going to the bathroom and getting some petroleum jelly or something that we can put in there so it's not dry as the Gobi Desert?"

"I have some cream," she said and swayed off. An underlying little bonus was calling the older woman in my life a little girl. I think it thrilled her, and it thrilled me that it pleased her. She brought a tube of some kind of Swedish sex paste. "I bought that on impulse last year because I get dry lips sometimes. It tastes like peaches and is okay to get in your mouth."

"I understand about the dry lips," I said. "You put this on while you watch TV?" She blushed, and I pulled her close. I whispered in her ear: "I watch you sometimes. You rub your oyster when you see a nice looking man or woman on TV."

"Not woman."

"Oh yes." I continued holding her prisoner in my arms and whispering the shameful truth in her ear. "You like seeing gorgeous women."

"No I don't."

"Then why do you rub yourself harder when those young girls in the sitcom are stalking around on high heels with their titties jiggling?" She couldn't answer. I had no idea what I was saying, only that it turned me on to say it, and I used my fantasy voice to let her know it was okay, it wasn't an accusation, it was maybe just another fantasy game even if maybe it was sort of true. I said: "You're not a lesbian, honey sweetheart, but I think many people have a little tinge of something inbetween."

"You mean bisexual?" she said.

"I'm not putting labels on anything."

"I have never made love to a woman."

"Have you thought about it?" I asked in my fantasy voice. As I did so, I let go and put a dab of cream on my fingertip. "Show me your oyster, baby." She sat on me, leaning backward and propping herself by her elbows against my raised knees. "I am a good chair for you," I said. She answered my question thoughtfully: "I used to get crushes on girls in high school."

"Did you take your electric pencil sharpener to school with you?"

She laughed and whacked me softly on the head. "I used to wait until I got home and then I'd masturbate in my bed. My mother would come in right during my orgasm and be all worried that I was sick or something. So after I was done masturbating I'd go out and she would have some steaming hot tea and cold remedies waiting for me. Being a girl, you can always get away with things like that by letting them

think it's your hormones. Which, come to think of it, it was."
While she spoke, I rubbed cream into her labia. I did her
whole pussy so it was slick and had a whitish coating. Then I
put my knees down and had her straddle me with her ass
toward me. I started applying the cream to her asshole while
we continued our little fantasy talk. "So when you were in bed
masturbating, did you think about being with those girls?"

"I think it I had a muddle of boys' and girls' pretty faces
and bodies in my head. Like the sitcom."

"Ah, I get it. It's a just a general sort of horny muddle."

"I think that's right. I mean—I've never actually thought
about making it with a woman. I'm too traditional, I guess. It
was hard being in school all day with the hormones and all
those nice looking people around me."

I worked cream into her asshole and watched it slowly
relax. She pulled away. "You're making me want to go poo."
She rose. "I'll be back in ten minutes." She disappeared into
the bathroom, and I sat watching a lingerie show with
beautiful women and soft music as they modeled various
skimpy outfits. *K* returned in 15 minutes. "I took care of it and
then did an enema and washed myself inside and out. I think
I'm squeaky clean for you. Let's go to bed." She extended a
hand, and led me to the bedroom. She giggled as we crawled
up on to the sheets: "I've never done this before."

I put on my fantasy voice (which was low, and
mysterious, and sensuous): "You promised I could touch or
lick any part of you because you were sorry for what you
did."

Her fantasy voice was also lower and slower and
sensuous. "Yes. I am very sorry that I whacked your nuts, and
I want to make up for it by giving you an extra special treat. I
was bad, and I want to be good."

I made her sit on all fours and wait submissively as I
crawled up to her rear. "I will show you how to be good. You
will stop being bad and be very good."

She sighed. "I hope I like being good."

"I will prove to you, my sweet little darling doll, that while you may enjoy being bad, you will really enjoy being good."

"What do I have to do?"

I lay under her looking up at her pussy. "You have to squat over me like you did before." She squatted again with her elbows on her knees, in a position that naturally spread her asshole for me. I first pulled her down close and sucked the irresistable little pink labia into my mouth. Tasting her pussy juice, and I had to force myself to stop. "I could go on sucking your pussy all day, but I am interested in playing with your asshole right now."

"I hope you will show me how to be good," she said.

I pulled her butt down and started licking the odorless, tasteless bloom of her super-clean asshole. I could feel her sphincter squirm as it grew wet from my spit. "Now you cleaned it really well?" I asked.

"If you smell anything, get away."

"That's a fair test." I had read that rimming is a fun thing, and many people discover it. It's called rimming because you run your tongue around and around the rim of your partner's anus, either on the outside, or on the inside edge. "Am I being good?" she asked.

"You are trying very hard, and I think you are on your way to becoming good." I continued rimming her, and felt her asshole loosen as she stopped being afraid and relaxed. Pressing my tongue like a little dick, I got the tip inside and pulled it in and out.

"Am I being good?"

"You are being good." I substituted my finger and finger-@ed her asshole. She smeared cream on her finger and worked that in. "Put your finger in next to mine," I said. Now we had two fingers in her asshole. She seemed to be enjoying it, for her eyes closed, and she did that swimming-the-head-around thing women do when they are feeling intense sexual gratification. "It makes me feel weak," she said. I helped her by pushing gently, so that she fell onto her side with one thigh cocked way up. We still had our fingers in her anus, and I crawled up close to lick around it.

These were the games we played during those rainy months when it wasn't much fun going outside, and there was so much to do by the fireplace or in the bathtub or in bed. Neither of us realized that there would be at least one visitor to our little fantasy world in the months ahead.

The Story of L

L was a nurse whom I met while getting a flu shot. She was a beautiful Latina, 31 years old, 5' 6", with long, thick black hair that was so glossy it almost looked blue. She had light olive skin and exotic features like one sees on Mayan wall frescoes-the swept back head, long curving nose, thin prominent lips, small chin, atop a long neck the color of caramel.

At this flu clinic, where she was moonlighting, she wore the traditional white nurses' uniform, complete with starchy cap, white nylons, sturdy white shoes, and a white dress buttoned up the front. She was one of those women with very skinny, almost stick legs but muscular, wiry, whippet-quick and strong—I mean her entire frame, not just her legs.

I was waiting in line for some minutes behind a nondescript assemblage of men and women, when she and I caught one another's eyes. What attracted me to her, aside from her exceptionally well toned body in that white uniform, was the humor and good nature in her eyes.

"How are you?" she said in a faintly accented voice. She managed to stick me quickly and painlessly. "Go sit over there," she ordered, and had me sit for observation on a plastic chair beside her. I watched with interest as she passed several more patients through. There was a lull, in which she stripped off her latex gloves and washed her hands. "What's your name?"

I told her, and she took her time filling out my chart. She admitted later that she was stalling in the hope I would summon up the courage to ask her out. I had that sixth sense about it, as always, and made some comment that led to a conversation which led to our having dinner that evening. I picked a nice, cozy steak house that I could afford, having just been paid from my librarian job. She ran home, changed into casual evening clothes, and came around to pick me up in her car.

We relaxed over a pair of margaritas, and talked about who we were. *L* was second generation American of Belizean and English descent, whose family had moved to the San Francisco area a generation earlier. Her father was a professor of Spanish Literature, and her mother was a nurse as she had become. "Why do you like nursing?" I asked. We were already holding hands, though I was not about to push things. It felt good, and I knew for sure all good things would come in time.

"I like helping people," she said as she squeezed my hand. "I like being in the middle of things. What I miss most is having someone to be friends with."

I put my hands around hers. "Someone who will be nice to you and enjoy spending some time with you?"

She rolled her eyes up. "If you would pay some attention to me and keep being nice like this, I would enjoy spending time with you, yes." She patted my hands, trumping my protective gesture. "I'm not needy, trust me. I'm very self-reliant, which is why I often push people away from me personally. I get so busy helping others that I end up sitting there alone most evenings." She leaned close with an embarrassed air. "Do you mind that I am so much older than you?"

"Six years?" I shook my head. "You aren't your chronological age, but however young you feel. Also, I think Latinas age so well, that you don't seem any older to me than I am."

"You are so flattering," she said. Her teeth flashed when she laughed, and she had pink gums. Her eyes were dark and beautiful, with the whites narrowing like almonds outward. "Are you full of it, Peter?"

I trumped her hands with mine again. "I wouldn't be sitting here if I thought anything less of you."

"Did you know I was older?"

"Only by your sophistication and maturity. I like that. It intrigues me, because you have so many secrets."

"I do?" She laughed, in a tone that suggested she knew I was full of blarney, and yet there was an element of truth to it, and I was certainly sincere.

"You were married? Had kids?"

She shook her head. "I dated someone for years. Actually, a few someones. One guy through college, another through my early nursing years, and I just broke up with someone a few months ago. Like I said, I am so busy that it takes me a long time to latch up, and then I just stay with a guy unless he leaves me."

"Did they leave you, those guys you were dating?"

"The first one and the last one. I got dumped real good recently. The middle guy—"

"Yes?" I waited. "Don't want to tell?"

She shook her head. "Maybe someday, if there is a someday."

I didn't care but I said: "See what I mean, secrets?"

"That's not a secret worth keeping. Okay, I'll tell you. He was kind of unsure about himself, and then after we dated for three years he decided he was gay and left me for a doctor at the hospital where we worked. I changed jobs soon after."

"You were embarrassed?"

She nodded. "I was. But more so I was scared about HIV. Luckily, we always used protection and he was careful about it. I don't think he had had sex with many men at that point..." She seemed to realize she was embarrassing herself again, so she waved her hands like a bird trying to take flight and squealed "Enough already, let me out of that conversation!" "Tell me about Belize," I said to change the topic, and she did. Dinner came, which was very enjoyable. We went to the mall and down by the water (maybe the classic test) and then she applied the 'not-on-the-first-date' rule by kissing me demurely good night as she dropped me off at my place, and then drove off in her nice little VW Passat. I stood waving, and she waved back and there was absolutely no mistaking the longing and interest in her gorgeous eyes—the hunger, I should say—as she drove off.

Our intimacy—my consummation with dear L—occurred that weekend after one or two lunch dates and a movie evening. She was a fulltime E.R. nurse and saw a lot of nasty things every day, so she had this mixed air of competence versus innocence, experience versus naïveté, hardness versus tenderness. She could probably bake you a cake and change the oil in your car while ironing—in other words, she was utterly feminine without being dependent. Having a relationship was not about being needy or codependent but about working out a kind of deal.

She told me at one point as we walked together arm in arm, after a movie one evening: "You can stay with me as long as you want, as long as you aren't mean or dishonest. I don't think you would ever be either of those things, but some men can be and I had to say it."

"It's okay. I understand."

"So what's your boundary?" She would ever be the deal-maker.

I had to think for a moment. "I can't think of anything more than what you asked me."

"That's fair." She was always about being fair and making deals and being on the up and up. She pulled me close and kissed me. Tongues talk to each other in various ways. Her tongue had a languid way of telling my tongue that she really liked being in the same mouth with it (hers or mine) and that it was just a plain pleasure to roll around together in all that spit and desire.

We drove to her place, which was a really neat high-tech themed apartment downtown. "Ta-dahh!" she said, flipping on the lights as we entered for the first time. "Wow," I said, gazing at the glossy wood floors, the glass and steel furniture with red, white, and blue cushions, the steel ceiling with greenish glass panes. "It's a loft," I said. "I've always wanted to live in one."

She turned proudly with her arms out. "Well, second best is having a friend who lives in one." She swept into my arms, bounced off, and dashed into her kitchen. "Want a drink? How about some juice?"

"Nurses always give juice," I said. "Yes." She threw things in a blender—ice, bananas, strawberries, vanilla cream—turned the gadget on High for a minute, and served up smoothies.

"Wow, that's good," I said, sipping creamy sweetness, wondering if her oyster would taste like this, as we sat in the living room area looking out of a broad picture window at a spectacular view of the city from the fifth or sixth floor. "Sixty or eighty years ago, this was a factory," she said. "Think of all those people who worked their lives away here, making shoes. That's what they made here. Shoes. Work boots. Combat boots."

She had her philosophical side that way. She also had the first threads of gray in her glossy hair, and a few wrinkles in the usual places. She was also direct and honest and fun and could sometimes read minds. She stood on tiptoe on those thin legs, with that whippet-thin body, and reached up for a bottle of white brandy. "I'm going to put a little spirits in there so that you don't see my wrinkles." That's not the kind of statement that begs a clever reply, or any reply, so I smiled reassuringly.

The skyline grew more magnificent as night deepened. She had a good place here under the haze of building lights and neons. Traffic noise was minimal. Laughter from party goers in the bars and restaurants below was more noticeable than the occasional honk of a horn or rev of an engine. She had this narrow stainless steel ledge that functioned as a counter top directly before the picture window, and we sat side by side on bar stools nursing our fruited brandies and looking outside. A cityscape isn't complete unless you have at least one rundown hotel from yesteryear to stare at, with a few bulbs missing in its lighted sign. There was such a place a block up the street.

L was a talker and a good listener, and buddy of a woman. For a while, she actually sat with her arm through mine. Or she would reach out suddenly and hold your hand for a while. She would gaze into your eyes as if it helped her listen more intently. I talked a little bit about my book that I was writing (portions of which would find their way into a detective novel I would publish years later).

L was a follower of the not-on-the-first-date rule, and had already tested me for predatory tendencies, so I was well vetted. I ended up walking part of the way home, and taking a bus the rest of the way. The light of the city were bright, and my heart was soaring.

Over the next week or two, we sat at her perch by the window and enjoyed the marvelous view, and soft music, and eventually slipped into each other's arms for a dance on the concrete floor. She had low-end Persian carpets, very tasteful and good on the bare feet, just didn't last a century like the high-end thing. On our third or fourth date, we undressed each other and danced naked in the soft glow of nearby red and pink and green neon signs. There were few possible Peeping Tom opportunities in the black windows of shuttered Victorian buildings around us, whose working staffs had long ago gone home for the night. Had anyone seen us, they might have seen faint sticks and squares of colored light moving about. I don't think *L* was into being watched. I think she was just carefree. There was also a secret side of her that I would get to know in time.

As we danced nude, we kissed, and petted. I enjoyed the feel of her wiry, girlish body in my arms. She had the smoothest skin, and a figure like that famous doll whose name begins with a B. I was {k} to her {b}, if I may bend the naming conventions of this book a bit.

As we danced closely, my erection became an issue. She laughed and held it for me. Remember, she was a nurse who held people's limbs and organs and puking throats all day. I had to laugh too at her pert humor. I had both arms around her, and her head on my right shoulder, while her right hand held aloft my pecker instead of my left hand; by aloft, I mean she pressed it against my stomach pointed upward. Okay, it was funny, but it was sexy too, and I could hear her steady breathing accelerate, getting harder, under my right ear. Again she read my mind. "Can you hear me breathing hard for you?"

I murmured in response, and she moved her palm around the head. "My hand is getting wet."

I had been feeling her thigh against my knee. "I feel something damp on my knee."

"That's me getting dewy for you."

"Dewy want to retire to someplace a little less vertical?"

She had been holding my penis against my abdomen, and now pressed close to me and held it against her belly. "I'm ready for the next step," she whispered in my ear and bit my ear lobe.

There wasn't really a bedroom—just a different corner of the loft, in the same darkly pinkish glow. Her bed was a large mattress, on the floor, covered with sheets and blankets. We crawled onto this together and made out.

Our petting grew more intimate—after all, she had been holding my schwantz already, so what secrets did have left to withhold? My hands roved over the sparse but shapely and incredibly smooth topography of her small brown body. She had small breasts and small nipples like raisins. I tasted them, sucked on them, and palmed the softness of her tits. Because she was light, there were special things we were able to do; like, she sat on my face. Actually, her butt was on my chest, and her vagina at my mouth, while her legs were bent at the knee, spread over my shoulders, feet flat on the sheets. She had a brownie outtie, from what I could tell in the dim reddish light. I felt as though I were in a bordello, which gave the situation an added bit of spice. She parted her good-sized labia for me so that I could penetrate with my tongue. I explored the geography of her little garden with curiosity and pleasure. At the top, under hard Venus mound topped by fragrant hair smelling of oyster sweat and bath soap musk, she had a nice clitoris like a little dog in a bun, waiting to come out and play.

Tracing the dewy path across the garden, I came to her well. This was a wobbly little swelling with an opening in top, and it had a vaguely salty flavor but even more faintly ammonia smell. I licked it with my tongue, and my spit made it more pleasant. She intook her breath sharply, while I diddled the masses of nerve endings that pleasured her, as my tongue waggled the opening of her urethra. From there, I wandered down into the cave mouth of her tunnel.

She was small and tight, and my tongue filled it as if I were @ing her. She reacted as if she were being @ed, and held my cheeks while her knees came together over me. She sank down on to her knees so that her oyster and my tongue formed a near-vacuum. She reached down and fanned her clit slowly, then more rapidly. She had this other way of playing with her clit. Holding its long hard shaft between her thumb and middle finger, she used the tip of her index finger to lightly raise the hood a tiny bit and then used the same fingertip to exercise the very tip of her clit.

I felt my penis growing painfully engorged seeing all this going on within inches of my face. My tongue came out with a pop, and her tunnel made a damp sucking sound as air rushed in. "Do it again," she urged in a tight tone that told me her voice box was constricted with tension and arousal. I worked my tongue in, again and again, to its root, so it was rolled up in her vagina. I could feel the vaginal walls throbbing around it.

She began to tremble lightly, and shifted about—squirm would be a better word to describe her motions. She was dripping wet, and I was swallowing her oyster juice, almost choking on it. Meanwhile, behind her back, I grasped the thick of my dick and felt it dribble on the connective skin between my thumb and index finger. "Sit on my dick," I said.

"Are you ready, darling?" She started to move, lifting a leg.

I nodded. "I wanted to stretch it out as long as possible, but I'm just going to shoot, and I don't want to waste a good orgasm." Compliantly, she backed down and straddled my waist. Her little rear end came down, and she held her labial door open as my head thundered into her shaft. Not a moment too soon, because her tunnel was already vibrating, and my dick was in its contractions. I sat up, laid her on her back, and proceeded to @ her hard in the missionary position.

I didn't even take time to put her ankles on my shoulders, as I liked to do, or kiss her. I just rammed into her the way a snow truck plows into a snow bank on a blizzard night. She tried to wrap her legs around my waist, but didn't get a chance.

She cried out and moaned with passion as I thumped her rapidly, bam bam bam, and the room was filled with fleshy splatting noises as our bodies collided.

Pulling her knees back to her shoulders with her hands, she opened up as fully as she could, all defenses down, desire all eyeballs on the ramparts, as I charged across under her portcullis. Bam bam bam, the steel girders and hard window surfaces without curtains echoed above us, and she must have slid an inch back with each collision.

She threw her head back and screamed my name. "Peter!" Then she just screamed, a short bark that trailed off into a wail and then a long deep moan like that of a wounded or impassioned animal. Meanwhile, I shot. They were big gouts, like lungfuls hurled from deep. On the best of orgasms, under the most passionate circumstances, a man feels the sperm squirting up from below, feels each hurled packet fly through the thickness of his tube, and out into the woman's receiving end. This was such a moment. When I was done, I collapsed on top of her.

I was afraid to hurt her with my weight. "Am I hurting you?"

She shook her head. "No, baby, I like feeling your weight on me." She stroked my buttocks absently. We were both sweaty, and both still breathing hard. I rested my head between her little breasts, and she stroked my hair—the buttocks now out of reach.

After a little nap, lying side by side, we slowly began to explore, and to be aroused again. This time, I took her from behind. She offered herself, holding her butt cheeks apart, while I walked on my knees holding my dong out like a probe, and inserted it between those loving labia.

She was good from behind, as she had been in front, and again the room rocked with the sounds of bam bam bam, louder because she had nice tight round butt cheeks. When I came, I pulled her up on to me. I had my arms around her waist, and lifted her backward while ramming my rod upward into her. She spilled backward with her arms and legs going in all directions, but she never stopped urging me to do it harder, faster, harder. Then I was on my back, she was on top, facing away, and I rocked her up and down while we both came. As I said, her lightness made for some unique acrobatics.

Speaking of acrobatics, she also straddled my face sideways with her hands propping her up by my left ear, and her feet beyond my right ear on the other side. She did this facing first one way, then the other, while her vagina hovered over my mouth. She loved having that pussy eaten, and I spent many hors with my mouth in it, and glad of it.

She could even straddle my head with her legs folded tightly against my ears, while she rested on her elbows above my head, and her vagina was open on my chin, mouth, and nose. That was a good position, because I loved cupping her buttocks while I drank from her chalice. She was one of those women who can tolerate pressure on their clits, so I tongued her hard. Ironically, she was very sensitive around her pee hole, so I had to go easier there.

An exciting moment was the first time I realized I should @ her while she wore her nurse uniform. I don't mean her baggy scrubs, but the crisp, traditional white one I'd first seen her in, skinny legs and all, with that starchy thing atop her head. We set aside an old pair of white hose that we cut a hole out of in the bottom, and sometimes we @ed with her wearing that under her uniform. Sometimes I had her @ with nothing on under her uniform. A few times, I had her wait for me at the front door, rather than near the bed, and I @ed her from the back and front in her uniform, standing, though she basically had to wrap her legs around my waist and have me lean her against a wall while we banged away.

She and I had a lot of fun going to movies and plays and having dinner in restaurants or just walking hand in hand downtown. This is where the other wrinkle in all this develops. Or, make that wrinkles, multiple.

One evening, we were walking hand in hand downtown, amid a heavy flow of pedestrians going and coming amid the bars, theaters, and restaurants of those several blocks. Who should be coming the opposite way, but my concurrent flame *K,* the gorgeous blonde who liked to rub herself, especially while watching that certain sitcom with beautiful young people of both genders.

She was with a man, a date I am sure, a @ buddy I'm not sure, and I know she saw us, but she looked the other way and passed. I generally was a one-woman guy. I couldn't handle with more than one woman the amount of passion I always invested. Also, oddly, though temporality was underwritten into all these dead-end love affairs, I wanted to remain true to the woman who was loving me. Later, when married, I never cheated. Like the vast majority of guys, the added work of having affairs has always been more than I can handle, both the work required for an average guy to chase a desirable woman, and the guilt. Oh God, the guilt. Not for me. But I never chose the timing of when these relationships started. Sometimes they overlapped. This was one such instance.

And, yes, I was jealous. Irrational to say, but I wished I had not seen *K* with another man. *K* grasped her male friend's hand, and passed with a look that is hard to forget. I saw shock in her eyes, jealousy in the half-parted mouth as she suppressed a gasp. Knowing her volatile temperament, I expected a bath of invective and a boot out of her life. I was in for a surprise.

L noticed the transaction. She felt my sudden stiffening, the tightening of my hand around hers, the exchange of looks or avoidance of looks. The other man even seemed startled. He looked like a very pleasant fellow a few years older than *K.* "Friend of yours?" my Belizean friend *L* asked.

"Someone I know."

"From how pale you suddenly look, I imagine someone you know intimately."

"It's a long story." I was suddenly worried that both women would dump me. I was very much in lust with both, and didn't relish the idea of losing either.

L didn't make more of it. She did stare over her shoulder once or twice. We went to our movie, and then sat in a bar afterward over margaritas. "Peter," *L* old me, "you've been looking worried. I want to assure you that I'm not upset that you bumped into an old flame or whatever."

I squirmed at the thought she might press me for information. Then I might have to reveal I was seeing them both. A violation, on the one hand. My perfect right, on the other hand, since I was not sworn to a commitment. In my confused and imperfect way, I think I had a streak of loyalty and fairness. I didn't want to hurt anyone.

"Maybe I should let you in on a secret," *L* said. "I don't have to, but maybe I will." She ordered us a second round of margaritas. She waited until the drinks came, and then had us move out of earshot to a private spot in a far corner. "Honey," she told me with one hand over mine, "I'm bisexual." She waited. "Are you shocked?" "Yes." I felt about an inch tall, then realized it was silly to feel that way, and popped back to my normal size.

I was still reeling—whether at her candor, or the breathtaking meaning of it, I'm not sure—when she said the next thing. "I've been having a relationship with another woman while I have been dating you." She waited for that to sink in, and sink it did. "You look a bit green," she said. "Sure you are okay? If it's something you ate, that's one thing. If it's about you're jealous or whatever, I'm like who cares, because this is who I am and it's my right to be who I am. As long as I am honest with you, as I am now, I think it's fine." She actually sounded a bit heated. "I hardly ever tell any partner that I am bi. It's none of their business, and most people can't grasp what it means. I am bi, and that stirs up animosity, whether from straights or gays, and I don't need the bullshit from either side. Okay, Peter, now you know."

"Why this moment to tell me?" I whispered when my breath came back.

"Because I got bowled over by your girlfriend. She is knock-out, drop-dead gorgeous. Not only that, but she is bi."

"I've suspected that she is bi."

"How would you know?" It was the first time *L* had sounded almost contemptuous to me. She was usually so even tempered. She caught herself immediately, but I wouldn't let her apologize. "No, it's okay," I said, "look, *L,* I love you or whatever the correct expression is to describe that I have these feelings for you, as someone I am intimate with, and I want to protect you from harm or hurt."

She put her hands over mine. "Sorry, Peter." She made a kissy mouth at me and winked both eyes shut reassuringly. "I will protect your tender little feelings too. On the one hand, baby, I have to tell you that my partner Marsha is lesbian and won't bed a man, so tough titty if you think we're going to end up in the sack all three of us. It ain't happening, poor sweet sugar cane. However, dear darling boy, that girl of yours is a walking closet case. Is she a little air headed?'"

"I don't think so. We have a very active fantasy relationship."

"I'm not good at those," *L* said wistfully. "I'm straightforward. Funny, Marsha is an actress and always tripping out in her fantasies, and I am the ground for her electricity. You and she would get along great if one of you had a sex change or something." We both laughed. She held my hands. "Baby, sweetheart, doll, I want to hold on to you. I hope you appreciate my secret."

I was baffled. "So, *L,* do bisexual people have two relationships going? I mean if you're bi, do you have to juggle two separate lives?" She grinned. "You devil, you. You're thinking, here I am struggling with two women, or however many of us you have on the hook at any moment—"

"—Usually one. I'm very monogamous," I said. "This is a unique—"

"—Okay, yeah. Unique case. No, Bobo, let me 'splain something that neither gays nor straights nor many bis understand. Remember that, though I'm a nurse, I actually majored in biology. I figured the sexuality thing out because I have the kind of personality that can step back and be neutral and figure things out. Also, I was very confused about myself and had to seek answers. Newsflash: Most people are bisexual. A small percentage are totally gay, and a small percentage are totally straight. At least 80% of the population are bisexual. One problem is that we're hung up on labels.

"First, society, driven by religious prejudices, wants to insist that everyone be heterosexual and @ only in the missionary position on certain nights when the moon is full or whatever. No fun, just mechanics, because women are evil and men are weak and we all have to be completely miserable at all times. That's just so much bullshit. That's asshole theology, but that's the groove where most people are stuck.

"Second, the majority of people are bisexual, but each person is a unique case. Statistically, I suspect while most people are bisexual, the skew is toward hetero, since that is biologically and evolutionarily what keeps the race going. Still, most people have some mix of hetero and same sex genes. If you're 90/10 or 80/20 or even 70/30, chances are you'll live most of your life in denial and will never stray across that gender boundary. But if you're 60/40 or 50/50, you're in my realm. Since society is so full of lies and bullshit and stupidity, you have to figure it out for yourself as I did."

I told *L* about *J's* television watching and diddling. *L* said: "Your gorgeous friend may eventually admit she is attracted to women as well as men, or not. I'd like to get her in the sack myself. I wonder if she would let me, and if you could be there and share in the passion."

I was too stunned to say anything. I was still naïve in some ways, and part of my universe was crumbling around my ears. I was, however, a logical sort, and would usually come around to the common sense of reality, as opposed to the wishful thinking of zealots who refuse to accept reality.

L said: "I don't know if you'll understand that, but for God's sake, please listen. When rightwing zealots claim to have changed gays to straights, they are I their own ignorance dealing with confused bisexuals. That is the tragedy of my kind. I know who I am and what I need. Most people aren't critical thinkers and cannot reason this kind of thing out for themselves, so they become victims of these cult leaders. Because we are such a pathologically rightwing society, those cult leaders are able to twist a lot of people to their agendas. That's all beyond the scope of you and me. What I want you to understand, Peter, is that every bi is different. Some have long-term relationships, and stay with a man or woman for life, or for years before flipping into another relationship. It's not the gender, but the loyalty, the fact of remaining true to one person. In the whole spectrum of things, yes there are opportunistic bis who play both sides of the fence. Most people are like you or me, Peter, and try to be kind and fair. I just want you to understand that being bisexual doesn't mean you necessarily have both a male and female partner, although when it happens it happens. At the moment, it seems to be happening for me. In my case, I am not in love with anyone right now. I am very fond of you, but you aren't in love with me, and I'm not in love with you. To be in love is to have a committed relationship, and neither of us has that. You certainly aren't ready for that, but you will be one day. I was seeing a woman who deeply turns me on, and I shared with her something I could never share with you. We've cooled off quite a bit, and I don't know where or if it's going. She doesn't know about you—that's how I prefer to play the game. I call it a 'need to know' basis. I have to always go back to who I am and what my needs are, and at the same time what's fair for my male and/or female lover." She shrugged. "That's the whole story."

"Is your female lover beautiful?" I asked.

She laughed. "You're not going to bed with her. She is a committed Lesbian."

"I didn't mean that. I many never get to talk like this with another bisexual, and I'm just curious, especially because I'm trying to figure out what is what with *K*."

"She'll never get past looking. She's a 20 maybe—just barely aware she is interested in women, but not enough to act it out. She'll go through life wondering why she gets a little hot when just the right gorgeous woman walks past her in the street, or flirts with her. She'll do that thing you said, rubbing herself, and some of the pictures in her head will be of a woman on the street who looked at her a certain way, or a woman on a passing bus who noticed *K* and turned her head to stare after her, or a totally straight woman who finds *K* looking at her kind of hard and blushes and looks away. *K* will have all those things, but never go past them." After some telephone games (she made it clear she was hurt or miffed or something about having seen me with *L,* though she herself was with another man), *K* invited me over a few evenings later. I had called her to initiate it, and she made it a little rough, but then she caved and told me to come over right away. She was waiting for me, kissing me as soon as I came in the doorway. She was exceptionally passionate and had both arms over my shoulders while Frenching me, then got her hand down my pants and led me to the bedroom, where she made love hot and heavy. As we lay together, she said: "I was afraid you had moved on."

"I am not moving on. I just happened to meet this woman. I'm still hot on our fantasy games."

"Does she play games with you like I do?"

"No, L honey, she is very straightforward. She's a nurse and gets right to the point."

"To your point."

"Yes that point. The point." I slipped my index finger in between her labia, and she squirmed her hips so that her oysterie seemed to suck on my finger. My finger and her oysterie were making a little light love there on their own, while **K** and I made pillow talk.

"Does she do everything to you that I do?"

"No, you are a better lover."

"How do I know you aren't lying?"

"You can't know. If I am telling the truth, you should feel good that you are the better lover. If I am not telling the truth, and please don't use the word 'lying' at me, then you should feel good that I care enough to spare your feelings."

"I'm sorry. 'Lying' was a bit harsh."

"You know it. And besides."

"What?"

"She couldn't steal me away from you."

"Why is that?" She cupped her hand over my hand, so that my finger was safe or trapped or something in her vagina where it belonged. Her finger. Her vagina. Her man. She leaned close to brush my lips, and I could feel the heat of her breath on my skin.

"She is bi."

"Oh really." After a momentary brightening of interest, she changed the subject, and we ended up petting for ten minutes or so. There was another storm of passion on the way, but we were resting up, saving ourselves for it. After a while, her hand, which had been cupped over mine, moved so that her fingers pushed another of my fingers into her slot. Now I had my index finger and middle finger both in the moist groove from her clit to her hole. My middle finger sensed the wet suction of her hole, and naturally wiggled in. She closed her sphincter and with her hand backed me out. "How do you know she is bi?" She was breathing a little harder, and I could tell she was fascinated.

"We talked about it."

"Is that all? Did you see her?"

"No. She has a lover but it's growing cool and she might be looking for someone else."

"Did she say that?"

"No, I'm just guessing."

"So you didn't see anything really hot and racy?"

"No, like I said, she is very straightforward. Not complicated like you, bunny. She doesn't watch television sitcoms and rub her labia with her finger and have all these little micro-orgasms whether it's over a boy or a girl actor."

"You only think you know what I am turned on by. I'm turned on by you."

"You are being extra hot and passionate tonight. I am happy that you are turned on by me."

She snuggled against me in such a way that not only did she want me to hug her, cover her, shelter her, baby her, protect her, but the movement made her hip ride up so that my finger slid back into her hole. She reached down and pushed all four fingers of my hand in, bundled so that index was next to baby, and on top of them middle next to third. She rocked her hip, which made her tunnel slide back and forth. Her head was against my chest, hidden, her face shadowed. I could smell her hair.

"Want to play?" I asked.

She nodded, a quick embarrassed shake of the head. She kept her face buried. She was waiting for me to take the fantasy where she knew I knew she wanted it to go. *L* would have called her (fondly) a chicken-shit.

"I am holding you," I murmured, and she preened at the knowledge a game was starting and I was going to be kind and hot with her. I kept murmuring on and on: "I am holding you, and you are getting turned on." She licked my nipple. "I am holding you, and you are having me put my fingers in your oyster." She tightened around my fingers, pulling the tips in deeper, while she gave my other nipple a lick. "You know that soon I will slide my thick dick into your wet hole, and you will squeeze your whole body around it because it just fills you up and turns you on." She gave my other nipple a lick. "I love holding you and feeling your figure in my arms. Then, while we are making love, you think about the boy and girl actors in that sitcom." Her oyster tightened excitedly. "You think about the dark-haired guy and the brown-haired guy. Then you think about the beautiful girl who has that hairdo and jiggles when she walks." Her oyster, still tight, wetly turned a few degrees each way, corkscrewing on my fingers.

She came out from inside my embrace and pushed herself up so her head was higher than mine, and she nibbled my earlobe. "She has a gorgeous little ass."

"Which one, the blonde or the redhead."

"The one you were with the other night."

I was a bit surprised, but shined it on. "We just passed each other in a flash."

"I looked back. I made my friend cross the street with me. I told him it was to look at a shop window, but it was really so I could stare after you too. I was mad at you, but I really liked her little ass."

"She does have a little ass."

"I'll bet you had your hands on it."

"Now, now, **K,** let's make a deal and stay off the jealousy stuff."

"I was very jealous of you. Now I'm not jealous. Well, maybe a little. I'm interested in the juicy details. Come here." She pulled my hand out of her oyster and had me rub the wetness on my member, getting it engorged. Then she rolled on top of me so that my head popped through her gate and slid up her tunnel. "See? I love you, Peter, fantasy bunny, and I want you to tell me all about it because I have never made love to a woman."

"Well," I said carefully, trying to keep it a game that would turn her on without hurting her feeling or making her angry or jealous. "She likes to get right to it."

"Did she @ you on the first date?"

"No, she held me at arms' length and checked me out long and hard."

"Long and hard, I'll bet. Well, then she has good sense. Good for her." She rode my dick slowly in a very preliminary way, getting herself ready to get ready to get heated up.

"Your nipples are big and hard," I said. "I am glad you approve of this woman and her good sense."

"She has good taste in men," *K* said as she continued rocking on my dick while she straddled my waist.

I fondled her soft, blunt knees and stroked the good curves of her thighs. "I think I have wonderful taste in women," I said.

"You do, you do."

"You approve of her?" "I think so. From afar."

I reached up with my lips and kissed her pinkie titties. She leaned forward to let me, and even held each one in turn for me so it would be easy to reach its pink nipple. "I'll bet you ended up kissing her titties," *K* said while she held hers and I sucked on it.

I pushed out on her knees to spread them a little, so that she rested harder and more helplessly on my groin. I reached around her and pressed with both palms flat on her tail so that her vagina pressed against my groin. "She has brown nipples, and a brownie outtie oyster."

K laid her face on my chest and fondled my arms absently. I could feel the tightening of her oyster with interest as I spoke of *L's* genitals. She wanted to hear more, but couldn't bring herself to urge me verbally. She didn't want me to see her face, but I know she licked her lips because her mouth got a little dry. Her palms tightened around the delicate skin of my ribs, which I liked, so I pressed my arms against her hands for a few minutes to hold them there—and to hold her, trap her, make her feel wanted. I forced her tailbone area down lightly.

"Her name is *L*," I said, "and she has a tight, wiry, very powerful little body."

"Does she know my name?"

"No," I lied. "I didn't tell her anything."

"Would she be jealous?"

"I didn't want to find out."

"I don't blame you." She still had her cheek pressed against my chest. She was thinking, and drawing circles in my skin with her fingertip. "If she doesn't know about me...well, tell me more about her. Did you enjoy it? Was she good?"

I put my arms around her back, stroking the back of her neck and her head lovingly. "She is small, and wiry. She has a nice tight pussy, and it gets very, very wet." *K* stopped drawing circles and pondering, and listened. Her own pussy tightened with interest and concern. I said: "She can lie on top of me just as you are doing right now, but there is less of her, and I prefer having more. Specifically, I prefer having more of you." As I spoke, *K* sat up and started rocking again. We were going for it. I rubbed her knees and said: "Do you know, honestly, I could get turned on just by kissing your soft round knees, especially when you have a tan?"

K lowered herself back onto my chest, but resting on crossed arms, and chin to chin. "Honey, Peter, would you pretend that I am her?"

"You want me to imagine her?" "No, I want you to make me do whatever she does." She sat up straight and waved her arms in the air dramatically. "How she does it. I want to be her."

"We can try. Will you be turned on?"

She nodded eagerly, as if I were finally catching on.

"I will have you be her, then. I have to pretend that you are she, however. Will that be okay with you?"

"As long as you don't forget who I am." Her oyster tightened on my cock and sucked on it with its interior muscles. She wanted this pretty badly.

I hugged her to me and, with her pinned in my embrace, beaming at me, I said: "I think you have been waiting for a long, long time to be this girl, and to have me pretend you are she." She nodded. "I think I know something else you would like me to show you." She knew what it was, and nodded. It was one of these flashes of genius, or telepathy that happens to two people as tuned in with their fantasies as she and I were. I said: "I am going to let you pretend that you are you, and I am going to pretend to be her, and you are going to let me do to you what she would do if she were here."

"Yes," *K* admitted, "that's what I would really, really like most of all."

I made love to her, keeping *L* in my thoughts. I tried to remember the things my little Mayan Indian had said and done to me. The way it worked, sometimes I did what *L* would have done to her, like sticking her tongue deep in *K's* blonde oyster and doing the glass woodpecker thing (head up and down, drinking from a glass while rocking on a fulcrum) to tongue-@ her. At other times, I had her pretend to be *L,* like when I had her sit on my chest and bring her pussy really close and hold her labia apart so I could get my tongue in there. We played Peter and the Maya for hours, and *K* never tired of it.

I had never had a threesome, and had no idea if either woman would be game, but this was intriguing. *K* thought that *L* did not know about her, so that *K* felt a certain stealthy sense of empowerment. I asked *K*: "Would you like to meet her?"

K lit up—sure she would, I could tell—but hid her face in my chest again.

"I mean, not meet her, if you are too shy."

"I'm embarrassed. Scared."

"Okay, not meet her, but sit near us if I were to have a date with her?"

"I might be jealous." "Not if I told her I could only see her for an hour, and that I have a date and have to go."

"Yes. That would work. Oh my God, Peter, that would be such a turn-on."

My next conversation was with *L.* We were sitting naked in bed in her loft, just before making love. I had worked at the bookstore, and she had come home exhausted from the E.R. We were resting, and drinking a pair of espresso coffees I had made. The neons outside winked on and off. We looked like reddish people. "Hey, we're both Indians tonight," she quipped. "Great espresso. Thanks, Peter. Good job."

"Remember I mentioned my friend K?"

"The closet dyke?"

"Bi."

"Sorry, yes. What about her?"

"She is interested in you."

L almost spit out her coffee.

"Sorry," I said. "I'm just the messenger." I was being a bit of a conniver, was more like it.

L laughed and set her cup aside. "Honey, did you talk with her about me?"

"A little."

L squealed. "You are a piece of work, man. Tell me every word."

"Well, she was jealous for a moment, then afraid I was leaving her, and in the end she told me she wasn't jealous of you (at first she was) but of me for having you."

L was incredulous. She waved her hand at her self. "She told you she likes me?"

"She said that she crossed the street to get a better look. She said you have an incredible tight little ass. Those were her words."

L held her hand to her head.

"What's the matter?"

L shook her head and sipped coffee. "I'm blown away. I just saw her for a moment. She is gorgeous."

"You like her?"

"The way you like a James Bond girl."

"You don't think she would go that far. That's what you said."

"My experience tells me she is all eyes and no action."

"Which gets her turned on, anyway."

"And me."

"You?" She held her hands out questioningly. "Duh, Peter. Doesn't it turn you on that your blonde girlfriend thinks your Maya jungle girl is hot eye candy?"

"It gives me a hard-on," I admitted.

"What are you driving at, Peter. What are you maneuvering us toward? You want a threesome?"

I hung my head, speechless. Did I? I had no idea.

"You are red as a whorehouse lamp."

"I don't know what I want. I—"

"You are a young guy drowning in your own hormones."

"And you're not full of hormones, Miss Belize?"

She smiled and put her hands on mine. "Listen, Peter. I don't mean a good, clean, honest game where nobody gets hurt. She might be interested in a Platonic date where you and I and she go out to dinner and a movie. A few drinks maybe. I pay a little attention and flirt with her, and she gets her rocks off that way, and then you take her home and @ her."

"That's your imagination at work, not mine."

She shrugged. "You brought the situation to me."

"I know. But wouldn't you feel used?"

"Yes."

"What if I preferred to take you home and @ you, and put her in a taxi?"

"She would be hurt to the end of the world. That will never happen."

"And you?"

"I can handle it, my good buddy." She wrapped her paw around my cock and squeezed reassuringly. "I know you'd come back to me."

"And feel used?"

"Don't you get it, Peter? Maybe I would enjoy being used. I am intrigued by a beautiful blonde who rubs herself while watching television. You know, honey..." Her voice lowered into a purr, and she slid closer while holding my dong. "...I might just come right then and there if I saw she was rubbing herself while looking at me. That would be a supreme turn-on from such an uptight little 20." She meant her supposition that *K* was too marginally bisexual (20/80 ratio bi/hetero) to cross over at all. I'm talking myself into doing this. Can you arrange it?"

"I'll see. I think so. She thinks you don't know about her. That gives her an edge into thinking she can be near you and you have no idea she is checking you out."

"I don't go for games, ordinarily, but this one is a scream." "So," I continued, "I could see if she'd be interested in something like this. You'll work with me?"

She said matter-of-factly "uh-huh," nodded, and crawled to my dick to give it a blowjob. She was so turned on that she initiated everything that evening, was on top the whole time, and we climaxed together in a chorus of passionate voices.

K liked the suggestion, but wanted to take baby steps. I got it worked out with *L,* and we met at a bar. *K* still had no idea that *L* knew about her, so I told *K* this: "I am going to meet her for a drink, with the understanding that I have somewhere I must go afterward."

"What if she wants to go with you? What if she is jealous?"

"I'll pick an evening when I know she has somewhere else to go."

"Her lesbian lover?"

"Don't be tatty, *K.*"

"What's tatty. Is that like catty?"

"It's small. It's when you are like a spoiled brat who needs a spanking."

"I'm sorry." She looked contrite (or played at looking so), unbuttoned my shirt, and give each of my nipples a lick. "I'll try to behave myself."

I held her to me and poured on a little sharper humor than I would have ordinarily dared: "Hey, listen, kiddo, this is going to be your big bisexual adventure, so don't get cocky. You are a scared little Bambi in the woods."

"Yes I am a scared Bambi. But I am not having a bisexual adventure. I'm having a sexual adventure with you."

"What we call things, and what they really are, is sometimes the same thing, and sometimes, when we want to pretend, it's not. But a thing with another woman is a bisexual adventure."

"Just checking her out."

"Right."

"I can't win," she said with a sigh. "What were you saying about spanking? Want to put me over your knees?"

I purred in her ear in my fantasy voice, and she caught on right away. "Has Bambi been bad?"

"Yes, Bambi has been very bad."

It went from there...a delicious fantasy, to be told another day.

K's big bisexual adventure happened in a fairly crowded corner dating bar. It was the kind of place that young urban professionals went to after work to have a beer or latte, check each other out, and maybe pair off. It had undertones of neighborhood hangout, depending on the evening, and was very tolerant. A few GLBTMs came and went (M being 'Miscellaneous') and you just noticed them for a minute before they blended into the crowd and the shadows. With all the intrigues that go on in a place like that, a twenty dollar bill took care of having a waiter keep two tables open by leaving one in need of bussing and the other with a Reserved sign on it.

When I arrived with *L, K* already sat at the table behind us nursing a latte in a big white ceramic mug.

K looked very nervous. Her eyes looked hunted, and she shivered while rubbing her hands together over her hot, steaming coffee. She had a silk scarf over her blond hair, which hung in a bob in front, and she wore a dark green loden coat with a heavy wool scarf.

I entered with *L* on my arm, gave the waiter another twenty, and guided *L* to the table. After some discussion, I had *L* and I sit laterally. There was actually one of those tall, pre-aged tannish vases on the wood floor with an arrangement of pussy willows and fake ficus to give *K* some shelter while she spied on us.

L and I ordered margaritas and sat with our faces close together. We played with one another's hands. At one point we told a joke and steepled our fingertips together. I never did

glance toward **K,** though I saw her shadow on the wall behind
the vase, and sensed that she was intently watching us. I
wondered if she felt jealous, intimidated, hurt—I had no idea,
and I hoped it wasn't something that would drive us apart
prematurely. I enjoyed having those fantasies together with
her. **L** meanwhile was direct and pert and fun. She too was
trying to play it straight, so to speak, and never made eye
contact with **K.**

"Do you think she knows I know?" **L** said softly. We
spoke in low voices under the general hubbub of clinking
dishes, rumbling foot-treads, and laughter.

"No, I don't think so."

"She is knock-out gorgeous."

"I know."

"I'd go to bed with her if she would."

"I'll work on it." I couldn't imagine what bliss there
might be. Or would there? Would **L** be able to tune into our
fantasies, or would a third person's presence actually dull
things down? I had never thought about such things before.

The hour passed quickly, and I rose with **L** to leave. I
notice with misgivings that the table behind the vase was
empty, and the busboy was already cleaning away the solitary
cup while a man and woman and the hostess and the waiter all
crowded around for the precious seats. **L** left a tip, and we
walked outside into the fresh cold air. "She was gone," **L** said
hugging and kissing me, standing on tiptoe on her skinny legs.

"I know. I hope she wasn't turned off."

"Maybe she went home to watch those sitcoms," **L** said
with a slightly harsh laugh, but not a mean one. It was more
ironic and helpless.

"I'll find out."

"I would take you with me and do dark things to you,"
she said ruefully as she pressed her forehead against my chest
(shades of K).

"I thought you said you'd be okay with this."

"Listen, I checked her out. She and I each went to the
bathroom at least five times. We almost bumped into each

other twice. I'm going to go home and get a cucumber, warm it between my thighs, and think about your lady friend." She kissed me and ran off before I could say another word.

K had arranged to pick me up in her car a few blocks away. As I got in, I was prepared for anything—being slapped, yelled at, whatever. Instead, *L* hugged me and kissed me passionately. She seemed aglow with pleasure. "What a gorgeous, exotic creature!"

"I was afraid you'd be upset."

"Oh no—I wouldn't have done this if I thought I would be upset."

"You weren't lonely sitting there by yourself?"

She put the car in gear and pulled out into traffic. "No, honey, I was fascinated. A few times I asked myself what I was doing there, you know, have I lost my mind, can this really be happening, but it went pretty quickly."

"Are you satisfied?"

She pursed her lips and nodded. "Yes I am."

We went to her place and turned out the lights and made passionate love. She had me pretend she was *L* when I licked her down below, or had me pretend that I was *L* when she licked my nipples and fondled my rear. We said no more about her great bisexual adventure, but she seemed exceptionally turned on. Maybe, I thought, that was what she had needed. She still rubbed herself in later weeks while watching television, and otherwise nothing seemed any different.

As I must sadly admit again, all these relationships ended after weeks or months. Hardly a one lasted over six months, none as long as a year. There were so many of them, and so many wonderful women among the average and dull and bad dates, that time seemed like a blender, sweeping me along with it.

Some time after I had moved on, when I was done with both *K* and *L,* I happened to be with a date, and happened to drive down the street where I had had all those wonderful, passionate fantasies with *K.* It was one of those drizzly early evenings, and my windshield wipers were going swish, swish, swish like in the children's song. My date was a girl my own age, who liked me and was interested in going to my place to hear more about my book and perhaps to check out some Mozart with wine and low lighting. I saw the familiar house, and glanced over—to see both *K* and *L* come out of the house, holding hands like a pair of star-struck lovers. Their faces were unmistakable, their glow that passed between them as readable as a book. I slowed briefly, which puzzled my date. *K* and *L* had not known me after I bought the car I was driving that evening, and a light rain obscured the windows, so I know they did not recognize me. I stared after them from behind the wipers, and I'm sure my face glowed with astonishment. Then I recalled *L's* comment that the two had gone to the ladies' room innumerable times and almost bumped into each other. Now I knew they had in fact probably exchanged phone numbers. I had remained with each for some time, never knowing about the "other woman" thing forming behind my back.

My date asked innocently: "Is something the matter?"

"No, just a little thing of the moment. Passing."

"Peter," she said primly, "it's not unusual nowadays to see two men or two women together."

"No," I said, "it's not. I heartily approve, but it's still a little surprising."

I wondered what tales *K* and *L* probably swapped about me as they sat laughing happily with wine glass in hand. So neither of them relished the idea of a threesome, and *K* had managed to overcome her hang-ups and become at least a 50/50 like *L.* Was there ever any end to surprises? I wondered if they had fantasy voices and could turn each other on in an instant. I tried to imagine my little Mayan nuzzling my blonde, blue-eyed Frisian's neck and saying "Has bunny been a bad girl?" and my Frisian writhing in the other's seductive charms saying "Oh yes, bunny has been very bad, and needs a firm lecture about how to be a better girl." I remembered what lovely soft round kneecaps *K* had and I hoped *L* would discover them for herself. When we were still a menage-a-trois without my knowing it, did *K* ever have *L* pretend she was I and have *L* enter her, *L,* (like with a strapped-on dildo) while they played a fantasy game? Did *K* ever pretend she was Peter as she seduced *L*? Were they ever both Peter? Did they ever swap identities just to see if it could be done?

"Merging traffic," my date warned as a traffic sign loomed in the rain, and I seemed to be driving like a man in a dream. Oh yes, the real world.

The Story of M

M was a college professor. We met one day when I was shopping. I saw this big woman in her mid-30s, wearing a wheat-and-silk ensemble, very bureau, striding slowly behind a shopping cart in the fruit and vegetable section of this big downtown supermarket. It was early afternoon, and I had come in for a bottled shake they carried. Her eyes met mine briefly. She wore large dark-rimmed glasses, and had straight, glossy mahogany hair in a long pageboy that came to her shoulders. I looked away. I found her at first glance imposing.

She walked off to the melons and bananas section, and I glanced after her. An athlete, aging, now successfully in the professions, so I thought. Something about her was, well, authoritative. I caught her glancing my way again and fixing her earring. I could swear her earrings were electronic and beamed signals at me. I caught a glimpse of reddish gold— she liked to dress well. I liked the crisp way the cuffs of her light-custard blouse extended past the sleeves of her wheat-colored jacket, revealing soft, big hands with gold rings.

I nodded, smiled, and picked out a red delicious apple to add to my lunch. The walk to the cooler took me directly through her line of sight, and she smiled at me and the apple. That was the moment when my sensor went off, and I said "Hi." She said "Hi," and stood behind the melons with her hands on a big one.

"Those look good," I said.

She looked down at herself and laughed. Neither of us dared repeat the *faux pas*: Your melons look good. Or, you have some nice looking melons there. When people flirt, it doesn't matter what they say. What matters is how they say it—their tone, their body language. I made some dumb remark about an apple keeping the doctor away. Maybe subliminally I had already known I would be talking with her and needing a prop. I'll skip the conversation, summarizing thus:

She taught History classes on certain mornings and evenings at the U, and was on her way home to prepare lunch for her teenage children, a boy and girl of high school age. I told her I was on my lunch break (true; I was employed selling watches at a jewelry store in the mall); that I was a graduate student (partly true, since I planned eventually to complete my Master's); and that I liked History (true; I read voluminously). She lowered those heavy glasses down her nose a trifle and asked me with a trace of supercilious amusement (as a test) "Have you had a chance to consider the similarity of our current national leader with Louis Napoleon?"

"You must mean during the Second Empire, as Napoleon III."

"Very astute. I meant from his contested election as President of the Republic in 1848 on the strength of conservative rural voters, versus the more progressive urban voters who hated him."

"Right, and then he declared the Republic finis in 1852, and made himself Emperor of the Second Empire. He made a total mess of things, in the end declaring war on the Germans, getting defeated in a matter of weeks, and actually being captured while sitting in his tent."

"Bravo. You should major in History."

"Thank you. Actually he was dying of cancer, and maybe he was committing suicide by Kaiser."

"An interesting hypothesis." Her cell phone warbled. "Excuse me." She spoke with someone, grew agitated, looked right and left and threw her arm up as she folded the phone away. "My son. He called to inform me that he is going to a friend's house, and my daughter is at cheerleading practice. Then why am I here trying to put a meal together."

"Because you are a mother."

"Thank you. Someone acknowledges my secret life."

"If you'd like, we could have coffee and a little lunch."

She looked at me thoughtfully. "I—"

"Sorry, I don't mean to seem pushy. I thought we could talk some more about Napoleon over a pair of Napoleons."

"Oh, the pastry," she said. "You have a good sense of humor." She looked down at her cart, which had a few things in it. "I guess I won't need to finish shopping then." She bit her tongue. "I can't just leave the cart, and I'm too lazy to put these things back. Oh hell, why don't you come home and I'll fix you lunch? Lunch for two, would that suit you?"

"If I'm not intruding."

"Not at all. I'm a single mother, and you look like you need a good meal."

There it was again—the gauntness thing, which apparently made me look sickly and needy, while also making me look very attractive. I ducked into a corner and cellphoned the store, saying I was having a personal emergency and wouldn't be back until tomorrow. The owner informed me it was my third absence in two weeks, and I should either come in or not bother ever returning. I said okay, which he took to mean I was coming back to his blasted store, and asked to be transferred to the bookkeeper. I asked the lady what address she had on file, and she read it to me. I said: "That's correct. You can send my check there." That's what it meant to be 23, in my shoes, caroming among the bumpers of life without a care in the world. I had a hot meal, a nice looking lady professor, and a ride home. What more could a guy ask for?

M was actually a very good looking woman. She needed the glasses to teach, and to select melons, but not to drive. When she took the glasses off, I saw a handsome, lightly tanned woman who (I found out) had played tennis, volleyball, and soccer during her undergraduate years. She was entirely of German extraction from the Midwest. "I moved here to escape Small Town Syndrome."

"What's that?"

"STS? You'd have to experience it. Remember what you said about the rural folks voting for Napoleon? They would vote for a horse thief if he promised them fundamentalism, the death penalty, and no more weird looking people of other skin tones allowed in town."

"I'm glad we think alike," I said. "You don't have to tell me any more about STS."

"Sorry, I don't want to spoil your lunch." She had blue eyes, a strong jaw and chin, a Romanesque nose, and an articulate mouth with wide, sort of thin lips that, if I didn't already know her better, one would expect to frown easily. Not that she didn't frown in her political outspokenness, but she knew how to turn it off. It came in waves—the sense that she was an imposing woman, this Doctor or Professor *M.* I was comfortable with her, sensing that she was a soft touch inside. She said: "In case you are wondering, I am divorced. There is no Mr. *M.*"

"I'm sorry to hear it." I was not sorry. I was glad. It made everything so much simpler. I looked at her and noticed that those intelligent blue eyes, under that high forehead, were making rapid calculations. I let her work it all out. We drove down a street of very imposing houses. Apparently professors lived quite well. "My ex is a surgeon," she said. "Am I reading your mind?"

"Quite." I grinned.

She took me into this air conditioned suburban villa in which everything gleamed and was new, except certain things that had been purchased as antiques like the carved Chinese ivory on the marble mantelpiece, or the cracked wooden window shades from Old Mexico that now served as wall ornaments. She fixed a light lunch—tuna salad on toast, accompanied by a tossed salad and iced tea. We talked, and got along quite well. As we got more cozy, at one point we impulsively started holding hands. "I hope you don't feel somehow—?"

"Oh no," I said. "I feel as if I have known you for years." I brought her hand to my mouth and kissed it. She smiled. "That's very gentlemanly." She cleaned up. "The silence sometimes bothers me. I feel empty nest syndrome coming on."

"Oh no, first STS, and now ENS."

"I'm just a psychological crater."

"You must have started young."

"Yes. My older one is 16, and I had him when I was 19. My ex and I ran away and got married during college. It was a dumb thing to do, but we stayed in love for quite a long time, and we both love our kids. He left me for a younger woman, but he provides well for us."

"Sounds rather classic," I said. I was sitting at a kitchen island, sipping my iced tea as she quickly and efficiently cleaned up. "Want to go in the hot tub?"

"Sure."

"Sit and rest for a bit. Let lunch settle. I'll go get some towels and trunks. Okay?" I wondered what her kids would say if they walked in. She seemed to read my mind again. "I have students over all the time, so nobody is going to raise an eyebrow."

I sat and watched the news for some time, until she came from the dark nether regions of the house carrying a basket with towels and keys and swim trunks in it. She said: "These are for you. They should fit." I put them on in the bathroom. Her ex had been more solid in the waist, and I had to cinch the drawstring tighter. "You look great in those," she said as I emerged.

At the back door, she reached into a shadowy alcove high up and took down a key ring with a brass plate two inches long, and several small brass keys on it. I followed her out the door, past their large pool, around a corner, through a neighbor's yard, and into a third yard beyond. There was another pool, big as hers. Same layout. "My girl friend, who is also divorced, lives here. We swapped keys long ago, and promised to keep it secret from our kids. Nobody will surprise us, because she and her kids are out of town."

M and I dove into the pool and swam around. The sun shone hard on the glittering water, and we were shielded by woven rattan fence covers all around. I began to appreciate *M* better now that she was practically nude except for a dark blue bikini that left little to the imagination.

She was, as I have said, an imposing, big, athletic woman. If there was much fat on her, it didn't show. She had early wrinkles around the eyes and mouth because of too much sun exposure—but nothing too drastic yet. She was as tall as I, and had shapely but heavy legs and a thicker waist from long-ago child bearing and perhaps a few quarts of ice cream to many. Or Napoleons. She was voluptuous and busty. As we played in the water, she felt chilly and slippery. We splashed around until we go a little tired and chilly. By now, we were touching each other lightly and innocently—I carried her down the length of the pool, with the water making her buoyant.

She squealed and held her nose as the water got deeper and we sank into its greenish depths. I ran across the pool floor in big bounding leaps, and just made it to the wall before we had to surface and cling together gasping. There, she kissed me. "I hope you understand," she whispered. She put her arms around my neck and held her face close to mine. "I am on the go a lot and this afternoon is a tiny niche of time I could carve out for myself. I think you are a sweet guy, and I would like to see you again. I want to make the most of this afternoon." She ran out of words and, mortified, lowered her head so her forehead rested on my chest and I couldn't see her face.

I put my finger under her chin and gently lifted. Her eyes rose hopefully and gazed into mine. "I understand, and I look forward to dating you a bit. Look, it's a little backwards, but can I take you to a movie this week?"

"You mean it?" She wrapped her legs around my waist and her arms around my neck.

"Absolutely. We keep it light and see where it goes, okay?"

"I like that." She pecked at my lips, my cheeks, my forehead with her lips. "I was worried that you might expect too much, too fast."

I shook my head. "I believe in lots of breathing room."

"That's really nice." She pulled my head closer and met my lips with a French kiss. This was the unveiling, the first contact, the opening of the first door. It was a wonderful moment of acceptance and trust. I really enjoyed standing there, as we were, with this magnificent woman wrapped around me. It was a moment for me, privately, that culminated a little hope that had stirred in me, maybe as early as when I picked that apple to tempt her with, so to speak. I had an apple and she had melons.

She had this amplitude about her. As I held her big thighs in my hands, caressed her full waist, and just brushed the edges of her heavy breasts, I thought to myself—this woman is a trophy. I know it sounds silly that a poor young student would think such thoughts, but she truly was a prize. Her ex had married her as an inexperienced young beauty, and now I held her as a magnificent, matured, sophisticated woman. She had awed me and intimidated me from the first, and I was still overwhelmed by her whole enchilada—her looks, her self-assurance, her brilliance, her success in life. I was not intimidated by her intellect—I enjoyed it. Had she overwhelmed me in that department, I would have written it off as a teacher/student thing. She had every right to be smarter than I. Actually, I didn't care.

"Let's warm up in the hot tub," she suggested after ten minutes of hungry, delighted French kissing and petting. She led me out of the pool and into a small side building enclosed in frosted glass. The glass was steamed up, and the air smelled of pool chlorine. She explained: "They circulate pool water through here, but heat it on the way in." We sat on the edge of the sunken, pool-like four seat Jacuzzi for a while, resuming our kissing and petting.

She had us climb in and relax in the warm water. After about ten minutes, the tub shut off automatically as it was supposed to. We showered, still wearing our bathing suits. *M* managed to be modest and hide behind the shower curtain to peel her wet trunks off and get into a long, plain jeans dress and T-shirt that she'd brought in the basket. "I'm sorry I forgot to bring your clothes," she said. "Do you mind wearing a towel?" She handed me an enormous, fluffy white terry towel that I put on somewhat like a toga. *M* led me into the house. Same prosperous interior, expensive décor, tasteful colors and textures and objects.

We stopped in the kitchen. "I'm going to fix us margaritas, if that's okay with you," she said. Margaritas were fine with me. As she fussed at her neighbor's counters, moving from sink to fridge and back and forth, I could stand the temptation no longer and embraced her from behind. "That feels so nice," she said. "I'm glad you are a mellow kind of guy. I was going to say mellow lover, but we aren't quite there yet, are we?"

"We are getting close," I said as I hugged her. I enjoyed the softness of her back with its swimmer's lard on the shoulder blades. I enjoyed the fullness of her ravaged stomach that jutted out slightly into my hands.

"I was afraid you would think I am too old for you." She paused in her busy activities and leaned on the dark marble counter top near the sink as if finally slowing down with her life and waiting for me to take control.

"No. I think you are a trophy wife. You were beautiful as a young girl when he married you, and you are still breathtaking." I held her from behind, feeling her big buttocks against my hardness. She stood facing away from me with her hands on the counter and looked over her shoulder.

"Thank you for saying that. I imagine you say things like that to all the girls you seduce, Peter."

"I only speak the truth from my heart."

"You make me feel very sexy, and that is really nice."

"Tell me what sexy means to you." "Honestly?" She looked scared.

"Honestly."

She swallowed hard, then started in a husky and raspy voice. She gained courage and conviction as she spoke. "I move around all the time. It's rare for me to stand still like this. When I'm moving around fixing lunches or teaching students, I sometimes daydream a little. Especially in class, when it's hot, and I'm looking at some exceptionally handsome young studs. I get horny, Peter. Is that bad?"

"No."

"Is it bad that I don't date much and don't have time to get involved with someone nice?"

"It's not bad, *M.* It's good that you have these thoughts."

"Sometimes, I just have this silly stray daydream that someone, a handsome guy like yourself, is waiting for me at home. Or he is looking up my dress. He—" She dropped her forehead on her folded hands in that mortified attitude again.

"Let me help you finish that daydream," I said.

Recovering her poise, she confessed: "It's a fantasy about being played with under my dress by someone standing behind me while I go about my business as if nothing were going on. Maybe it's someone lying behind the podium as I give my lecture, and that someone is looking up my dress. I'm not wearing any underpanties, and he is fascinated by my labia and starts playing with them."

I stroked her and murmured, continuing her train of thought: "You are teaching your class, or you are moving around in your kitchen, and you aren't wearing any underwear. For some reason today, you forgot to put on underpants. But people never do anything by accident. You were thinking that some guy, like me, would notice how beautiful and sexy you look."

She moaned slightly as I embraced her, as I moved my hands up and cupped her breasts. She put her hands over mine and rubbed her breasts with my hands. They were full, firm breasts still hidden from me. They were big but in proportion, not exaggerated melons. These were real industrial working tits that had suckled two robust children. This woman was German and a professor and a big one at that. I could feel her huge nipples now. My dick pressed against the back of her jeans dress as I felt those nipple plums turn into prunes between my fingers. "Keep saying these things to me," she said.

"You dream of having someone behind you, fingering you under your dress. That's what you hoped for when you came to the lecture hall without underwear." I reached under her dress, so that the heavy denim material gathered on my forearm, and explored upward. My hands encountered the hams of her thighs, and my fingers explored further until they found the dry fault line between her legs. "The problem now," I whispered into her ear as I leaned my chin by her neck, "is that you have forgotten how to really turn on. You have this guy who is fingering your pussy, but your pussy is all dry." She whimpered, and I diddled the dry pussy top with my fingertips. "You have a lot of wet pussy juice in there, but we need to wake your pussy up. Your pussy is asleep down there because nobody has paid any attention to it in such a long time. Do you not play with it at all?"

She reached with one arm over her shoulder and spread her hand against the back of my head. She leaned her head back so that we were cheek to cheek. She said: "Oh yes, I do when I am not too tired." Her voice got that tremulous fantasy tone to it, which assured me she was getting turned on.

"Will you show me later?"

"Oh yes, I will gladly show you."

"Maybe we can do it together."

"Oh yes, we can do it together."

"For now, though, darling, I want us to focus on how you are getting horny under this wonderful dress. That's the fantasy we are doing right now. You are in a kitchen, making margaritas, and someone is @ing your oyster from underneath, right under your dress."

"I find it so hard to believe," she cried.

I lifted her dress, dropped my towel, and slid my cock up into that pussy of hers. It wasn't dry anymore. When my head touched those dry labia, those lips sprouted wetness and grew slippery in a second. My erect cock slipped up into that glorious hole of hers. I had not planned to move this quickly, but she was an emergency in progress. Lights and sirens. @ing a big woman like this was sweet. Your cock slid into this warm, wet cave. There were two ways of looking at it. She was big, and her oyster was a little loose, but she had meaty thighs that could crush my cock into a tight tube.

"Are you inside of me?"

"Oh yes, but not for long, baby. I just wanted to show you how hot I am for you."

"Oh God." She almost cried, I think, as she gripped the counter again.

I didn't want to shoot yet, so I backed out. I sent my fingers up there instead. By now, she was a dripping mess. I could insert four fingers sideways halfway up her snatch. "Make the margaritas," I said. She started to protest, but I told her: "Baby, this is your fantasy. Someone is finger-@ing your wonderful pussy while you are going about your business. Make the margaritas." So she obediently went about the normal motions of making these drinks, while wearing her jeans dress, and having my fingers up her oyster. I felt a bit like a puppet master. "This is good for you," I said. "This is going to reinforce in your mind that getting @ed is a wonderful thing. In all of your duties and obligations, you have no doubt forgotten the pleasure of having a man enjoy your body."

She moved about as best she could, throwing ice in the mixer, pouring tequila, cutting up limes. All the while, I had one or more fingers up her hole. She surprised me by saying through gritted teeth: "I'm going to come soon."

I felt the flutters in her oyster. "Then come, baby, do it all over my hand."

"It may be wet."

"Are you going to ejaculate, baby?"

"Oh Peter, do you know about that? I would be so mortified if you didn't."

"I know all about it, *M.* I want you to feel free and cut loose."

"Then you understand?"

"Yes, *M.* Let it go." Female ejaculation, which relatively few women know they can do, consists of releasing juice from an organ inside the front of the vagina. In some women it's a foamy froth. In others it is a spray of clear liquid. If it's yellow it is not ejaculate, but urine—she gets so excited she loses her bladder, and squirts pee in your face. *M* knew what was coming.

As she moved around the kitchen with my hand between her heavy buttocks, she grew aroused to a resounding climax. I felt her begin shuddering and quaking as she struggled with her margarita procedure. She laughed uproariously: "This would really be so much easier without the good @ing sex, but don't stop now." Then her eyes rolled up and fluttered. I was diddling *M's* long slit fast, when she started to shudder and tremble. Her pussy stiffened and tightened around my fingers as she started to come.

All at once, she sprayed—I felt her clear, warm ejaculate on my hand. I lifted her dress so that her solid thighs and buttocks were visible. She leaned forward over the counter, thus raising her behind, to oblige me with an easier look. I saw that her softness had closed up on itself, but the wiggly line where her lips met was soaked with a whitish, foaming liquid. I had seen this foaming in a girl I knew, who didn't understand why her oyster produced foam when she was aroused. It was part of her ejaculate, I was sure.

"You like what you see?" she asked.

"It is beautiful. High art. This is what should hang in art galleries. There would be no more wars. People would beat their swords into plowshares as they beat their meat."

She giggled. "With your humor I could easily flip and start thinking I look silly like this."

"Oh no," I said fervently, "I am just about to start licking you."

As I licked her, she murmured her own self-arousal, while massaging her breasts. In fact, as I shifted position at one point, I saw that she had opened the top of her dress and pulled both breasts forward so that they rested on her forearm while she sucked them by turns. She murmured: "You did it for me, Peter, you made my fantasy come true about being played with under my dress by someone under me or behind me while I went about my business as if nothing were going on."

I turned my attentions back to her big ass, slapping it gently and rubbing it, admiring its creases and curves, and then licking open her lips to taste and smell the juice. The edges still smelled cleanly of chlorine and salt. I licked until I noticed that her clitoral hood was spreading, and the pink bud was pushing its way forward. I gave it a few licks to see how sensitive my love partner was, and she squirmed and gave a tiny animal cry of discomfort.

So I eased up and ran the tip of my tongue around and around the 'little girl' and that made the big girl groan with growing satisfaction. She started leaking tiny suds again, and I wasn't sure if this come was new or still in her from a short while ago. Or maybe she had been continually pumping this stuff out from the pores in her tunnel.

"Come into me, baby," she said over her back. "Come with me. I'm coming again. I think this is going to be the big one. Please, baby, please, put it in."

Her legs were long, her ass high, and I had to hook a little wooden footstool over and stand on it. She was foaming as I pushed my head into that slick tunnel. I grabbed her glorious hips, just under her thick, hanging belly, and pulled her against me. I slammed her bouncing fleshy behind against my hard thighs so that the kitchen filled with slapping and slamming noises. Her oyster gurgled and popped as my cock-head formed and broke a vacuum in her tunnel several times. It sounded also like a fish breaking the surface of its pond, coming up for food or just to look around in curiosity. *M* was moaning continuously now and unable to lean over and suck her nipples. Her cries rose in pitch, and she pleaded with me to hit her harder, though I was at the height of my strength and didn't want to bruise her. Slamming steadily like that, we headed for orgasm together. She let out the first of a deep, throaty yells, "oh!" or "aw!" and hearing her pushed me over he edge. I shouted, and my shout propelled her to shout more vehemently. For the next minute or two, we filled the kitchen not only with the slamming of our flesh, but also with those interlocking shouts as we were each overcome by our own passion and the other's. My penis and testicles were soaked as her ejaculate gushed out.

She rested belly down on the counter with her naked tits and nipples crushed between her arms and face. I breathlessly clung to her as long as I could, until my beaten and exhausted member slipped out of her and sat shriveled on top of my scrotum like a little howitzer. Bending down to give each of her buttocks at least a dozen kisses, I watched her oyster dribble a combination of my come and her come. I watched the flow alternate with a yellow trickle, and opened her labia for a look. Sure enough. "Honey," I said, "you are dribbling piss on the floor." I looked down at the soaked footstool and the puddle gathering around my feet on the linoleum tiles. "It's not a lot, but there is a puddle growing here." She had become so overwhelmed that she'd also lost control of her pee-sphincter.

"I don't care," she gasped. "I'll mop it up before we leave." So saying, as she continued to lean over the counter top, her hole gooshed. A yellow arc appeared in the air, and the floor splattered merrily. "It's sterile," she gasped, "so it's not doing any harm. I just don't care right now. When I'm done, will you put your dick in me just once more."

"Sure." I stepped up and rubbed myself stiff again. As I did so, she squirted a few times. I didn't care enough to get out of the way. I felt the warmth of her golden shower on my belly and groin, then running down my legs and over my feet. It wasn't a bad feeling, and the frankness and honesty of that action made my fish erect again as it jumped upstream into her waiting cleft. We rested like that for a good ten or fifteen minutes before leaving the scene.

She wanted to get into high gear, clean the floor, lock the house, all that busy stuff, but I convinced her to give herself one more hour of rest on this wonderful day of freedom. So we went back to the shower, rinsed, and lay on the warm, moist Jacuzzi room floor. While the green water near us steamed and bubbled, we nestled together and kissed. We both fell asleep for a while. Languidly, I got on top of her and kissed her when I woke. My dick found her hole and crawled in without hand-help. I enjoyed feeling the cushion of her stomach under my body. When we rolled over and she straddled me with me still inside her, she closed her eyes and visibly enjoyed the feel of me under her. It was I who whispered in her ear: "Please, let's do this again."

"As often as you want," she said and surprised me by jamming her tongue in my ear and reaming it while breathing hard. She switched positions and started licking, gobbling, hungrily nibbling at my dick and balls. She crawled down and sucked on my ball sac. She pushed under it and licked my asshole. She pushed my thigh out of the way so she could get her face in between the cheeks of my ass. I felt her tongue mauling my sphincter as she tongue-@ed my asshole.

With one hand she rubbed my nipples as she reamed me. Her butt was next to me, and I worked my fingers into her asshole. She uttered a mouthful-little cry of passion as I got her sphincter to relax and played in there.

All this happened with total spontaneity. I held her big muscular strong ass with both hands, as I shifted around and plunged my rod into her asshole. Getting in took a moment's paused, and I had to spit into it several times to get a lube in there as the gate opened for my ram. She held herself open, rubbed herself, slapped her buttocks, all to relax the muscles so nothing would tear.

Once I was in, she moved the focus to her oyster. She rubbed a finger along each side of her clit while I gently ass-@ed her until I could feel the tremors growing, then the bucking as she started to be overcome, and finally the all-out collapse as she fell forward in her orgasm letting me finish until I got my whang all the way in, up to the root, and then squirted her anus full of come. We would have many passionate moments together in days and weeks to come (no pun intended).

The Story of N

I was taking a Classics course at the University, evenings, when I met *N*. You went in by this neo-Gothic archway, through a garden of bushes and round modern light globes, and into a classroom with wooden floors and stone walls. It is a genre environment, a museum of scholasticism, a container whose shape spoke of its purpose, sui generis. It was a nostrum and a stupediction, by some lights, because not everyone who went in there as meat and came out as sausage was actually an educated person capable of critical thinking. Anyway, into this lovely, lovable cliché marched a dozen of us to be read to be a fussy little white-haired man with liver spots, a too-young looking blue blazer and khakis, and the early trembling of, sadly, Parkinson's. He was very erudite, and had mothball breath under jaundiced skin. He spoke of ancient Athens and Rome as if he had walked their streets, and judging by his age, perhaps he had.

Sitting beside me was a leggy woman with skin the color of cocoa and a broad smile and mischievous eyes: *N*. During the break, we walked past the smokers and those who insisted on showing their sophistication by badmouthing the University. She seemed as out of place among the rest of the class as I felt. "What are you doing here?" *N* asked as if we had long known each other.

"I'm actually sort of interested in ancient history," I confided. "You?"

"I'm taking this as an elective," she said. "I'm actually a graduate student in Chemistry. I was missing one undergraduate class in Liberal Arts. I work during the day, and I have a child in grammar school, so this night course seemed like the perfect thing. It's actually pretty interesting."

"Must be a nice break for you from all those molecules and their bonding."

She had an infectious little laugh, and nice white teeth in a wide mouth. If you teased her with even the most obtuse word play, she read right into it.

"Would you like to team up as study buddies?"

"You being my study buddy?" She laughed. She said brightly: "Okay."

We started that very evening, and the subtext was unspoken but clear to both of us. Her little girl, Nminor, stayed at *N's* mom's house on school nights. That created an obvious set of windows, two evenings a week and Saturday mornings, for about sixteen weeks. Actually, four of us teamed up after about a week, which gave us really nice coverage as we pooled our knowledge and insights. *N* always signaled for me to stay after. By then, we were burned out on Classics and preferred to numb out. So she always made cocoa with marshmallows, and we would sit together on the big leather couch near the fireplace in her old Victorian apartment. We particularly liked watching cartoons or really old movies, anything that took our minds as far away from the present as possible.

There is, in the beginning of every relationship, that brief time of getting to know the other's broad preferences. Later, there is the point you cross where you admit whatever it is that you like that's a little kinkier, from toe sucking to the more complex penetration fantasies and so on. *N* was a straightforward, kind girl (woman; older woman; she was 29 but could pass for my age easily). Her finely knotty black hair was shaped in a simple but elegant kind of Afro, not too big, but sculpted so that it rose toward the back and widened across the sides, kind of like a pheasant's tail. She wore a white band in it across the front. She had a narrow forehead, high and intellectual, and a small wide nose, and prowed pink lips. She had a dimple in her small brown chin. I describe her in detail because she was really statuesque.

When we first became intimate, she smiled (her gums were so pink they almost shone against the fine-grained, dry cocoa of her downy skin) and said "I'm easy," meaning a whole bunch of things (and some, not). She got right to it, she could cut from A to Z in analyzing a situation, she was sometimes too logical and analytical. The latter meant she didn't do well at fantasies, but she had a different quality—she could be mischievous when it suited her, or regal and aloof at other times. By deceiver, I mean if you saw her in street clothes—jeans, blouse, short jacket, you might notice that she had long legs and a pert behind, but she was breathtaking when naked. I had not gotten that far when we became intimate. This happened on our third or fourth study date, because *N* was also a tease who liked to stretch out anticipation and desire. When she said "I'm easy," it really meant she wasn't easy until she was ready to be easy.

We had been watching our usual Porky Pig and Bugs Bunny cartoons, laughing at our own silliness, when I had enough of being nudged away and avoided. I crawled across the couch to her. She said "What do you think you are doing?" but did not try to escape from the lion who was stalking her. This was a hungry lion by now, who had been teased with dusky shadows under white blouse, and scarred ankle with gold chain on it, and other tantalizing glimpses. She gave that mischievous laugh and swung her legs off the couch so that she knelt before me. "You stand up here before me, honey," she commanded.

I rose obediently and stood before her, cupping the gorgeously formed back of her skull in my palm through the soft frizz of her hair. "Now, honey, I'm going to open this zipper here, and I expect to find a nice dinner bun in the oven. Am I going to be a happy woman?"

"I think that you already know the answer."

She giggled. She gave a nod. "Um-huh."

"I know you have felt the bulge in my pants brushing against your leg or your arm as we were watching cartoons. I've been sitting here with this big hard-on next to you, and you must have felt the heat emanating from it."

She fumbled with my zipper. "Come to think of it, I once had a boyfriend with a big noisy Corvette and, yes, when he came over to see me, the heat just emanated off that big red car. What is this?" She got my zipper open and pushed down my underpants. My dong flopped out. "My, my, Peter, this is definitely a thick dick. You have a handful here, my beloved friend. It's not a long dong, but this dick is thick. Look at that. I feel as if I am at a ballpark." She held it in both hands, like a dog in a bun, and opened her mouth wide.

I made two or three baby steps forward, and that cruiser went right into her schmoozer. She moaned lightly as she sucked on it. I mentioned this girl had pink gums. Those gums fit around my dick as if the two had been made for each other. She was not a deep throat kind of woman. She was a head-turner, meaning she sinuously wrapped herself one way and then the other around that pink, wet gearshift knob.

I held her frizzy hair in my hands, enjoying the feel of her skull like a shapely vase or container, or work of art. It was sexy to think of such a brilliant mind in that vase, focused on exchanging maximum pleasure with my regenerative organ. If that sounds esoteric—she and I could have conversations like that when we were not watching Porky Pig cartoons. She palmed my balls and fondled them, rubbing them lightly while she sucked on me. "Baby," said in a voice grown tight and faint with sensuous overload, "you know that I am going to suck your little pussy all wet and good."

She had small chocolate breasts with smooth bluish nipples that stiffened into handles as her breasts bobbed around with her every motion.

"Mm-hmm," she murmured, nodding, without missing a stroke. She held it and licked underneath it, and then bobbled my balls with her tongue, creating a shiver of sensation that ran through my entire body. She pushed my thighs apart and licked under my balls. She pushed her tongue up into the darkness between my scrotum and my thigh, first on one side and then on the other.

She seemed to take great pleasure in treating the looseness of my scrotal sac almost as a food item to be played with. She sucked and nibbled on my scrotal sac that way I would play with a woman's labia. She made loud smacking noises as she did so, and I grasped my rod in both hands because I was beginning to think I was going to ejaculate. She looked up at me with a mouthful of nut and murmured "Mmm?" Seeing my face, she pushed down her jeans. She stepped out of them on long, dark, elegant legs. She twisted around and showed me her white panties, which had little flowers on them. She slapped them slightly to show me how round and tight her buttocks were.

In one motion, I let my pants drop. I pulled those delicious panties down, noting the wideness of her hips, and gave her oyster a quick rub to check it out. "You are dripping wet," I said. "You bad girl. You have been hiding a wet oyster from me."

I was going to say more, but I was overcome with the first throes of an orgasm that wasn't going to stay out of town another minute. I turned toward the couch, and she circled around so that she could lean her fingers on the cushions. I slipped into her, appreciating and loving the warmth and moisture of that tunnel. Given how long her legs were, I did not have to bend down. All she had to do was support herself and be comfortable. Had she been wearing almost any kind of shoes, I would have had to stand on something to get inside her.

I thrust rapidly and deeply, and she started moaning. "Baby," she said, "did I make you wait?" ("Yes.") "Did it make you hard?" ("Yes.") "Does it feel good now?" ("Yes.") "Are you glad I made you wait?" ("Yes.") "Are you glad I am letting you @ me?" ("Yes.") She slapped herself on her buttock and told me: "I want you to @ me all night so that you have enough to last until next class night. Want to do that?"

I started to answer my chorus ("Yes.") but was overcome by my orgasm. As I thumped against her in a rapid series of slapping sounds that echoed in the room like rocks dropping in water, each stroke weakened me. She sensed my coming collapse, and bend her knees, letting me guide her beautiful plum-colored ass cheeks down on the couch. She ended up sitting on my dick as I pumped the last few strokes into her. She wasn't very heavy. She wanted to get off me for fear of hurting me, but I held on to her buttocks and hips and kept her there. "You are so precious," I told her in the delirium of the moment, "I want to keep you there forever."

Ever the wit, she flashed a laugh over one bony shoulder. "We'd starve to death here. People would find us here a thousand years from now and wonder what strange ancient American ritual we were engaged in."

I said: "The ancient rituals of @us-comus."

"That's the Classical scholar talking. Muckus-suckus."

"I am going to suck your lips," I told her.

"You and what energy, White Boy?"

"Me and this big Enron between my thighs, Black Girl."

She wiggled her bottom and squealed. This was going to be the first of many nights that I stayed over until morning. Grandma was taking little [N-minor] over to grammar school, and *N* would pick her up after school. Until late into the night, *N* and I could play.

When we had recovered a bit, she had me sit on the edge of the couch. *N* had that peculiarity, that she wasn't so into fantasies as the queen of them, *K,* but she had a way of orchestrating little things that we ought to do. So she got on all fours sideways to me, and had me spit on my middle finger and insert it in her anus.

She rocked her long lithe body back and forth, touching herself below, so that she was @ing herself with my finger in her ass while she masturbated. I stroked the long, lightly-muscled surfaces of her back, which gleamed dry and brown before me. I bent down and licked along her spine and around her shoulder blades.

Suddenly, she uttered a series of shuddering breaths and collapsed on the floor before me. "I just came," she said breathlessly. "Stay there. Be very still and look at me." She lay on the floor with her heels beside my thighs on the couch. As lay looking up at me, with her left hand she pulled her dark left labia open and with the fingers of her other hand rubbed the bright pinkness of her pee hole and clitoris.

I watched her clitoris grow like a little bubblegum-colored bee hive with a swollen kind of tiny head on it.

"Just watch me," she said. She stared at me intently. Her eyes grew large and beseeching as her fingers moved faster. She alternated hands a few times.

I was allowed to fondle her feet at my sides, and nothing more. Much as I wanted to get down and lick her torso—anything, to be closer to that wondrous action—I had to stay between her feet. I looked down through her spread legs and watched the pink bud in her clam grow larger and harder.

Her mouth opened in a silent cry as she stared at me with big, hungry eyes. Her eyes beseeched me, even if I could not touch her, they beseeched me to send her the relief that she so desperately needed. She was going into the throes of another orgasm, but it was slow and moving deliberately the way a massive storm crawls over the landscape, enveloping hills and trees in its foggy thrashing fury. She cocked her head this way and that. I rubbed her feet, pulling them against me. I felt her big toes stroking my ribs as she tried to caress me with her feet. I lifted her feet away, spreading her legs even more, but brought her feet to my mouth so I could like their orange bottoms. The sensation in the pits of her arches made her start moaning. "Yes, baby, that's good, you found the way to help me. Oh, baby," she wailed, "I need you to do that so badly...please lick them hard...push your tongue in there so I feel it rippling all the way up my legs into my oyster and up my tummy to my titties. Oh!" Her cries became loud, almost tearful, and incoherent, as her tight behind thrashed around on the hard wood floor. Her wide hips moved up and down as she @ed her fingers, and her buttocks slapped on the wooden floor in rapid strokes, pop pop pop... or, looser if she shifted positions, plop plop plop...

I stood up and hugged both of her ankles while continuing to lick the bottoms of her feet.

"Lower me!" she cried.

I squatted so my balls hung down. She reached around and fondled them with one hand while sticking her fingers deep in her oyster. Then she stiffened. Silent for a moment. She yelled, a truncated scream. Fell silent again. Turned, so that she faced to my right, staring away along the floor. Twitched. Then her contractions began, and she doubled over in a fetal position while stuffing her hands between her legs and mangling her clitoris among several ravenously wiggling fingers that seemed to want to gangbang her all together. She let out a choked, truncated shout with each contraction, and shoved her fingers deep into her hole, before she stopped moving.

We moved into the bedroom, where we threw ourselves on the bed. I watched her lithe body streak across the sheets and land on a pillow. She turned, with open arms, and invited me into her embrace. I reached out with my left hand so that our fingers entwined, while I kissed my way to her mouth inch by inch after sucking on her toes a while. As I drew near, her other hand welcomed my free hand, and now both hands were entwined. I walked on my knees into the simple paradise of a missionary position @ that lasted about another forty minutes. A quaint little clock somewhere in the dark, still corridors chimed midnight as we pulled up the blankets, spooned as tightly as we could with me behind her, hugging her, and fell asleep together after a few awkward but sincere kisses over her shoulder. This is some of what we did during those long, delirious evenings after studying the ancient Romans and Greeks, who would have been proud of our inventiveness and our ardor for one another.

The Story of O

I met *O* in a bar, where she was crying. Here's how this happened. It was a sticky hot summer afternoon, and there was this little downstairs hole in the wall drinking place where my cronies and I liked to go. The beer was cheap, nobody was pretentious, and the clientele was interesting. There was a lesbian table deep in one corner, where women would hang out if they couldn't get into the Bookends. That was a pair of gay bars, with men in the left and women in the right establishment—two long, dark, narrow divisions in a long Victorian brick house that stretched a block.

My friends and I were strictly straight, but the downtown scene with its trendy eateries, mixed bars, and attractive women was our draw. It was amazing how many attractive straight (and, I assume, bi) women came down here of an evening to seek companionship. With our impoverished means, my pals and I usually went home slightly drunk and very much without companionship of the sort one craved. I did very well, of course, with my Summers, so I wasn't complaining too loudly.

Fact was, too, I was stealthy and really didn't spread the word. It wasn't that I was trying to corner the market on Summers, as much as I would be in for some amount of ribbing. Also, show-and-tell went against my grain. I had no intention of ever sharing with another man, even my best friend, the details of what went on in the bedroom with me and my Summers.

One day, then, I came down to the Cavern alone. My male friends were all away or working or with girls. I was between Summers. It was hot and sticky, and I was waiting for the day's heat to subside. The Cavern was too poor to have air conditioning, but it was cool among those heavy walls downstairs. The semi-darkness alone lifted about ten degrees from the air. I washed my face and hair in cold water in a grimy bathroom sink, dried myself with paper towels, and came back into the peanut shell-strewn bar for a cold beer.

I saw this very attractive, slim blonde sitting alone in the middle of the bar. She had a skinny beer slowly sweating between her elbows, and she had this big brown purse that she seemed to be using for a rampart to hide behind. She had thick hair, cut short and trimmed up into a kind of high porcupine with dark and silver highlights instead of quills. She had quarter-sized earrings of beaten brass. She wore jeans, a brown blouse, and high-heeled shoes whose bare backs revealed her oiled, sanded heels and a tiny gold chain with a love charm on each ankle. I sat a few seats down and nursed a skinny one of my own. As I sat, I watched every guy who walked past try to hit on her, without result. Our eyes met several times and finally she took her beer and her purse and walked down to me. "Would you mind if I sit beside you? I'm not trying to hit on you."

"Oh, by all means," I said. "Make yourself at home. I'm just killing time."

She slid in beside me. I could smell the expensive perfume, and saw the tiny golden hairs on her bare arms. She didn't seem like a working lady. Maybe a high-end prostitute like you rarely saw around this part of town. Not that I knew much about it, but as a taxi driver I'd ferried a lot of nightlife around, including girls going to motels for pay, and...well, it doesn't bear talking about. "What do you do?" she asked.

"I am a graduate student. I get by."

"Graduate student of what?"

I wasn't sure yet, but I gave it my best shot. "Ancient history."

She laughed a bitter little laugh from the throat deep. "That's fitting."

I didn't ask. I had not seen the eye interplay that usually told me the Summer was interested in me. I wasn't sure if I was interested enough, or had the energy on this hot day, to pursue her. In another moment I noticed she was crying silently and hiding her bleary face behind her purse. I offered her a small stack of drink doilies. "Sweetheart, whatever it is, it can't be all that terrible."

She thanked me and blew her nose. She dabbed at eyes. "I'll have to do a touch-up in the ladies' room," she said. "Excuse me." She left, and came back five minutes later. "Do my eyes look puffy?"

As she slid back into her seat I examined her. "You look just fine to me."

"How old are you?"

"I'm 24."

"Mmm."

"Mmm?"

She opened a little pocket mirror and looked at her eyes, then snapped it shut and put it away. "Do you know a—" and she said some guy's name.

"No, sorry. Doesn't ring a bell."

"Do you come down here a lot?"

"No," I said, "maybe twice a week, evenings, at most. I work at a bookstore and attend classes, which keeps me pretty busy." I wasn't taking any classes at the moment, but I was officially enrolled in the system, so it wasn't a lie—just a fib. "Is this guy a friend of yours?" "Was," she said ruefully. "I just got dumped."

"Oh geez, no wonder you were crying."

"I should have seen it coming." She wasn't bitter, really. She folded her hands together on the bar and looked at them pragmatically. "There are always nice people in the world. Like yourself." She gave me a big blue look full of vulnerability.

"You seem like a pretty nice person, yourself," I said. "Who would want to be mean to you?"

"It's the silliest story," she said.

"Try me."

She shook her head. "I would have to be really drunk to have the nerve."

"Don't get drunk. It sucks. Just tell me if you want to get it off your chest."

She put her hand on my wrist, very innocently and lightly. "Are you one of those people who listen?"

"I'm a good listener. I used to drive a taxi, and people told me their life's stories."

"I'll bet. Weren't you scared?"

"What, of their stories?"

She burst out laughing and hit me on the shoulder. "No, of being mugged."

I shook my head. "I relied on luck, and nothing happened."

"Would you like to pretend you're a cabbie and I'm telling you my story?"

"Sure, why not?"

"I'll buy you a beer for a tip."

"Aw go on, not necessary. I work for free. Pro bono."

"You are an educated man. Young man, but educated. Are you embarrassed to be with a woman ten years your senior?"

I shook my head and looked her over. She was no bouncing college sophomore with baby skin, but she was okay. "I had you figured for maybe a few years older, but not ten."

She beamed. "Oh, you flatterer."

"I'm serious. No, I feel perfectly fine, two adults having a conversation. Are you awkward about being with a younger man?"

She shook her head. "No, not if he is a nice, sweet guy, which you seem to be."

"I try hard not to offend."

"Well, here's the story. My boyfriend had a choice to make and he made it." "Oh, another woman?"

"Another man."

"Yikes."

"Yikes is right."

"How long was this brewing?"

"He and I went together for two years. The past year, he realized he had other interests, and came out of the closet. We started drifting apart, because he started seeing the guy who opened the door for him."

"You tolerated that?" I asked. "I don't mean like I'm putting you down. On the contrary, I think your patience and kindness were admirable."

"Thanks." She sat hunched in thought, with her ankles cross and her fists between her thighs as if she were cold. "Why did I wait? Why did I not move on? Why did I let him dump me? Why Why why."

"You're not worried about HIV and so on?"

"I was. I stopped having sex with him months ago, and I've had two checkups. Lucky girl. I'm clean."

I swiveled around, holding my beer. "Are you sure you're done with him?"

She nodded. "I've made up my mind for sure. First there are the risks. Then there's the history between us with him and this other guy. Finally there's today. I called to find out where I stand, and he told me."

"Told you what."

She shook her head. "You're going to think I'm nuts."

"Try me."

"He said—go to this place around the corner downstairs, near Bookends. The Cavern. Wait for me there. If I don't show up, it means I decided to go with my boyfriend. I told him, if you do that, we're done. He said I understand that. If you don't see me there for our usual, then I'm going to be a man and let you go. He didn't say he was sorry, and I don't imagine he'll ever even apologize. He was really a spoiled momma's boy entirely concerned with himself."

"You said—twice—'the usual.' May I ask what that means?"

She looked at me in a funny way, her eyes brimming with secrets, and her shaking head finally told me she wasn't coming forth about it. "Maybe sometime if we get to be friends."

As my instinct informed me over those two skinny beers, we did become friends and then lovers. *O* was a complex person who made love in a very simple manner, which somehow jarred me a bit. She was passionate, but always seemed to be holding back. She had the not-on-the-first-date rule, and she checked me out by walking down dark streets with me to see if I grew hair on my hands and face a la Lon Chaney. I laugh, but you can't blame women for their caution.

O was a medical doctor, of all things. Made over a hundred grand a year without trying. Lived in a nice three-story townhouse, drove a Jaguar, dressed nice, could take a trip on vacation without sweating the money. She was an OB/GYN on staff at the University Medical Center, where she also taught a graduate class in the Medicine Department. In short, *O* was a very impressive and accomplished woman. So what was she doing in a dump like the Cavern, sitting next to a blowing leaf like me who didn't have enough scratch to buy her a cheap beer that afternoon? I thought I knew the answer—needy—and therefore didn't ask. I made it clear that I wasn't pressing her for anything—money, information, state secrets, sex; nothing. I was just interested in her company.

She sat with me on the couch in her living room under a single reading lamp, so that we were bright islands amid soft shadows. She held both my hands in hers and said: "I can't tell you how much it has meant to me that you have been a good friend the past few weeks."

"Is this goodbye?"

Her face grew sad, and she squeezed my hands. "Oh no, Peter, I'm just opening up to you a lot more now that I know you and trust you. I hope that doesn't push you away?"

"No, of course not, *O.* I'm beginning to trust you also."

"Thanks." She leaned forward and kissed my cheek. She really was a very attractive woman, even with her age showing a little (I had downplayed it at the Cavern). "Maybe it's time that I level with you a little bit." She was off work for two or three days, and relaxing at home. She was barefoot, wearing only a mid-thigh blue jeans skirt, a white blouse that hung loosely on her thin frame with its small, protrusive breasts. I had not made love to her yet, but we were kissing and petting, and had reached a nice comfort zone about our bodies and each other's. "Will you sleep with me tonight, Peter?"

I was a little startled by the directness, after all the coyness. "Yes, I have been hoping you'd ask."

"You didn't press me for it," she said fondly, kissing my other cheek. She squeezed close to me.

"I knew you were probably hurting inside and I thought it would be inappropriate to push myself on you."

"You are really thoughtful."

"I hoped things would go in this direction, and it seems they have. I'm very glad I met you." "Me too, Peter. I need a break. I think you're the guy who will help me get my breathing room and—"

"Yes?"

"Pamper me a little bit?"

"Why certainly."

"I'm supposed to be a doctor and be in charge and never let my guard down." She started to cry. "I'm very lonely, and my boyfriend—ex-boyfriend—was selfish and jerked me around for two years." She burst out crying and I held her close.

She cried for a good ten minutes and then, blinded by tears, rummaged in her purse kind of helplessly until I found her some tissues.

She honked her nose. "Thanks, Peter." She cleared her throat to try and talk. She still had some sobs and sniffles in her, but the worst seemed to be past. "I won't be a pest or make demands or lean on you." She almost cried again. I knelt at her knees as she sat on the couch. I held her hands and looked into her eyes and tried to convey supportiveness. I was a bit worried that she might still be rebounding and depressed and who knew what. I did want to bed her, but as a simple thing, not a complicated issues thing.

We ended up not making love that night. I just held her, and she sobbed a little now and then before falling into a deep, exhausted sleep. It was 'that awful night' that we would mention in horrified whispers during our time together.

We were bonded, and went on little trips together—to New York City, to Boston, even to Montreal by air. She paid for everything, and never threw a reproach my way. She encouraged my researches, pushed me toward my interest in ancient history and Classics, was really a lifelong influence on me. We weren't having fun yet, however.

Making love with her, as I may have mentioned, was like playing piano with the cover half closed. I got to play the white keys, but not the dark keys. Then that changed.

First, the white keys. She was recovering from a miserable affair, and taking time to heal. We spent a lot of time together, many a night, and we started having sex. It was passionate, nice, pleasant, a turn-on—but something wasn't quite in place. She didn't do anal sex because it was bad for the sphincter.

She didn't do rimming because there were bacteria. Basically, her bum hole was off-limits, as was mine. She did a small amount of oral sex, but she seemed to prefer the missionary position. She did like to get oyster-@ed from behind, but (ssshh!) we didn't use explicit words. I concluded that she was a pent-up, prissy, overly intelligent and overly analytical woman who was too stiff and rigid to ever let go and enjoy herself. We had a big fight, didn't talk for three days, and I was about ready to move on. I'd about had it.

Before I could start trawling the city, she came to my room at the Maison Piano Music with her purse dragging and the scent of about three or four scotches and a half pack of cigarettes on her breath. I took her in, held her head as she puked out the third story window, and made her one of my coil tea specials—Lipton on the run, palmed secretly while having the tea I actually paid for at the deli around the block. She fell asleep for an hour, then woke up and seemed sober enough to drive. We went over to her place, and she 'splained.

Turns out that her ex-boyfriend had something a little special on her, because she had unloaded her secret sex life on him, and she felt extremely dependent on him. I could also see that maybe he got tired of all the energy and found simpler, easier going in the brawny, hairy arms of his new boy buddy.

We took a long, leisurely bath together in her warm tub at midnight. She had taken some cola syrup and other homeopathies, and was feeling better. She made a face at the mention of either scotch or smoking, and neither ever came up again (literally or figuratively). We lay at opposite ends of this huge tub, and played footsies while she explained. "Honey, I don't know if you'll understand this, or if it will drive you away from me. The time has come to be honest, and to let you decide if you want to do this with me."

"'The usual,'" I guessed, recalling the afternoon's conversation at the Cavern they day we'd met.

She nodded. "Yes. So what is the usual? Well, it has to do with what it takes to turn me on. I mean, really turn me on. You've never seen me turned on. Frankly, I was hoping it was over and I would never go there again, but you can see—"

I interrupted: "You were like a different person when you showed up drunk and reeking of tobacco at my place earlier. And you're a doctor."

"I know, isn't it a shame?" She grinned. "I promise not to drink or smoke again. That was just the bad girl in me trying to get out."

"So what is this 'usual' that you want to tell me about?"

"It's a sexual thing."

"Okay?"

She swallowed hard. "If you laugh at me I'm going to—to—pour cold water on you and make you go away."

"I won't laugh at you. If anything, it will probably turn me on." She frowned at me speculatively. "You do have a huge imagination. Maybe you'll appreciate this in a different light than that poor dodo I wasted two years on."

"Try me."

"Well, it's very simple, Peter. I like being picked up."

After a silence, I said: "That's it?"

"Yep. Nothing really terrible. No violence, no rape, nothing like that. Just a kind of role playing. You can have your sex one way or the other with me. There's the vanilla, Miss Prim way that you've known, which I know you're sick of; or you can meet me at some bar we agree on, and flirt with me, and pick me up, and I'll butt @ you with your own dick or with my foot."

"Honestly?" I was amazed.

She closed her eyes and nodded portentously. "Wait until I get warmed up, yet. You ain't seen nothin' yet."

She could not have been more right.

The first time, I met *O* at ten p.m. at a clean, well-lit tavern with a stately old bar, a rather sterile pink-looking faux brick wall, some hanging plants, mirrors, and a pool table frequented by cowboy types in denim and white or black Stetsons. There were about fifty people in there, mostly hanging bars or walls. Very few tables. Good mixed crowd, different age groups, some married couples, a few singles looking around hard while nursing drinks, a few pickups in progress. When I walked in, I spotted *O's* blond head. She was sitting at the bar, and a beefy guy with red hair, twice my size, was avidly leaning over her in a conversation that suggested pickup in progress. I had a little worried thing in the pit of my stomach, not knowing how she liked to play the game, and if I had to become a bloodied pulp in the process to be rescued by her.

I walked up to the bar, sidling among some guys in black leather jackets holding a beer in one hand and their helmet in the other. They were laid back, though, and there was no trouble.

The big beefy guy was getting closer to *O.* His hand slid down her back and rested on her buttocks. I was sick to my gut. Next thing, she had told him to take a hike and he stomped out of the place. He had a dazed look on his face, and almost took the inner swinging saloon doors with him, but he disappeared. Next, I wasn't quick enough, and a seedy looking man in his 50s, with gray hair and a rumpled dark suit, stood by her holding a beer mug and saying something idiotic. He was sent packing in a few minutes. I was on my way over to her, when a young black guy (twice my size) walked over with a strange, insistent expression on his eyes. He pulled out three multicolored balls and started juggling for her. He also got his hands on her ass (inbetween juggling) before being sent packing. As I drew near, *O* flew from her seat for the bathroom, spitting at me in a rage: "What's taking you so long, Custer?"

I stood by her seat and nursed my beer until she returned. "Do I know you?"

"No ma'am. I'm George Custer."

She was still angry. "You got the Seventh Cavalry with you?"

"No, Ma'am, ah came alone."

She looked almost humored. "You think you're big enough?"

"Yes, ma'am, I am endowed by my creator with all the goods and services you need to be rescued from this Big Horn here."

"Well, George, my name is—why should I tell you my name? I don't even know you."

"Yes ma'm, we don't know each other, but I reckon I could save you and we could ride out of here on my hoss together."

"Let's hang around a little," she muttered—not to George Custer, but to Peter Spring. The first huge guy came back in, almost taking the saloon doors with him again, and he got himself a boilermaker and stood not far away eyeing me with tiny lead eyes full of hate and violence. I saw the black guy juggling for some other woman across the room, and he looked at me with a strange stare.

"Have a beer, George, and relax," *O* said. She put on this persona of a slightly tough babe. I figured this all had something to do with her self-worth and some childhood rejection. She wanted the attention, and she enjoyed the sexual tension and violence in the air. It was like predators in the wild sharing a watering hole and competing for food and their own kind of the opposite sex. I drank my beer and after a few minutes had to go real bad. So walked down this long, narrow, dark hallway to the Men's Room and went in already unzipping my fly. There was the guy with the lead eyes, coming out. He looked down at me over the acreage of his chest and stopped.

"Hello," I said.

He nudged me out of his way. I walked to the urinal and hung myself out. He pushed open the bathroom door on an afterthought—a sheet of paper couldn't have fit there between him and the frame. "Hey, dude—what's the secret?"

"Huh?"

"The bitch you picked up."

My dick was so frozen I thought it would be a week before I ever pissed again.

"I'm talking to you." "Sorry."

"What did you do to score?"

I shrugged. "Want to know? For real?"

"Yeah." He hung his shoulders.

"Well, for one thing, I don't put my hands on a woman's ass in public. That's when she send you away."

He stared at me, and I couldn't' tell whether he was going to beat me senseless and spray blood all over the walls, or if he was going to cry. He meekly whispered "thanks" and strode off.

I stood trembling and alone in the bathroom and almost cried myself. There was no piss coming out of me just then. Despite having drunk a beer and needing to go, I was like a dry creek here. I flushed anyway, so nobody would think I was weird, even though nobody was in there. I went back and joined *O,* who was fighting off another guy. I walked up to her, took her arm, and yanked. She managed to grab her purse. "@ the drink," I said as I propelled her to the door. Outside, I let go her arm.

"Where are you taking me?"

"Home."

"What if I don't want to go?"

"I'm taking you home."

I was to tell her we were through, when the door opened and out came the black guy juggling this balls. He pointed at me: "You! I want this bitch." He looked at *O* and pointed like Zeus: "...and you ain't leaving with this pencil-dick."

The door of this inexplicable nightmare place opened, and several men burst out. "What's going on?" "Onion!" The black guy's nickname was Onion. "Onion, you going back to prison if you @ with them people." I saw the crowd gather round to restrain him, saw the balls juggled in the air, grabbed *O* by the hand, and started running. We ran around the corner, jumped into her car, and she gunned the engine and pulled out just as the men came tearing around the corner. In the lead was Onion, looking for mayhem and juggling while he ran. I'm serious—you couldn't make this up in a book of fiction. It's the real world. Nobody would believe you.

"What the hell was that all about?" I asked.

"Don't talk," she said. She held up her palm. "Please." She looked rigid and pale as she drove with both hands on the wheel. The only words spoken in the car were by her: "I'm carrying it with me." She almost seemed to be holding her breath.

We got to her house, and she instructed me: "Wait in the car about ten minutes, and then come up. Okay?" "Okay." I was dubious, to say the least, but I was giving her a chance.

Ten minutes later, I let myself into the lobby of her secure place with a spare key she'd given me. I went up in the elevator, got out, crossed the hall, and knocked. "Come in!" So I let myself in with a spare key, closed the door, and turned around. The entry way was dark, and music poured out of a throbbing, pulsing back area lit red like a bar. The music poured out around me the way smoke pours out thick and black from a raging house fire. Only it was cool in here. With a few tricks of lighting, she had transformed one of her living spaces into a pickup bar. She turned to look at me—still wearing the blue jeans miniskirt that showed off her thin legs and fine ass. I began to get turned on as I walked into the room and saw her there. She turned and looked at me, a totally transformed person. She waggled a finger for me to come closer. "Hi, Peter."

"Are you *O?*"

"I am *O,* and I want to prove to you that everything is different now."

"Yes?" I walked up and started to take her in my arms.

Her eyes had a glazed look, and her teeth showed a little bit in a grimace of animal tension. "I want you to @ me, Peter."

"Yes," I said, not sure how I could do this without first embracing her, kissing her, working my way up to it.

"I want you to take me." She got down, pulled my cock out, and started sucking it while twirling her hand around it. She looked up: "You're hard."

I shrugged and let her take me. I went with the flow. In the throbbing red lights and music, she had a bottle and two glasses on the counter. There was also some sort of strap-on dildo thing that puzzled me. I closed my eyes with pleasure as this newly released wild woman sucked my tube. "Peter, do you like this little dress?"

"Yes."

"I want you to pull it up and @ my ass." She stood and pulled on my dick. "Now."

I didn't know if I was ready yet, but she bent over a chair and lifted that little dress, and there was her asshole. Whatever was missing from my hard-on, it instantly returned to maximum tensile strength. She leaned over the back of that chair with her feet dangling by my ears as I got closer for a visual inspection. She was holding her ass cheeks apart with four red fingernails spayed on each hand, like landing lights directing a plane in. Her pussy was a pink hanging garden of labia under that. I put my finger in her oyster hole, which was wet, and licked her asshole. I couldn't help myself. Those cheeks were pale and perfect, and she held them open for me to get inside. "I am licking your asshole," I said.

"Yes!" she shouted hoarsely.

"I am rimming you."

"Yes!"

"And then I am going to @ you."

"Yes! Do it! Go on."

After licking her, I knelt behind her and shoved my train up her tunnel. She shouted hoarsely. Her hands flailed on the seat back as she steadied herself, then half unbuttoned, half tore her blouse off. No bra. My groin kept slapping hard against that soft little ass of hers. She reached behind and pulled me to her as I butt-@ed her and came. When she felt me coming, she yelled hoarsely and doubled over, which made it easier to get in and out of her. "@ the bacteria," she shouted, "get into my oyster. I want to feel that donkey dick inside of me. Go on! Do it!" So I got into the pink of her pussy and whaled away until a while later we both climaxed again.

The way to *O's* sexual switch was to pick her up. We did it a bunch more times. It was never again as weird as that night with Tiny and Onion. Mostly it was subtle, the way I liked things. I would walk in out of the cold, see her at a bar, work my way slowly over to her, maybe watch her dismiss one or two clumsy overtures (no jugglers, no giants), and be sure she was getting pre-orgasmic knowing her big bad baby boy was sidling closer for his wet spot. I would get close so it would look to onlookers (and they really did look on) that we were just exchanging pleasantries.

I was talking dirty to her. "Is your little pussy wet?" ("Oh yes.") "You are sitting there all prim and proper, Miss Goody Two-Shoes, but if I were that barstool I'll bet I would be smelling some oyster juice by now." ("Oh yes.") "I saw your tight little ass the minute I came in the door, and my cock got hard, so I had to come over and tell you that I have a wet spot in my shorts where I spewed a little thinking about you." ("Oh yes," she would murmur, "I have a soggy place in my panties that I want you to lick up later. Will you take me home in a while and @ me?") "Little lady, I am going to take you home to that bar and I am going to put you on the chair, because you are a bad little girl, and I am going to look at your asshole. I am going to touch your asshole. I am going to lick your asshole. I am going to @ you in the asshole." ("Oh yes, please.") "But I have a very large dick." ("Oh yes, I am sure that you do.") "I am going to fill your asshole up with my dick." (I think she had a little mini-orgasm right there, because she closed her eyes, gritted her teeth in taut cheeks and emitted a tiny mouse-like eek). "I'm going to pull that huge old dick right out of your asshole and shove it in your pink pussy hole." ("Oh yes. That's what I want.")

So it went. Dear little *O.* We played this game, and I got good at it. I had a talent for this kind of thing. Too bad a slightly younger man ages and stops being what a young older woman wants. It was good while it lasted. *O* was challenging, to say the least, and high-energy, but it was fun for a while. I think I tired of it before she did. I think she sensed it and wasn't about to waste another two years of her life on a fading thrill.

One night, I met her at a new bar (it was never the same place twice) and there she was talking to some handsome guy in a business suit. He had long dark hair, and was schmoozing closely with her. She looked delighted, transformed, and stroked his long brown hair. This time, she was not the one dumped.

I watched them leave the bar, arm in arm, and I never heard from her again. I didn't try to contact her. I hope they lived happily ever after.

The Story of P

I was in a local branch public library one blustery Fall afternoon, reading the epigrams of Martial in translation and testing my Latin between the translator's rendition and the original. I always felt a sense of awe when something written 2,000 years ago in a long ago and far away time and place became fresh again for modern eyes. In the midst of my concentration, I heard the cries of excited children, and heard a wondrously soothing voice.

My first glimpse of *P* was a noble, beautiful one. She was a dark-haired beauty, sitting regally among a roomful of children to whom she was about to read a story. She was the Queen of Story Hour, and the children huddled excitedly around her as she held up a large children's book. "Can anyone tell me what this is a picture of?" She pointed with a pale hand to a picture of several cartoon animals living in harmony in a garden.

"Lions! Tigers! Zebras!" the children cried, enumerating about half a dozen animals who were having a tea party. "That is right," *P* said in a careful, kindly voice with the crisp bite of authority in it (like when one bits into a fresh apple). "What are the animals doing?" She paused. "They are having a tea party."

The children laughed. I smiled, and *P* noticed me.

I saw the instant change, the camera flash deep in her green eyes, the interested lingering of her eyes on me even as her head, with its high full dark hairdo, already turned away. I smiled and caught her eye again a few times during the reading of her story.

When she was done, she stood and spoke with several of the children. I saw a pale, exotic woman of about 30, with Mediterranean features, pale olive skin, freckles the color of golden raisins but tiny, and that glossy dark hair done like a Greek helmet tilted back. She wore a loose dark denim dress with overalls-style top. Under that she wore black ballet tights. I saw that she was full-breasted and ripe in the hips and rear, and firm. I wandered over, holding my Loeb's Martial, and said something charming that set up a conversation.

She slipped easily into the conversation, and we soon established that she was a substitute teacher who volunteered to do story hour once a week. One of the children was her five year old son, whom she briefly introduced. He stayed with his dad, her ex, on certain days of the week. There were several afternoons when *P* was interested in having coffee, or going to a movie, or maybe having me along for company at the mall. Like most men, I hate shopping, so I became impatient, and she'd laugh and send me to the bookstore.

P was of mixed Italian and Brazilian extraction, with one of those wonderful Italian names that end in -ini and sound like something good to eat. She was 30, as I had guessed, and had been married several years to a fellow Italian-American who had dumped her for a blonde from the Midwest. *P's* father had been a businessman from stylish Milan who had moved to Rio and set up a chain of department stores. [P-senior] had married a German-Indio Brazilian model who had come starving down from Sao Paulo to find work in Rio de Janeiro and lucked out—on her first runway assignment at the department store, the owner had fallen in love with her and ended up marrying her for the rest of their lives.

They had sold their considerably holdings and moved to the United States, where *P's* father felt the business climate was healthier. He'd ended up losing his fortune in the stock market and retired as the manager of a small bank. *P* could speak English, Italian, and Portuguese. An only child, she had inherited enough money from her parents to be able to pay off a condo and live on a small monthly dividend. She worked partially because she had to, and partially because she wanted to live a purposeful life. Being careful with solid though meager resources, she was able to enjoy some leisure. Her ex was fairly good about paying child support and a small amount of alimony, so *P* and her child were pretty well set in the grander scheme of things.

P was still young, and her body smooth and firm. She wasn't exceptionally tall, nor would she ever be slender or skinny. Her face had that sharp, pale exotic form, and her eyes were a deep, crystal green. With her high, sculptured face, roundish cheeks and soft outlines, and dark, somewhat wanton mouth, she invited the poet in me to gaze deep and reach across the age difference. Like many Young older women, she had some gray already, but a simple rinse every month or so masked that. She seemed to have genes for good aging, and didn't show crows' feet or wrinkles yet.

One afternoon, I met her at the mall. It was maybe our fourth or fifth date. *P* had tested me and found me not to be a predator or otherwise distasteful. She had introduced me to a man and woman who taught school with her, and probably asked them their opinion of me. I must have gotten a passing grade from these teachers, because she kept seeing me. Of course she did not believe in crossing the line until around the fifth date or so—in short, a careful woman. From what kissing and petting we did, I knew she was very passionate. I felt full, firm breasts under her dresses, and smooth ripe thighs under bluntly rounded thighs. She had slightly larger ankles and slightly smaller feet, from what I saw of her, bare, under the loosely flowing dresses she liked to wear. From other glimpses I'd had, I saw that she liked colorful underpanties cut in that thong style below the waist elastic.

But these were fleeting glimpses, and I made quiet, patient suppositions from them. I learned much from observation, and of course whatever a man sees, the woman lets him see—there are no accidental glimpses in this world. What you see or glimpse under a woman's dress is revealed to you for a reason. Either she wants to tease you, or she wants to arouse your interest, or just wants to make you horny and punish you or keep you waiting until the pain becomes exquisite. If she pushes this agenda too far, she stands the risk of having you drift away.

On the big day, we met at the mall, as we liked to do, and walked arm in arm, window shopping. It was really nice for me to do this, and meant a lot. It was wonderful to pretend, even for an hour, that the gorgeous woman with her arm through mine really was mine. I was adrift in life, with little money and few prospects (my interest in academics good for conversation but not for finances). At some level, *P* sensed that I needed this perhaps more than I needed to get laid, and so she steered us onto the slow path. Whether she had another lover who was satisfying her, I will never know. I suspect not. She had plenty keeping her busy, and she spent a good part of her free time with me.

We had already done a lot of kissing and petting during our time up to then, and I had tasted the passion in her mouth, the sharp darting of her tongue, the way she moaned when I ran my hand down her waist. She controlled things pretty closely, and only allowed this when she drove me home. We'd sit outside the Maison Piano Music, in a shaded spot away from the street light, which was smothered in a tree crown, and there we would steam up the windows like a pair of high school kids. It was pretty neat, actually, to go slow and let the hunger build.

This day would be different. Everything would be different from now on. Like so many Summers balancing work, a (alternately horny and violent) ex, a small child, two sets of parents, and so forth, she had made certain slots of time for herself. Into those slots she put what she needed and wanted, and no ex or parents or other distraction was allowed. The only exception might be if her son was sick at home. Then she was off limits, though this only happened one time and I lost two days' time with her.

She had invited me up for a light dinner, which was a first. She had cleaned house in her condo, and everything sparkled. It was a pretty nice town home with three bedrooms upstairs, so it was roomy. It had a picture window overlooking a park near the University, and modern appliances. The Milanese flair for design must have come down through her genes, because the place had cohesion. She owned good, pricey things, and a lot of it was modern, abstract, sparse, with splashes of that hot Italian color: a red handle on a sleek brushed-steel kettle; a pair of gleaming black onyx candelabra; jade knobs on all the cupboards; blue stone napkin rings; a blue neon wall clock.

She had set a nice table with linen and silver, Japanese china (which sounds odd), and an electronic coffee maker that filled the cathedral ceiling with a fragrant hush. We started with a small drink in the kitchen. I volunteered to help, but she had me sit in the husband-chair with my feet up. She massaged my feet for a few minutes, kissed me, and left me to watch the news while she went into the kitchen to finish preparing dinner. We had a light, lovely meal (soup, salad, small teriyaki steaks with string beans and mashed potatoes) followed by a fairly rare, tartly sweet after dinner Eiswein. We cleaned up together, rested quietly for a bit (I let her invent all this; it was her show), and then took a walk by the nearby river park. I liked having her on my arm. She was very wifely as these things go. I would never admit such a thing, but she probably sensed that I liked it. There was an autumn hush in the air, and the Milky Way spread its river of stars over the emptying trees. I wanted to hold her, but she whispered: "Let's go back."

When we got to her home, she turned on romantic music created a soft background. She turned and opened her arms. I took her gently and kissed her. She closed her eyes, looking very pale, and said: "What do you like?"

Not entirely sure what to say, I looked quizzically down into her eyes.

She had kicked off her shoes, and stood looking up at me from a six inch disadvantage. It was a look I had not yet had from here, but one I had dreamed would come. Her green eyes were frank as they met my gaze, and her face turned up to me in an offer of surrender. She put her hands up on my shoulders and had this look—she was letting me look into her heart for the first time, and I saw that her cautions were now to the wind. "What do you like?"

"I like you."

She seemed pleased, and acknowledged by a faint, shadowy smile. "Be gentle."

"I promise."

"Do whatever you like."

I bent to kiss her, and found her surging up at me on tiptoes. There was a new hunger in her mouth that I had not yet been privy to. This was a wonderful moment, because she had held out and done all the right ceremonies (candles, dinner, saying no all this time), and I wanted it to be special in a sensual way. "What I like..."

"Yes?" She was a bit breathless, and eager. One hand stole around my neck and under the back of my head. "Yes?"

I was slowing it down now. "What I like," I said as I embraced her, as I rocked her gently in my arms and pulled her face against my chest, "what I have been wanting to do is to play with your dress—I mean, hold you, hold it, lift it, peek, drop it, run a finger up your leg, kiss your nipples."

"We have all night," she whispered. "I hope you are staying."

"I have eagerly awaited such an invitation."

"Tonight's the night." Her eyes were big, her mouth slightly open.

I sat down in a chrome-rimmed canvas chair and pulled her toward me. She was compliant. "Do what you like," she urged again.

I put my hands on the back of her legs. I almost didn't want to raise her dress, which I really wanted to do, for the sake of preserving and stretching this moment as long as possible. She put her arms around my ears and kissed me on the forehead. "Do with me whatever you like," she said.

I hugged her to me in her dress, inhaling the fragrance of her bush under the dress and under her panties. Oops, I now noticed that she was not wearing panties. I felt around her good full ass cheeks in vein for the telltale little elastic lines.

"I took them off," she said, resting her cheek on my head as if I were a work of art and she were creating me.

"I like when you tell me to do what I like," I said as I palmed her buttocks through the dress.

"We have all night, and you can take your time. Do whatever you want, and take me when you are ready."

I pulled her to me and stuck my nose against the material so I could smell her bush and feel my nose pressing into the hair. "I smell your bush."

She stroked my head, running her fingers like a comb through my rich, long waves. "Do you like it?"

"I like it very much. I think it likes me too."

She giggled in her solemnity. We were happening like a poem together, and neither of us wanted to chance its stately pace. "I think it likes you too."

I hugged her to me so that my arms were around her full bottom and my cheek rested on the hard curve of her abdomen.

She grew impatient, took my hand, and put it under her dress so that my fingers touched her hair. "Does it feel wet, Peter?"

I put my finger in the crease and she lifted one thigh slightly to help. My middle finger slipped into a wetness that felt like a slimy rock under water in a forest stream, only warm instead of chilly. She tightened her rich thighs around my hand and forearm. "It feels very, very wet," I said.

"It's waiting for you. Take your time and do whatever you want to me. Take me when you are ready. I can wait a long time, even if I am dripping wet."

"In a little while," I said, "I am going to lick your pussy." I wiggled my finger in her. "I am going to put my tongue here, rolled up like a drinking straw, and I am going to suck you like a cola bottle."

"I can make all the cola you want." She stroked my hair steadily, as if it too could become aroused.

"I am going to want a lot of juice," I said.

"I can make a lot of juice," she intoned.

I put my hands on her dress, outside, on her hips, and had her turn slowly. As she did, I started lifting that loose dress in which her shape had been enticingly moving around since that day in the library. Now, at last, I was getting under there.

"Do whatever you like."

"This is what I like." I lifted the dress slowly, fondling her ankles, her calves, her thighs. They looked pale. She was richly shaped and pale in this light, though her skin was really a very soft honey color. "I watched you and saw the shadows of you under your dress." When I had the dress up, and her two cheeks stared at me, I stopped her. I laid my cheek against one warm buttock, then turned my head and laid my other cheek on her other ass cheek.

"Do you like them?" she asked.

"Yes." I kissed each one.

Her hands pulled them apart an inch or two, and she bent forward. "Do you like it?"

I touched it with my finger, pushing lightly against the brown flower in its beige concavity. "I like it very much."

"Is it pretty?" ("Yes.") "Is it what you like?" ("Yes.") "When you are ready, you can play with it." ("Wonderful.") "You can do whatever you like." ("Thank you for being so generous.") "I am not only generous, I am hungry for you." ("I have been stretching it out and taking it slow to let you enjoy being hungry.") "Promise me that you will do what you like." ("I promise I will do what I like.") "That you will do everything. Everything you like." ("I promise, and I think you will like it too.") Her groan of anticipation was almost a sob, shuddering intake of breath as she massaged her breasts with her hands and rolled her head back. "I know I will."

I turned her around so that my face was in her bush. She held up her dress for me. I embraced her bare legs and pulled them toward me so that my mouth was in the mouth of her river delta. "Lift your dress high." She lifted it to just under her breasts. "Lift it higher. Take it off." She struggled with it for a moment, but I stood and helped her take it off. She puffed. "I am so hot—it's time I got naked. I am so hot for you."

"I wanted to stop and look at your titties."

"Oh, yes, here they are, waiting for you." She held them in her hands. They were full and a little limp, with big brown nipples. I kissed her navel—an innie—and then her titties—they were beige and had great almost sorrowfully shaped nipples the color of chestnuts. As she held her titties for me to bite, she moaned softly and her aureoles rose in a garden all around the nipple stems. "These are long nipples," I said. I sucked on them, licked them, pushed them this way and that with my tongue. They folded over and snapped back. She twirled each nipple between thumb and side of hand. "I'll make them longer for you. Watch." They became engorged and almost doubled in length.

She giggled. "They're like Tootsie Rolls, huh?"

"Oh yes. You know what?"

"What?" She suddenly felt an ardor and pulled my face to her and kissed me passionately. Her tongue invaded my mouth (the way she wanted me to do anything) and poked this way and that. "What?" she said, letting go. She held my cheeks in her palms and looked at my lips as if eager to kiss more.

"I didn't dare dream when I saw you, *P,* looking so beautiful and regal and elegant and magnificent in that library, that I would ever get under that dress and kiss everything you have under there."

"I saw you looking at me."

"Did you think I would get under your dress?"

"I wasn't sure I would let you. I didn't know what kind of guy you are, but now I know you're very nice. I wasn't sure you would turn me on so much. But I did look at the bulge in your pants."

"Did you want to touch it?"

"I wanted to suck it." She looked down shyly. Then she gave me that frank look again. "I'm almost ready to start exploring you while you explore me."

"I'm ready any time you are. What I was going to say was—do anything you want with me."

"Honest?"

"Yes."

She looked a bit squirmy as if she wasn't sure. Or maybe this wasn't the time yet. There are two points of realization in a love affair, as regards sex. The first is when the woman first opens the gate. The man comes in and looks at the flowers in her yard. Their conversation is conventional. The second point of discovery is when they exhaust their formalities, and their hunger overcomes their caution. Then he reveals to her, and she reveals to him, what really turns them on. The first element of discovery had come when she let me under her dress. Were we rushing it now to reach the point where she was going to reveal her closest secrets, her most intimate fantasies and desires, to me?

"You mean anything?" She had her palms on my nipples.

"Anything. That's our deal."

"Okay, well, I am so horny now that I want you to just @ me straight out, missionary, and then we'll rest a while. Maybe we'll try a few other things." I had been dribbling ejaculate without realizing it, until she pointed it out to me in her master bedroom upstairs. On the bed, while I lay on my back, she licked the head of my dick, while I caressed her thigh. Wasting no more time, she lay back and spread her knees. With her small, blunt fingers, she parted her labia and I crawled closer to the golden gate. She had an innie brownie. A layer of baby fat under hard skin made her pussy look like a girl's hairless slit, even as her Venus mound was a thicket of heavy hair. As her fingertips pulled apart the fleshy cleft, I saw small brown labia hidden in the valley, and deeper down, the pink cave my finger had earlier visited. She had brown freckles around the pee hole opening of her urethra, and a brownish clit under a tight little hood. I know it has been hard for you since we first kissed this evening. Now you get in there, quick. I want to feel you inside of me. Oh, look at the size of that thing. Come, here, Peter."

I was in, not a second too soon. Through the gate, which resisted for a second before opening wide, and into the tunnel I went. *P* let out one of those deeply, deeply affected moans again and pulled me toward her by my elbows, then by hands around my ribs. We wailed together, and she slapped my buttocks repeatedly, making me come even harder. This wasn't the night for the second revelation, but next time would do the trick.

We saw each other several times a week, and each time we enjoyed the long, slow buildup. She liked to tell me "Do whatever you like," and I loved telling her "I want to have you." We'd build up slowly. I always liked her to wear one of those loose dresses. She would ask me on the phone: "Want them on or off?" It was secret code for, did I want her to wear panties and a bra or not. I changed the answer regularly, to have the best of both worlds. Sometimes I liked to @ her as she wore her dress. Sometimes I liked to @ her as she wore both her dress and her panties, and at those times I liked to pull her panties bottom aside to slide my dong inside.

What came next now got me even more hot for her. After we made love, and lay resting, she got that silver dildo out. "I want you to warm this up by putting it in your mouth."

I shrugged and stuck the tip in my mouth. She watched me avidly, while putting a hand behind her. When I looked quizzical, she turned partially around so I could see she was putting her index finger in her butt hole. I didn't ask, because I figured out what she wanted, and she didn't explain. She took the dildo from me and rubbed a lot of petroleum jelly on it. She reached behind herself and started massaging the rim of her asshole. The silver tip had a vibrator in it, which sounded like a little buzzer.

She closed her eyes and rocked her body gently as she became aroused. I kissed her and pulled on the hem of her dress to make it ride up over her titties. While she was masturbating her asshole, I held her titties and kissed them. I sucked on her nipples and made her moan. By now she showed me, holding two fingers up, she had two fingers in there. She kissed me avidly on the mouth, and I couldn't resist—my cock was hard again and I slipped it into her oysterie. But she wouldn't let me stroke her hard. She had another plan in mind. She took her fingers out and put the dildo back in. Finally, she pulled my dick out of her, tossed the dildo aside, and turned around to show me her asshole. It was open and relaxed about a half inch or more. "It's nice and ready now," she said. "Slip inside me, honey."

Careful not to tear anything or hurt her, I slipped my head through and got my shaft into her rectum. Her sphincter was tight around my shaft. It took another three or four minutes, and generous amounts of petroleum jelly, to get that tight sphincter of hers loose around me. I @ed her long and slowly, going in and out while she encouraged me and fluttered her fingers over her clitoris. We came together with great timing.

Then I turned her over and put my tongue into her innie. I was after that little pickle that had pointed so insolently at me. She watched me while she kneaded her breasts. Her nipples were huge. I saw her glazed, aroused eyes staring down over her bush as I sucked on her pickle and pushed her thighs back.

Afterward, we lay quietly together in the lights that glowed in the park outside her condo window. During the night, she must have had a little dream. Her cry woke me, and I held her. She sighed with satisfaction. I slipped my penis into her asshole again, which was still packed with petroleum jelly, and I whacked away, in and out, while she reached behind her and held one of my buttocks. "That is very nice," she said. "Do me again in the morning, okay?"

In the morning I woke up with a hard-on. She had gotten up to pee but came back under the covers and fell back to sleep. I scooted down a bit, bent her over, and slipped into her wet vagina. Her oyster was still wet with pee, and her bush had pee on it like dew. "I didn't dab myself, on purpose," she whispered. "Do to me whatever you want."

The Story of Q and R

Q was a somewhat coarse but really majestic woman. She was an authority figure—a karate instructor, a nature hike leader, a professor of biology and ecology. She was the unreachable to the many who knew her, saw her in the news, on TV—and I more than reached her. There had been a husband, and then a boyfriend, and then just a gap in her life that she was filling with a new research project.

I was sitting on the patio outside the bookstore, reading Dickens of all things (Hard Times) when this nondescript female in purple sweats and a mismatched shawl came trundling up the walkway. She had a straw hat on, and sunglasses, and hurt my eyes to look at, so I dropped my sunglasses down and raised my copy of Dickens.

About ten minutes later, I heard a scraping sound. Someone had sat down at the table beside mine. I glanced over my book, and saw it was she. Before I could hide again, she swept hat off, and the sunglasses. She hung the shawl on the chair beside hers, and took off the purple top because the day was warming up. What emerged from under those layers of bundling was what one would call a handsome woman. She wasn't pretty in the accepted sense, but she had a strong, athletic looking face.

She had gray eyes like rain clouds in a sunny sky. She had a strong jaw line and a little rectangular chin and these little blue lips that were already, at 32, torn at the edges with sun wrinkles. Same with her eyes. She looked older than her age, and yet she was stunning. She caught me staring at her and winked. I nodded. She sipped her hot coffee and unfurled the day's newspaper. Out came a pair of horn-rimmed reading glasses.

As she read, she glanced up, and our eyes met. She smiled and quickly looked down again. I was interested, and I thought she was too. How right I was. She initiated the conversation. "Dickens," she said. "Love the man. That's one hellacious little heroine." I held up the book questioningly, and she nodded. "Sissy Jupe," she said, "a woman after my heart. The bold little girl who shows grown men right from wrong."

"A real heroine," I agreed. Our conversation meandered through its expected twists and turns, and I was beginning to admire the hard, athletic body under her dark blue T-shirt and those loose gray sweats. She resembled one of those sunburned vixens you saw with braids wrapped around their blond heads like crowns. They had climbed mountains and were now looking into the camera with chapped, reddened cheeks as they devoured bread and cheese. Their flower was the edelweiss. Their teeth were white as snow. Their thoughts were almost that pure, until you got to know them better.

Q, who would have brushed most men away like insects, had me follow her to her house in the suburbs. We made a pretense of wanting to find her Dickens books or something—the exact charade didn't matter. The fact was that we were interested in the comforts and adventures of one another's bodies. Then there was the matter of the roommate.

Q lived in an old ranch style house. I didn't have a car, so she drove and I sat in the passenger seat with the wind whipping through my hair. "You have nice hair," she said at one point. I thanked her. We spent an hour or two in her living room watching reruns of very old programs—The Twilight Zone, Gilligan's Island, Clutch Cargo. She plied me with beer, popcorn, pretzels, even a good ham and cheese sandwich on rye. I absorbed the atmosphere of almost boyish neglect and clutter, complete with wet suits and surf boards on the walls.

The roommate showed up. That was *R,* a tasty looking Eurasian mix of about 30, tall, with almond eyes and long glossy black hair. *R* had that same robust, chapped aura, and she wasn't going away. I began to think I was misreading the cues, and considered how long of a walk it might be to the nearest bus stop if I bailed out of there. All the while, I had been gauging the attractiveness of **Q's** athletic body with its full breasts and sturdy hips and thighs. This was a woman who could power a bike uphill or a luge sled downhill. This was the kind of woman whose thighs could crush your head with vise-like strength while you sucked at her clam.

Q and I had just begun to get cozy when **R** showed up. **Q** and I were on the couch, watching some ancient black and white romance with Cary Grant and somebody. I was following **Q's** lead as she brought me to her sexy place. Then this tall Eurasian walked in, greeted us as if there were nothing unusual about us both being under the same blanket on the couch with our popcorn and beer and movie. **Q** was a warm woman, a regular oven, a generator, and I was almost sweating, except that she had her hand on my cock under the blanket and a hungry look in her eyes. So now the tall Kyoto Krusher walks in and sits down on the love seat. I would have expected **Q** to recoil in modesty, but the hand on my cock kept cranking. Pretty soon, she was rubbing her palm under my balls. There was this hump in the blanket that kept moving up and down, but **R** appeared not to notice. "Cool movie," she said.

"Oh..." **Q** replied. "Yes." The first was a moan because I slipped my hand into her pants and found that she had an enormous clitoris that interested me and made my cock double in size instantly in her loving hand.

"Who's in it?" **R** asked while hoisting a palmful of popcorn over her lower lip and following that with a wash of beer from a glass mug.

Q could only reply by looking at **R** with her mouth open and a stricken look, as if she'd been hit by lightning. That was me, four fingers in her dripping wet vagina, hoisting moisture over her clitoris and rubbing it like a tiny dick.

"Don't know?" **R** said as she tossed another few kernels over her lower lip, and washed that down with suds. She was longer, thinner, smaller breasted than **Q,** and more graceful, less dikey.

Q had enough. She couldn't take anymore. Rising with the blanket wrapped around herself, she pulled me up. "Into bed."

R watched the movie obliviously as we wandered off into the back of the house. There, on a huge bed, *Q* stripped off the last of her clothing and lay under the sheets waiting for me to join her. I was naked in seconds, and eager to explore what she had there. First we kissed—passionately, and she was very good. She offered me first one breast, then the other, and I sucked on her big brown nipples. She was a brownie. Brownish lips, brown nipples the color of chocolate, brown oyster, brown asshole pucker.

I went down under the sheets while she pressed on my head, moaning, and I explored. What I was most intent on seeing was that clitoris, and I was not disappointed. What a wonder it was! I had the dear girl pull her knees back so I could enjoy the full expanse of her powerful buttocks and thighs. Her oyster sort of melted in its own juices as I stroked it with my tongue. I tasted something like mushrooms. I felt the ripples hit her, and heard her crying out softly, and knew she was on the first orgasm. At that moment, her little clitoral hood parted, and a tender grayish bud popped out. I rubbed my fingertip over her pee hole while licking that erupting mushroom, that kernel of her sexual pleasure.

She made a lot of noise, all of it dear to me and welcome as I sated the idleness of my hands by gently twisting her naked tits. Then she took over with both hands, massaging her tits with their brown nipples, while I pushed her thighs back against her stomach and got my tongue into the full pungent stew of her oyster. I marvel to this day, thinking of that gray, pinkish clitoris growing as my tongue lapped against it. It grew to the size of a very large peanut before dear *Q* collapsed in a shower of contractions and spasms and double over so that she landed hard on top of me. Big gentle girl, she apologized in her daze and confusion. I kissed her fluttering hand as it brushed over my head.

The other woman came in--*R,* who sat on the edge of the bed looking at us. Dear gentle *Q,* unreachable heroine of ecology and saving the world, was apologetic again, speaking as if *R* was not there. "We aren't gay or anything. My friend and I enjoy watching each other get @ed, if that's okay with you."

I was more than eager to help out, and told them so in a casual manner that suggested I did this every day. I asked them which one would like to go first, and then answered my own question. "*Q,* you already came hard, so why not let me play with *R* so she can catch up with us." They agreed to this, and so *R* took off all her clothes and slid underneath me while *Q* curled up to watch. I wasn't going to let it be that simple. "Look at her pussy," I told *R.* "Look at her clitoris. Isn't that little lady a marvel?" *R* nodded as she looked to one side, at *Q's* oyster.

As I played with *R,* I kept a finger on *Q's* marvelous clit. With my fingertip, I massaged the soft flesh around it to keep it as upright and protruding as possible. *Q* helped by bringing her middle finger up from under her ass, to thrust it in her oyster. She reached her other arm down her belly, and inserting that @-finger in her oyster from above, so that both hands worked wetly and noisily.

R's oyster was nice, in that she had a little tiny kernel that grew hard as stone in the moment before orgasm, and slight labial sails, nothing remarkable. I didn't buy the not-gay thing. I suspected that one or both were bisexual but had no idea how that worked. If anything, I suspected *R* of being bi, although *Q* was probably a good candidate. Who cares about labels? I don't. I'll never know, and it doesn't matter. I think a lot of confused people are really bisexual and don't know it. I @ed them each in turn, and they each came—noisily, and wetly. *Q* licked her Asian partner's oyster while holding my hard, erect dick as I knelt beside them. I got them each to lick the other's oyster, and they each had a huge climax. The Asian woman had been at *Q's* great clitoris before, and they had not been entirely honest with me. I note this with humor, because

I don't expect people to be honest with strangers about their most private and intimate passions. People often aren't honest with themselves about their innermost desires. *Q* sat back and let *R* tongue her swollen peanut, while rubbing the Asian's hair with her rough and horny hand and squeezing herself on the nipples and fluttering her eyelids in pleasure. *Q* readily took my offered cock in her mouth and deep-throated it while the other woman lipped *Q's* clitoris. When *Q* dropped me off at the Piano Music house late that night, I climbed weakly up to my floor, entered my gray little cell there, and slept a long exhausted time.

The Story of S (An Introspection)

As with *I*, *S* is not one woman but a collection of experiences. So many of these Summers were good (some not so good) to be with, that they collectively deserve some mention in this book. In this chapter I will summarize some of the glorious hours they presented to me. I should have mentioned that, by now, I had gone from owning one pair of jeans and one shirt to owning a collection of designer clothing. This came about because one of the hallmarks of the Summer relationship is that the young older woman invariably feels she must dress her younger guy. It's part of the nurturing syndrome. It's not about mothering at all, I'm sure, a type of relationship that would have repelled me. It's about being seen in public. The Summer is, collectively, a giver and a taker, a user or a toy, a player or an instrument. She has a galaxy of reasons to be in a relationship with her slightly younger man (or Spring), but almost invariably she will initially take him to a department store (depending on her finances) and treat herself to having a well-dressed stud muffin.

Thus, by this point in the story, her younger guy is no longer a kind of dazed hippie wandering around in a single torn suite of casual clothing (preppified by wearing a sports coat with elbow patches, like the graduate student that he is in theory). He has become conscious of his appearance and is striving toward the classier look. He is becoming sleeker, less gaunt, and increasingly invisible as a poor mouse to be put in her pocket and taken home for nurture.

Gradually, as I built up credits on my Master's, and started seeing more prestigious work, I became less noticeable to the sort of woman with whom I had been mutually attuned and a magnet. For many Summers, the age difference remained a magnet. Don't think for a moment that women do not make trophies of men. It is a delusion to claim otherwise.

I have been the trophy—I know. On the less pleasant side, I was occasionally used as a weapon to instill jealousy. On one occasion I found myself running down a snowy street in my bare feet to thump the head of an ex-husband whom I had been manipulated into hating; luckily for me, and probably him, he got away.

Most of the time, when she is on your arm in a public place, glowing and beaming, pressing herself against you, she is having some much deserved and innocent fun. Maybe she is divorced and full of anger, bitterness, loneliness. Maybe, as in one or two cases, she is a young widow—whose final glimpse of her handsome 30-something husband was as he manages his sailboat in a shallow sea near shore, and another boat clips him, the tall sail moving over him with horrific slowness and grace like a white angel. I have gazed into that abyss with her, lain on her slender ship, tacked through the breakwaters of our mutual passion. Life goes on. We know what lies beneath.

For example, *S1* was a bird more gamey than suited me, and I felt an odd foreboding from the first. *S1* was a woman in her early 30s who had never been slender, but was still formidably sexy in a robust way. It was as if her baby fat had gone hard. She was as tall as I, had a good figure, strong in a muscular way without being athletic. We met during the hot cocoa and glogg hour after skiing (I don't ski, but I enjoyed hanging out at the lodge, not the same one in Vermont mentioned earlier, but closer to home). She looked like a sturdy Finn, this *S1*, as she tromped in on her boots, in her black ski pants, and in her white sweater with red reindeer. She was aglow from her exertions, and the cold had made her cheeks and nose red. Her short blonde hair was awry as if someone had ruffled it; she had ski-cap-hair.

Putting her skis aside, she noticed me and beamed this huge smile that was the signal—on first eye contact—that she was interested in me. She was very interested, and within a short time she and I sat by the big fireplace with our drinks. She pressed close to me, and soon had her hand resting on the inside of my thigh. What did we talk about? As is often the case in such encounters, nothing memorable. She was an insurance underwriter, made good money, and lived in a stone house with a three-car garage and a 300 foot driveway full of snow and ice. I can't even remember if I ended up at her place that night or the next. I remember her driving in this white Mercedes whose interior was all white leather and leather cowgirl trim. She was into Country, and I sat amid twanging guitar music and Dixie drawlin' from deep, whiskey-scoured throats the whole way to her Connecticut estate. She took me into this twelve-room marvel, whose den was as big as my single room at the Maison Piano Music.

She poured me a foofy drink (something brandy and chocolate with artificial nut flavoring that lingered on the back of the palate like one of the early, detergent diet drinks). We went into a large marble bathroom, where she undressed me and knelt before me amid the gleaming tiles and warm air, and thoroughly blowjobbed me.

She cupped my nuts, held them on her hands as if she had a tray of sacred objects, while her mouth cranked on me like a torque wrench. She was very skilled, and I must have squirted a bit, because she looked up at me, beaming, with semen on her lips, and then went at it all the stronger. When she rose, we stood kissing for a short while, and I touched her long, flat breasts and explored in the drizzle of her rainforest.

I remember encountering a good-sized 'little girl' down there peeking out from its hood. She had me get into a warm, bubbling Jacuzzi, Frenched me for another minute, and told me, with this strange air of excitement that tightened her voice box and made her feel trembly to my touch: "I'm going to get ready. I'll call you, and you come in."

"Okay." It was more of an okay with foreboding.

Ten minutes elapsed, while I lay with my eyes closed and enjoyed the water. My pecker, who is usually dumber than I but this time may have known something I didn't, was utterly limp.

When he call came ("Peter, darling, come in now!") I dried myself off, wrapped a huge towel around myself that covered me like a Masai cloak, and stepped into the vastness of her bedroom. It was dark in there, and I heard movement. "Come in, darling," she said.

I saw something moving on the bed there in the dark, and hesitated.

The room was comfortably warm as a heater hissed soothingly nearby. A faint light fell in from the moon in a barren tree outside, and I saw *S1* on the bed with her legs up. A young man in white jockey shorts and a wool ski cap was on her knees banging her away. I saw the chub and muscle on the guy's buttocks and back, and the weight-trained sausages of his biceps and triceps.

"Come on, Peter," she said, "let me take you in my mouth." At the same time, a door opened to my right. From one of the plethora of bathrooms in her house came another young athlete, and he winked at me while raising his hands to pinch his nipples at me.

I didn't scream. I just started running. I don't know if anyone ran after me. It was the fastest I have ever run in my life. I scooped up my clothes and somehow jumped into them while running—down the stairs, through her living room, and into the front hallway.

On the cold slate floor, I realized I had taken my shoes off. Screw the socks. I grabbed my shoes, which sat in a collection of hers and I don't know how many men's pairs, and ran out the door without tying them. Laces flapping, I ran out into the freezing driveway. My hair was wet and instantly snapped into ice atop my head. I knew I was at least a mile from the nearest house and would die out there. I felt the icy cold squeeze me like a giant fist.

This was life and death. I turned, ran into the vestibule, found her car keys, and raced outside. I thought of locking the door and breaking the key off in the lock to slow my pursuers, but was shaking so badly that the keys rattled and I couldn't manage—it would have required my eyes focusing, which at the moment they couldn't. I stole her car. It was that simple. I knew her studs must own some of the other cars in the driveway, so it's not like I left them marooned.

I flew out of there backwards, slid on the ice, almost went into a ditch on the country road below, and hauled ass toward the edge of town. As I drove along, in that white leather interior full of cowgirl fringe and effects, the music loudly cut in. Whiskey voices in chorus, slide guitars, bemoaned the tragic loss of an unfaithful lover who 'tried on a pair o' boots too many' and 'left me a broken and down like an old pair o' leathers on that long, lonely bayou road.' @! This was no bayou. It was ten below, and this was New England. That broad had no business... oh well. All's well that ends well. I parked her car at a restaurant, turned in the keys as lost at the hostess desk, and got on the last bus into the city.

Not all encounters were even funny. There was *S2* (let's call her) who seemed slightly dotty from the start, though she was slender and dark-haired (with a lot of white streaks that I weren't sure came from age or the hair dresser). She was a kissing fury when I met her in the park, as she was walking her dog and I was out jogging on a mild spring afternoon under the great university's neo-Gothic spires. With carillon bells tinkling in the air, she and I and the frisky Irish Setter romped happily. She took me to dinner in a little steak and ale pub. We went to a movie, and off to her apartment downtown. I smelled the dog poop even as we went up the stairs. She wasn't a good dog owner, but that wasn't the worst of it. The scariest part was soon after we had gotten into bed, and I was just starting to enjoy the spread of her legs and the tilt of her purplish oyster, when she called the dog in and it ran right toward that oyster from long experience...well, I was on my way down the stairs with my shirt in one hand and my shoes in the other, while pulling my pants up.

S3 represents a formation of women who took me home in order to bridge the gap between their previous bitter marriage and the next bitter marriage. I caught on early— when the woman has a cutting tongue, and is full of anger, and obviously hates men, I back away as quickly as my heel propel me. I was naïve the first time, enjoying a pleasant first visit, just getting ready to woo this woman, when she started arguing with me.

I had no idea why she was picking on me, and tried to reason with her, but in fifteen minutes she had reached the point of screaming at me.

That was when I realized she called me Scott, and I already knew Scott was her ex. I reached for my clothes, and she hit me across the face so that my cheek bled where it had cut my tooth. Then she started sobbing and sat down in a chair and begged me to forgive her. She was loudly crying when I left. I went from confused to angry to sick to my stomach and let myself out.

I was half a block away when I heard her wailing and heard her feet on the sidewalk. She was actually running after me. "I'm sorry, Peter. Please forgive me." Yeah. Sorry too. I hid in a bush until she was past, then stood by a wooden fence and vomited my dinner out. Finally, I ran two or three city blocks and caught a bus home.

S4, therefore, came as one of the nicer surprises. She was the girl next door. Never mind that it was during a chilly time of year—she warmed me. Here was this straight-forward girl who could have been 18 or 20 but was 32. She wore a ski parka and a wool cap over her straight, thin ash-blonde hair. She had light blue eyes in an almost gamine, squarish soft face with those incipient wrinkles in her laugh lines, just faintly there. The crows' feet around her eyes could just as well have been the smile lines or laugh lines of a much younger woman. She was uncomplicated, thank God. Just a sweet, pleasant companion who asked little and sought to please.

Art galleries and museums she enjoyed, especially when I explained everything to her. She was a high school grad with a year of college, working as a secretary for the university and thinking of going to school to become a dental assistant. *S3* had a little apartment within the sound of the university carillon, in a street of rambling, multi-story Victorian houses hidden behind great tree crowns.

She could have been a great erotic chapter in this erotic memoir, but she had absolutely no imagination. She liked to @, but just once at sort of the peak of a date. There was almost this schedule: meet, eat, movie, apartment. The latter subdivided into: drink a beer while watching a funny program, start petting and end up hot and bothered, move to the bedroom and pet a little more, then @ in the missionary position, and finally wind down.

It wasn't all that cut and dried. Some evenings she was hornier than others. Sometimes we went several rounds. She'd let me bang her from behind, or she would blow me, or I would eat her out. There were no quickies, no night @s, no morning @s. Everything was pastel and vanilla and pleasant and sweet.

She was beautiful to be with. Men turned to look. I felt she was a trophy, yes. I moved on to someone else, and I saw her a week later arm in arm with a short man with a big head of frizzy brown hair. He wore a suit and white shirt and bowtie, and was obviously a professor she had bagged. He looked proud, she was a trophy, and she pretended not to recognize me. I was happy for both of them.

I should mention *S5*, who also tripped some hidden alarm bells. Everything seemed kosher on the surface, and I didn't listen to the faint voice of unease. *S5* seemed a bit too facile for what she was—a straight-laced Puritan housewife divorced from a wealthy minister of some fundamentalist church. They were very wealthy, and appeared at all the right sorts of fund raisers, Christmas choirs, and what have you. In my naïveté, I never questioned that they were seen together in public as husband and wife, and that he later ran for mayor and nearly won, and for years has exerted huge behind the scenes financial and political influence at the state house.

What attracted me about *S4* were her own contradictions: she felt she had to be so pseudo-religious, so chaste and controlled and self-righteous, yet the more that demon poked her with pitchforks, the more Faunus and Bacchus and Eros laughed inside of her and nudged her with their horns.

She was a robust mare, a jock's dream, a Viking of a woman with coppery red hair that fell over her pale shoulders, and a full body with big ripe melon breasts and nipples on them like little red apples. She had the face of a cheerleader who has grown thick in the cheeks, but was still pretty with a small nose and pink cheeks. Her ex, whom I had seen on local news on TV, was an older, white-haired man with glasses and a reedy voice that suggested low testosterone levels. She wore bright, flashy dresses, while he always wore his trademark dark rumpled suit and spoke in a light, sanctimonious tone the way people who write shitty poetry read it aloud in a high, singsong voice. There was no way I pass up the opportunity to bite those apples, and to wrestle with that big woman in bed, and suck on the might of her genital florage.

When I @ed her oyster from behind, and she knelt facing away from me on the bed, I had to stand on the wooden sideboard and hang on to an ass the size of a motorcycle. Everything about this woman was abundant, overflowing, rich—even her throaty voice and the copious pussy cider she cranked out. One of her favorite things was to have me stand over her while she turned her face up to suck my balls while she massaged her breasts with one hand and rubbed herself to climax with the other. She took me in every one of her orifices and climaxed with equal sonority. She had me stand before her while she lay back and walked her heels up my body so her heavy calves lay against my shoulders.

With the help of a few tactically placed cushions, she got her oyster high enough for me to @ her, and @ I did, whacking my abdomen noisily against her full thighs while she sobbed with passion. I galloped on her. I yelled with my own passion. It was good.

Then her husband coughed behind the one-way mirror.

I got it.

I got it in an instant.

I wasn't going to let anyone take from me the massive orgasm building up at that moment. She faltered, but I whanged on. I was a pile driver, doubling her over backward. She shrieked as I piled on, bounced on her, @ed her in that huge brimming wet vat against whose panoramic vastness even my thick dick was a mere steel toothpick (I exaggerate a bit, but in mid-orgasm my exploding brain saw her as a kind of earth mother, cosmic bang, betrayer, greedy oyster, false oyster, yet passionate she-bear into whose cave I had strayed). When I finished, and we had come together, I rolled her onto her knees and gave her just a few more strokes to let the engine cool down a bit. I stroked her buttocks and said I was going to the bathroom, and I'd be right back. Instead, I grabbed my clothes and ran through their house. I dressed along the way, put my shoes on one hop at a time as I sped away to the nearest bus stop.

Now a wiser man, I occasionally saw her around town with other studs (very discreet; of course I knew) and a few young women who might be church vestals or bacchantes, I had no idea. They came and went at that big white house of purity on, let's call it Cherry Lane, while she and her husband renewed their 20th wedding vows and donated money for creationism and other fringe causes. I still don't know whether to laugh or cry at the human condition. I do know that I got out of there with the benefit of that one last huge orgasm, which is built on the impossible tension between religious zeal and the lure of forbidden fruit, which are like fire and gasoline to one another. Avoid either, and you don't get singed. Avoid both, and you can have a peaceful life. Sorry, banging such a scriptural horse makes a person want to spout aphorisms and conceits.

So you see, gentle reader, whether male or female—no two love stories are ever the same. There may be similarities, but each has its own unique licks and grace notes. I was a drifting leaf, and blew against many a tree. Stay true to a loving partner, and count your blessings that you don't know all that goes on in other bedrooms. Don't be jealous of the sexual adventurer. With all such medieval woodcut advice behind, I can only say once again that (borrowing the words of Thomas Wolfe in reflecting on his own youthful drinking partnerships): "We were young and drunk and twenty/And could never die!"

When I was not coupling with my Summers or chasing younger tail, or working ridiculous jobs or pursuing esoteric researches, I was out carousing and drinking...as in the medieval drinking song *Gaudeamus igitur ("Let us therefore rejoice")*:

*Gaudeamus igitur Juvenes
dum sumus Post jucundum
juventutem Post molestam
senectutem Nos habebit humus.
Ubi sunt qui ante nos In mundo
fuere? Vadite ad superos Transite
in inferos Hos si vis videre
Vita nostra brevis est Brevi
finietur. Venit mors velociter
Rapit nos atrociter Nemini
Parcetur
Vivat academia Vivant professores
Vivat membrum quodlibet Vivat
membra quaelibet Semper sint in
flore.
Vivant omnes virgines Faciles, formosae. Vivant et mulieres
Tenerae amabiles Bonae laboriosae.*

Which translates as:

Let us therefore rejoice
While we are young. After a
pleasant youth After a
troubled old age The soil will have us.
Where are they who before
us were in the world? Go to
heaven Go to hell If you want
to see them.
Our life is brief shortly to be
finished. Death speeds
toward us Tears us away in
its claws. Nobody can escape.
Long live the university! Long live
the professors! Long live each
male student! Long live each
female student! May they ever
stay in bloom!
Long live all young virgins their

easy grace, so comely! Hurray
also for mature women, tender
lovers who work so hard to please us.

There it is, in the fifth stanza of this thousand-year-old student drinking song, in a supposedly dead language, this great universal truth—the reference to Summers—and, by implication, their Springs (there are two more stanzas, but they do not concern us here). This song was howled and growled by drunken Springs and would-be Springs for many centuries. They banged their beer mugs on wooden benches in university taverns across Europe from the age of Crusades until well into the modern era, at Victorian Oxford and Cambridge, and certainly pre-World War II Yale and Harvard, Stanford and Berkeley, to name just a few—as long as Latin was taught and the Classical world remained cherished and rediscovered—for in the distant past and its charms I would eventually find my niche in life and become a portly professor unnoticed by any woman of the age whose women used to ravish and lavish me long ago. That is the reason for this book—celebration, monument, remembrance, closure.

The Story of T and U

I was once in a shopping mall in town, in the early afternoon of a chilly but dry winter day. I was looking for a small gift for an aunt who sometimes treated me to a hot meal. While I was in a jewelry store, an older woman in her early 30s kept glancing toward me. I ignored her at first, noticing that she was with another woman about the same age. They had that ripe, domesticated look of wives and mothers. They were bundled in expensive clothes and wore fur hats. One was a blonde with straight hair cut in a flouncy page boy. She had bright blue eyes and a pink lipsticky mouth curved in a bemused near-smile. The first one was dark-haired and dark-eyed. Her mouth was small and hungry, pursed in what I first took to be disapproval but later found was disappointment. Her eyes had a deep, dark greenness, a jungle spark, just an ember from a fire that had been let go and was near going out. They looked expensive and pampered. Some of their many paper shopping bags held clothes they had bought for themselves, while a few contained clothing and toys for little children. They did not seem to have bought gifts for the men in their lives.

I gradually began to pay less attention to the small gold charms in the display case before me, and started to listen to their whispered conversation. I caught only phrases and snatches, but it was enough to build a picture.

"I can't get him to spend an afternoon with the kids, much less me..." said the brunette. It became clear that she was the slightly older and more experienced.

"I feel like I don't exist anymore," said the blonde. "It's not right."

"You just can't get relief. I know the feeling. I think sometimes I am going to explode," said the brunette. "We do have needs."

"Oh, I know," said the blonde. She looked at the other with pleading eyes. "Is it so wrong to...?" "To want to be held? To hold someone? No, it's perfectly all right," said the brunette. "When you feel alone..."

"I just touch myself sometimes and don't know if I should start crying..."

The brunette patted the other's shoulder. "Not crying, honey. Life is too short for that."

I sighed deeply and resumed my search for just the right charm bracelet. When I looked up, the two women had left the store. I inhaled the rich scents of their passing—leather from expensive gloves and handbags, perfume filled with mystery and promise, even a dash of alkaline something that told me they'd had their hair done that morning. They were trapped in privileged lives, obligated to children they loved and men they still bedded with affection when asked for a quick @ between football and poker night. In my idealism and naiveté, I felt repelled by their dilemma.

I noticed them two or three times as I cruised the mall for my gift. Each time, I could swear—or was I nuts?—that green-eyes glanced in my direction. I saw my reflection in a store window—tall, dark-haired, with a gaunt face under thick wavy flying dark hair—and I saw green-eyes staring after me as if I must be good to eat. Both women were very attractive. The money would not marry anyone who wasn't. I considered making a pass, though I didn't quite have the nerve, not with two of them together.

I turned around, thinking to either walk away or contemplate the possibility of reaching out to that yearning in the older woman's eyes. Green-eyes—or T—saw me looking at her, caught the moment of hesitation in my eyes, and raised a gloved hand for me to wait. She spoke aside with Blondie for a moment. Blondie brightened, nodded, smiled with those sweet pink lips, and cast a mischievous glance in my direction. I saw mischief in her blue eyes, but it was the kind that says 'not me, not this time, but I'll watch you to see how it's done,' as if she'd never flirted before. She probably was a terrible flirt, but not after marriage. Not yet, anyway. And not today.

Green-eyes left her shopping bags with Blondie—or U— who stood guard over their purchases while pretending to be looking at the wares in a toy store for small children. I saw her looking at us in the reflection of the toy store window. Green-eyes had her hands in the pockets of her coat and looked older than her years, which was pretty old for me, as she strode toward me. She looked domesticated, pragmatic, scary in her courage. She was far prettier than I had realized, when she swept her fur hat off and touched her stiffly manufactured curls with long pale fingers. What a pick-up line she had. Walking directly up to me so I could see the microscopic wrinkles around her lips and the rouge lipstick nestling in them, she said: "Excuse me, I am wondering if you know me."

"I am wondering the same thing," I said.

"You are so beautiful," she said. She had a really mellow, full voice. It was almost husky. If she were a perfume, she would be musk. The perfume that faintly emanated from her was dark and ripe, as if it was cooking in the secret spaces like under her arms, or under the strap of her underpants, or in the swamp of her crotch. "I have very little time, and I would like to just...talk with you."

"I would enjoy that."

She looked a bit dazed at her own audacity and success. "Just to talk, nothing more."

"Of course. I'll be fascinated to talk with you."

"Good. Then I can tell my girlfriend to catch a cab and take my bags with her."

"That's fine. I don't have a car to take you home later."

She looked horrified at the prospect of even thinking such a thing. "That won't be necessary. I have a car here in the mall garage." She turned and walked away. She and Blondie had an excited conversation. Blondie went "oh!" and held her fingers to her mouth and jumped up and down a bit. Then, glancing at me through the very corners of the corners of her eyeballs, and stifling an incredulous laugh, Blondie loaded all the bags into her hands so she looked like a baggage tree, and staggered away toward the still-daylight exit hall, beyond which I could see the line of yellow and blue taxis.

T walked toward me with her hands in her pockets, hardened like a criminal—a woman who knew what she wanted, how far she wanted to go, and where she wanted to take it. "You probably get someone like me once in a while," she said as we walked through the throngs side by side. "How old are you?" I told her. "You're a boy, but so handsome, so beautiful. Do you feel funny having an older woman flirt with you?"

"How old are you?" I asked, and she shook her head. Thirty-five at most, I guessed, but I managed later to learn she was just a mature looking 32. She continued: "I had an affair last year. It ended badly. I was glad to be free of him. My husband never found out. I decided never to have another affair, and to just take cold showers."

"Doesn't your husband take care of you?" I asked. I had visions of a berserker chasing me with a cleaver, and was being very cautious.

"My husband is a very wealthy man and he's usually gone on business. I know he has women everywhere he goes, but as long as he doesn't bring them or anything they may have home, I don't say anything. He is—kind. He is just—empty." She walked in silence for a minute or two. "I didn't ask for your company to complain. I wanted to enjoy a few carefree hours with you. In case you are wondering, my friend and I live two hours from here in another city, and I don't expect anyone here will recognize me." She laughed for the first time—a husky, tart laugh—and said: "If anyone does see me and comment, I'll say you are a younger cousin." She took me to a pastry place that smelled of fresh coffee, whipped cream, and candied fruit. There, we sipped black espresso with orange peel. She offered to buy me something sweet, but I thanked her and declined. "No wonder you are so thin," she said. "You don't eat sweets. You make a woman want to feed you."

"I have an aunt who will be doing that in the next day or two. I came to the mall looking for a gift."

"How sweet." In the process of our coffee and subsequent wanderings, she asked a lot of questions and got to know all there was about me. She was beginning to warm to me, and I to her. She was doing this thing women do—testing me. She had me go here and there with her, even pretending to be lost in a big department store and ending up alone together in a back stairwell amid dust and cardboard boxes. Anything to offer me opportunities to grab her, scare her, show what a cad I might be. I was congenial and well-intentioned, and would never think of acting offensively. I offered my arm, and she took it, as we made our way back to the main shopping floors. By now, she pressed against me. I felt her trembling, and asked: "Are you okay?" She looked at me shivering as if she were cold. Her lips were slightly blue. "I'm okay," she said in a still, soft voice. "Are you?"

I shrugged. "Sure. I'm fine. I am thinking I should hold you. You look kind of lost. Or cold."

"Not here." She tightened her grip on my arm and towed me along. I had known for some time where this was going—not exactly, but in a general manner—and I went with the program. We took an elevator that smelled of fresh linen and other choice goods. We rode upward and emerged on the topmost floor of a parking garage. She had a sleek new forest green Jaguar with beige leather interior. The car beeped as she rattled her keys. "You sure you don't mind?"

"I'm fine. Just don't abduct me or anything."

She laughed. "You silly boy." We climbed in. The car smelled of leather and expensive carpets and, well, money. It started up with a muffled roar. Lights popped on (like, in the carpeting for example) and hidden fans began to whisper as lukewarm air poured in with a hint of machine oil. She backed the car out, and I got my first glimpse of a pair of strong tennis legs as her coat parted and her black skirt rode up to

mid-thigh. Out of habit, she demurely covered herself up.
"We have a place here in town. It's something wealthy people
like my husband do. It's called a pied-a-terre, a foot on the
ground."

"Wow. What does he do?"

"He," she said, carefully weighing how much to reveal,
"is a lawyer and an import/export entrepreneur. He is from a
very wealthy Armenian family. They are very successful."

"And you?"

"I am his prize Italian-German wife." She uttered that
deep laugh again. It was fraught with bitterness and self-pity,
which I didn't much like. "I am the trophy bitch, the saint on a
pedestal. I cannot have an impure thought." She handled the
wheel deftly with strong gloved hands as we bobbed and
weaved through traffic. The sunlight was just beginning to
fade a bit. Street lights began to flicker on in long parallel
rows as we left the center of town for a section of stately old
brick houses clustered around the edges of the great
university. It was where I would have expected a wealthy
woman to drive.

"And your friend?"

"Same thing, only her owner is a wealthy Arab from
Lebanon. Much older than her."

"Why do you marry guys like that?"

She laughed. "I don't know. Money. Comfort. It's a
decision not everyone regrets. I don't regret it much, except
that I never get any affection. Men like that don't marry
women for love or even sex. They get all the sex they want
from mistresses and prostitutes."

"This is America," I said softly, thinking of all those
ideals.

"This is life," she said.

"So your friend—?"

She put a leather fingertip on my lips. "Sshh!" We were
still as she wheeled the car into a driveway, down a ramp, and
into an underground three-car garage whose door opened and
shut at a command from a gadget in the Jaguar's sun visor.

She pulled the parking brake with a loud grinding noise that echoed in the bare concrete garage. There was very little in this place, and the floor had almost no telltale oil stains that spoke of frequent use. "We don't come here much," she said. "Mostly it's for his cousins when they come here from Manhattan or Boston or Montreal."

"Any chance of them showing up today?" She laughed. "No. They have to arrange weeks in advance. Don't worry."

I followed her up the stairs to a little lobby with mirror walls and a butterscotch marble floor. There, we took an elevator lined with velvet up several floors. We emerged in a penthouse apartment that glowed indigo with that last fading light of day. "Wow," I said, walking from picture window to picture window on thickly carpeted floors. She put down her purse and jangling keys.

She peeled off her coat, revealing a whipcrack body in a short black dress. She was small-breasted, thin—about 5' 6" when she slipped her high heels off. Padding around in nylon-stocking feet and legs, she flicked on indirect lights in a kitchen of shadows from which I had glimpses of dark marble counters, glass cabinets with interior lighting and stainless steel edges, and ultra-modern everything from can openers to wine bottle opener.

The décor of the place in general was ultra-modern, with bare smooth concrete walls almost like marble or dark glass, and long abstract wall hangings. Lots of little touches, like garnet and olive stained glass shooting slot windows in the thick walls, and fresh flowers on the sills. The fresh flowers and juice should have tipped me off.

She poured us each a heavy glass tumbler of fresh orange juice. "Here, this will freshen you up."

It did. The O.J. was fresh and cool, and quenched a burning thirst I had barely known I had. "Come sit with me," she said and plopped in a sitting area under a sun roof. The sitting area was composed of four blue corduroy chairs with chrome piping, flanked by two long couches of the same material and design, centered on a thick, smoky-glass coffee table.

She sat opposite me with one stocking foot up on the end of her couch. I sat in a chair hear her head, holding my juice. "No lights," I observed. Only the distant kitchen light and the starlight above illumined us.

"We have almost a full moon," she said waving her arm toward the bright citrine disk high up in a sky that was turning from dark blue to jet black. Like the moon, her forehead glistened with reflected and re-reflected sunlight (if one thought of it). Her facial features underwent a metamorphosis from a subdued, domesticated housewife to a fierce night predator. The weird light played odd tricks like that, and my own hands looked like they'd been dipped in that liquid green radium used to paint numbers on watch dials. I had a pleasantly spooky, expectant feeling in my gut.

She rose and went to a liquor cabinet. "Would you like a drink?" "Sure, something light."

She poured us each a tiny, long-stemmed glass of white crème de menthe in which an ice cube floated. "Cheers." We clinked glasses. She stood before me like a high school girl. "Do you like me?"

I took a sip and set the glass aside. "Yes." I leaned forward and put my hands on the sharpness of her hips.

"If this works out," she said, "I can see you again. Not often, but maybe once a month. Never call my house."

"You call me. I'll be totally discreet."

"Bring your drink." She offered her hand, and towed me across the room, through a long dark corridor, and to a huge bedroom at the other end of the floor. Across the shadowy hall was a bathroom. She reached in to flick on a light. "Gotta go?"

"Thanks." I did. I whizzed, flushed, and stepped outside. She was waiting to take her turn. As she stepped past me in that little black dress that made her look half her age, she pointed pertly across the hall. "Don't go in yet."

I caught a glimpse of the bedroom opposite. I saw a king-size bed covered in expensive white quilts, with ruffled lacy borders around the base. A sheer silky curtain surrounded the bed on overhead tracks, but had been pushed back to expose the bed to full view from the doorway. When the bathroom light shone into the otherwise dark room, the curtain looked opaque. When the bathroom door shut, I could see right through the curtain, and through the plate glass window beyond. I could see the dark sky with stars and moon, and the straight lines and quadrilles of city lights. The city twinkled with moving traffic like a windy night sky ripples with stars.

T came out of the bathroom, leaving the light on and the door half open. The sound of flushing water dwindled behind us as we entered into the bedroom. She took me aside and stood on tiptoes to kiss my mouth—our first kiss. She whispered: "Whatever we do in there, stay on the bed and work with me, because we don't have long." She led me into the bedroom. "Take off your clothes," she said while reaching up behind the back of her neck to remove a necklace of jade blocks.

As I stripped, her eyes roved up and down. She was transformed, no longer the uptight matron I'd first noticed at the mall. "You liked the blonde, did you?"

I shrugged. "You're both very pretty." I was diplomatic.

She let the little black dress fall to the floor. Off came a small baby blue bra that was loose even on those tiny breasts. Her matching silk panties fluttered to the ground, leaving me to see all there was, and I saw that it was exceedingly good. For a moment she stood with her hands behind her back, which made her flat belly protrude forward slightly. She twisted left and right. "I have to be home soon. We don't have a lot of time, and I apologize for that. I want you to make me happy for an hour."

"I'll do my best." I knelt down, and bent to the floor, with my hands caressing her small tanned feet.

She had even, pretty toes lacquered rouge to match her fingernails. I caressed her ankles, with their petite bones. I ran my palms up over the smoothness of her foreleg, and down around the taut muscles of her calves.

I kissed the inside of each thigh just above the knees, enjoying the softness of her skin. At this point, I heard her breathing hard and she grasped my thick, curly hair with both hands. I worked my way up her thighs inside and out, kissing. As I got hear her pubic hair, her grip tightened and I could feel her pulling me gently closer. I smelled dampness on her panties, and licked up the faint dew of oyster juice that had dampened her thigh.

"I've been craving you for hours," she said. "Come up here." She patted the bed. "Stand up."

I climbed onto the bed. She walked around the bed smiling as she pulled the sheer curtain closed around us.

We were trapped inside a lantern of indirect light that reflected softly on us from all sides. She crawled onto the bed, came across to me on all fours like an animal, and took the head of my cock in her mouth. Sitting between my feet, she held my cock in both hands and worked her mouth around it, twisting her head this way and that, until I felt like a ball bearing inside a speeding wheel. She licked my dangling balls. She wrapped her arms around my legs to support them, and tongued my balls so they swung back and forth. She raised her face under me so she could like the crack between my scrotum and my dong. She held my aching, huge dong up so she could get her tongue under it. Her arms had a vise-grip on my legs.

This girl was strong, and she did tongue. Oh, Mrs. *T,* I sang silently in my mind behind closed eyes—I'd like to take you home with me and keep you under my bed so I can call you anytime for a royal blow job. I felt her pointy tongue flick up the backs of my balls and over that little ridge that is full of sensitive nerve endings, just before my ass pucker. I felt the heat of her palms as she cupped my butt cheeks. "Small ass," she whispered breathlessly, "nice strong thighs, tiny ass cheeks, nice, nice," she whispered until her voice diminished in busy tonguing and sucking. She kissed every inch of each buttock. She did it the way a man kisses a woman's breasts—squeeze one, kiss the other. Squeeze the left, kiss the right; kiss the left, squeeze the right... She moaned as she kissed the huge dimple in the side of the left buttock, and then the similar dimple in the right buttock. I heard the splash of her fingers in her oyster, and began to massage my cock in preparation for putting it in the swim. It was still wet with her spit as I stroked it. She was behind me now, on her knees still, cupping my buttocks with her hands while running her tongue up and down my ass crack.

She rose up and stood behind me so that I felt the flat of her stomach against my tingling behind. She embraced me with her left arm, brushing my left nipple with her fingers, while her right hand reached around and took my penis as if she were helping me point it for a leak.

At that moment, due to some trick of the light—just a momentary flash—I saw through the opaque, soft light of the sheer curtain. She was pointing my dick directly at a third person in the room, and I instantly figured who that was, although I caught only a fleeting glimpse of a shadowy female figure and a blonde page boy hairdo. I glimpsed a pale face upturned to look at me, and a pair of somber eyes and an open mouth. A little lower down, I saw a dark bush between long, parted legs whose bony knees were pulled back.

I saw a blurry movement over that bush as she fanned her sex organ with rapid fingers.

It was the only glimpse I had of her.

I must have stiffened, changed my posture, stood staring—whatever—so *T* moved quickly in front of me. She made a frantic face, shook her head sharply, and showed me 'don't' teeth. I raised my hands in a 'whatever' gesture. She pulled me down, and I sank onto the bed. I lay on my back, groaning with pleasure as *T* sucked on my cock. What was going on? I rested for a few minutes and let *T* work on me while I tried to puzzle this out. For a moment I was alarmed, thinking there might be a husband or two beating his meat in the shadows.

T seemed to sense my disconcertment and whispered faintly in my ear: "It's only her. She wants to but she is still afraid. If you play along you might get to @ her some time soon."

I nodded. That would be fine with me. We put on a show for *U* for a while longer.

I heard an occasional rustling sound—I had no idea if she was on a couch or bed or futons or what. A few times, when I listened carefully—because the thought of her intrigued me— I heard splashing sounds. At some point she must have climaxed, not for the first time, but the big bang to end all bangs. She shuddered out there, made a moaning sound, maybe doubled up on her side in a fetal position with several fingers still in the stone hole of her peach. Then there was silence, except for the sound of a door closing, and minutes later the distant and muted sound of a car starting and driving away outside.

T heard it too and pulled the curtain back. "You were a success!" She swept nakedly across the room, with two fingers in her oyster, and examined the cushions that the two women must have pulled over two nearby wheat-colored couches nearby. "You're a hero!"

I rose and joined her squatting by the place where *U* had lain to watch us. I leaned down and sniffed, and *T* did too. There was a faint lingering aroma of oyster milk. *T* smelled it too, moving the fingers inside her as she did so."

She came over here," she told me.

We leaned down together and smelled the faintly salty, fishy spot in the material where *U's* juice had poured out during her exertions. It must be the place where she doubled over and turned so that juices welling up spilled from her.

I pushed *T* over so that her ass was in my face and her oyster was directly over where her friend's had been. I stuck my rod into her oyster and took her right there, hard, like a celebration.

"Yes," she said, "yes, Peter, do it, hard. Push me hard. Like that, yes." I could feel her fingertips brushing against my shaft as she whisked her clit. We cried out together, and the room filled with sounds of smacking and oh! Oh! as we orgasmed together right on the spot where Blondie had spasmed out a great climax minutes earlier.

T sat opposite me, laughing as she rubbed her fingertips through all my cum and her oyster dribbles that now joined *U's* secretions on the cushions. "I'll put these in the wash." She took my face between her hands. "I have to have you again." She kissed me on the forehead.

When *U* did decide it was time, she orchestrated an interesting way for us. Money was no object, and these women wanted to hide their tracks. Their husbands were away, the Arab to London, the Armenian to Tokyo, and so the women decided to visit a cousin of *T's* in Canada.

They had their mothers fly in to take care of the children. I received a small package in the mail. Inside was a gift-wrapped package, which I opened to find a brand-new wallet. The wallet was fragrant dark-blond leather and contained $1000 in twenties and fifties. There was also a two-way plane ticket to Toronto, and a gift certificate to eat the most expensive meal offered in the restaurants of the Toronto Marriott Eaton Centre. Like several other Canadian cities, Toronto has an extensive system of heated underground pedestrian tunnels. As in Montreal, a person could theoretically live in central Toronto, work, play, and live without ever going outside during the winter months. My wallet had no note, no signature—but the dinner certificate had a scribbled reservation time, 7:30 p.m. on the date of my flight. There was also a faint rouge kiss-print whose maker I was sure to have been *T*. Amused, I took this roundabout flight from JFK to Washington D.C. and thence to Toronto. I was seated at a corner booth in the dark-paneled Consort Bar, which resembles a pub of sorts. The hostess took my reservation and seated me alone in a bench booth, secreted against an interior brick wall.

I confined myself to a light salad and a beer, when I smelled that same perfume I had noticed in the mall back home before looking into those wild forest-green eyes. Moments later, my two preppy looking older women slid into the benches. *T* was on my left, Blondie opposite. They wore scarves, light tan loden overcoats, and wool berets. Their cheeks were flushed from the cold outside, and they brought fresh air with them in their coats. It was obvious they shopped together a lot. "I should have waited," I started to apologize, but Blondie waved me off. "Oh, don't mind, we grabbed a huge lunch in Detroit."

"You go ahead and enjoy yourself," *T* said as she slipped her arm through mine. For several minutes, before they settled in, they were kind of hyper, looking around at the people and the menu and what not. They each ordered Dubonnet on the rocks, with a twist, while I finished my beer and switched to spring water.

The drinks relaxed them, and pretty soon we were feeling cozy in our booth. *T* told me: "We have rooms at the Marriott of Bay Street near the Eaton Centre. Now this all has to happen like a military plan, okay?" I agreed. "He is so nice and easy going," Blondie said. "I wish I were married to someone like you." It was the first time I had actually committed to a tryst with a married woman, knowingly, and I wished she wouldn't mention that again, in that acidy tone, but it was reality. "Sorry," she added, downing her drink. She ordered another. *T* squeezed my arm. "Be patient. She's a little high strung. Something new for her."

"For me too," I whispered back. For a moment, I thought *U* was going to bolt. But she unexpectedly reached across the table with soft, square pale hands and patted my hand. She didn't say anything. Her drink came, and she had it to her lips in a moment. *T* reached across the table and took it from her. "You won't need this. Trust me." She gave my arm a tug. "Let's walk." And so we did. It started getting dark, and a thousand neon lights danced around us. It wasn't dreadfully cold, and we walked surface streets from King Street East, north on Yonge Street, and into the vast Eaton Centre. This is a fabulous mall with a high glass ceiling that covers a big city block. We didn't linger among the thousands of shoppers, diners, and movie goers, but walked a brief stretch in clean and well-lit underground passages to the bowels of my hotel, the Toronto Marriott Eaton Centre. We rode up many flights and walked down acres of corridors to reach the suite in which they were setting me up for the night.

While *U* disappeared into the bathroom, *T* took me aside. "She's still very nervous. It's the first time she's done anything like this. You see what a production it is. You'll be gentle with her, won't you?"

"If you two are gentle with me, I won't run away," I quipped.

She laughed. "That's all we need. Now let me clarify. She and I do not make love. I want some time with you, honey, but I want you to help her relax and enjoy herself a bit."

"I overheard your conversation the day we met," I said. "I know she is lonely."

"Then you understand. We both made a mistake in life from which we can't turn back. Really, it's the children. I'd give up the money in a heartbeat. I'm trying to make sure she doesn't start drinking to ease her pain, and you see that I'm a pretty strong person." She stroked my hair. "You are a sensitive, good young man. My advice to you is not to think about us except as girls your age, if you can manage that, having a fling. Don't think about anything else. You won't want or need for anything on this trip."

"Thank you."

She kissed me on the cheek like a friend. "No, thank you for turning out to be a very decent guy."

The suite they had rented for me, for us, had two bedrooms, a central sitting room, and a huge marble bathroom with gleaming floors. It had a sunken tub big enough to float a yacht, and a separate four-seater Jacuzzi with jets. I changed into a short white bathing suit, boxers-style, nothing grotesque. I donned a white terry bathrobe over that, which was thick and fluffy and came to my knees.

T donned a similar robe over a dark blue bikini. She turned on the Jacuzzi, which filled the room with chlorinated steam and loud bubbling. "We only have this night and maybe some time in the morning," she said as she started filling the bathtub. "Let's make the most of it. If she gets nervous and starts to drink again, I'll sneak it away from her and pour it out. I don't want her to ruin her big night out."

"This looks like a nice room to start our evening in," I said. *U* entered the room as if nothing had happened. She was several inches taller than *T,* a little fuller, but still thin. She wore a turban and a robe. I expected things would be uncomfortable for a while, but she acted nonchalantly as she stepped into the Jacuzzi. She swept her turban off and left the robe on the steps below. She wore a white bikini. Her back was long and sinuous, as was her neck.

The page boy swung this way and that, almost looking small on her finely formed skull. With her long arms and legs, she was statuesque. Her skin was milky and soft. *T* and I exchanged awkward looks. What to do? How to start things rolling?

I walked slowly toward the Jacuzzi, in which *U* was relaxing with her eyes closed and her head lying back. I walked slowly, the way one does in order not to startle a pet animal. With her ripe lips and softly sculpted cheeks and small, rounded, almost streamlined nose, she was imposingly beautiful and that slowed my step.

T took my advance as a signal to clear the room, so she left us alone. I climbed up into the Jacuzzi, saying "May I join you?"

"Mmm," *U* said without opening her eyes. She smiled happily. I was a bit surprised, thinking we'd have a scene. I made small talk, and she invited me to sit beside her. I let her take the lead at her comfort, and sat quietly beside her. She took my hand, and so we sat holding hands quietly for a minute or two.

Then she pulled my hand toward her, and brought her face close to mine. She made a kissy-mouth, and I gently leaned down to kiss her. She didn't open her eyes, and her face was flushed. "I'm still buzzed from the King Eddie," she ground out without losing the kissy-mouth. "Don't worry, I'm not sloshed." I smelled something sharp, sour. "I went into the bathroom and threw up." I wrinkled my nose. She opened her bright blue eyes. "What's the matter?"

"You smell of toothpaste and barf." I tried to say it with a smile, and without being critical.

"Oh, is that all?" She ducked under the water, and emerged in mid-Jacuzzi sputtering and wiping her wet hair back. Tilting her face up, she opened her mouth and gargled loudly with a huge mouthful of hot chlorinated water she had filled her cheeks with. She spat it out when her face started turning blue from lack of oxygen, and paddled over toward me so that her face came within inches of mine. "Better?"

I laughed and pulled her close so that our lips were in inch apart. "Now you smell like the YMCA swimming pool." She laughed, and I pulled her the last inch closer so that our mouths joined and my tongue found hers. The bad breath was gone. I lay back and pulled her softly onto me, still trying not to spook her just in case. She straddled my lap, and stroked the sides of my face with her hands. She studied me with suddenly serious eyes. "I wish you would hurry up and be older so we could get serious. I'm leaving him."

"You are?"

She nodded. "I haven't told *T* yet." She put a finger on my lip. "Don't you say anything either. I am the only person she has, but I can't play this game any longer. I didn't want to do this, but now that I know what I really want to do, I want us to have a blowout here tonight. I want you to be the @ I will never forget, unless we see each other again. I want you to be the period at the end of my sentence."

"I'll be better than that," I said. "I'll be the carriage return at the end of a very long, dark paragraph in the book of your life. Better yet, a chapter ending."

She twiddled the tip of my nose. "End of Book One, beginning of Book Two."

I sat there with this gorgeous blonde on my lap, and just looked at her enjoying every pixel of her spread. I ran my palms lightly up and down the stem of her long torso. I cupped her small buttocks and pulled her toward me. She moved compliantly, lightly, as if buoyant not only in the water but in her new happiness. She poked at my navel. "Innie."

I poked at hers. "Outtie."

She put her finger lower. "Boner."

I squirmed. "Very." Her fingertip felt like fire on my swollen head.

She slid down and pulled at my swim trunks. "Let me fix."

I reached down into her bikini and felt for the little bead I expected. It was tiny but it was there and it was hard. "Peanut," I said.

She palmed my finger down further into her and slid up to kiss me. A long french one while my finger wiggled in her sweet pussy.

Then she slid down and started giving me head. "God, you have a big meaty dick here." She ran her tongue around it, studied it, cranked it like a five-speed in overdrive. "What a great machine this is. If it were longer, I'd shriek and run from the room."

"Or not," I said grinning.

"I'm on fire tonight, baby. I might make you shriek and run from the room."

"Only if I see you chasing me. I'd let you catch me."

"You won't escape, not tonight."

"Okay, I'm yours. Please, do what you want. Tell me what you want, and I will lay it on you." "I like that word lay." She played with my dong. The Jacuzzi cut off, and she sloshed over on long legs to press the button for another ten minute go. Then she sloshed back and held out her arms. I rose to join her, and we stood like two slow dancers amid the bubbling, frothy water, with the steam rising around us while we kissed long and arduously.

T peered in once or twice and vanished again. *U* called out to her friend. *T* peeked again and asked: "Any seconds for me later maybe?"

U said: "I am going to wear him down to a toothpick and then throw him to you." She hugged me to make sure I wasn't offended. She asked her friend: "Are you exceptionally horny?"

"I could eat him alive."

U said "Okay, hold on." She put her hand on my buttocks and led me out of the Jacuzzi with my dong pointing straight ahead. Laughing, she grabbed it. "It looks swollen and heavy. Does sit hurt when it's purple like that? I'll lift it for you so it doesn't get hurt." As we walked, she kept it in her hand and it felt good.

I let her play. I felt goodnatured about it. Being a sex object wasn't so bad if they just weren't rude or mean about it. I could fully understand a woman's position in this regard. I knew what assholes men could be at times, and was determined to do my best not to be one. I wouldn't let anyone push me around or make fun of me, but I had become sure of myself and my ego felt like velvet over steel. I slid my hand into *U's* panties and cupped one of her tight little apple buttocks, maybe to enjoy, and maybe to send a little message subliminally. Her ass felt good in my hand. Maybe she was sending me a message too.

We entered a large bedroom that contained a master bed, and then a smaller single against a wall. Tall as she was, *U* took a chair and slid it under the huge plate glass window that overlooked a twinkling galaxy of Toronto's skyline by night.

"Turn off the lights," she instructed *T.* Standing on the chair, she took down a twelve foot section of the sheer curtain, which was attached to a little steel track with about a dozen little steel wheels.

I said "The skyline looks far better naked" as *U* strode on long legs around the big bed, pulled some tacks out of a bulletin board, got onto the big bed, and tacked the curtain to the ceiling.

"Good job," we both said and clapped as *U* sprang down
and made a nude curtsy. She had small, tight breasts with
little pink nipples—a pinkie to *T's* brownie—and they bobbed
tautly just once as she jumped down. *U* said "Voila" and
pointed to the large bed. She made herself comfortable on the
smaller bed a few feet away alongside. *T* slipped out of her
robe, dropped the bikini parts, and joined me on the bed. I
could see the faint outline of *U's* long body as she lay on her
side, fondling her breasts slowly and absently waiting for a
long, leisurely warmup. *T* and I repeated our sequence of the
earlier balling. We did much of it standing on the bed so that
U could have a clear view and enjoy herself.

As things heated up, *T* had me turn with my rear end
pointing toward her friend, and started licking the crack of my
ass while fondling my buttocks and slapping them lightly. I
had my finger on her clitoris and massaged it briskly the way
she liked it. Some women like it hard, others light, and some
are so sensitive they can't stand to have the little olive
touched. Some just want to do that part themselves. *T* was
very wet and liked a brisk rub.

"Whoah," I heard *U* say. "This is getting hard to take."

Just then, *T* began to orgasm. She spasmed, bending over,
lower each time, until she collapsed on the bed beside me and
held my wrist with both of hers to make my finger stop what
it was doing.

U walked up the bed on her knees while *T* crawled away
under the curtain to take her place on the narrow bed. There
she lay, curled up, with one hand buried in her crotch, and the
other hand idly holding up her chin on the pillow as she gazed
through the curtain at me and *U*.

U and I crawled around each other like a pair of animals
inspecting, sniffing at each other's cracks, licking each other's
genitals. I remembered what *T* and I had found after *U's*
orgasm, and I knew that this page-boy blonde churned out
some juice, some oyster milk, mare's milk, when she got hot. I
sniffed her behind as she waited for me on hands and knees.

Aside from a little blonde tuft of hair in front, she was naturally bare. Her labia were a complex tangle of pink folds. Some women have outtie oysters, while others have innie oysters. The innies are more rare. Heavier women sometimes have fatty outer lips that hide the little flossies inside. This woman, while long and thin, had an innie oyster. It was taut as a peach, and I had to work my tongue through the firm outer area, to penetrate into the (very wet already) inner region. Her lesser labia were firm and small, like peach slices from a can. Hidden beneath it all was a firm little bud that flowered for me as the tip of my tongue found it.

"That's the spot," she gasped. "Go for it."

She tossed her head left and right as I drilled down on her clitoris, coaxing it out from its heavy hood, seeking it with my tongue. At the same time, I lightly ran my finger around the rim of her outer labia, then her inner labia, and finally into her oyster hole. Then I brought some of her heavy juice up to push into her asshole. I kept sliding my finger into that underwater, kelpy flesh inside her vaginal canal, and bringing out wet slick fingers which I pushed gently through the door of her pink pucker, parting and loosening the tightness of her sphincter. Soon her clitoris lay in the fold of the tip of my tongue as if the two wanted to spend the night entwined. At the same time, I had her back door all softened and moistened.

She liked this, and reached back over her buttocks to insert a finger in her anus, just the first joint of her @ finger. I brought more mucus up on my finger and rubbed it on her fingertip, so that it was transported into her asshole. She began to spasm. She pulled out the finger and grasped her breasts, left, right, left, right. She was sinking. She was crashing. Her face contorted with the anguish of pleasure as she sobbed loudly. I rolled up my tongue like a jungle plant leaf around her clitoris and sucked lightly, so that the strong vacuum drove her nuts. I was careful not to hurt her, and I didn't want her clit to be sore, because I wanted it handy for more pleasure later. She lay looking back at me, with one leg pulled up, and her oyster area looking at me pinkly under a dangling hand. I threw myself at those pink folds, but she intercepted me with a hand on my forehead.

"Easy," she gasped. "You are going to wear us out tonight."

They switched places. Now *T* was back in bed with me, while *U* went to the small bed. "Let's see, where were you?" *T* said playfully. She assumed the exact pose *U* had just abandoned, though of course her body was more compact and petite. I went from looking at a pinkie innie oyster to a brownie outtie oyster. It was a pleasant switch.

Though she was smaller, *T* had larger labia that I enjoyed pulling in between my gums and sucking as if they were covered with honey. If you do this one way, it annoys the woman and can even hurt. If you do it right, depending on the size and shape of the lips, you can make her shiver with pleasure and she will writhe with her eyes closed and a sigh or a smile. That was what *T* did as I concentrated on her labia. At the same time, I stroked her tight, round little buttocks. I pushed her up so she was on all fours as *U* had been, and nosed around her rear as I had done with *U.*

T moaned and sighed, wriggling contentedly on folded arms with her tits hanging down and her nipples like hard little nuts. I tongued her clitoris, which was bigger and more available than the other woman's. At the same time, I used my index finger and then two fingers to ferry prodigious amounts of vaginal syrup to her butt pucker. To get closer and see better, I slid under her so that her behind pointed directly at my face. She was on her knees, bent over, and sucking on my cock. I could lick her clit and at the same time take pleasure in watching my fingers working on her asshole.

I pushed in my spit and her oyster juice until her sphincter relaxed so totally that her asshole opened slightly. I cupped her splayed buttocks and pulled her closer so that I could insert the tip of my tongue in her asshole. In this way, I tongue-@ed her asshole while she massaged her breasts. As her passion grew, she threw her head back though she remained well bent forward to allow me maximum tongue-purchase on her rear. She began pulling her hair with both hands while wailing in the throes of another orgasm.

Right there, I could hold myself no longer. I ejaculated spurt after spurt of milky cum that flew up onto her face. She bent down and sucked my cock dry. Then she rubbed her face with it to spread the cum all around. I lay on my belly, exhausted, while the two women switched places. Now *T* was the one on the small bed, and she looked over at us while gently massaging her pubic area with all ten fingers flat. She too was gasping for breath and red in the cheeks, with a dazed glow in her eyes—the forest green eyes in which I had seen so much wildness through all those layers of disguise and submission.

U now sat beside me, idly rubbing my back, my buttocks, my thighs. I was too tired to move for the moment. She sat quietly looking down on me with a happy glow on her face. My hand lay limply at my side. She managed to twist her long, agile body around so that she could lift my hand and insert two fingers into her damp and ready oyster. That was all she wanted for now. She pressed her legs shut around my hand, and the two fingers stayed nicely trapped in the warmth of her pussy while I faded away.

We made love several times before noon the next day, when we had to fly our separate ways. Of all the women I had met in this way, I came closest to genuinely falling in love with U—by which I mean, among other things, the age difference would not have mattered to me. Shh! Sadly, though, she did leave her husband and she disappeared into the far west, where she became an editor at a fashion magazine. She went through years of an ugly and sometimes violent divorce. *T* and her husband moved to London. I'm not sure that *U* and *T* ever saw each other again. I didn't pursue the matter either, but drifted on. It was quite a while before I fell back into this older woman, Summer mode. There were some younger women for a while, but they do not figure in the scope of this book.

The Story of V and W

I had gotten a six week stint as a research assistant to a wheelchair-bound historian. He lived with his wife in a snowy little mountain village in northwestern New Hampshire. Each day, I would drive down to Berlin or Littleton, or even as far away as Montpelier, Vermont, to photograph documents that could not be checked out, and artifacts that could not be adequately captured otherwise. I was learning a lot about the discipline of research, and the disciplines needed in my scattered life.

Each morning, I would set out from the village and drive along winding roads cut into the sides of mountains. In the mornings, it was pleasant to sit in the warm VW Kombi van with a hot cup of coffee and see the passing hillsides over 3,000 feet altitude, with their snowy-covered pines. Against a backdrop of gray atmosphere, it was spectacular to see gray clouds drifting in and silently breaking up against those mountainsides the way galaxies in space collide.

Every afternoon, I would drive back toward the village with an armload of books and movies to see me through the night. The professor had a chalet overlooking a small valley, and I had a small suite off the garage. It was comfortable and warm but quiet and lonely. On my way home, it would get dark early, and I would stop for dinner at this restaurant snuggled in the toehills of the White Mountains.

The restaurant, a gas station, and a few stores formed an impromptu village of their own about five miles from where I was staying. I only had another fifteen minutes to go, but it was tortuous uphill driving. Some evenings the roads were already slick with ice. It would snow in the early morning hours, so that my drive out was beautiful—the leaden sky dappled with Bambi spots of snow flakes—but during the day the sun might come out for a few hours. Temps would rise, the stuff melted, and as the sub-Arctic winter night set in, it froze. Nevertheless, I would always stop for dinner, and I carried with me a menu so I'd know hours ahead what the special of the day was.

The waitress was *V,* a ski enthusiast and part-time sports instructor at a nearby high school. She was 28, and gorgeous, and best of all, she liked me. She had a shapely, solid body that looked cute in her yellow waitress dress. She had wonderful dark-blue eyes framed in dark brown hair. Her wide, pale face was faintly freckled and had that exotic touch of Indian and French-Canadian so common in the region. *V* seemed to await my coming. She knew approximately when I would arrive, and sometimes I could see her setting up table services (napkins, fresh cutlery, cups, saucers, clean glasses with paper covers, etc.) while looking out one of the big picture windows as my van arrived. Often it was still snowing, and there would be white atop the van. I always loved walking in to the warm chalet-like atmosphere, clapping my cold hands together, blowing steamy breath over them, and stamping ice off my boots.

V would appear with a menu in hand and sweep me along to a table she tried to put me in—a small two seater, isolated near the kitchen entrance, where she could grab a few words with me while rushing out with armloads of plates or rushing in to get more of the same. Bus boys passed, other waitresses pressed past, and *V* managed to get a good 20 minutes of chat time with me each evening.

Pretty soon, we timed it so I arrived a bit later, and she'd put on a thick gray sweater to cover her uniform top (kind of like a taxi turning its in-service lights out). She'd bring a cup of coffee and a salad and join me. Until then, I'd always bought the evening paper, and she originally started asking about stories. Now she'd slide in with her dinner, and we'd talk. Pretty soon, she was sitting with her thigh pressed against mine, and we were on our way to being good friends. I had a good idea that we were working up to something nice. But there were some odd complications.

For one thing, the first evening I came in, before *V* and I became chummy, where were three butch looking women who came to visit, and I happened to notice that there was a lot of extremely fond hugging and glowing conversation, including *V* and *W* in sort of a brief, milling exchange that soon evaporated in the bustle of the busy restaurant. I wondered—were they lovers, or were they robust ski women who weren't lovers?

Or both?

For another thing, there was a roommate, *W*. *V* had *W* join us one evening during her break—the testing thing, I assumed (correctly). *W* was to give *V* a second opinion to make sure I wasn't really some body snatcher. *W* was a smaller, thinner woman, also lithe, a skier like *V*. *W* was gamine, boyish, with tousled caramel hair and gray eyes in an interesting, rectangular face with a wide, sensuous mouth, thin high nose, and still-soft, but squarish jaws. Her other job was as an aerobics instructor at a private gym. We made pleasant conversation (part of which drew me out on social issues and I admitted I had been a student activist and favored progressive causes) and I forgot about her. Soon enough came the first date with *V*. She was off on a Saturday, and so was I. We met around ten and had breakfast (anywhere but her restaurant, so we went into Berlin). From there, we walked a bit, sat through a good suspense movie, wandered through the mall, and then the bookstore, before I took her home. She was a warm companion, and clung attentively to me.

We stole our first furtive kiss in the movie.

By the time we were in the mall, we were French-kissing with ardor. At the bookstore, we tittered over erotic manuals and I could hear her breath grow shorter and hotter as she became aroused (which she tried to hide from me). She spoke briefly on the phone (to ask *W* to carve out some space for us), and had me up to their apartment. They lived in a modern, blond-wood upstairs flat, with stores below. Their front windows looked out over the main road, while the rear looked out into a nebulous, snowy expanse of forest.

W was there—wearing jeans, soft boots, and a turtleneck sweater. They exchanged hugs and kisses. At that moment I remembered the glowing and hugging on the first day, and thought maybe their fondness was a little extra. There were photos of them on the bureau and on desks and window sills, and they seemed to share a lot. What I did not realize, on that first date, was that they shared one bedroom. That's a pretty sure tipoff, when there is only one large bed. *V* herded me into the small living room, and the three of us watched TV for a while.

W brought out popcorn and ice cream, and *V* opened a bottle of sparkling apple cider. We had a cozy time together. After an hour or so, *W* announced that she had someplace to go, and left. She hugged *V* with a kiss on the cheek, and did the same to me. "Nice meeting you," she said with those bright gray eyes and that plain, healthy skier's face. They both seemed to have matching slight cases of ski burn (a mix of air and sun peeling and redness) on their cheeks, foreheads, and chins.

"We have about two hours alone," *V* announced as she took my hand and towed me into the bedroom, which overlooked empty forests. She turned off the lights and opened the curtains, so that we were illumined by a silvery light from both a half moon and the reflected light on the snow fields. Both fully dressed, we plopped on the bed and started petting.

We pulled each other to one another, and I saw the eagerness in her eyes as she gave me her lips to kiss. I had already been inside that hungry mouth with my tongue, and our tongues were like old friends picking up where they had left off. My hand strayed along the curves of her strong body, down a smooth back and waist, up over the hill of her hip, and down the broad, firm slope of her thigh. As I palmed her thigh, she took it as a signal and pressed closer, so that her corduroy-clad leg rode over my knee.

I pulled her thigh closer yet, so that the warm cleft between her legs rode on my thigh. The muscular hardness of my thigh excited her, because her breathing got excited. Her hand crept up my sweater and rested on a nipple. The nipple was startled and grew hard, which made her hand palm it, finger it, wiggle it, and I thrust my tongue hard into her mouth while pulling my thigh up against her vulva. Soon, my hand was in her shirt and up on her breast. She had smallish but full breasts. I maneuvered her silky bra off and found large nipples that wanted to fill my hand.

Clothing was now extraneous. She motioned for a time out for both of us to undress. When we were naked, I lay on the bed and looked up at her. She stood in the silvery light and let me admire her. I could read the pleasure in her heavy-lidded eyes and slightly parted, almost smiling lips as she looked down at me in utter sensuous enjoyment. Her body was full and strong, with good curves. Her thighs were strong, her belly a little full like a ripe fruit, but taut. She had a huge innie belly button. Her breasts, as I said, were small but full and lay somewhat flat, with huge nipples pointing upward, brown, from a wide oval full of aroused aureoles. Her bush was oval, like her Venus mound, and as she crawled up on the bed and turned her buttocks toward me, I saw that she had a brownie outtie oysterie. She had a tight little pucker between goodly buttocks, and a tangle of brown folds, labia, with a clitoral bundle that would summon my attention soon.

"You look good," she said in a breathy, emphatic low voice.

"So do you," I said as I ran my hands over her buttocks and my fingers through the folds between buttock and thigh, and between both of those and her vulva.

"Like what you see?" she said, and squirmed her shoulders pleasurably knowing what the answer would be. "You look ravishing," I said. "I like when you say that," she said with a smile. I put my fingertip to her lips. "Wet it." She chowed her mouth around my finger as if it were my dick. She turned her head this way and that, and I felt her tongue slide around my finger. "Nice and wet," I said. She soaked it in thick spit, moving her head up and down as if @ing the finger. I took the wet finger and ran it down the line between her labia. Her lips parted. She barked out and grasped the sheets with her fists. I ran my fingers through the parted space, which was parted partly because of the finger wet with her spit, and also because her labia were engorged and heavy. I maneuvered her gently, so that I lay on my back and pulled her big thighs toward me until I could smell the snailness of her oyster. "Like it?" she said.

"I like it. I am looking at it and loving it."

She moaned and lowered her face onto the sheets while wiggling her rear. She grasped the sheets tighter in her fists. "It's all yours," she said, "all yours. Everything you see."

What I saw was wonderful. She lifted her leg over my torso and moved closer yet, so that she was squatting with her genitals an inch from my face. I could count the hairs, and the myriad skin pores on folds outside her labia, as well as the glistening pinkness inside. It smelled damp like the forest, but also faintly briny and fishy like a pond at the edge of the tidal swamps where I grew up, which had mixed sea and fresh water. Her skin smelled clean, almost hinting at lavender, as if she had just soaked in her bath, though we'd been on the go all day.

Positioned thus, she took my cock in both hands and closed her mouth around it. I groaned as I felt her take possession of me with her strong mouth and sure hands. Every woman has her own, unique way of pleasuring herself when she is alone, and just as unique ways of pleasuring her lover. As she sucked and blew me, she held it with both hands but kept one long middle finger in the crack between my buttocks—not a penetration, but a pleasant suggestion she might push it in, but for now let it rest amid the sparking nerve endings around my anus.

I could not stretch the desire any further, but parted her vaginal lips with my fingers of both hands, and got my tongue into her hole. I tongue-@ed her strongly, but alternated with licking her pee-hole, and licking circles around her aroused clit. My hands roved under her, seeking the generally flat but (in the middle) bulging plane of her stomach. I grasped the wide bones of her hips from behind, from underneath, wondering at their breadth and strength and beauty.

As she sucked me closer to climax, I grasped her buttocks and hips and pulled myself up so I could lick her anus. She moaned with pleasure but made protesting sounds that she liked that but needed me far more in her oyster. So I returned to penetration of her hole with my tongue. I felt tremors and fits start to race through her like an electric current. Her sucking noises were loud and randy and echoed in the room. She cupped one hand under my ass while circling my dick with her index and middle fingers of the other hand, and keeping her third finger in the crack as before. Twisting her hand around, she diddled my sphincter with her third finger. I held her ass and drank from that pink, dripping cup until I felt the fits of orgasm start to shake her. That brought me on, and I could feel her teeth (gently) as my cock rammed up and down throwing wads of come into her mouth and on her face. Her clitoris was like a little girl-weenie in my mouth as I puckered and sucked on it, with loud smacking sounds, the way she had sucked on my penis, and I brought her to orgasm. She hollered brokenly in her passion, and held her ass with one hand, my dick with the other, as she rocked her torso up and down. Her ass moved this way and that, but I clung to it like a sea creature and delivered tongue thrusts into her contracting, quivering oyster box until she squealed and rolled away, unable to stand any more.

As we lay resting, she looked at me strangely. "Peter, I want to tell you something." It was a moment of truth. "I hope you like this." She looked into my eyes and her face said she wasn't sure how I was going to react. " the best way to tell you is directly. I'm bisexual." She studied me. "*W* and I are lovers."

I shrugged. "Okay. Now a few things I noticed make more sense."

She laughed. "You're not—upset?"

I shook my head. "I just made love to a beautiful, loving woman. I'm just totally all over you."

"I'm all over you too, Peter." She kissed me. "There is a silly thing. Let's see what you think. You know how girls will be girls."

"Mmmm?" What did that mean?

"We are both bisexual. We happen to have been lovers for the past year, since we met and really fell for each other. Look, there is no such thing as a simple bi pattern. We're not lesbians, and we're not straight. Those are each complicated enough, but sort of easier to define, at the ends of a spectrum." I had learned some of this already, and wasn't surprised.

V continued: "Every bi woman has her own twists and turns. I usually stay monogamous with either a man or a woman. Once in a while both, never both together. If I do both, they won't know the other exists. That's just how it has to be. That's how I keep my world sane and stop it from falling apart, or falling together. It's about the same with *W,* except she's more apt to be with a woman, and occasionally with a man. So we were having this talk about the time you happened on the scene." She stopped and looked down, as if this were hard to say.

"Go on," I said, stroking her hair gently.

"We talked about you and we were wondering if it might not be fun to have sex with you." She added quickly: "If you don't mind."

I kept stroking her hair. "If that is what you would like, I would certainly try to please you both." She grasped my chin and pushed me back, down, to kiss me roughly on the mouth. "You are such a diplomat, Peter. You said that so carefully and with such diplomacy!"

"The only thing is—"

"What?"

"I don't want to do anything that would cause me to lose you."

She put her finger on my nose, a subtle hint that she was still the older woman and I the naïve younger man. "Honey, if I didn't want to do this, I wouldn't have said it. Besides, I was terrified that I might lose you." She looked down suddenly as if ashamed to have admitted that. It meant she liked me a lot.

I laughed. "Come here." I pulled her on top of me, and slipped my hard cock into her. "On the topic of just you and me for the moment, I am still horny for that good little pussy of yours." She wiggled it to show me that her good little pussy was horny for me too. I said: "I would be the happiest guy in the world just making love to you, because you are gorgeous. I think your roommate is a very sweet person, very cute, and if you want to invite her along, that might just turn out to be a real turn-on. I've never slept with two women."

"Neither of us has ever slept together with a man."

"Want to try it?"

"I'll talk to *W* and see if she wants to."

"Do you want to, or is this something you're being talked into?" It was a silly question. I knew the answer. She knew I knew. We were just making horny talk, which helped us start getting hot for each other again, embracing, tossing on the bed together with my cock inside her warm hole, and her solid hips wrapped around my smaller, harder thighs and ass.

We heard the sound of *W* quietly letting herself in, and it was time to shower, and for me to leave. *W* was in the bathroom when *V* kissed me at the door and told me: "I loved having you this evening." She rubbed my buttock and thigh as we kissed goodnight. "I'll be looking forward to seeing you at dinner tomorrow as usual."

"Me too," I said. "What a treasure you are, especially up here in Santa's frozen North Pole."

W agreed. So *V* said the next evening at dinner. "Want to come over this evening?"

"I'd love to. I'll need to drop off some books and tapes for the Professor, so his wife can help him with transcriptions. As soon as I drop the box of stuff off, I'm done for the day. That's our arrangement."

"Good—then drive over to our place and come on up." Less than two hours later, I knocked on their door on the second floor. *V* opened the door with a coy, expectant look. She wore a long pink night gown that was opaque but revealed her rich figure. "Come on in, Peter. We have been waiting for you."

W came over and kissed me on the cheek. She wore a similar nightie, but light blue, that came down to her ankles. She accepted a chaste, sisterly start. She was, too, a gamine, a tomboy. She said: "I didn't know if I would feel shy or embarrassed or whatever, so I thought I would break the ice by giving you a hug."

I took her in my arms and chastely kissed her forehead. I could feel that she was tense as a steel coil, but she quickly relaxed. *V* put on some soft music and turned off the lights. We were bathed in that same silvery moonlight plus the red and green glow of flashing lights in the entertainment system. *V* said "Why don't you kids dance for a bit."

W and I slow danced. "This is nice," I said.

W nodded. She rested her head on my shoulder. "*V* said you are a sweet boy."

"Thanks," I said in the direction of *V's* faint shadow sitting on the couch.

"It's the truth," *V* said.

W and I slow danced for a while. We started to kiss. She was slower to arouse, but steady as she let me make my small advances a step at a time. She was cool, and not breathing any differently, but her eyes were big and lustrous, and their lids were languid as if her eyes were the moon and her lids slow clouds drifting before the moon. She was bewitching in her own way. Her body felt long and thin in my arms, her waist boyish, but her hips were side and delicate, and her buttocks soft and girlish. Womanish. Both women were about five years older than I, a lot for any of us at that age, and yet they were of the type that age well and seem younger. Maybe that's because women like that stay fit and keep a positive attitude and don't get too wrapped around the axle over small stuff. I took turns dancing with each of them. *V* was horny already, breathing in my ear, and I kept my knee between her thighs so that she rode on me as we swayed in the air. *W* sat on the couch with her knees up and her arms wrapped around them. She looked comfortable and relaxed and interested. Soft rock music throbbed quietly in the air, and I danced with thin *W* and handful *V.*

W and I talked a little. I said: "This is nice, like high school."

"I liked to dance, but boys confused me."

"Did you like boys?" "Sometimes. But I liked girls too. Took me a while to figure out. In college, I got it all ironed out by second semester. Plenty of help from the right older girls."

"Me too," *V* said from the couch. She was so close, really, that she could almost have reached out to touch our legs.

"Why don't you and *V* dance while I watch?" I said. The women silently made the switch, so I sat on the couch and I watched them. It occurred to me I should watch what they did so I would know what they liked, at least for a start.

The two women danced slowly, and *V* held *W* as I had held *W. V* said over *W's* reclining head and tousled hair, "she is a slow bun in the oven, but wait when she gets hot."

W said: "I don't mind taking my time, especially when something good is coming."

"That's the spirit," I said.

They were about the same height, *V* being maybe an inch taller, but *V* was fuller and presented an illusion of being taller. She lifted *W's* chin and kissed her. They kissed long and slow, turning their heads slowly so their tongues could frisk around one another, hidden from me by their lips. In a few quick little motions, they shed their nightgowns, so that they were nude as chalk in the moonlight.

I watched to see if either was the more aggressive, or if they played any he/she nuances, or whatever—I saw nothing like that. They simply were two women making love, and alternately one or the other would be more vigorous. I watched as *V* palmed *W's* smaller, still round and soft, buttocks, while *W* seemed more interested in touching, cupping, kissing *V's* saggy little breasts with their large nipples. Alternately, *V* touched *W's* tiny breasts with their pinkie nipples. Where *V* was a brownie, *W* was utterly a pinkie, from her delicate oval nipples to her hard little outtie belly button to what was hidden in her big ash-gray bush.

At one point, *V* sounded a little embarrassed or, to put it more mildly, unsure. "Are we doing okay, Peter?"

"You're doing perfect. Let's take our time, enjoy each other, do what's fun and not do what's not fun. I'm looking forward to making love with both of you."

"And you will," *W* said reassuringly. "I've never done this before, but I think it will be just fine."

"I think so too," *V* said. She stopped dancing and turned *W* toward me. "Isn't she precious?" *W* stood like a doll and let herself be gazed at.

I said: "She is very pretty and precious, yes." I could tell that *V* loved her, truly. *W* closed her eyes with deep pleasure and laid one hand loosely on one of *V's* breasts. *V* nuzzled the back of *W's* neck, moaned, and rubbed *W's* genitals for me. *W* had a big bush for a small woman, and now *V* gave me a foretaste by fingering *W's* bush so that I glimpsed pink. *W* had a surprisingly large oyster with large pink labia in intriguing folds between her legs. I sat on the floor cross-legged so I could look up, and see *W's* pussy framed by her narrower thighs and the round ends of both buttocks visible through the wide spread between her hips. She was one of those women who have a wide ass but legs set far enough apart so you can see daylight between them.

W moaned a little as *V* fingered her.

"She likes being looked at," *V* said.

"I like looking at her," I said. I feasted on the sight of her long, thin torso and those faint mounds, her breasts, and their subtle pink nipples.

V kept fingering her, showing her to me, saying: "Isn't she precious?"

W reached with both hands down to her bush and rubbed so that *V's* hand was between her hands, and *V's* finger between her fingers as they massaged *W's* labia.

I rose and stepped closer. I put my left hand lightly on *W's* waist, my right hand on the fullness of *V's* buttock and thigh.

V said: "Kiss her nipples."

I bent down and licked the soft little mounds on *W's* chest and was surprised at how her nipples wrinkled up into little pink prunes like plants sucking up the wetness of the gardener's hose on a hot day. I ran my fingertip up and down the shallow groove of her front, each time over her hard little outtie belly button. "Do you like having your boobies kissed?" I asked.

"Oh yes," *W* said. "Kiss them like that. My nipples get nipply when you do."

V said: "Let's go into the bedroom."

I stood and watched them as they went, the fuller one and the leaner one, both lovely to watch. I followed them. When I got to the bedroom, *W* was in the bathroom and *V* stood shivering with both hands pressed over her groin. "We both have to pee, now that we're getting excited." We took turns going in to pee, but nobody watched anyone.

In bed, I watched them tangle and kiss. First, *W* was on the bottom and *V* straddled her and kissed her on the mouth while *W's* fingers worked in *V's* snatch and the air was filled with wet sounds from the snatch. I liked watching *V's* breasts hang, dangling a bit, heavier and fuller at the bottom than in the middle, and with brown nipples sticking out. I liked watching *V's* boobies rocking back and forth like the clappers of bells. *W* liked *V's* nipples too, because she sucked on them each for several minutes in turn. *V* held each breast for *W* to suck, while *W's* fingers kept working in *V's* oyster. In minutes, they were both twitching and writhing as their first orgasm rolled through them simultaneously. They lay beside me, the two women, intertwined and resting, while I lightly massaged their firm backs and buttocks. My cock was hard as a rod.

W crawled over to me and sucked my cock. *V* lay nearby watching and idly fingering herself. I lay on my back and pulled her backside over so that she straddled my shoulders as *V* had the first night. I inhaled the scent of *W's* lavish pink pussy. She had a big pussy for a small woman. She had a bigger pussy than *V*. Sometimes smaller women surprise you because they have big loose oysters.

W had a big oyster, and I pulled it over my mouth. I sucked on each labia, then on her pee hole, and I tongued her clitoris. *V's* clit was bigger. However, *W* had a bigger, longer shaft disappearing up under her clitoral hood and into her Venus mound. Touching her shaft made *W* writhe with sensitivity and pleasure. She was one of those women who quickly orgasm when you gum the shaft of their clit. So I tongued it and gummed it, this long hard line under her skin, and she sucked on my cock exactly as *V* had done on the first night.

They had probably exchanged notes about me. I started to feel that warmth down below that signals orgasm is on the way. *V* meanwhile, nearby, was rubbing herself faster and moaning as she saw what we were doing. After all, I had watched my two girls dancing, and I had watched my two girls as *V* showed me *W's* oyster, and I had not touched myself for fear of coming early and by myself. Here I was with this lovely gray-eyed girl (okay, older woman, but she was like a girl) who had my dick deep in her mouth, and I stuck my tongue in her loose pink oyster that was foamy with oyster soup, and I started coming. *W* had plenty of experience with men, and she did cunnilinguis with women, so she expertly wrapped her wiry arms around my ass and kept that dick in her mouth as I thrust up and down. At the same time, overwhelmed with passion at the wealth of that large, loose pink pussy on my face, I held her hips in a vise grip while I tongue-@ed her quivering cavern.

"@ her," *V* said to me.

I was still limp and awash in come. "I'll work my way up to it. Why don't you @ her in the meantime, until I'm ready?" I turned to *W* and gripped her arms. "Do you want to be @ed by *V?*"

"I want her to eat my pussy while you watch." So I lay on my side within smelling distance while *V* lay on her back and *W* sat on *V's* face with her ass on *V's* forehead. The three of us were wrapped in a scent like fishy sea water as *V* held *W's* pale buttocks apart and sucked on her pussy. I wished men could have more orgasms as I helplessly watched from the sidelines as these two went on. They had what I called rolling orgasms, maybe one each ten or fifteen minutes. I remained exhausted from my first orgasm, and half-hard as I hovered around them. With luck I could get one more orgasm in, with time maybe two.

A dildo came into play. *W* was the man wearing the dildo, while she @ed *V* in the oyster from behind, and I watched *V's* breasts swinging back and forth as the two gradually climaxed.

I was ready by then, and chose to take *W* in the missionary position. *W* held my head to her chest as I @ed her hard, rocking back and forth on top of her. I sucked *W's* little tits when I was able to slow down. *V* slipped in to help me, sucking those tiny titties. I rolled onto my back, taking *W* with me, so that I had my cock up her oyster, while *V* slipped behind and fingered *W's* anal rim.

Then *V* strapped on the dildo and straddle *W,* so that I was @ing *W's* oyster with my dick, while *V* rocked on top and @ed *W's* asshole with that dildo. We were both whacking away in tandem, and poor sweet little *W* splayed like a tadpole, wailing in a broken voice as she made thrashing, swimming motions and I and *V* both attacked her in both holes with the vehemence and need of our passions and desires.

V and I both noticed at the same time that *W* was crying. She had tears running down her cheeks and was sobbing. "Is anything the matter?" I asked. *V* was all over her. "Darling sweet baby, are you okay?"

"Yes," *W* said, "I'm fine. I'm just so wanting you both that I can't get high enough. I just want to melt in a big orgasm, and I don't think people are designed to go this high this fast and this hard. I wish you would both eat me."

I and *V* put *W* before us, missionary, and licked her smooth pale buttocks and big pink oyster. Meanwhile, I squirmed around so that *W* could take my cock in her mouth, and she sucked on me like a lollipop. I saw *V's* dangling titties and sucked on those, and then moved down to her tight brownie oyster and tongued her. Pretty soon, all three of us came in a massive climax.

I was up there for six weeks in all, and for five of those weeks I had the most ungodly wonderful sex with these two older young women. We played and played, trying everything there is to try. Then, we went our separate ways for reasons that are too long to contain in the margins of this notebook.

The Story of X, Y, and Z

I have said that my Summers came in styles and flavors,
complex as good wines, richly textured. One such was *Z.* I
learned a lot from her. You've heard people describe gourmet
wines, and they talk about the head, the aromas—coffee,
chocolate, ash, tobacco, prune, vanilla, walnut, what have
you—and the after-palate or whatever. In *Z,* a whole package
came with the woman. She had money, style, elegance,
everything. Seeing her on the street—striding down Fifth
Avenue in Manhattan, let's say, in high heels and dark nylons,
in a $1000 overcoat from the best department store—her full,
wavy reddish-brown hair under a pillbox hat in dented plum
with a broach of antique beaten silver and a mother of pearl
hat pin—you would never imagine what happened behind
closed doors. Most men would consider her unreachable,
beyond sex, beyond anything so earthy as a kiss or an orgasm.

I was in Manhattan one rainy afternoon in early Fall. I
had gone into the city on a job interview that had ended
ambiguously—I might hear the result in a week, and it turned
out I didn't get the job—but for the moment I was satisfied
and window shopping before heading down to the Transit
Terminal for my bus back to New England. I enjoyed the
glitz, the glitter, the neon, the sullen reflections in plate glass
windows. I enjoyed the fresh air, the smell of cars and passing
perfumes and the occasional furtive cigar, as I wandered
among rushing pedestrians. It was a dreary, dark-early, drippy
day.

Coming toward me was this elegant, reserved woman in a
plum hat. She strode on heels that made her look taller than
she was. Nice coat, fine figure, fine everything, but it was her
face that captured the imagination. There was drama in her
expression. She had high cheekbones with smoldering dark
eyes behind them. She had a tapering lower face with a large,
aquiline nose and a strong, red-lipsticked mouth. Her mouth

was large and determined, as if she insisted on having her way. From either arm hung the string handles of shopping bags emblazoned with great retail names. Her dark coat was slightly open at the top, revealing a subdued brown or mauve blouse that matched the hat. Dark coppery wavy hair spilled from the hat and she pushed the hair back. Her eyebrows were arched and supercilious. She looked, in fact, quite miffed. "Scoundrel!" I heard her say under her breath. "Is anything the matter?" I asked as she bumped into me, and one of her packages fell on the wet sidewalk. I quickly bent to pick it up, and tried to find a way to hang it back on her among the others.

"I'm having a terrible day," she said. "Could you please help me get these into a dry place so I can call a taxi?"

"Sure." I took several from her and we hurried into the nearest department store entrance. She whispered thanks and slipped her arm through mine. I almost felt faint—I'd had nothing to eat, and the interview had been a strain, and now this woman's sensuous perfume wafted around me and I felt the lightness of her suede-gloved arm against my ribs.

"I am so embarrassed," she said. "Thank you so much."

"Not at all," I said. "There is a phone over there. Here, I'll carry your bags over there while you call." This happened in Manhattan, which unfairly has the reputation of being fast and hard. It is both things, but the people are fundamentally good as people are everywhere. Same proportion of creeps, thieves, and other scoundrels. Well, too, it was my older woman phenomenon at work. She told me later that she had liked and trusted me from the very first moment, and that was something that never happened with her. She was a seasoned Manhattanite with a nose for danger and deceit. I struck her, I am embarrassed to say, as a lost puppy—as she put it, a good looking one, needing a meal and a bed.

It took an hour and a half for her cab to come. I assured her I had time, since my bus was not due to leave for hours yet. I had some sixth sense that this was going somewhere. She seemed to enjoy having me there to talk with, to protect her from unwanted advances. She was divorced and a former model, now an occasional actress in small off-Broadway pieces. She had been the only child of a German father and a Cuban mother, both very wealthy, and the wife of a newspaper publisher in Ohio. The publisher apparently collected women the way some people collect umbrellas or thimbles, so in five years with no children, the affair ended in a divorce. That left *Z* to fend for herself, a millionairess many times over, in the wilds of Manhattan. Whatever she did, she did well—she was, after all, an honors graduate of both Andover and Yale, with a degree in Art Appreciation—but whatever she did, she did because she wanted to, not because she had to. She did not do, she dabbled.

"I was supposed to be picked up by my boyfriend, but he chose to stand me up," she explained as we waited. The floors around us were beige wood, the display cases loaded with expensive clothing and jewelry, the sales people elegantly dressed in dark suits. "At least we are in a suitable location. Are you sure I am not inconveniencing you too much?"

"I am alone in Manhattan, with no place to go while I wait for my bus. I can't think of a more pleasant place to be standing than right here. If I bother you, please send me away."

"Oh no," she said with a wink, "you are helping me greatly." She pointed with her chin toward a pair of men in jeans and cheap jackets who wandered by leering in her direction.

"Must be difficult being a beautiful woman," I said.

"How old are you?"

"Twenty-four." I would be in two months. I didn't ask her age. I took her to be about 31 or 32.

"You seem mature for your age, and you certainly have good manners. How would you like to have a first-class dinner, followed by a glass of $100 wine, and maybe a show off Broadway?"

"Are you in the show?"

She laughed. "Not tonight. I'll be in MacBeth downtown starting next week. Right now I'm just enjoying a much deserved little bit of time off. Relaxing."

"The boyfriend—he doesn't want to relax with you?"

"Pah." She waved a hand. "He's an older, married man. I've made a few mistakes in my time. That's one of them. Was. I gave him the high sign when he called to tell me he has to take his wife to a podiatrist's appointment and can't see me."

"That doesn't sound very romantic."

"No, it doesn't. Are you a romantic?"

"I look for adventure in life," I prattled. I was in over my head, but swimming for my life. "We are here today, gone tomorrow. We must make the most of what there is at the moment."

"An Epicure?"

"Certainly no pedicure."

She stared at me, then burst out laughing. "A wit!"

"Not a twit."

She laughed until she had to hold her arms over her stomach. "Thank you. That's the first time in a long time I've had such a good laugh." She collected herself. "Look, Peter, if you'll help me get home, and help with all these things I bought to console myself, I'll feed you, wine you and dine you, and have you driven home all by yourself in total comfort in a long black limousine rather than a smelly old bus. That appeal to you?"

"Sounds great." "Oh thank you, sweetheart." She planted a kiss on my cheek. It left a faint waxy smell of lipstick. "You're such a cheerer-uppper. Do you come to New York City often?" She looked triste as I shook my head.

So the not-on-the-first-date rule would have to be modified, she must have realized as we sat in the back seat of a very clean, very expensive, very sharply tailored black car driven by a uniformed chauffeur. It was no touch as we sat on opposite sides of the back seat with piles of packages between us. She spoke at length on a cell phone with another woman.

She briefly called schlepperman and read him the riot act before snapping the cell shut. Then she called another woman and chatted about her shopping. Once or twice, she reached across to pat my hand and nod reassuringly with a big friendly smile so I shouldn't feel ignored.

The limousine cruised along one river or the other, with piles of vast buildings and thousands of tiny rectangular lights. The wipers went swish-swish-swish, and the driver sat erect like some Brazilian army colonel. He drove as smoothly as I imagined a $100 wine must taste.

We alighted outside a kind of Venetian confection, a building that looked like the backdrop for an opera. I was to learn that she had a vast apartment in there, an entire floor to herself, in a building originally built as a four story hotel, and now turned into townhouses worth millions. The exterior was brick, with white marble trim including laugh/cry masks under carriage lamps on either side of an impressive entrance atop a flight of orange-slice stairs. The driver carried her parcels and accepted a wad of paper money in payment, for which he thanked her—a nod, a touch to the cap—before driving off in a wash of bleary red taillights. The rain picked up as she rattled keys and unlocked the door. A gust of wind drove us inside. We got the packages in just as the downpour started.

What a place. Mahogany floors, dark wood-paneled walls, Victorian wainscoting, faux electric candles in sconces. Oriental carpets, in some spots piled two or three deep for lack of space. Mirrors. Araeca palms in several varieties. "Let's sit here," she said, taking me into a large den. She waved a wand, and a wall opened to reveal a total entertainment complex. "I like movies and I hate that idiot who always sits in theaters and talks, so I had this installed. Want to see this?" The latest cable release was playing.

"I would enjoy just talking with you," I said.

"That's nice." She shut the thing down, and the wall slid shut. "I hope I am half as entertaining."

"I'm easy to please." An older woman, who looked short and dark and Mediterranean, entered the room. "This is my cook." The woman and I nodded to each other. "What have you prepared for us?"

"I have made julienned carrots, a light salad, some green tea ice cream, and now you must tell me how you like your New York steaks."

"Medium rare," I said, while **Z** said "the bloodier the better."

We sat and talked, and then talked some more in a room shaped like a box car, totally paneled in age-blackened oak. We sat at one corner of a long table on which two silver candelabras flickered with dozens of white candles. The room smelled faintly of wood, like in a wine cask, and burning wax, and salted bloody pan drippings. The meat was tender, the salad fresh, the carrots sweet and sour. It was a light meal, accompanied by a well-aired Pinot Noir.

Afterward, as the old woman cleaned up, we wandered into a great room in which a hundred people would easily fit. Same polished floors, dark walls, elegant furniture, portraits on the walls, general air of gloom. "I bought this place from a stock broker who lost millions and retired upstate to become a small town banker."

I was speechless. She took my hand and led me to a smaller room beyond—totally modern, with a large screen on one wall. "Like to play computer games?"

We held joysticks and played for an hour or two while cartoon cars and cats and planes careened across the huge screen. The old lady brought a silver service with a bottle of wine and two simple crystal glasses on it. The cork lay beside the bottle. She bade us goodnight and left.

"We are alone," **Z** announced dramatically as she poured us each a half glass of Chateau Lafite-Rothschild Pauillac. I dared not ask what the bottle had cost, but it was well up into the three and almost four digits. We toasted each other and sipped sparingly. I rolled it around on my tongue—a moody, full swirl of drama in several layers, with fancy edges and a delightfully breezy end-scroll.

She looked me up and down. "I'm going to get into something more comfortable. I think you could fit into a men's sweat suit I have from my ex." She disappeared, and I played a few more runs on the machine while sipping sunlight from a Bordeaux summer of twenty or more years ago. She returned wearing a simple gray dress that hung loosely to her knees, decorative strips of lace on each sleeve. She wore high gray wool socks, black ballet slippers, and a wine-red pullover with a hood down the back. She handed me a men's dark green sweat combo and pointed to a bathroom nearby. When I emerged from the bathroom, she had put away the games and was playing romantic violin-driven orchestral music. The sound system was so true that it sounded as if a dozen or more musicians were in the room. "Do you like to dance?" Seeing that I had no such education, she said: "I will teach you."

A half hour later, we were tired. "It's been a long day," she said. I walked over to the sound system, switched to radio, and found a station playing soft, slow rock. She walked toward me before I had to gesture. She folded into my arms, rested her head on my shoulder, and slow danced with me. I had been careful not to overdo either the food or the wine, and she seemed to be a light eater and drinker, which is why she had a fine figure and beautiful face worthy of the stage. She was, in her own right, a very fine wine.

At first we held each other and swayed gently. As we warmed each other with our body heat, she looked up at me. Her eyes looked into mine, then down at my lips, and I leaned down to touch her lips with mine. She had removed most of her lipstick, though a faint, waxy residue remained. Her breath smelled of wine, and came in hot little bursts. I could feel her heart pounding against my chest. As our lips locked, our mouths opened full and hungry. We were in no hurry, but we were hungry for this. Her tongue met mine, and they wanted to devour each other. Our tongues danced together, and it was not a slow dance. She had her hand on my crotch before I could get my hand on her behind. We were still locked in that heavy, wild kiss as she squeezed my privates, almost as if to weigh them.

"We'd better retire for the night," she said and led me through that great, empty house. She pulled me by the hand—down carpeted halls, around corners where sconces illumined singing putti in the crown moldings, through other large rooms in which it almost seemed the band had just stopped playing. "The private section," she explained as we came to a small parlor with a dully shining brass door. She pressed a button, and the elevator slipped open. We stepped into an ancient wrought-iron cage and rode up inside a stainless steel shaft toward sanitized fluorescent lighting. "I think you'll like it."

We emerged in a wondrous place—round, modern, indirectly lit, very techno and Continental. "I had a team of designers fly over from Milan," she said with a bright look and a shrug. "And look here." She walked over to a kind of window in the wall and slid a door open. It was a dumbwaiter. There stood the silver tray with our wine and our glasses. The cork was gone, but a crystal tray of chocolates sat in its place. "I stuck in here. Easier than carrying it." She poured us afresh and brought me my glass while holding hers. She pressed a button, and soft guitar chords filled the air. "It's a little sentimental silliness from Jerez."

"That's in Spain," I said.

She stood on tiptoe and brushed her lips against mine. "You are a man of surprises."

"Home of flamenco as well as sherry. The word sherry comes from Jerez, down there on the sun-beaten horn of Spain, a quick leap to Morocco."

"I love it when you talk smart." She reached out with one hand to undo my shirt. I had no objection. She was short, now that the high heels were gone, but she had a way of striding authoritatively. She pulled me by my half-open shirt front toward a cube hanging from the high ceiling. On each of the cube's six sides was a photograph of a woman. Hers was one of them. They were all gorgeous. "Which one do you like best?"

That was a no-brainer. I pointed to her picture.

"Well done. Now which do you like next-best?"

The cube hung at eye level to her, chin level to me. Each side was about 8 x 10 inches. A slender steel cable was attached to a hook on one corner, and the cable receded into the shadows of the ceiling. I studied the pictures while slowly turning the cube. They were all beautiful women—young, probably all wealthy like her. "That is a hard choice because they are all so beautiful."

"Take your time, and make a good choice. You may be surprised." That was the moment when I realized this evening was a spectacular event I had never bargained for while killing time in the rain, hungry and waiting for my bus.

Since I had only faces to work with, I picked the one with the most alluring eyes. There was a black woman, two Asians, a blonde, a redhead, and a brunette. I turned it around and asked her: "Which do you liked best?"

She pointed to the redhead. I nodded. "That's the one." She pointed to one of the Asians. I said "Yes." She pulled out a cell phone and walked away from me, speaking into it. Her walk took her across the room, where she turned and walked back toward me. "Yes," she said, "put it on the silver account." She snapped the phone shut and took my hand. "Come with me, Peter. Let's wash off the sweat and grime of the real world. All that dancing has made us like animals."

She took me into an antique sort of bathhouse portion of her home. The air here was warm, moist, and smelled of chlorine. She flicked lights on as we went. There were rooms beyond rooms, and some of the switches made lights in further rooms flicker on. One entered the complex by heavy white doors with medicinally frosted windows. Inside, the floors were done in tiny black and white tile squares. The walls were in larger blue and white tiles, not Delft, but close—designs in tulips and other flowers. "Looks almost Turkish," I said in the dim greenish glow.

"You're close, darling." She undressed me and laid my clothes over a chair. Then she took hers off and laid them over another chair. Taking me by the hand, she led me down a hall that had two saunas on each side. We walked through a hot room in which steam drifted over wooden benches on either side. "That's your Turkish bath," she said. My eyes were all over her café-au-lait body with its firmly turning buttocks that were dimpled on the sides. She had firm calves, firm full thighs without any signs of aging, and a nice nice arched back with a shiny spinal arc. I liked the way the skin on her shoulder blades dimpled when she moved her arms, and the erect way she carried herself.

We came into a round room with a rectangular pool set into the floor. The floor was done in Roman-style mosaic tiles: a hunt in a fantastic garden, with tame lions and tigers running alongside fast dogs. Peacocks spread their glorious feathers in displays of their sexuality, while pink nymphs and sunburned farm hands or yahoos or whatever followed them with white eyes and unchaste grins. *Z* walked to the edge of the pool, which was about fifteen feet wide and twenty feet long. A number of tiny rectangular white lights gleamed in tiled pods along the poolside at regular intervals. Steam drifted lightly over the water's still surface. As *Z* stepped in, she touched a bank of controls. Lights winked on in the water creating an aqua glow like inside a lantern. "Come," she said, holding out her hand. I followed her into the rippled water, down some light green steps. "The water is specially warmed," she said. Still holding me by the hand, she pulled me along so that we walked around the pool waist deep on a ledge that ran around the edges. I noticed one or two Jacuzzi-like jets propelling heavy amounts of water against my legs. There was a ledge for sitting chest-deep, and another ledge for walking, also chest-deep on me, neck-deep on her.

"It feels very comfortable," I said.

"It should be. It is set to average normal human body temperature. Let me show you the controls." She showed me: there were six stations—two on each short end, and three along the long edges of the rectangle. The master light switch was on the station where the handrail and the main steps were. Each station had a sort of metal elevator button set in. "Watch me," she said. She pressed the button, and it when from white to blue. "Blue means it is about seven degrees below normal body temperature." She pressed again and it turned red. "Red is seven degrees above. If you get out of the pool and need to warm up a little, press until you see red. Feel the jet kicking in?" I noticed warm water being thrown against my legs. "If you get a little overheated," press for blue and it will cool you down a bit." She sat down on the topmost ledge, and had me sit beside her. She had small but full, hanging breasts and brown nipples. She had a long Venus mound that terminated in a dark bush between the fullness of her thighs. "I hope you like what you see," she said softly, opening her palms in the air.

"I do, very much." For me, as fine as she looked, the things that turned me on most were (first and foremost) the sultry Spanish-German elegance of her face, followed by her youthful tush, and then both the fine articulation of her shoulder blades and upper back, as well as the firmness of her caramel calves and thighs.

She picked up a silvery electronic wand that lay near the pool, by a stack of towels. "I think we will listen to some soft, nice music, if that is okay with you." Momentarily a magnificent sound system cut in, and the coy little darting advances and retreats of a Mozart symphony poured through the humid air. "Let's relax a little bit, shall we?" She spread her arms so that her elbows rested on the pool's concrete rim. Her breasts stuck out with firm nutty nipples. She let me come to her and kiss her. We were like kids petting in a parked car. "Honey," she murmured, "let's talk a few moments. You know that we're about to have guests?"

"Yes?" I was trying to figure out how, diplomatically and preemptively, to say no gay stuff for me if that came up at all.

She must have read my mind. "First of all, you are my date and I am yours. This is going to seem very strange to

you, but I don't really need or want to have sex with anyone."
Seeing my baffled look, she said matter of factly: "I plan to
have sex with you, but if you don't want to—"

"—I do, I do—"

"—Good. Then I don't need to elaborate in that direction.
Anyway, there are two very attractive young fashion models
coming. This is where I thought I should explain. I'm into
being watched. Can you understand that?"

I couldn't, but I shrugged lightly trying to accommodate
her.

She laughed gently. "You are young and pure, in your
own little sexed-up boyish way, Peter. No offense, you are
sweet, and I hope I am not a bit too gamey for you. Yes, when
you are very, very wealthy, you can indulge in many appetites
denied to the average citizen. You have to be very, very
discreet. There are a small number of very, very discreet
entrepreneurs whom you pay very, very large sums of money
to provide you with very, very covert services. It's all very,
very natural if you think about it logically."

"Yes."

"You haven't been in a position where you needed to
think about it, Peter. I need you to be very, very discreet."

"I promise I will be."

"I have nobody in my life right now, as in steady dating,
so there is an opportunity here for you to have a foot on the
ground in the city and some remarkable comforts for a while.
You may get tired of it or I may get tired of it first, and we'll
cross that bridge when we get to it. Fair enough?"

"Sounds good to me," I said lightly. It did sound exciting,
mysterious, and a bit scary.

"You are a very, very nice guy. You are very handsome
and intelligent, and you will be a big man someday. Right
now, you are a charming, lovable kid with a huge dick and an
appetite to match." She laughed in a fun, girlish way and
grabbed my swollen cock. Pulling gently, she propelled me
toward her. She still looked very elegant and attractive. If she
weren't letting me into her defenses, she would be a

forbiddingly beautiful piece of exotica. "What do you think of me, Peter?"

I stood between her knees with my arms over her shoulders, getting ready to kiss her. She held my cock as if she were shaking hands with it, and looked up at me awaiting an answer. "Well," I said, "you are a beautiful, alluring woman." With each compliment, I felt her fingers squeeze my dick unconsciously, lightly, thrilled at what I told her. "You would intimidate many men, I think."

"Oh really?" Something told me she knew that. She rubbed my buttocks and pulled me down to sit on her lap. In the water, I was buoyant enough. She held me as I sat sideways, and continued to grip my cock. "I really love holding your cock," said. "Continue." She slipped her free hand down between my buttock and her Venus mound to play with her aroused organs as I told her things that turned her on.

"**Z,** you came down that street looking so gorgeous and wealthy...you are an exotic breed, you know, and you look very elegant. Were you a fashion model?"

"Faces," she said with a laugh. "I wasn't tall or thin enough for the full body stuff. They loved my face."

"I'll be," I said. I ran a fingertip lightly along her cheek. "You are the kind of woman who looks like she comes from somewhere where the men are cruel to their women but guard them with fanatical jealousy." "Oh, keep talking to me," she gasped.

"You are a woman that I would think twice about approaching, because I'd be afraid some guy with a huge black mustache and a cleaver would chase me away."

"What would you think about my ass, my legs, my private secret parts?"

"If I were not afraid to, I would picture running my tongue up along those firm legs of yours. I watched you as you walked ahead of me."

She stroked herself. "I was hoping you would be turned on."

"I was. I was turned on by your whole back, especially your shoulder blades and the brownish tops of your arms."

She rubbed herself and laid her cheek against my upper arm. She rubbed her cheekbone against my triceps, realized my muscles were strong, and kissed them before resuming brushing her cheek against my arm and continuing to arouse herself below. "When I was younger," she said, "I could come at the drop of a hat. Now it takes a lot more playing to get me up the slope."

"I'll help you," I said. I massaged her breasts, which just filled my palms, while telling her more imaginative stories. She continued arousing herself. At the same time, even wet, she maintained this brittle, contained beauty. Her lipstick was still red, her fingernails still glossy, her hair thick and dark-red. We kissed some more. Her tongue was wild for mine, and her hand stole up around my back while the other hand retained its grip on my cock. I reached down toward her privates, but she trapped my hand. "Slow and easy," she murmured. "We want the evening to last."

I was French kissing with her—she kneeling on the step beside me with her arms wrapped over my shoulders—when we heard the patter of naked feet. I looked up, startled, to see a man coming from one direction, and two women from the other. He wore a black tuxedo with a purple flower in the lapel. The two women, both tall and shapely, wore dark shiny evening sheaths. *Z* whispered to me: "Don't worry about Daniel. He is discreet and docile and does what he is told. He has no interest in men either, which is why I had him sent. The women will do anything you want, as long as you don't hurt them or scare them. You don't seem like the type to hurt anyone."

"That I can assure you," I said. "I am naked and embarrassed."

"Don't worry. They'll keep their distance. I just like them to show up in good form, and warm up my eyeballs with some attractiveness. Whets the appetite." The three very attractive young newcomers greeted us with cheery hellos, like old friends. Everyone greeted each other by name. *Z* introduced me as Peter, and I had no idea if these people's given names were real. The redhead was *Y,* and the Asian was *X.*

Z pointed to a cabinet in the wall. "Daniel, if you would be so kind, there are drinks in the fridge. " Daniel came from the fridge, lumbering with a tray of tall, thin glasses that appeared rimed with frost and contained juice. "Orange juice, fresh, not spiked," *Z* assured me. Daniel put two drinks by the poolside, squatting for a moment so that his shiny black shoes creaked. He took the tray with the remaining three drinks to the women, who stood quietly waiting by a small round table some distance away. They reminded me of young women who have gone out to the evening and are waiting to be asked to dance. They looked mildly full of ennui.

"I sent out for two," *Z* said with a quiet laugh, "thinking it might be more interesting for you." She dropped down under the water, took my cock in her mouth, and formed a perfect suction around the head. It almost hurt as she turned her head this way and that, like a mechanical socket on a ball bearing. All the while, the two women stood there quietly conversing while they held their drinks, maybe folding one long-gloved arm around the other. *Z* surfaced, pushing her hair back. She spewed a little cone of water. "I tasted a little shot of sperm, Peter. You are very hard." She wrapped herself around me and I held her as if we were slow-dancing, which is odd when Mozart is playing. She cupped my buttocks and nipped at my nipples with her teeth. I shuddered and bent a little, feeling both fire and pleasure. She said: "I invite you to use me, to explore every little place on my body that fascinates you." She added: "I'm not looking for an acrobat, darling, just a good @ from a young boy with wild flying hair and the attention span of, well, a young boy who keeps looking over at the redhead and the slant. Which one interests you more?"

"I think the redhead. But you are the center of this evening for me."

"Thank you." She stood on tiptoes and kissed me. "You will make me happy tonight. Hold me." I wrapped my arms around her. She was small, and had hard edges with soft surfaces, that probably had all been hard when she was my age. She squirmed in the shelter of my embrace. She reached down and cupped my balls, weighing them, thinking about them. She slid her middle finger back a bit, past my balls, and tickled my sphincter. She looked downward, and I saw her face in profile. Someone seeing her in her subdued, expensive clothing, maybe at a fashion show, would never guess how she spent her evenings. Maybe there were many people like her in the ruling structure of our world.

Maybe I would never drive through a city at night again and see the magnificent skyline, skyscrapers aswim in hazy light, and think of it the same way again. I saw in her the height of power and arrogance, mollified by the absence of any need to be cruel, just the absoluteness of her power, or the power of her vast fortune. I saw in her the caudillo, the Negro, the Indio, the German Juncker with his dueling scar, all the components of mastery and slavery, all the oreo layers of power and submission. Here was the power and the ownership—in this chlorinated space where aquamarine light wiggled in big blobs and reflected on the ceiling—sublimated into sex as a catering business. I did not turn away from it, or think badly of her, because she was as much a victim of the system as I or the blond guy or the two starving young models who hired themselves out for a thousand bucks a night.

"You think too much," Z said to me suddenly, flatly, as if she were reading a bus schedule to me. "That's what killed my husband. Learn to unwind, relax, go with the flow."

"I plan to do just that," I promised her. "Thank you for your concern."

She looked serious as she reached out to touch my cheek with trembling fingers. "You are a silly boy now, but you'll become a serious old man with an ulcer and a lot of financial worries. The more money you have, the more you'll worry. Don't let it do that to you. Enjoy life."

"You are being too serious now," I said, lightly pinching her nipple.

"I'm so silly," she breathed. She patted the edge of the pool. Daniel, who had been sitting on a stool by the two women, reading a book, rose and fetched a white foam rubber futon, which he lumberingly brought to the poolside before returning to his reading. Mozart played on and on, and the pumps in the pool seethed in their chlorinated churning. "Let's lie up there," Z said. We climbed out of the pool and lay on the spacious mattress. "Lie down," she said, and I lay on my back. She stood over me, looking down, and I saw hunger in her eyes, and wasn't sure what she was going to do next.

The two young women watched from a distance. Daniel kept reading that textbook of his without ever looking our way. All three remained dressed and somehow imprisoned in their expensive evening clothes as if they had turned to statues. The two women never took their eyes off us.

Z said: "Give me your foot. The right one." I lifted it, and she took it. She straddled me and my foot, so that the bottom of my foot was against her vagina. Legs apart, slightly bowed, she began grinding her oyster on my heel. Then she shifted her attention to the ball of my foot, which had more nerve endings, so that I could feel it nestled in the wet softness of her oyster.

Her eyes flickered and rolled up slightly, as if she were having spasms, and her lips were lightly parted and trembling with unheard words. I pressed up against her, supporting almost her whole weight at times, so that there was pressure on her clitoris. She moved up and down, grinding the ball of my foot in the wet, pink hole of her oyster entry, and then moving the ball of my foot so that she could deposit all that oyster soup on her clitoris.

The women watching sipped their drinks and looked on with rapt attention.

Z spoke in a faint, tiny voice. She spoke not to me, but to herself, as if at a séance. "I like when they watch. I like when they see me. I like to think that their oysters are wet and they wish they had your foot. I like how young and elegant they are." She was beginning to quake. The climax was arriving. She jerked and spasmed, tried to keep up the foot massage and the monologue, but her eyes rolled up and fluttered, and she grew weak. She talked as long as she could. "I like when they watch. I like when they see me. I like when they look at my ass. I like when you look up my oyster. I—" And there she started faltering.

I felt her grow limp, and pushed hard with the ball of my foot in her oyster hole to keep her from falling down. She was going down, slowly, coming toward me. Her arms were parted, and she wanted me to hold her. I lay back and held her as she fell into my arms. "@ me now," she whispered feebly. She straddled me, and I worked my dong around to slip it into her. She reached down with both hands to guide it in. I cupped her hanging tits in my palms. Her nipples were engorged as if she had milk for a baby. My cock-head crossed her threshhold, a wet and messy place, and traveled up into the dark corridor of her vagina. She moaned as my fullness pushed into her insides. I filled her up, the way a tree grows roots and fills the soil with its ever-expanding rootball. Resting her knees on the mat on either side of my hips, she rocked herself back and forth and cried while she held onto my shoulders. "Let me help you, baby," I said, raising and lowering my hips so my dick rode in and out on her foam. I was careful to time my swing with hers.

Together, we were an awesome machine rushing toward a grand tunnel climax. She was in ecstasy, with her eyes closed and face upraised, as she half-coherently gummed the words "I'm onna umm" and I cried "Let's come together baby" and we did. Great shuddering gasps, holding each other, we rocked through it and then collapsed side by side still holding each other. She grinned and said breathlessly: "Thank you, Peter, that was great." She breathed hard for a minute or two. "Darling, that wasn't planned. I was going to stretch it out for hours, but you got me all turned on and I just wanted to @ and suck and have this huge fireworks orgasm!"

"And you did," I said.

She rested her arms on my shoulders. We lay face to face, my cheek resting on her right forearm. She glowed at me. "Darling, you deserve a little candy. I'd like to watch you @ the redhead."

"Only if you are sure you are satisfied."

"I'm very satisfied. If I need more, I can jump in."

"I thought you said you didn't need the sex."

"I don't."

"Oh." Realization flooded in. For a person who can have anything, need is not an operative word. Want is the thing. When, and if. "How do I—?"

"*Y,*" *Z* said in a crisp voice.

"I'm not ready," I whispered. "I just mega-super-@ed you, and I'm limp. My noodle is down. My hardware has turned into software."

"It doesn't matter," *Z* said. "*Y* and *X* will understand and provide whatever you need. It's okay if you can't come. Everything is okay. Nothing matters. It's all play. It's all air." We slid back into the water.

The two young women strode toward us as if they were on a runway with strobing lights and throbbing music. Their eyes were dark, their faces gaunt, their heads like those of cats on the hunt. They came to the edge of the pool, stepped out of their heels, and started undoing their dresses.

Y was a tall, slender woman with a fiery carrot top, lots of orange freckles, and large blue eyes. She was gaunt, and pale, with those hollow model eyes. *X* was a little, with thick, glossy black hair, almond eyes, and smooth custard skin instead of freckles.

Dropping their clothes on the dry concrete and tile, they walked around the rim of the pool until they came to the aluminum railings that curved like matching mastodon tusks of chrome.

They stepped down into the water and dove down to wet themselves. I saw their twin shapes approaching underwater like parallel sea animals. They were good swimmers, in this tiny space, and all this happened in seconds.

They surfaced once for air, and then dove down and swam around our legs. As *Z* and I stood holding each other, *Y* and *X* nosed around the calves of our legs. I felt hands on my thighs, my buttocks. I felt fingers gently touching my balls and dick as if minnows were swimming past. The girls surfaced with great grins. Apparently they felt at home with *Z.* "Hi, darlings," *Z* said. They kissed her one by one, and then embraced me. I had two women hanging from me as I sat back in the top underwater bench.

On my right was the Japanese girl, *X.* Her name meant hydrangea, a beautiful species of flower, and she was tall for her nationality. *Y,* the redhead on my left, was from Kent in the U.K., and struggling to make a go of it in Manhattan. Both girls were 22—two years younger than I. We moved about in slow motion, touching and feeling lightly, kissing each other and exploring orifices with a gentle fingertip, an inquisitive tongue.

I noticed out of a corner of my eye that the big blond man, Daniel, was sitting on a stool reading a book. He was still in his tux, and when I went to find the bathroom for a whiz, I noticed that he had a U.S.M.C. tattoo on one hand and was reading College Algebra, an Introduction. I stopped and quipped: "Going to night school, are we?" He didn't take well to my flippancy. "Listen, Peter," he said in a laboring tone, pointing toward Z: "If she tells me to @ you, I will @ you whether you like it or not. If she doesn't, I will study for my math test tomorrow. Whether I end up @ing you or not, it's just a job, okay? To me, you look like just another piece of roadkill, got it?"

"Got it. Thank you."

"So @ off."

I felt relieved that he didn't seem to have designs on me. When I returned to the pool, the two girls had *Z* between them and were kissing her nipples while *Z* lay back with her eyes closed. I slipped into the water and hung back for some minutes, watching them pleasure her. Soon, *Z* rose from the water and picked up one of the hand towels in a pile. The two girls followed her, each with her own towel. *Z* waggled a finger for me to follow.

We went into a room in which there was a huge round bed. The walls and ceiling were covered with mirrors. We crawled onto the bed together. *Z* lay back and let the two girls work on her. She signaled for me to join. I had no idea where to start. *Y* was the longer, leaner, harder of the two girls, and she was licking *Z's* oyster at the moment. *X,* meanwhile, alternated between Frenching *Z's* mouth and kissing her nipples. *Y* pushed *Z's* thighs back so that *Z's* knees touched her cheeks.

Doing this, *Y* exposed the entire juicy panorama of *Z's* privates to our view. I crawled up behind *Y,* and under her, under her small bobbing breasts, to watch her licking *Z's* twat. *Z* had a brownie outtie smothered in hair like a Smith Brothers cough drop picture. I crawled up close and inhaled the wild forest smell of all that oyster hair. I dove in next to *Y* so that she and I were both licking the juice out of *Z's* oyster.

"I'm going to have Peter @ me soon," *Z* wailed as the two girls pinned her and immobilized her in pleasure. As I was brushing tongues with *Y,* it occurred to me that her ass was pointing into space, and I moved back until I could inspect her skinny rack with its satisfying little pockets of meat. She had a pinkie outtie oyster. In fact she had nice pink labia, and she was really turned on over *Z's* twat. I had only to start my tongue licking up and down the moist canyons of *Y's* labia.

I was about to stuff my thick dick in *Y's* open and available oyster, or maybe her little pink asshole pucker, when I noticed *X.* The Japanese girl was a little shorter, a little meatier, a little more on the dark side, and she had a brownie innie oyster. That is, her oyster lips tended toward the brown end of the oyster lips scale, and her oyster was one of those that doesn't show much on the outside. No folded hands labia, no loosely open hole, but hairless, fatty skin parting in a slit covered the wet little treasures inside.

As *X* sucked on *Z's* nipples, her legs were pointed down parallel to *Z's* and a lick of my tongue around *Y's* asshole pucker afforded me a view of *X's* precious little apricot oyster. Given so many orifices, I chose at that moment to park my dick in *Y's* oyster while I leaned over to get my tongue into *X's* hidden treasure house.

At first, I thought *X* was totally ignoring me. Then, she reached down with a finger and parted the little ramparts to let me find the bud that was almost hard. My tongue encountered a lost little clitoris under a smooth, fatty hood, and I coaxed it with the tip of my tongue until it got bigger and moister and bigger yet and damper, until it was dripping wet. *X* began to moan with pleasure, and I helped her by putting the tip of my finger in her anus.

Soon, I was able to add a second finger as her sphincter loosened and her moans increased. During all of this, *Z* had turned onto her belly. *Y* was still sucking at *Z's* clit, but now *X* had *Z's* ass to occupy her. So she used her fingertips to part *Z's* ass cheeks so she could get her tongue down into *Z's* asshole, past the pucker and into the soft interior which of course *Z* had cleaned with copious enemas and fruit washes.

We made love for what seemed like hours, until first *X* and then *Y* fell asleep. Daniel read his book for a long time, until he grew tired. He fell asleep on the concrete still in his tuxedo, with his ankles crossed and one arm over his chest and the other arm pointed into eternity, in the same direction his snoring face appeared to be looking.

Only *Z* was still awake, the little bee, having taken a nap, and now gorging herself on my cock. She pushed me onto my back, mounted me, and had yet another orgasm while massaging her boobs and looking up into heaven.

Right about there, I didn't fall asleep—I passed out—and yet I woke during the night to the sound of cries, and saw *Z* giving Daniel a blowjob. Daniel, who had shed his tux and creaky shoes finally, was a very big, wrestler-looking blond man with blue eyes and very little body hair except a wavy slick on top and a bit of fuzz below. He was very pale, and had one of those banana whangs that curve slightly to one side. It was huge, with a tiny head on it, and probably half erect most of the time. *Z* had him standing over her with his powerful legs spread while she tongued his banana in huge lapping motions. I only caught a glimpse of all this before I feel back to sleep.

In the morning, I woke, dressed in my street clothes. They were all gone. There was in fact no sign they had ever been there. Also, I wasn't where I had fallen asleep. I was in a single-wide bed in what looked like a cell. I sat up and studied my surroundings with some alarm. Sunlight slanted in through heavy wooden blinds. The little room had white-washed walls and was barren except for the bed, a little desk, a chair, and my clothing neatly folded in a pile on the chair. I staggered to the door and turned the handle, afraid I might be locked in, but the door opened quite readily onto a silent, vacant hallway. I was reminded of an exclusive university club I had once visited with one of my older women. The walls were paneled in a kind of dark-red wood, much like *Z's* hair. The floors were carpeted, the windows barred, the ceilings bright with cold fluoro lighting.

As I peered left and right, a door opened and Daniel in his tuxedo lumbered out. "Peter," he said with that deadly serious voice, "she likes you and wants to see you again." He handed me a business card with her name and a phone number on it. "Keep this with you. Let's go." I had nothing to go back and get. "The driver will take you where you need to go."

"How will I ever find my way back here?"

"You won't," Daniel said. "Not even *Y* and *X* or any other girls know how to get here, or who *Z* is. The driver is the husband of the old woman who left the drinks in the fridge, and who cooked your meal last night. They are sworn to secrecy about this place and its owner. I am too. I would give my life for *Z,* and she is taking good care of me in her will. What this means to you is that you will take the elevator down, get into a van, and be driven away from here never knowing where you have been. You will be brought here and

taken away blindly, never knowing where you are. That helps
Z keep her affairs private." He poked me in the chest for
emphasis. "Come here and enjoy yourself, but don't ever @
with me, or this place, or any of the women here. It'll be the
last think you ever do."

"I promise, I'll be good."

The funny part was that, when I arrived deep in the earth
at a very private loading zone in the semidark, the redhead *Y*
was waiting there too. She had overslept, and was about to
take the same blind van ride. Having made love in a most
intimate manner just hours earlier, we were quickly on
personal terms.

The van arrived, driven by a Hispanic man of severe
mien.

The van had no windows, and there was no way for us to
know where we had been or to find our way back. *Y* took me
by the arm when we arrived at her apartment in midtown
Manhattan. She towed me out of the van and into her multi-
female-roommate fun apartment. The roommates were all
gone to work or classes. We had breakfast and then made love
some more. That afternoon, I called *Z's* number, and
requested a ride home into New England if possible. The
service was provided without demur. I was part of *Z's* fabric
now.

An even greater irony was that *X,* the Asian woman, had
a connection who was a historian, and through them (with a
recommendation from the wheel-chair bound professor in
New Hampshire) I eventually secured a little graduate
teaching assistantship that got me started on the road to a
stable course of life. Thus, the blue doorway into *Z's* steam
rooms became the doorway to my eventual success. What I
did not know until I was to occupy it many years later, after I
had lost all touch with her, was that *Z* had endowed the chair I
would one day occupy, and she had been the force acting
through *X.* It had not been *X's* connection, but *Z's*. Though
she left me no money, *Z* had taken good care of me.

Epilog: Sea Writing in Sand

Years ago, when I was divorced and dating again, near 40, one of my girlfriends was a beautiful young woman of 34. This was in the San Francisco area, far from the Northeast where my youth and the stories in this book took place. I'll call this woman Eve—both because she was young and the Eve of her personal world and future, but also because I'm far along on the eve of reflection and stillness. Of my intimacies with Eve, there is little I want to tell.

She was (is, wherever she may now be) a remarkable woman. She was pretty in a sort of a softly chiseled, athletic way. She was a skier, swimmer, scuba diver, anything fast or exhilarating. I have always been, was then, and am now, a writer. We writers often lead dull lives. Mostly we walk, we think, and we type.

Very few women, with the best of intentions, can sustain themselves in their needs with such a man for a long time. Eve, though she had the best of intentions, did finally leave me for someone more like herself. I understood he had was a combat flight instructor, martial artist, parachutist—the kind of man she would take hiking or deep sea diving.

She did admit, though, that she had acquired from me insight into a totally different world of thought and expression. For almost a year, we complemented each other well. During that year, we spent much time together, and made love passionately. I was past the rebound from a disappointing marriage and a mildly embittered divorce.

Eve was good for me in many ways, and she caught me at the right time, not on the rebound, but back on my feet. She was actually the last great fling before the long marriage in which I have grown mature, and with which spouse I will be lucky to find the sunset many years hence.

Yes, I did end up marrying a woman just a few years older. My first wife, ironically, was many years younger than

I, and even less mature though beautiful. So I have had the best of all worlds in women both younger and older and I have no complaints. The only reason for this epilog, mainly, is to say that Eve gave me the nudge, the insight, to record the adventures of my early twenties.

Parenthetically, I should note that I was already a man of substance. I was no longer a stray leaf blown against every October tree. I had a wife and children, and a nice salary, and a seat by the warm bench at the fireplace on the other side of the window, while outside the cold wind blew. I always remained an outsider and a lone operator, only my hunt took me not to the Summers of this world (a state of being from which I was permanently barred when I stopped being a Spring in my late 20s). My hunt took me to the attenuated air and refined philology of the Classics.

I realized, as I lay beside Eve one night, this beautiful athlete five or six years younger than I, that she was the older woman, the Summer. That is, she was in the age bracket of the women I had romanced in that phase of my life. She was a young woman, who might have dated me as a younger man. As the younger man, I moved in a world of confusion and short-term gratification. I bounced from job to job, place to place, woman to woman.

The older woman, the Eve I might have dated, was mysterious to me, alluring, accomplished, a teacher, a bringer of forbidden fruits. Now I was years older than Eve, and I could see her from the other angle—a girl still. She was young, still possessing that freshness and that blush of innocence. It's all relative, of course. Every person ages differently, gains wisdom otherly. We can only generalize as we try to grasp this life with its sometimes subtle, sometimes brutal rules that we must each figure out on the fly.

I see Eve in my memory as a serious young blonde with a swimmer's wide shoulders, crisp gray eyes looking almost fiercely at the waves rolling in at Redondo Beach as she stands holding her surfboard like a Greek goddess holding a spear. I see her with damp, tousled locks over her forehead, as she wipes a blue-wetsuited wrist draped with a sprig of kelp across her runny nose. As spots her wave and starts to trot, leaving an arc of dark, torn footprints in the wet sand. Faster and faster she runs, drops her board, throws herself on and starts to paddle into the wall of water still on the horizon but coming fast.

She told me one evening, as we sipped wine by a hot fire in the stone cottage, that she did have a young boyfriend once. I told her I had been such a lover to one or two women almost twenty years earlier. She laughed. I asked her why she laughed. She shook her head. I prodded, and she reluctantly answered with diplomatic honesty: "He was like a child. A real challenge. He was fantastic in bed, and he could out-run and out-play me at most things. But he was just a kid. He was kind, but he was self-centered. It was all he knew. He was groping his way forward through life, and I helped him a little, but it's hard to be a younger man's lover, older sister, sometimes a little touch of mom even."

"So you moved on," I said.

She nodded. "I moved on with life. I had my little play time, and he grew bored and probably found someone else like me. I think he had an easy time with older women."

"Older girls," I corrected.

She shrugged and looked perplexed. When does a girl start being a woman? When does a woman stop being a girl? Is it relative? Is there some date and time when she punches a ticket, goes into a booth as a girl, and comes out as a woman? She didn't know, and neither did I. She grinned. "All I know is that, at the moment, I am enjoying being with an older man." "I'm enjoying it too," I said, and we clinked glasses. I lay back on the rug, dressed in my jeans and sweater, and she crawled close beside me with one arm over my chest and her lips by my ear.

I listened to the rhythm of her breathing, and thought of the waves splashing back and forth in the changing tides. I thought of the arc of abandoned footprints out on the sand, not far away, probably already erased by the water to leave the sand blank and fresh for new writing.

~ END ~

Other Literotic Titles

Clocktower Books is an omnibus publisher, active and innovating on the Web since 1996. Among our imprints, we publish the erotic literature collection Erotic Memoir.

Learn more about us online at **www.clocktowerbooks.com/**.

We define literotica as erotica that is authored at a level of artfulness we call Fine Writing, as in Fine Arts. Having studied literature, we tend to avoid loaded terms like 'literature', which can mean many things to many people (who, like religious fundamentalists) often vehemently insist that they possess the only true answer. Please refer to Ezra Pound's article on Literachoor for an examination of pretentiousness.

We offer a very small selection to date, believing as we do, in quality rather than quantity.

At this time, we offer the novel *A Perfect Ass: Muriel and Sarah's Summer of Wonder in a Year of Bummer*.

We also offer a small trilogy (Limewood) by Max Ready, which consists of an entertaining and sexy romp by a film crew on a fictional Adriatic island.

We hope you will visit our websites, or find our titles online, and enjoy happy hours of reading. Note: our erotic fiction is largely straight, adult MF, with a smattering of spicy FF at times. A Perfect Ass is, of course, a love story between two women who are friends in the dark and terrifying period of the 1950s, with the Cold War, McCarthyism, and nightmarish bomb drills as well as public book burnings and other social throwbacks to the age of Kafka and Orwell.

Learn more about us online at **www.clocktowerbooks.com/**.